The New Writing in Russia

The New Writing in Russia

Translated, with an Introduction,
by Thomas P. Whitney

Ann Arbor   The University of Michigan Press

Permissions
Appreciation is expressed to *Encounter* magazine for permission
to quote from its account—April 1963, pp. 102–3—of Khrushchev's
remarks on modern art made in December 1962; and to *Survey,*
A Journal of Soviet and East European Studies (No. 48), for
permission to quote from Professor R. Etiemble's article,
"Pictures from an Exhibition"; and also to *Survey* (No. 36,
pp. 7–8), for permission to quote from Gene Sosin's article,
"Talks With Soviet Writers."

Book design by Quentin Fiore
Drawing by Judy Nathanson

With much love to my mother,
Louise Metzger Whitney,
and to the memory of my father,
Herbert Porter Whitney.

Preface

When I set out to compile the material for this book in the late spring of 1962 I was anxious to avoid involvement in the political aspects of current Russian literature.

This is, and was, an important subject, and I would be the last person to attempt to disregard it. And, indeed, how can one disregard it so long as the Soviet Establishment itself persists in making an eternal political question of art and the function of the artist in society?

Still, it seemed to me that quite enough was being written by others on this, and that for anyone interested in it there was a mass of competently written critical literature as well as a great deal of source material in the form of translations of relevant political documents and of Russian "literature of protest"—which was usually interesting as protest but not always interesting as literature.

I wished—for the moment at least in this one collection—to get outside this ubiquitous political framework in which Russian literature of the Soviet era is perpetually treated both inside and outside the Soviet Union.

For one thing I wanted to make the point to at least a limited number of American readers of something I discovered for myself —that at long last there were being written and published in the Soviet Union works of prose fiction worth reading for their own sake and not as political sensations or exposures of the seamy side of Soviet life.

I wanted to introduce American readers to a handful of newer prose writers who are already important and popular literary figures in Russia itself and from whom—it seems likely—much more will be heard in the future. More than anything else I wanted to make available to readers some of the more interesting and vivid insights into the hearts and lives of modern-day Russians available in contemporary Russian fiction. To me they are fascinating, and I cannot help but think that for some others they will seem so too.

So within this general framework and with these purposes I have compiled this collection—picked the writers and the works included. I have *not* felt under any compulsion whatsoever to find a set of "great masterpieces." I have deliberately left out the poets and poetry—not because they are not important, for they most surely *are*—but partly because they are a very special field and deserve special treatment, and more relevantly because they did not have what I wanted for this anthology.

I wanted stories. I wanted them to be interesting reading and as modern and up-to-date in style and subject matter as possible.

In particular, while by no means wishing to bypass or skip major themes and questions of Soviet society, I wanted the works included to be *apolitical* in the sense that they would be concerned primarily with *Russians as human beings* rather than with Russians as patriots, Soviet citizens, or embodiments of the aspirations of the Soviet Communist Party. I wanted them to be concerned with the hearts, minds, perceptions, feelings, pains, and joys of contemporary individuals among Russian people, rather than with the physical and material problems and tasks of the "building of Communism."

And this orientation was not a matter of whim, for it was my own deep conviction that the future of Russian letters—like its past—lay precisely in this type of literature, and that it was in the only very recent emergence of the beginnings of this kind of apolitical writing from out of the still long-lingering smog of Stalinism in the Russian literary field that there was good reason for compiling this book. So the works I included were *apolitical*.

And yet politics do have a way of intruding themselves into the Russian literary scene—at times rather forcibly. At the end of November 1962 I had completed the first drafts of my translations of the stories which are included in this book and was ready to set to work on a general introduction for the book.

At this point the Soviet Communist Party intervened in literary activity to inaugurate a noisy, full-scale, long-continued campaign to reassert Party authority over Russian writers and to reaffirm the Party's right and "obligation" to provide direction and guidance for literary effort in the Soviet Union. There were scoldings and vituperations and recriminations galore! This campaign lasted into June 1963. Since then it has apparently slackened off somewhat. But the whole episode threw a great deal of bright light on the complicated and difficult relationship existing between Russian literature and Soviet politics—and made it obligatory for me to discuss this relationship in detail in my introduction to the book. The Soviet communist politics of literature are, after all, the environment in which contemporary Russian literature breathes— or, as has sometimes happened, suffocates. And if one wishes to put the literature being written today into perspective in the cultural development and directions of the country one certainly has to have some of the elementary facts on this part of the literary situation.

At the same time, notwithstanding this necessary spotlight on the politics of Russian literature in my general introduction, I have adhered in the anthology as a whole to my original and never-abandoned intent of presenting a collection of Russian writers and writings worth reading for no other reason than that they are interesting.

But whether I have succeeded in this the reader will have to be the judge.

Contents

Russian Literature
and Soviet Politics*

* Parts of this introduction are adapted from chapters in a book being written by the editor of this anthology, on the subject of Russian writers and writing in the nineteen sixties.

1. The Historical Background

Russia's most important contribution to world culture is unquestionably Russian classical literature. It is properly the pride of the nation. The works of great Russian writers of the nineteenth century are known and loved all over the world and have had enormous influence on world literature. Given the international renown and significance of Russian literature there is nothing surprising in the fact that many non-Russians still watch current Russian writing expectantly—in hopes of the appearance of able writers and important works. The Russians of today also judge their contemporary literature by the standards of Russian classical literature, which they read copiously and to which they have long looked for inspiration and spiritual sustenance.

Russian classical literature is not old compared to that of other European countries. It is almost entirely a product of the last century—specifically of the period from 1820 to 1917. The most productive years were the 1860's and 1870's, partly because those years were the freest in all Russian history, partly because several writers of unusual talent were writing during those decades. But even in the most oppressive and difficult years of the period there were also excellent works written and published.

After all, tyranny has always up to the present time been the rule rather than the exception in Russia. And there has almost always been tension and bad feeling between writers and the political authority. Most of the great Russian writers of the classic period suffered from one or another form of political persecution. All of them had serious problems with censorship.

Considering these factors and also that Russian literature was always a principal channel of presentation and dissemination of new thoughts and ideas in the country, it is not to be wondered at that Russian writers were in the front ranks of Russian progressives seeking changes in the political and social system. And it was natural, too, for the Russian monarchy always to have strong misgivings about literature and writers. But Russian tsarism was not efficient or effective in dealing with literature. It had a narrow and short-sighted view of the question. It consistently aroused the hostility of writers—but fortunately failed to suppress their progressively oriented works. And Russian writers were consistently unanimous in their desire to see the end of all aspects of censorship, suppression of literature, and interference with writers and intellectuals by the

3

autocracy. This platform was a principal theme of Russian literary life in the entire period.

Russian writers of the nineteenth and early twentieth centuries did not by any means avoid themes taken from Russian life or from contemporary national problems and issues. Some important works had an immediate political foundation and immediate political impact. Nor were the Russian writers of the classic period by any means all unskilled in the fine art of propaganda. Yet, in general, Russian classical writing did not have a political or ideological platform as a mainspring of its being. Russian classical writers mostly kept clear of adulation of despotism. The great Russian classical writers were in the first place artists, interested mainly in people, not politics. Russian classical literature is outstanding for its deep insights, through art, into human beings and history. And it was this that gave Russian literature such universality of appeal inside and outside Russia.

The crucial fact about Russia in this period was that it was a European country, a full participant in European cultural life. Enlightened Russians of the era were also Europeans. They, many of them, spoke or read French, German, or English—and all educated Russians of the time read Western European literature either in the original or in translation. There was mass travel by educated Russians to Western Europe in the last part of the nineteenth century and right up to World War I. Tens of thousands of Russian young people went to Western Europe to get their education. And there were also large colonies of Western Europeans in Russia itself.

The closeness of the Russian tie with Western Europe, the membership of Russia in the European community at the time, conditioned the Russian literature of the period. It was mostly about Russia and Russians, of course, and this endowed it with a full measure of the native Russian freshness, strength, and color. But it was also, in its basic assumptions, European literature. Russian writing was in the mainstream of international culture—and an important part of it. And as a result Russian classical literature very quickly found readership in Europe and throughout the world for itself. And this was, of course, a source of its great international influence and prestige.

The Bolshevik Revolution of November 1917 and the events which followed—turning Russia's face away from Western Europe and back upon itself—had a profound effect on Russian literature.

Russian writers generally took a hostile attitude toward the communist coup d'etat at first. In fact, almost to a man they boycotted it. Indicative was the position of Maxim Gorki, the most important and popular living Russian writer, a friend of Vladimir

Ilich Lenin who had himself for a time been friendly to the Bolshevik cause. He was so hostile, in fact, that Lenin closed down his newspaper, *Novaya Zhizn,* in mid-1918 and encouraged Gorki to emigrate in 1921. Gorki made his peace with the Bolsheviks after a time, but didn't return to Russia to reside till the early 1930's. Other writers found the adjustment to the radical communist regime much more difficult. Many emigrated and remained abroad the rest of their lives. Some others emigrated initially and later returned. Only a few individual writers with established reputations supported the Bolsheviks from the beginning. Among them were several outstanding poets—Vladimir Mayakovski, Sergei Yesenin, and Alexander Blok. The initial days of the communist regime were in general a better time for poets than for other writers. There was little paper— and poets could get along without paper by public recitations of their works.

The early period of the Revolution saw, as a dire prophecy of things to come, the beginnings of the Soviet censorship system. But after the civil war was over and the difficult period of war came to an end things improved. Under the New Economic Policy—the NEP —there was substantial relaxation. Paper on which to print books soon reappeared. To be sure censorship was permanently institutionalized in the form of the notorious *Glavlit* in 1922—but it was not severe at first. The government began to seek more active support among writers, and Russian writers began to take a more tolerant view of the new government which was then, as later, lavish in its monetary support for literature, the arts, and education. Also important in the new situation in encouraging literary activity was the heady, hopeful spirit of the times in the new revolutionary Soviet Russia, which appeared to be blazing new trails in human and social development. It was a fascinating, vivid age and a colorful revolutionary country, and there had never really been anything quite like it. It is not surprising that this found its reflection in Russian art and literature in which much experiment was taking place. The NEP period resulted in the rapid revival of Russian prose —it poured forth in torrents, mostly absorbed in the Revolution and civil war as primary subjects.

Then came the First Five Year Plan from 1928 to 1932—and for a time enthusiasm for the daring scope of the plan was reflected in literature. But, meanwhile, in the countryside as the collectivization program proceeded, a horrible tragedy was taking place and news of this gradually began to filter into the public conscience.

One of the marked characteristics of Soviet literary life in the first years of the new regime was the fever of writers for organizing themselves into a multitude of groups and spending great amounts of time and energy on the discussion of public and literary issues and problems. There were all kinds of organizations and factions. The group in particular known as the Proletkult tried to get dictatorial powers over literature. It did not succeed, but for a time its strong position enabled it to persecute other writers. On the opposite side from the Proletkult were the "fellow travelers"—who for the most part came from the ranks of the traditional Russian writers who were professionally established to some extent before the Revolution. They were not, for the most part, communists, but neither were they against the regime, and as things progressed some of them evolved into active propagandists for the new order of things.

At first the Party permitted the proliferation of various literary groups. As time went on, however, and as Stalin consolidated his power over the Party (from 1924 on) it began to take an ever more direct hand in literary affairs. In 1929 the Party demonstrated its power by inciting a bitter campaign to discredit two outstanding Russian writers who were deemed to be insufficiently sympathetic to the regime—Boris Pilnyak and Yevgeni Zamyatin. The former was forced to recant sins abjectly and the latter departed, after intercession for him by Gorki, from Russia. Grounds for persecution of both were publication outside the Soviet Union of works by them which had not been authorized for publication inside the Soviet Union. This campaign of vilification was an ominous precedent. The "proletarian" writers in this period were being allowed to attack nonpolitical writers viciously—as, for instance, Boris Pasternak, the poet. However, they were not long allowed to maintain their predominant role. In 1932 the government organized all writers in one organization known as the Union of Soviet Writers. This could thenceforth serve as the organizational instrument for Party control over literature. Meanwhile, the Party's ideological system for control was also being worked out. This was given the label of "socialist-realism" —proclaimed as the official literary dogma in 1934 at the First Writers' Congress. Socialist-realism meant that artists should express themselves in a generally recognized and accepted realist form and that their works must possess pro-Soviet content. In other words, they must deliver *propaganda* for the system in artistic language comprehensible to the masses. Literary works were expected to be optimistic. Under Stalin socialist-realism was a straitjacket for the arts.

Gorki, then residing in Russia, was also drawn into the tightening system as one of its sponsors. Yet the single brightest and most vivid personality of the first decade and more of the new regime was not Gorki—but Vladimir Mayakovski, the poet who lived a stormy life and declaimed his propaganda verses at workers' meetings and on street corners. He committed suicide in 1930 as things began to close in on Russian writers.

Russian literature in the years from 1917 to 1934 was rich—particularly in poetry but also in prose. It was a flamboyant time and this was reflected in writing. The dominating characteristic of the literature of the period was its deep absorption in the overwhelming and specifically Russian experience of the Revolution. And this was a barrier between the literature of Russia and that of Western Europe. More and more as Stalin established himself firmly in power the connections between Russia and the West were being cut and barriers built separating Russia from Western Europe.

In December 1934 Stalin's rule of terror began—and continued on one or another plane of intensity for the rest of his life. Stalin's awesome personality dominated the age. He demanded unending sycophancy—and he took upon himself to exercise the most direct dictatorship over Soviet literary-artistic life. Unfortunately, his taste was atrocious. The history of Russian literature, under the circumstances, was not so much a chronicle of achievements as of obstacles to creative effort put up by the political authority under Stalin. And yet the regime desperately wanted "art" and "literature"—and even while making it most difficult for writers to operate, it was continually demanding that they produce.

To give Russian writers an example of what they were expected to produce the Party selected a particular model in the form of an autobiographical novel written by a communist of working-class origin, and propagandized and publicized it with all the possibilities which mass communications gave. The novel, entitled *How the Steel Was Tempered,* was by Nikolai Ostrovski. It was interesting, but not, of course, a great piece of literature.

Meanwhile, the Party made clear that no more experimentation in literary form would be permitted and that the most direct hand would be taken in guidance of literature and the arts.

As Stalin's purge raged, many writers, including some of the greatest, became victims. The rest were terrorized into total submissiveness to the Party's and Stalin's dictates.

Into this atmosphere burst the war. With its very genuine dangers and with the possibilities for writers, as for all Russians, to devote themselves wholeheartedly to the struggle for national survival, it brought relief from this atmosphere of terror and fear—and in its sacrifices and feats a new Russia was born. War literature in some measure immediately reflected this.

After the war, however, the relaxation and freedom so ardently desired by Russian writers and all Russians were not forthcoming. Instead, in a period of renewed rigid dictatorship over literature, all writing was subjected to the magnifying glass of Party ideological control and supervision. The basic Party decree on this subject was the 1946 report by Party Secretary Andrei Zhdanov, and the whole trend exemplified has been called Zhdanovism. Behind it, of course, stood Stalin. The particular elements of which it consisted included Russian chauvinism, hate for things foreign and especially Western, a demand that literature devote its energies to the indoctrination and depiction of a "new Soviet man," and the requirement that the arts should urge Russians on to more sacrifice, "to storm more heights" in the name of the Motherland. One of the principal facts of Soviet life in the period was the iron curtain cutting Russia off from Western Europe and America. Russian literature, too, was cut off from Western literature. Procommunist Western authors were almost the only ones translated. Under Zhdanovism the Party leadership developed some highly original concepts of the literary process: works should be written to the order of the Party on selected themes; works which were unsatisfactory from an ideological point of view for one reason or another should be rewritten—also to order —even if they were in the category of Soviet "classics"; works should see contemporary life through rose-colored glasses, exaggerating to an absurd extent Russian standards of living; they should flatter Stalin by depicting him personally in a God-like image, rewriting history wherever necessary for this purpose. As the end of Stalin's rule approached there were menacing outbreaks of anti-Semitism in official policy toward literature—and other ominous phenomena.

Stalin's death was a good thing for Russian literature—as for Russian life in general. Under the circumstances of the last two decades of Stalin's rule it is not surprising that very little significant literature was produced. And yet works of permanent value were written and published. This is a tribute to the stubbornness and talent of Russian writers—to their determined will to create.

When Stalin died a new era came for Russian arts and letters— but it did not come all of a sudden. Its first manifestation consisted in articles of literary criticism in 1953: by poet Olga Berggolts—on the absence of lyricism in contemporary poetry—by novelist and essayist Ilya Ehrenburg—attacking the system of writing works to order—and most importantly by critic Vladimir Pomerantsev—calling for sincerity in writing. This last article in particular immediately drew down strong attacks from other, officially inspired critics. But these articles showed there was a new atmosphere.

This new atmosphere began to appear in new literary works. Writers very quickly acquired much broader freedom of expression of emotions and ideas. The name for the new period of Russian literary development was given by Ilya Ehrenburg in a novella called

The Thaw. In his story Ehrenburg's chief characters expressed thoughts and feelings which for this time were startling and daring. They talked freely of the seamy side of life under and just after Stalin and spoke hopefully of what might come, namely *change.* Ehrenburg's novel was also bitterly attacked. But the author made no recantation and was subjected to no sanctions or punishment. Other writers, seeing this, themselves took heart and began to write more freely and more frankly. And even though at the Second Congress of Writers in December 1954 strong criticism of Ehrenburg and Pomerantsev was a main theme of the gathering and was voiced by many official spokesmen, there were many writers, including even official rapporteurs, who spoke out vigorously at the meeting demanding changes in the literary milieu. All of these demands taken together added up to a demand for more freedom for writers.

The big breakthrough for Russian literature, however, came in 1956, after Nikita Khrushchev's denunciation at the 20th Party Congress of the Stalin "personality cult." At this point a whole flood of writing expressing strong protest against inhuman bureaucracy and the presence of dishonesty and insincerity in official attitudes toward life poured forth. Many works described with vivid realism the bad living conditions of Russian people, particularly in the countryside. Stories by Alexander Yashin, Nikolai Zhdanov, Yuri Nagibin, Dmitri Granin, and others bore down heavily on these themes with surprising frankness. A number of excellently written, startling works appeared in volume II of the almanac *Literary Moscow,* edited by a group of Moscow writers.

At the same time the literary reputations and some of the works of some of the writers who had perished in or as a result of the purges were being "rehabilitated." Some individual writers who had been in exile but who had not perished appeared again on the literary scene and in print.

There was broadened translation of foreign writers—including some of those most advanced in terms of style and subject matter, who had previously been on the forbidden list. Soviet writers began to go abroad more frequently and foreign writers to visit the Soviet Union. In general a period began when there was renewal of contacts on all levels with Western Europe and the United States—and this had strong influence on literature.

Literarily speaking, the most important development by far was in the field of poetry. Under Stalin ordinary unpolitical lyrical poetry had been virtually forbidden. After Stalin this prohibition was gradually lifted. As a result there was a torrent of new, excellent lyric poetry in 1956, much of it completely unconcerned with political causes and questions.

Among the poets to appear in print were such senior figures as the much-criticized Anna Akhmatova and Boris Pasternak (who had published some of the verses from his novel *Doctor Zhivago* as far back as 1954). There were poets such as Boris Slutsky, Nikolai Zabolitski, and Leonid Martynov, who had been unable to publish their works for years. Most important, a galaxy of newer, younger poets headed by Yevgeny Yevtushenko, Robert Rozhdestvensky, and Yevgeny Vinokurov began to acquire artistic maturity in their works. Alexander Tvardovsky of the older generation, who had been silent almost since the war, wrote his *Distance Beyond Distance,* in which he touched on the delicate and important theme of people returning from exile and imprisonment. At the end of 1955 there arose the annual custom of a poetry day at which poets read their verses aloud, and this set in motion a general wave of public poetry readings and recitations which gave a whole new life to Russian poetry and served —for poetry—the immediate purpose of effectively bypassing the literary censorship.

The culmination of the important literary year of 1956 was publication of the strongly written novel attacking the bureaucrats of science and industry—*Not By Bread Alone* by Vladimir Dudintsev. This aroused the most lively discussion in Moscow's literary history, and, in conjunction with the political crisis which arose out of the Soviet Union's suppression by armed force of the Hungarian revolution and the consequent move to tighten political controls at home in the Soviet Union, it brought down the wrath of the Communist Party on Dudintsev. In the year 1957—a year of suppression of the tendencies and literary activity of the kind seen in 1956—the Dudintsev book and *Literary Moscow* were more or less constant targets of officially inspired condemnation. It was one of the objects of the campaign taking place at the time to make the writers who had been guilty of getting furthest out of line—including Dudintsev and the editors of *Literary Moscow*—repent and recant their sins in public. But this campaign encountered strong and stubborn resistance. Some of the writers involved refused in effect to recognize that they were wrong. This was a direct challenge to the authority of the Party. As a result administrative measures were taken to put trusted individuals in key positions in literature, and a new writers' organization —Union of Writers of the Russian Republic—was formed to assist the Party in reasserting its authority. Some of the younger writers were disciplined through Party channels. Yet no important literary figures were arrested or otherwise subjected to physical punishment.

Meanwhile, sides were forming among the writers themselves. There was a liberal wing led by Ilya Ehrenburg, Konstantin Paustovsky, and Alexander Tvardovsky among the elder statesmen of literature—which had very strong support among Moscow writers, particularly among the younger more advanced writers who had been those most criticized in the aftermath of 1956. They were united in seeking greater freedom of expression for writers. They were opposed by a conservative or "Stalinist" or "dogmatist" wing led by Vsevolod Kochetov and some other individuals known for their vociferous and noisy support of the Party and its special causes in and out of literature. These conservative writers were "Stalinist" probably not so much in the sense that they wanted to see a new Stalin, but as wanting to be the "chosen instrument" themselves—in other words the official policemen of the Party in literature with authority to judge other writers, to decide what was proper and permissible communist literature and what was not, and in general to preserve a "Stalinist" atmosphere of Party control and guidance of literary activity.

Perhaps the heart of the problem for these "Stalinist" writers lay in the fact that few of them really had talent, and their whole position in literature rested on the Party's willingness to support them and their works in competition with the more talented liberal writers.

In 1958 Kochetov provided the "Stalinists" with a "program document" in the form of an anti-intellectual novel, *The Brothers Yershov*, which attacked the concept of freedom for art and literature. Feelings between the two camps began to become very bitter indeed as a result of the attacks by the "Stalinist" camp on the liberals during the period of Party backwatering in 1957 and 1958.

But though these two years were a time of tightening of official policy they were also years in which younger and older writers alike were busy writing new and interesting works.

In particular, it was the period when a completely new type of prose literature began to break into print in quantity: stories, often short stories but sometimes of novella or short novel length, which were unconcerned with politics and political "protest" and which attempted to penetrate in depth into the heart and soul of individual Russians. In a sense the symbol of this new school was Yuri Kazakov, some of whose recent stories are presented here. His work was often much influenced by Western models, and it represented a new departure in contemporary Russian writing. Other outstanding writers of this school emerging into importance in this period included the veteran writer Yuri Nagibin, who for many years had been well-known for his war stories, and another thoughtful and experienced veteran writer, Vladimir Tendryakov.

Late in 1958 the Pasternak scandal burst on the Soviet literary world. Resulting from the award of a Nobel Prize in literature to

Boris Pasternak, whose great novel *Doctor Zhivago* had been published outside the Soviet Union in 1957, it saw a rising series of
bitter attacks on the quiet writer and threats to expel him from the
Soviet Union. The scandal died down, however, when Pasternak
himself begged Khrushchev not to expel him from Russia, declaring that this would be the equivalent of death. At about this point
Khrushchev evidently began to have some second thoughts about
the whole thing.

And in a very real way this set the scene for a much more relaxed
and conciliatory atmosphere for Russian writers when the Third
Writers' Congress met in early 1959. It was this Third Writers' Congress which set the tone for the subsequent auspicious literary developments of the next three years—to December 1962—which are
the subject of this essay.

2. *Soviet Literary Policy: 1959–62*

The Third Writers' Congress held in Moscow in May 1959 was
not particularly important for what happened at it, and yet it is regarded by students of Russian literature as a "turning point." *

The meeting had been originally scheduled for December 1958,
but was postponed. It has been suggested that the reason for the
postponement was that Nikita Khrushchev, in view of his delayed
negative reaction to the inflation of the Pasternak Nobel Prize
scandale into a major public issue, did not want the Congress held
so close to this episode and ordered it delayed so as to give things
a chance to settle down before it met.† At any rate to the extent
that the "Stalinist"—or, as they might more properly be called, "the
dogmatist"—camp of writers counted on the Party's help in stacking
things in such a way that the Third Congress would confirm or
increase the great power they were wielding in literary affairs in the
post-Hungary reaction of 1957–58, they were keenly disappointed.
In the aftermath of the Pasternak affair they suffered a severe setback.
One of their key points of control had been the editorship of the
Literary Gazette, the leading literary newspaper and the official
organ of the Soviet Writers' Union—held by Vsevolod Kochetov.
Kochetov was removed from this position, and in his place a relative
moderate, S. S. Smirnov, was appointed.

This then set the scene for the publication of an important

---

* Max Hayward, "Conflict and Change in Literature," *Survey, a Magazine of
Soviet and East European Affairs,* No. 46 (Jan. 1963), p. 12.
† Harrison E. Salisbury, *To Moscow and Beyond, A Reporter's Narrative* (New
York, 1960), pp. 104–5.

article in the *Literary Gazette* which appeared in connection with the Congress. The author was Konstantin Paustovsky, one of the "elder statesmen" of Russian literature, a distinguished writer 67 years old at the time, who had gotten himself involved in the storm over the Dudintsev novel *Not By Bread Alone* and who could speak effectively for the whole liberal camp in literature. Paustovsky's basic point was much the same as that of Pomerantsev in 1953—it was an even stronger appeal for sincerity and honesty in writing.

In the literary magazine *Novy Mir*, there appeared about the same time another important article by Ilya Ehrenburg. This time he discussed the work of the outstanding Russian writer Anton Chekhov—his article being entitled "On Rereading Chekhov." The points which Ehrenburg made were clear enough to anyone accustomed to this oblique approach to discussion of contemporary literary problems and issues. Ehrenburg dealt a very heavy blow indeed at the school of "optimism" in literature—in the form of a pointed Chekhov quotation. Chekhov had declared that the "bourgeoisie" loved happy endings and goody-goody heroes, both items being, of course, typical of socialist-realism in literature.

The Ehrenburg and Paustovsky pieces were strong stuff. Yet they drew down no immediate lightning on their authors' heads. Other liberal writers watched with interest.

And under the circumstances the dry-as-dust speeches at the Congress went largely unnoticed—all except the address of Nikita Khrushchev, which was certainly not dry-as-dust and which was one of the more important literary-political documents of the decade. It was a very different kind of utterance from some of his previous— and subsequent—declarations on writing or art. He did, of course, restate many of the fundamental Party theses on literature. But instead of demanding abject acceptance and submission from his listeners he talked with a certain amount of diffidence about his literary concepts. He suggested there should be tolerance for the efforts of younger writers who were just learning. In fact the suggestion of tolerance in literary controversies permeated the entire speech, and this was bad medicine for the "dogmatists." After all, their whole position was based on a right, given them at times by the Party, to be "intolerant" of everyone they did not like. Khrushchev told the writers in effect to run their own affairs and not to be perpetually troubling the government and Party with their controversies. This was right down the line for the liberals, because they were the ones who wanted to run their own affairs. Since they also had great strength among writers, particularly in Moscow, they didn't need to keep running to the government so long as they were permitted some kind of self-government. Khrushchev asked the writers to get together and settle their quarrels among themselves by themselves. He obviously wanted an end to the bitter factionalism—at least he was acting as if he did. And this may have been sincere enough at the time.

The Writers' Congress responded rather promptly to the Khrushchev "offer." Konstantin Fedin was elected as the new First Secretary of the Writers' Union in place of Alexei Surkov. Since Fedin was well known both as a close personal friend of Boris Pasternak and as a relative moderate in literary affairs this was a very indicative move. Fedin, though not himself a member of the Party, was, of course, unquestionably loyal to the Party and notably unrebellious. But he was a very different kind of a person from Surkov, who had often been more vociferous than the Party required him to be, and, who therefore, had made no few enemies in the process. Some of them —writers he had persecuted—he now found alongside himself on the Board of the Writers' Union as equals. One of these was Alexander Tvardovsky, once again editor-in-chief of *Novy Mir,* a post from which Surkov had helped get him removed back in 1954.

This then was the way things added up at the end of the Third Writers' Congress, and as a result there were no particularly sensational controversies in literature for a considerable period. There was, however, great literary productivity. The "fat" journals—the literary magazines—came out steadily with interesting and unusual works, and, as the months went on, there was constantly a greater breadth of freedom of writers' self-expression. Many new writers appeared on the scene. True, the overwhelmingly dominant *mise en scene* of almost all the Russian literary works published continued to be—for fiction—factory, farm, and laboratory. This kind of milieu was seemingly very socialist-realist—and yet writers were using this milieu with a good deal of verve and imagination, carrying it beyond the bounds of socialist-realism. They were opening up new areas for literary exploration.

The year 1961 brought several specific interesting literary events.

In February a very tiny booklet of lyrical verse by the poetess Anna Akhmatova was issued. This was an indicative development. Akhmatova, after all, had been one of the two main targets of Andrei Zhdanov in his notorious report of 1946. From time to time a few of her poems had later appeared in literary magazines or other publications—some of them in *Literary Moscow* in 1956. But that shadow of Party disapproval was never fully off Akhmatova. Her verses had been scheduled, it was indicated at the time, to come out in book form in 1956. But this didn't happen. So it was a notable day when finally an Akhmatova collection did appear in an edition of 50,000 copies, which was quickly snapped up by eager Russian readers.

Later that same year—in early autumn—an event of very similar but greater significance took place. A booklet was published—in an edition of some 25,000 copies—of the poetry of Marina Tsvetayeva. If Akhmatova had been considered all along relatively undesirable by the powers-that-were, then Tsvetayeva's lyricism had been thought of as positively subversive. Of course, there were no politics in Tsvetayeva's poetry—other than a burning hate for German Fascism expressed in some of her pieces. The thing was that Tsvetayeva's very talent and greatness were apparently deemed to be extremely dangerous—because she was certainly in every respect the very antithesis of socialist-realism. She herself had long been dead—a suicide in provincial exile during wartime—but her spirit was very much alive. And there was the rub. At any rate because of the peculiar political meaning of this very unpolitical poetess—something quite difficult for any non-Russian to grasp, so utterly harmless she seems—the appearance of this volume of her verse, promised back in 1956 but held up for five full years, was a unique sign of the times.

If the publication of the Akhmatova and Tsvetayeva volumes was a manifestation of the increasing influence of the liberal faction of Russian writers, the appointment of Vsevolod Kochetov as the editor-in-chief of the literary journal *Oktyabr* was obviously a victory for the "dogmatists," of whom he was the recognized leader. *Oktyabr* had previously been edited by F. I. Panferov, who, though very party-line himself, was a moderate in the literary controversies and had suffered at the hands of Alexei Surkov in the 1954 reaction. After Panferov died in the summer of 1960 the post as editor-in-chief of *Oktyabr* remained vacant for a time. Obviously, there was a continuing dispute over who should get it. When Kochetov won out in early 1961, it meant that the "dogmatists" had, so to speak, an "official" organ among the literary journals. They already had their newspaper—*Literature and Life*—which was a rival of the *Literary Gazette* and which usually took a more conservative view than did the latter.

Kochetov who had written the "Stalinist" writers' platform in the form of his novel, which was in essence a political tract, *The Brothers Yershov*, published in 1958, now came out with a new novel, which was entitled *The Provincial Party Secretary*. This work was similar in character to *The Brothers Yershov* but even stronger—even more anti-intellectual, anti-liberal, and bitter in tone.

There is in the book a scene in which the hero of the novel, the Party secretary named Denisov, returns from the 20th Party Congress and stands, together with his wife, in front of Stalin's portrait—tears streaming copiously down their cheeks. And Denisov declares, overcome with his emotion: "But no, I can't judge him."

One of the villains of the book is the young poet, Ptushkov, a more or less out-and-out takeoff on young poet Yevgeny Yevtushenko. He is flamboyant, active—and terribly liberal. And his verses have "no possible use" under socialism. Says a Party official who has come to headquarters seeking guidance on literature which will help him in his work:

"Well, now how can one use such verses (Ptushkov's) for purposes of heightening the indoctrination role of propaganda work? I would like to have you explain that to me. Because when I get asked about that I am stuck in a blind alley—I can't explain it. I consider that our historical tasks are too great, and our responsibility too heavy to our people and to the whole communist movement in the entire world..."

Then there is another scene in the book, typifying yet another aspect of the Kochetov program, in which a communist is hauled on the carpet and given a collective tongue lashing—because he has built himself, absolutely legally, and according to his rights under Soviet law, an eight-room two-story privately owned house. This, in the judgment of the critics of the given communist, and obviously of the author Kochetov as well, means that the man has already become a "capitalist."

The whole controversy between the liberals and the "dogmatists" in literature broke out into the open in an ugly, ominous way over the issue of the poem entitled "Babi Yar," written by Yevgeny Yevtushenko. The poem is named for the ravine outside Kiev where thousands of Jews were massacred by the Nazis during World War II. It was a site and an event which had never been commemorated by the Soviet government till Yevtushenko took it upon himself to write a poem on the subject which was not merely an historical exercise—but a burning condemnation of anti-Semitism in Russia, including the Russia of right now.

Yevtushenko declared ringingly:

"Whenever the last anti-Semite of all on earth is buried once and for all/ Then let the International resound/ I have no Jewish blood/ And yet I'm as badly hated/ By every last anti-Semite/ As if I myself were Jewish/ And by this token/ I am a Russian."

It is difficult to imagine what a storm this poem stirred up.* It was interpreted by the Soviet right-wing extremists—among whom Russian chauvinism is closely related to anti-Semitism, and anti-Semitism to anti-intellectualism, and both to antiforeign feeling, or

---

* Yevtushenko in his *Precocious Autobiography* (New York, 1963) has vividly told the story of how the poem went to press in the *Literary Gazette* on Sept. 19, 1961, and his thoughts as he waited to see it in print. He knew there would be a strong reaction.

anticosmopolitanism—as a direct challenge and a slap in the face. And five days later in their organ *Literature and Life,* the "dogmatists" answered Yevtushenko in a set of verses by Alexei Markov.*

"What kind of a real Russian are you anyway/ When you've forgotten all about your own people . . ."

Literature and Life returned to the assault on Yevtushenko a few days later, in an article written by D. Starikov, with the assertion that not only Jews were massacred at Babi Yar. (This was more or less like saying that not only Jews were killed in the gas chambers at Auschwitz.)

On October 8, 1961, on Poetry Day that year, ten thousand people turned out—and turned the whole meeting into an ovation for Yevtushenko, thereby registering their feelings about "Babi Yar."

A little later the editor of *Literature and Life* who had published the replies of Markov and Starikov was dropped. For the time being the Russian liberal writers were on the top.

This fact was emphasized in a rather unique and startling way by the publication of a book in October of that same year. Entitled *Pages from Tarusa,*† it was issued by a provincial publishing house —in the town of Kaluga.

Tarusa was a small town on the Oka River, not far from the city of Serpukhov and maybe a hundred miles south of Moscow. It was a quiet, sleepy little place and off the beaten track. As Konstantin Paustovsky had written of it:

"Tarusa has its own glory . . . Perhaps nowhere close to Moscow were there such places so typically and touchingly Russian in their landscapes . . . It was not for nothing that even at the end of the 19th century Tarusa became a city of artists, sort of our own national Barbizon . . . After the artists came the writers and scholars, and Tarusa became its own kind of creative laboratory and refuge for people of art and science . . . To this one must add that, thanks to the attraction to Tarusa, during almost a century, for writers and artists there gradually accumulated here valuable art collections and literary archives. During the last five years there have settled down in Tarusa still more people of science and art. For many writers Tarusa has become a unique creative corner, refuge, where they can work fruitfully and well."

Paustovsky was one of the moving spirits in compilation of this

---

* Markov quickly became known among liberal intellectuals in Moscow as "Markov the Third"—since a character known as "Markov the Second" had been a notorious Jew-baiter under the tsars. See Harrison Salisbury, *A New Russia?* (New York, 1962), p. 73.

† *Pages from Tarusa* is now available in a translation edited by Andrew Field and published by Little, Brown.

volume which consisted of works, most of them previously unpublished, by writers who had lived and worked in Tarusa. But it was more than just an ordinary compilation. It included works by some people of the older generation such as Paustovsky himself. It included works by a certain number of people who had suffered from repression or from suppression of their works under—and for a time after—Stalin. Among them were the late Marina Tsvetayeva, represented by a lengthy collection of previously unpublished verses, Nikolai Zabolitsky, who for a time had been under arrest, Boris Slutsky, who had spent the years of Stalinism and Zhdanovism from 1940 on writing "for his desk drawer"—in other words, not for publication—and N. Korzhavin, who had been exiled. Then, alongside these there were included works written by a whole constellation of younger writers, including Yuri Kazakov, Yevgeni Vinokurov, Bulat Okudzhava, Boris Balter, and others.

What it all really added up to, in spirit and deed, was an affirmation of a certain Russian literary tradition, of the liberal heritage of the Russian enlightenment. And the implication of the inclusion of relative newcomers to writing alongside older and battle-scarred veterans in a collection dedicated to a place deemed to be the "most typically Russian" of anything in the surroundings of Moscow and possessing the most venerable of Russian literary-artistic backgrounds was that the publication of the work was a sort of symbolic act of the laying on of hands. Paustovsky was seeming to pass on to the writers of the new generation whom he had picked for inclusion the mantle of "the Russian literary future." The book itself was interesting, containing some excellent stories and verse previously unpublished. Some 75,000 copies were published—but this was a small edition for Russia, and the book disappeared from circulation nearly as fast as it appeared.

The 22nd Congress of the Soviet Communist Party was convened on October 17 and continued right on till October 31. From the literary point of view its main feature was the sharp contrast between the literary positions set forth before this distinguished gathering by the exponent of the liberal platform, Alexander Tvardovsky, and of the conservative or "dogmatist" platform by Vsevolod Kochetov. Nikita Khrushchev himself in his own very lengthy keynote address to the Congress, devoted largely to economic progress, international affairs, the new Party Program which the Congress adopted, and to attacks on the Albanian—i.e. Chinese —heresy, did not devote but a paragraph or two to literature. He uttered one or two standard phrases: "The Party bases itself on the position that art must indoctrinate people first of all on positive examples in life, indoctrinate people in the spirit of communism.

The strength of Soviet literature and art—the method of socialist-realism—is in the truthful depiction of the chief and decisive elements in reality."

This, of course, is the same old unchanging Party position on literature and art—the socialist-realist definition of the function of the artist in Soviet society. But Khrushchev did not select particular literary works for criticism and attack—nor others for favorable comment—not on this occasion.

His friend, the writer Mikhail Sholokhov, spoke at the session. Sholokhov had earned the right as a result of his fame, his age, and his performances at previous solemn assemblages, to be usually less than serious and almost always less than wise. His talk at the 22nd Party Congress was not an exception to this tradition. He used this occasion—as he had used similar occasions in the past—to take a few random pokes at pet hates. In particular he dwelt this time on writers who, unlike himself, enjoyed city life and didn't feel like hanging about all their lives in their native villages as he did. "A hopeless cause!" he declared of the plea of the Minister of Culture, Mme Furtseva, for more writers to live outside the biggest cities. "Let Mme Furtseva garner for herself in this noble cause lumps and bumps—I've already had enough!" And Sholokhov in discoursing on this theme gave vent to hard feelings about the popularity of the young Russian poets—presumably Yevtushenko, Andrei Voznesensky, and the like—when he declared:

"One can't really forbid the young creators of 'permanent values,' those who live in the provinces, entry to Moscow or other large cities. They hear with what acclaim literary evenings of our currently fashionable boudoir poets take place in Moscow—always with a detail of mounted police and with hysterical yells of young *stilyagi* screamers. They also want to shine before undemanding 'girls' in improbably narrow britches and unjustifiably broad-shouldered jackets. They also want to taste the fruits of fame. And so they crowd into Moscow like believers to Mecca."

At any rate his feelings were clear.

Alexander Korneichuk, another writer close to Khrushchev, and a man who had always kept closely attuned to current political tendencies—and in particular to official policy on literature—also gave a talk. And he made in it one indicative remark: "I want to say only one thing. It seems to me that our Soviet literary figures should worry less about what pedestal they are going to be put on and work more, work, work and work, study life."

This statement could certainly be interpreted as a plea for less controversy in literature.

The principal address on literature at the Congress was delivered by Alexander Tvardovsky—it was an appeal for truth in literature. He said the personality cult had not yet been outlived in literature—it appeared in a tendency toward immoderate braggartism and a "striving to see in life only Sundays, only red-letter days, and to somehow leave out of account weekdays..." A principal theme of his speech was the contention that writers could not be viewed as mere illustrators of the current Party line. He did not deny the importance of political writing, but he said that the demands which Russian society was making of literature were much much broader than merely that: they relate "to the spiritual life of our human being, to all his happiness and grief, his concerns and desires not only in his productive life, but also in all his life, in family relationships, in love, fatherhood and motherhood, in a word in the whole complexity of life, as it is."

He objected to the thesis that writers could not work effectively in big cities, pointing out that these were the cultural centers of the nation. He objected to the concept that writers must stick to very contemporary and immediate happenings only in their work. He objected to the absence of "human charm" in the heroes of Soviet literary works.

His address constituted a strong, moving statement of the liberal program in Russian literature—kept, of course, carefully within the framework imposed both by the Soviet system as a whole and the particular gathering which he was addressing.

The last speaker at the Congress was Kochetov. The fact he had this position in the discussion presumably indicated that he had not been originally scheduled to speak, that he must have sought specially the opportunity to reply to Tvardosvky, and that he had received it at the very last moment. There was in his speech a deep tone of injured outrage at the current literary scene.

He struck out at Ehrenburg: "Truth demands that the facts be stated about the gloomy writers of memoirs among our writers who look more backward than at today or the future, and as a result of such distortion of point of view with energy worthy of a better purpose dig down into the trash bucket of their wandering memories in order to drag out into the light long since rotted corpses and to present them as something still capable of life..."

He struck out at the young poets: "Truth demands that the fact be stated that there are in the literary milieu chicks who have hardly yet grown their first yellow down who want like fury to appear to be dangerous fighting cocks."

He struck out at the Writers' Union: "If we speak out conscientiously then we must say that the leadership of the Writers' Union should have told the Congress about the state of our literary affairs. But, we have to constitute the sad fact, speaking in fighting language, that it has lost, you see, its capability of giving battle and needs a decisive reforming."

In other words the leadership of the Writers' Union needs to be changed—and Kochetov put in charge of it.

But he wasn't. That was the real burden of the Congress and its aftermath. Kochetov was listened to—and no doubt among important Party officials some approved what he had to say. But for the time being he had no decisive support.

Not that the Party was happy about everything going on in Soviet literature. There was particular concern about the kind of works which were being published for and about young people. And this came out in a very specific form—after the Congress, in late December of that same year. A meeting on the subject of Party ideological work was held in order to bring Party propagandists up to the minute on the new lines of effort which they were to make as a result of the Party Congress. The chief speaker was Leonid F. Ilyichev, one of the secretaries of the Central Committee who headed the Party's work in the field of propaganda—an area which included culture and literature. Ilyichev spoke out on the subject of some recent youth literature appearing in the magazine *Yunost* previously that year. *Pravda,* on December 27, 1961, reported his remarks in summary form:

"Underlining the great indoctrination role of literature and art, the rapporteur particularly dwelt on some erroneous works on youth. In particular, he said that the novel of V. Aksenov entitled *Ticket to the Stars* and the scenario of V. Rozov entitled *A B C* had been subjected to just criticism in the press. A characteristic feature of the young people described by V. Aksenov and V. Rozov is skepticism. The authors did not dethrone it—but took a sympathetic attitude toward it. And after all this is that same skepticism which puts in doubt everything in the world ... The art of socialist-realism opens broad possibilities for the manifestation of creative initiative, high skill, multiplicity of artistic forms, styles, and genres. However, searchings for innovation—must not become formalistic gimmickry which was always a manifestation of bourgeois lack of taste."

One key phrase here—"formalistic gimmickry"—was identical in the Ilyichev speech with a phrase in the Kochetov speech at the Congress.

The matter was not carried much further at that time. One immediate effect was to hold up a motion picture based on *Ticket to the Stars* till it could be revised so as to be satisfactory to the Party propaganda authorities. Similarly, there was a need for changes in Rozov's popular stage version of his scenario. And there was a change in the editorial control over the magazine *Yunost*—a journal for young people which often printed younger writers and which in 1960 and 1961 had been rather in the forefront of the move toward modernization of styles and subject matter in Russian writing. Valentin Katayev, a famous writer for young people, was dismissed as editor-in-chief and replaced by Boris Polevoi, a faithful Communist Party man who had also done some interesting writing himself. But Polevoi did not make any abrupt about-face in the orientation of the journal.

These moves were a reminder that the Party was still there— and keeping a watchful eye peeled for "unhealthy phenomena," but they did not change the general trend—not for the time being.

In the first half of 1962 the liberal faction of writers strengthened its position in Moscow considerably—by use of the vote. This was an extraordinary event. The Moscow branch of the Union of Writers met in early April and elected a new board. According to a report from the French correspondent of *Le Monde,* Tatu, the result was a virtually complete exclusion of the "dogmatist" faction's leaders—including Kochetov himself, Nikolai Gribachev, Anatoly Sofronov, Leonid Sobolev, and others—from the large board consisting of more than threescore members.*

The "dogmatists" were then forced, in order to maintain their control over the Union of Writers of the Russian Republic—originally set up in 1958 as a counterweight to the Moscow Union of Writers' organization—to retreat from Moscow to Rostov-on-the-Don to hold their board meeting. One has the impression that had they dared to hold their session in Moscow they might have lost their foothold in this association too—or that the session might have turned into a riot. But in Rostov they could continue to thunder out at such liberals as Yevtushenko and his colleagues with impunity—and they did. Leonid Sobolev gave vent to a particularly strong attack on the liberal writers.

At this point it is interesting to dwell for a moment on the fascinating question of just how a situation like this could arise in Soviet literature.

It had always been an established principle of the Soviet type of totalitarian social organization, once its basic outlines had been worked out, that every organization in the country from a club of stamp collectors right on up to the Council of Ministers itself *must* be under the direct and active control of the Soviet Communist Party. This applied likewise to all writers' organizations—including the Soviet Writers' Union, the Moscow organization of the Writers'

---

* Max Hayward, "Conflict and Change in Literature, Survey," No. 46 (Jan. 1963), p. 20.

Union, the Writers' Union of the Russian Republic, the publishing houses, the literary magazines, the censorship, *Glavlit,* the Ministry of Culture, etc., etc. There had been no indication of any kind that the Soviet Communist Party had any intention of abandoning this prerogative—a self-assigned obligation—of exercising an active control over every sector of life, including literature. There had been not the slightest indication that the Soviet Communist Party was prepared to make some kind of a grant of a charter of self-government to any sector of the social system—including writers—in any formal sense. There had been no sign whatsoever that the Soviet Communist Party leadership had any idea of an abandonment of the principle of socialist-realism in culture, or of the constant Party supervision, guidance, and control which that principle implied.

So how then, we have to ask, could it happen that things were allowed in the period from 1959 to 1962, particularly in this latter year, to move so far in the direction of self-government of Russian writers, of control by the overwhelming, liberal majority of writers over Soviet literary affairs, and of a shift away from the dogma of social-realism to the extent that a whole series of important works were written which one can, only by the broadest stretch of the imagination, consider to be socialist-realist? And what are the possible implications of this for the Russian literary future—and for the Soviet future in general?

That there are such implications one can imagine and ponder—though certainly one cannot postulate them in any self-confident way.

One more or less obvious factor in this situation was the tactical need of a national political leadership—of Khrushchev—committed to a policy of continued relative liberalization of the system, to a policy of "destalinization." Because of these policies Khrushchev's leadership was continually under fire from the elements within the body politic—and from the system in a broader sense—whose power or authority was under one or another kind of threat from this policy. In this situation the political leadership was forced to look for support where it could find it—and certainly it did find some valiant assistance on the part of the liberal writers in assailing the pillars of Stalinism. Therefore, it was natural for the national political leadership to be inclined to give the liberal writers a free rein from time to time—until they seemed to be endangering the system or at least the political position of the national leadership, at which point there would have to be a clampdown.

Another perhaps significant factor was that the nation, and its political leadership, wanted the international and internal prestige deriving from the creation of significant literature—and it was clearly only the liberal writers who could deliver that and who were actually beginning to deliver it. So here again the country's political leadership, to get the kudos it wanted, had to rely on the liberal writers and—since they required it as their condition for producing—let them to some extent run their own literary affairs. But the political leadership kept periodically finding it could not have its cake and eat it. The better the literature that appeared the more it contributed to spiritual unrest and ferment in the nation—and that was a price which seemed always too high. So again there was a kind of dilemma, "solved" by a periodic clampdown.

But behind this and underlying it was there operating another factor of longer-range significance? Could it be that there was in the Soviet system a gradual and developing shift from full totalitarianism—with the initiative always emerging from the dictatorial national control center, with that control directly, constantly, actively exercised over all organizations of all kinds by the one big superorganization, the Party, and over the Party itself by its leadership—to a kind of authoritarian system in which there was much greater autonomy of the constituent elements, perhaps even reaching eventually in the future to a broad grant of self-government for some of the elements? This has to be left as a mere question—but it's the most important question one can ask about the Soviet Union.

And perhaps it is the literary scene which is a key point in the whole picture—one of the reasons for watching it so closely. The significance of Soviet literary policy, it is true, always seems to transcend pure literature itself.

The year 1962 was notable for Russian literature. In the atmosphere of the times many interesting things were written and published. It was also notable—in a different sense—for a decisive series of events which took place in the area of literary policy.

On October 21 *Pravda* published a poem by Yevgeny Yevtushenko entitled *Stalin's Heirs*. It was a moving work. In it Yevtushenko depicted Stalin's bier being removed from the mausoleum on Red Square with the dead Stalin clenching his fists and planning to rise up from his resting place again:

> "And I turn to our government with a request:
> Double, triple, the guard at that gravestone,
> So Stalin may not arise, and with Stalin the past."

And Yevtushenko then pictured unreformed Stalinists picking roses in retirement and considering their retirement temporary, other Stalinists making speeches against Stalin but hoping secretly for the return of Stalin's times and his concentration camps, hating in the meanwhile all the Moscow halls overflowing with people listening to poetry.

"And so long as there are the heirs of Stalin on earth
It will seem to me, that Stalin is still in the Mausoleum."

This was strong medicine. And after a time it became known that the poem had been printed with Khrushchev's own personal approval.

Another event which took place about this time was the decision to discontinue publication of the relatively conservative thrice-a-week literary newspaper *Literature and Life,* and to replace it with a new periodical, a literary weekly, entitled *Literary Russia.*

This looked at first glance like a blow at the conservative faction of writers. Similarly interpreted was a change in the editorial board of *Yunost,* the literary journal for youth which had been attacked by L. F. Ilyichev in December 1961. In the November issue of the magazine it was revealed that the writer criticized by Ilyichev for the novel *Ticket to the Stars,* Vasily Aksenov, had been named to the editorial board of the magazine, and along with him Yevgeny Yevtushenko. This seemed likely to increase the already liberal orientation of the magazine.

It seemed also of significance that somewhat earlier a new view had evidently been taken of the motion picture based on *Ticket to the Stars,* which was released in a film version retaining at least a good deal of the essentially frank and outspoken atmosphere of the novel in its approach to the moods and feelings of Russian young people. Much the same had happened with the other work criticized by Ilyichev at the same time, Rozov's *A B C,* which was in the repertoires of a number of Soviet theaters—in a somewhat revised edition. Rozov, incidentally, despite the Ilyichev criticism of his scenario, had never been deprived of his post on the *Yunost* editorial board.

On November 6 the leading newspaper, *Izvestia,* published a very short story entitled "The Nugget." On November 11 *Pravda* followed with a short story entitled "Good Memory." The latter work, by Valeriya Gerasimova, depicted the touching scene of return to her old home, to what little was left of her family, by a woman communist who had been arrested and exiled for many long years in Stalin's terror. The woman, who did not in the course of the story disclose her identity, encountered her own daughter who was being brought up by relatives. "The Nugget," written by Georgi Shelest, however, came even closer to treatment of previously unmentionable aspects of the Stalin terror by picturing a scene in an arctic concentration camp in the Soviet Far East during World War II in which four former Communist Party members were struggling to survive in the most difficult and cruel conditions. Neither of these two short stories was in any sense so vivid or annihilating in its frankness and pathos as such a work as Yuri Bondarev's novel *Stillness,* which had appeared earlier in 1962 with a scene portraying the after-midnight arrest on a false denunciation of an old and honorable Russian communist in the year 1949. But "The Nugget," by *actually giving a literary fictional treatment* for the first time in a Soviet publication of concentration-camp conditions seemed to be suggesting that this important previously untouchable subject had been thrown open at least on a trial basis for creative writers.

Another work which appeared in November was the play by Samuel Alyeshin entitled *The Ward.* Through discussions among patients in a hospital ward it presented a vivid denunciation of Soviet communists who were still devoted to Stalinist terroristic methods. In the context of this period it also was regarded not only as an assault on the vestiges of Stalinism and the so-called "personality cult" but also as one more development in the trend toward freer literary expression.

However, by all odds the most important and decisive development in this whole series of happenings was the publication in the literary magazine *Novy Mir* in late November 1962 of the novel by Alexander Solzhenitsyn entitled *One Day in the Life of Ivan Denisovich.* This work described in fictional form the life of a political prisoner in one of Stalin's hard-labor concentration camps from awakening in the morning until sleep at night on a cold day of January 1951 in Siberia. It created in the person of its hero, Ivan Denisovich Shukhov, a peasant carpenter emprisoned because he had briefly been a prisoner of the Germans, an unforgettable character. And it dwelt for page after page on the small details and cruelties of hopeless prison life in the long period of the Stalin terror. It was something completely new and epochal in Soviet Russian literature.

When *One Day in the Life of Ivan Denisovich* came out it was greeted by enthusiastic reviews in leading Soviet press organs. *Pravda* compared the author to Tolstoi. *The Moscow News* ran it serially in translation, and the Soviet official publication *Soviet Literature Monthly* also carried it in English. Subsequent to its appearance it was reportedly revealed by Nikita Khrushchev himself * that he had personally sanctioned the appearance of the novel in print without, allegedly, any deletions.

A juxtaposition of dates shows that in all probability there was a decision of the Soviet leadership, possibly even some kind of formal

* *The New York Times,* Nov. 29, 1962, p. 4.

but unpublished decision, authorizing the publication of certain works dealing with the "concentration camp" theme. The issue of *Novy Mir* which carried *One Day in the Life of Ivan Denisovich* went to press on November 3. (It did not, of course, appear on the newsstands in Moscow till November 20.) The paper *Izvestia* carried its concentration camp story, "The Nugget," on November 6, while *Pravda* ran its story, "Good Memory," about the tragedy of the woman returned from emprisonment on November 11. The fact that both of the newspaper short stories dealt with the camp theme in a way stressing loyalty to the ideals of communism and faith in the Soviet Communist Party, contrasting in this respect with the Solzhenitsyn novel which carefully avoided any political context, seemed to be a deliberate signpost to other Soviet writers who might in the future wish to write in this area, telling them how and in what way the Party would like them to approach it. Yet such an indication of continued Party interest in the way touchy and difficult subjects were handled was hardly surprising—and could in no sense diminish the significance of the fact that the introduction of this new and vital theme into the scope of creative work of Russian writers meant a very important accretion to their breadth of freedom for self-expression.

This then was the way things stood at the end of November: there were a number of different developments indicating that the Soviet Communist Party leadership was acceding in some important respects to the desires of the overwhelming majority of Russian writers represented by the liberal wing of literature for further liberalization of controls over literary and other artistic activity.

It was precisely at this moment of highest hopes both among observers of Russian literature and politics outside the Soviet Union and among Russian writers and intellectuals inside Russia that the Soviet leadership chose to hurl a thunderbolt at the creative arts which signaled a dramatic and abrupt reversal of official policy in literature.

This is a full story in its own right.

3. *Clampdown: December 1962–June 1963*

On December 2, 1962, the paper *Pravda* published a front-page report on a tour by Nikita Khrushchev and other Soviet leaders of an exhibit of works of Moscow artists at the Moscow Central Exhibition Hall, sometimes known as "The Old Riding School" or more simply as the "Manezh." The press report of the tour constituted in fact a most important declaration of principles for Soviet art. And even though the specific target of the remarks by Khrushchev in the course of it was representational art—painting and sculpture—it obviously, from the very beginning, had a much broader significance than just these fields and was aimed with equal force at literature.

Soviet art, declared the *Pravda* report, citing Khrushchev, must faithfully depict the life of the people, inspire people to build communism, indoctrinate people in the best and most noble feelings, and arouse in them a deep understanding of the beautiful. The *Pravda* news "story" went on to deliver a bitter attack on abstract painting and sculpture: "It is impossible to observe without disturbance and outrage the smears on canvas (of the abstractionists) which are deprived of meaning, content, and form. These pathological eccentricities are a pitiful imitation of degenerate formalist art of the bourgeois West."

Pravda said that such creativity is alien to our people. Russians "reject it." Khrushchev went on to say, repeating that ancient banality of cartoonists and traditional critics when faced with modern art for the first time, that one could not tell whether the abstracts were upside down or rightside up, whether they were painted by human hands or by the tail of a jackass. Criticizing the organizers of the exhibition, Khrushchev condemned their "liberalism" and declared: "In the leadership of art there is required ideological consistency, adherence to principles, clarity, precision, and implacability toward any waverings or deviations from the main line of development of our art—the art of the people building communism."

Actually, Khrushchev's remarks which were apparently made in the presence of a goodly number of people were evidently much more blunt than *Pravda* reported them—and even profane. The magazine *Encounter* for April 1963 quotes from an alleged stenographic report of the statements made at the Old Riding Hall—with Khrushchev * declaring:

"People tell me that I am behind the times and don't realize it, that our contemporary artists will be appreciated in 100 years. Well, I don't know what will happen in 100 years, but now we have to adopt a definite policy in art, emphasizing it in the press and encouraging it materially. We won't spare a kopeck of government money for any artistic daubing . . .

"As long as I am president of the Council of Ministers, we are going to support genuine art. We aren't going to give a kopeck for pictures painted by jackasses. History can be our judge. For the time being history has put us at the head of this state, and we have to answer for everything that goes on in it. Therefore, we are going to

* *Encounter*, April 1963.

maintain a strict policy in art. I could mention that when I was in England I reached an understanding with Eden. He showed me a picture by a contemporary abstractionist and asked me how I liked it. I said I didn't understand it. He said he didn't understand it either, and asked me what I thought of Picasso. I said I didn't understand Picasso, and Eden said he couldn't understand Picasso either."

Khrushchev was quoted as declaring to the artist Zheltovsky: "We should take down your pants and set you down in a clump of nettles until you understand your mistakes. You should be ashamed. Are you a pederast or a normal man? Do you want to live abroad? Go on, then; we'll take you free as far as the border ... We have the right to send you to cut trees until you've paid back the money the state has spent on you. The people and the government have taken a lot of trouble with you, and you pay them back with this shit. They say you like to associate with foreigners. A lot of them are our enemies, don't forget."

The next day after the report of the visit to the Old Riding School *Pravda* set off a press editorial campaign on the themes set by Khrushchev. The paper broadened the scope of the offensive to include literature and music. In music *Pravda* assailed Soviet musicians who devote themselves "exclusively" to imitations of "rumbling jazz" modeled after Western jazz leaders.

Wrote *Pravda:* "The correct policy in the field of art is the Leninist policy of Party content, of communist ideological content. On the firm basis of just such a policy which has nothing in common either with wishy-washy all-forgiving liberalism nor with rotten sentimental complacency, the great art of socialist-realism has grown and become strong. It is precisely this fact which those artists who, under the pretext of bold artistic searchings and allegedly brave innovation, depart from the glorious traditions of our realistic art and betray them, forget ... True innovation is by no means bound up with anarchistic denial of the advanced traditions of national artistic culture. Pseudo-innovators, turning away from the life, struggle, and labor of their own people, thoughtlessly chase after Western 'fashions' and occupy themselves with pitiful imitations of the degraded formalist art of the bourgeois world which by its very nature is deeply alien to our perception of the world, to our aesthetic ideals, to our concept of beauty, of the lovely."

The *Pravda* report of December 2, 1962, on the Khrushchev visit to the Old Riding School art exhibit and the same paper's lead editorial of the next day were then immediately followed by publication of the same report and of similar lead editorials in all the principal organs of the Soviet press.

Here, obviously, was the beginning of a major ideological campaign, guided and directed by the propaganda authorities of the Communist Party. Its slogans and its themes were clear. They added up to a vigorous reassertion of the same theses of socialist realism in art and literature which the Soviet Communist Party had so often repeated during and after Stalin.

How far would this go? What did it mean for writing?

A most ominous sign for the Russian writers and artists fully initiated into the intrigues of the Soviet artistic world—and who among them was not?—came on December 4, 1962, with the word that Academician V. A. Serov had been elected the new president of the Academy of Fine Arts.* Serov's name was enough to frighten any liberal writer or artist in Moscow. He was an academic and socialist-realist painter *par excellence*. He had specialized in painting scenes from the revolution and other phases of the communist movement—and during the Stalin period the image of Joseph Stalin could sometimes be seen in them, as for example in the painting which won him a Stalin prize, which showed the young Stalin standing behind Lenin at the time of the proclamation of Soviet seizure of power in 1917. He represented to the liberals pretty much the worst in the aesthetics of the personality-cult period, and from his new position he would certainly be able to hinder the work and attack the style of anyone who desired to paint or sculpt in a modern style on politically neutral or apolitical subjects.

Worst of all to show his new influence *Pravda* on December 9 published a major editorial by him on the theme of socialist-realism in graphic arts.

The storm warnings were up!

To a much greater extent than in the field of writing the dogmatists had managed to maintain in the field of the fine arts their positions of control over the major institutions and organizations of the system. As things had proceeded the liberal artists—and the liberal writers as well for they were nearly as concerned over the situation in the fine arts as in literature itself—had hoped that now there might be a change. But instead back went Serov into the saddle, and the prospect looked grim indeed.

The immediate result of all this was that two separate groups of prominent creative artists—principally writers—alarmed by the whole course of the new campaign, afraid for the loss of their newly won and insecure liberties, got together to compose letters to Khrushchev expressing the hope that there would not be any return to Stalinism in the arts and letters.

One of these groups—including, it has been reported, some of the leaders of Soviet culture, Dmitri Shostakovich, Konstantin

* Reported *Sovetskoye Iskusstvo*, Dec. 5, 1962.

Simonov, Ilya Ehrenburg, and fourteen others *—was extremely out-spoken in expression of fears lest the artists and writers of the "dog-matist" faction should now once again be given free license by the Party to persecute all those with whom they did not agree:

"We are now seeing how artists of the very trend that was the only one to prosper under Stalin, allowing others no chance to work or even exist, are commencing to interpret the remarks which you made at the art exhibit.

"We are deeply convinced that this was not your intention and that you are opposed to this. We beg you to put an end to the trend in graphic art to the former methods which are against the entire spirit of our times."† The individuals signing the letter went so far in their communication as actually to defend the Old Riding School exhibit:

"Such an exhibit became possible only after the 20th and 22nd Party Congresses. We can have various judgments of one or another work exhibited at the show. If we all appeal to you through this letter, it is solely for the reason that we want to say in honesty that unless there is the possibility for existence of various trends in art then art is doomed."

The other communication to Khrushchev was rather similar in character—and no text of it has become available, nor any direct quotes. But as Ilyichev described it, it contained, he said, "even an appeal for peaceful coexistance of *all* trends in the arts, which sounds objectively like a plea for peaceful coexistence in the area of ide-ology."

According to Ilyichev this letter was withdrawn by those who had sent it shortly after it was dispatched to the Soviet Premier. With-drawn or not it was already on the record, and it was referred to frequently in the subsequent debates on literature, and those who did sign it were now and then called on to explain just why they had.‡

Because of the great alarm obviously existing among the artistic intelligentsia, and in order to explain the new line, the Party lead-ership promptly called a meeting of Party political leaders, including Khrushchev and the Central Committee secretary in charge of ide-ological questions, L. F. Ilyichev, together with leading personalities

---

* Michel Tatu in *Le Monde,* Paris, Dec. 28, 1962.
† Part of the text of this letter was quoted by L. F. Ilyichev in his speech of Dec. 17. *Pravda,* Dec. 18, 1962.
‡ See the attack on Alexei Surkov, evidently for signing this letter. *Literaturnaya Gazeta,* April 2, p. 3 (speech by M. Sokolov). Surkov, from being one of the leaders of the "dogmatist" position in 1954, has evidently reconsidered in some degree his position in more recent years.

from art and literature. Such meetings of political leaders with writers had occurred before—during the post-Hungary clampdown in 1957.

From this meeting, held at the Reception House on the Lenin Hills on December 17, there emerged two official documents. One was a short report that such a session had taken place, listing a few of the individuals who had spoken, including Khrushchev himself, giving nothing of the content of the discussion. The other was the text of the keynote report delivered there not by Khrushchev but by Ilyichev.

It apparently was a drama-packed gathering which lasted, it has been reported, for some ten hours! And it evidently saw some sharp exchanges. The usually well-informed correspondent of the Paris newspaper *Le Monde,* Michel Tatu, in a dispatch published in his paper on December 28, revealed that one work attacked was the new Thirteenth Symphony of Dmitri Shostakovich because it used, among a group of poems by Yevgeny Yevtushenko included with the music, the controversial verse about Babi Yar. Tatu's report on this was clearly accurate—since the Shostakovich symphony was later publicly attacked on exactly this ground after having been originally received by the Soviet press and radio in complete silence, except for one hostile innuendo aimed at it on December 25 in a lead editorial in the paper *Soviet Art.*

Tatu also reported an exchange between Yevtushenko and Khrushchev on the subject of the Soviet sculptor Ernst Neizvestny, who had been attacked by Khrushchev. Yevtushenko assertedly made a vigorous defense of his sculptor friend's patriotism and integrity. The article in *Le Monde* also reported some alleged strange charges said to have been made against Ilya Ehrenburg by the writer, Galina Serebryakova, which were supposedly too horrible to repeat and which were reportedly based on memoirs being written by the head of Stalin's former personal secretariat, Alexander Poskrebyshev. In reply to this it was said that the writer Mikhail Sholokhov, long hostile to Ehrenburg, had gone up to him and shaken him ostentatiously by the hand. This last incident, it must be said, seems a little unlikely.*

The officially published text of the Ilyichev report at the meeting, at any rate, did not reflect any of the byplay and fireworks which clearly took place there. It was, in comparison with the original Khrushchev statements at the Old Riding School exhibit, rather

* Tatu's reportage on this and other aspects of the Russian literary crisis was later bitterly attacked by Yuri Zhukov in *Pravda,* March 17. Zhukov accused Tatu of falsification.

less blunt and outspoken and had a slightly more tolerant tone. In art Ilyichev attacked, for the most part, only those same artists named in the original story of December 2. In literature the only personality whom he singled out for attack was a poet named Alexander Yesenin-Volpin, who had published some anti-regime verses in America. He had bitter words for this individual, but he did not extend his remarks to others. Basically, Ilyichev tried to build up a case to the effect that "formalists" in art were attempting to sneak into the graphic arts alien, bourgeois ideology, that not only were the "formalists" seeking a free way for their own works but that there was a plot to impose "formalism" on all the Soviet arts as the only tolerated trend.

Ilyichev had some strong words for Russian writers who hoped to be allowed to write as they please: "There are people who think thus and so: Since there is no longer arbitrary treatment in our country and since people are not arrested for political dissent, this then means that everything is permitted, and there are no limitations on what one wishes. One may not only paint ugly paintings, but one may praise them to the heavens as original searchings. One may slander the progressive traditions of our arts, but evidently one cannot defend them, because this, clearly, would be a 'limitation' of freedom, 'pressure' or the use of 'administrative' methods."

No, declared Ilyichev firmly, Soviet writers and artists must adhere to the principles of socialist-realism in their work. This, he said, did not exclude different approaches in form or searchings for new ways of expression. It did not mean that works could not be critical.

"The point is that while boldly exposing everything that stands in our way we must not deal blows at Soviet society itself."

The Party, Ilyichev indicated in no uncertain terms, would guide artistic processes in the Soviet Union.

Ilyichev was clearly the man who had been picked to carry the ball for the Party in this question of art. He made another important speech before a meeting of the Party's Central Committee's ideological commission, of which he was the chairman, with young writers, artists, etc., on December 26. This was a more detailed exposition of the Party position, naming a number of names among the writers. With a certain amount of moderation he criticized Yevgeny Yevtushenko and Andrei Voznesensky, for example. But he stated more strongly than before the basic line:

"The penetration of distortions and abnormalities into the world of art must come to an end, an atmosphere of intolerance toward manifestations of alien ideology, toward formalist gimmickry and tricks in art, must be established and a situation brought about which encourages the further consolidation of all the forces of the intelligentsia in the arts on one basis, the foundation of Marxism-Leninism."

Once more he came down heavily on the concept of freedom of expression:

"Loud shouting about 'domestic freedom of self-expression' and haughty efforts to picture oneself as being 'in the vanguard of progress' and up above the people—who evidently are expected to strain their brains to comprehend the full 'depth' of artistic concepts and aesthetic 'subtleties' of certain persons who have wandered off the right path and are often nothing but fakers—these are simply anti-humanism of the purest type and the conceit that arises from lack of talent."

The year 1963 arrived with thundering utterances in *Pravda* by leaders of the "dogmatist" faction of writers and artists: on January 1 V. Kochetov, on January 2 G. Serebryakova and the sculptor S. Konenkov, on January 3 Alexander Chakovsky, and on January 4 the painter A. Laktionov. The series amounted to a whole barrage. The dogmatists were on the attack—and they were out for vengeance for the indignities they considered they had suffered from the liberals during the previous year or so.*

That the "dogmatists" would have easier access to the important newspaper the *Literary Gazette* was assured by an "administrative" measure (obviously taken on the basis of an unpublished Party decree) which reorganized the editorial board of that publication during the last week of December. The paper's editor-in-chief, V. A. Kosolapov, who had been running the publication was dismissed. Then there were fired—in January, a little later—six other editors of the paper out of fifteen. The editors dismissed were replaced.

This then was the situation as it stood in mid-January: There had been a dramatic reversal of the policy of liberalization in the field of art and literature. The "dogmatist" faction of the writers was engaged, with strong Party support, in an active offensive against liberal writers. The campaign was obviously only at its very begin-

---

* The whole atmosphere of this period of December and January is colorfully and feelingly transmitted in the article written by the outstanding authority on comparative literature, Professor R. Etiemble of the Sorbonne, for *France Observateur* and carried, in slightly abbreviated form, in English translation in the magazine *Survey*, No. 48, July 1963.

Wrote Etiemble: "The main thing that the Old Riding School affair proves is the extent to which official art in the Soviet Union is bogged down in tradition, not the best tradition of the ikons, of Kandinsky, or Chagall, but the tradition of Repin, Briulov, and Venetsianov. As a Polish acquaintance once said to me in this connection: 'Be patient! The windmills of God turn slowly.' May the wind of freedom already blowing speed them up a bit."

ning, and it was impossible to say how far it would go—but it looked
to be in dead earnest. At the same time, up to the middle of January
only a few particular targets for attack had been specifically named
among the liberal writers—including the young poet Yevgeny
Yevtushenko, and the senior writer, Ilya Ehrenburg.

How and why had this reversal of policy come about? It's worth
examining this question closely since it illustrates so vividly the
process of formulation of literary policy by the Party.

Two individual observers of the Soviet cultural scene have advanced some particular suggestions or theories on what happened.
Professor R. Etiemble of the Sorbonne is one of these.* He sees one
particular villain in the piece—Academician Serov:

"Oddly enough there was hardly any reference in the press to
the man who was most involved in the Old Riding School intrigues.
He's no fool, this man, who is the pet aversion of all thinking people in Moscow. I mean by this Mr. Serov (he already knew whom I
meant). Everyone knows, and everyone says that, having been beaten
in the Moscow elections, and forced to take himself off to an obscure
corner of the Urals, he swore he would have the blood of the insolent
Muscovites. He is every bit as talented as Gerasimova and Laktionov
and, as he did fairly well for himself in the happy days of the Personality, he is doing everything in his power to restore for his own
ends the cult of that Personality.

"With this in view, he cunningly contrived the Old Riding
School scandal, and induced the 'abstractionists' who were exhibit-
ing their work privately to appear before the authorities. Taking advantage of the scandal, he had himself made president of the Academy of Fine Arts without any competition and there hopes to break
the back of everyone who is any good as a painter or sculptor."

A different suggestion was made by the able commentator Alexander Werth, writing in *The Nation*.† Werth considers that the
"spark" that set off the fireworks of the Old Riding School exhibit
and everything that followed was the " 'Poets' Evening' of November
30" at the Luzhniki Stadium in Moscow, attended by some 14,000
people with an overflow of some thousands outside. At this gathering the biggest ovation of all went to poet Andrei Voznesensky—and
Werth considers that this was too much for the authorities to take
—because Voznesensky was the most "formalist" and "modern" of
all the young poets. This event, he suggests, decided them to take
decisive action to stem the "formalist," "modernist," "liberal" tide
and impose a return to socialist-realism in all fields.

Now, both the demonstration for the most modern among the

* *Survey,* No. 48, July 1963, pp. 13–14.
† "Letter from Paris," *The Nation,* Feb. 2, 1963, pp. 104–6.

younger poets at the Luzhniki poetry declamation * and the thoroughly effective political maneuvering of Academician Serov presumably played their role. But, I would submit, they have to be looked at as parts of a far broader picture.

As has already been pointed out, the year 1962 was one of rapidly moving liberalization in the field of Russian literature. The liberals had taken a full measure of control over the Moscow Writers Organization—and excluded the dogmatists from any voice in the organization's affairs. The *Literary Gazette* was under relatively liberal editorship, and the literary journal *Novy Mir* was practically a party organ for the liberals, under the management of Alexander Tvardovsky, one of their leaders. In this situation writers had steadily become more and more outspoken—and this had culminated in the venturing into a new and very touchy field of writing—that selected by Alexander Solzhenitsyn in his novel on life in a Stalinist concentration camp. In painting too the liberal movement was well under way. In November the Moscow abstractionists held a private exhibit of their own—and it was well noted by Western journalists, as it was quite probably intended to be by its organizers, including a painter named E. Belyutin.† Not only this but the abstractionist painters went so far as to defend their kind of art in a letter to the Central Committee of the Party.‡

Meanwhile, there cannot be the slightest doubt whatsoever that the great popularity of poetry recitations and readings on a large and small scale § was causing alarm in official circles. These readings had several characteristics which were certain to raise the hackles of antagonism among people entrusted with indoctrination, propaganda, and security. In the first place there was an atmosphere of

---

* Some idea of the measure of feeling in the higher ranks of national leadership on the impact of the poetry declamations in public and the chance for demonstration of popular feelings which they gave can be gleaned from a speech made by the outstanding Soviet journalist and editor, Alexei Adzhubei, son-in-law of Premier Khrushchev, in which he used the following terms of description: "It is difficult to be convinced that not one Soviet journalist among the 36,000 members of the Journalists' Union was present at any of the numerous gatherings of rabble at which our own home-grown 'angry young men' recited their poems and sang their songs! But who among the journalists got up to deliver a rebuff to the ideological garbage that smelled from the stages?" *Sovietskaya Pechat*, May, 1963.

† The exhibit was referred to in the Ilyichev speech of Dec. 17—*Pravda*, Dec. 18, 1962.

‡ *Ibid.*

§ There is a description of one in *Encounter*, April 1963, in the introduction by Patricia Blake to the selection of Soviet literature contained in that issue of the magazine (pp. 30–33). There have been a number of other descriptions by foreign observers of these sessions.

quasipublic demonstration about some of the gatherings. How could security people be certain things might not on some occasion get out of hand? In the second place, there was a kind of air of uncontrolled emotional tension quite contrary to the accepted official feelings of what public gatherings might be like. And third, the poetry readings provided the young poets with a means, evidently, of circumventing the censorship. This was an extremely significant loophole in the Soviet scheme of things. Poems printed in the press must have some kind of approval before they appear. Songs sung on stages must also have, under Soviet regulations, a "visa" from the artistic censorship—Glavrepertkom—by and large, at least that was the way it certainly always was. But the young poets' poems? The poets often recited—often at public demand—verses which had not been published or given a visa for public recital. Thus, Yevtushenko recited "Babi Yar" before it was shown to any editor, if one believes his account.* Even more significantly, Yevtushenko, if one believes his own account and there is every reason to believe it, was reciting his quite political poem entitled "Stalin's Heirs" for a year before it was given a visa for publication—at the instance of Khrushchev himself, no less, to whom Yevtushenko had sent the poem.† Not only were Party and other officials aroused by this sort of thing, but it also raised the keenest jealousy among the older established writers of the country, people like Mikhail Sholokhov, for example, who made an invidious reference to public poetry recitations at the Third Writers' Congress. After all, such people considered, naturally, that the young poets who had won themselves such enormous and quick popularity were upstarts and popularity-seekers. Such established writers, being themselves quite unlikely to inspire anything like a riot, naturally in some particular cases tended to take a dismal view.

All in all and adding everything up there certainly must have been by November 1962 a good number of rather alarmed people among those with most influence in the Soviet Establishment: officials in the propaganda and agitation apparatus, security people, Party secretaries, established writers and other artists whose personal positions were perhaps being affected adversely as they conceived it, and others, including even some of the topmost leaders of the body politic—all of whom had their sense of Soviet propriety wounded and their misgivings aroused by all the seemingly completely uninhibited and unrestricted "freedom" which was floating around Moscow.

But then there was another set of circumstances in the immediate picture—and this related to policy in the larger sense. The Cuban

* Yevgeny Yevtushenko, *A Precocious Autobiography* (New York, 1963), pp. 116–17.
† *Ibid.*, p. 122.

crisis burst upon the Soviet government at the end of September, and Khrushchev, to avoid war, surrendered to American demands to remove Soviet missiles from Cuban emplacements. Although in the long run this certainly meant no loss of a position essential to Soviet security—in the short run it was a blow to the prestige of Khrushchev at home and abroad. Furthermore, in the immediate sense it played into the hands of the Chinese communists who were already carrying on an intense political warfare against Khrushchev —hoping with the aid of "Stalinist" elements within the Soviet Communist Party to remove him from power. This continually more acute Chinese situation was a factor aggravating tensions within the Soviet Party. Khrushchev had other serious problems on his hands in 1962, for instance, problems of administration in agriculture and industry, which caused the leadership to convene a Central Committee meeting in late November to consider proposals for a radical reform of the Party organization and administration in the provinces.

The Soviet Premier was undoubtedly in a difficult position politically when the Central Committee met. It was in this particular situation that the question of Party policy in art and literature was raised in an urgent fashion before the Central Committee.

As Ilyichev later revealed in his own speech of December 17:

"A large group of artists sent a letter to the presidium of the recent Plenum of the Party Central Committee. They declared:

" 'V. I. Lenin's theses and decisions of the Party on realist art are at present being contested by the formalists as obsolete. The formalists are aiming their declarations and actions at resurrecting formalist trends condemned in decisions of the Party.

" 'We request the Party Central Committee to state just what in these decisions has become obsolete. If they have not become obsolete the declarations being made against these decisions in the press, on the radio, and over television have to be considered as revisionist and conducive to the infiltration of an ideology alien to us.' "

One can imagine that one of the leading spirits in the sending of this message was Academician Serov, of course. And one can also imagine that it was *not* sent without the knowledge of some elements in the topmost Party leadership—and perhaps even of the entire leadership.

It was rather reliably reported that Khrushchev in his final and concluding remarks at the November Plenum of the Central Committee touched among other things on the subject of literature.*

Since at the time this report was published the spirit of the times seemed to be favorable to further liberalization it was pre-

* *The New York Times*, Nov. 29, p. 4.

sumed in the particular news report that Khrushchev's remarks were along these lines. In fact the text of Khrushchev's remarks was not published. And one can, in the light of the known fact that the question of the Party position on socialist-realism had been formally raised by "a large group of artists" before the Plenum—through its presidium—hypothesize that there was possibly an unpublished discussion of this problem at the Plenum—and a decision reflected in the events beginning December 2 at the Old Riding Stable. One is left wondering whether—if this hypothesis is correct—this was brought up at the Plenum with or without the knowledge and participation of Nikita Khrushchev himself—whether he was faced unwillingly and unwittingly with a situation in which others in the leadership forced him to reverse his policies or whether he himself perhaps had initiated this reversal, sensing the political need for a dramatic change in order to placate the more conservative elements in the Party. In a sense it is idle to speculate about this, though it is certainly an interesting and rather relevant question.

For the purposes of this introduction it will be sufficient to chronicle in brief compass the further events from January to August 1963 in the Soviet literary-political arena.

During the month of January the campaign for socialist-realism in the arts and literature rolled on. It had various manifestations such as *Pravda*'s article on January 22 by Mikhail Sholokhov on the centenary of the birth of the Bolshevik writer, A. S. Serafimovich, author of one of the Soviet "classics" on the civil war. Sholokhov, putting himself on the side of the Party campaign, evidently declared in his tribute to Serafimovich that "only art which serves the interests of the people remains alive among the popular masses and has a right to live." He tried to draw a contrast—not very successfully, one feels—between Serafimovich who, he claimed, was popular and Ivan Bunin who died an emigré and who, Sholokhov claimed, was unpopular.

But this sort of thing was mere sniping. The big artillery was rolled out toward the end of the month and aimed at the main targets of the campaign. Thus, in *Izvestia* on January 30 V. Yermilov, a well-known Party representative in literary criticism, attacked Ilya Ehrenburg. His thesis was that Ehrenburg in suggesting or rather actually picturing himself during the years of Stalin's terror as constrained to silence for fear of doing harm to his country was being less than sincere and frank. According to Yermilov most Russians did not know that abuses of legality were taking place during the personality cult period. If, as Ehrenburg claimed he had, they had known about this then it was their duty to have spoken up. This in essence, as Ehrenburg pointed out in his reply published on February 6, was an attack on him as a person rather than as a writer. It impugned his courage and honesty. Ehrenburg replied rather pointedly that he knew of none who did speak out—none left alive anyway. Yermilov, who was granted the last word in the argument, returned to the attack on the same grounds as at first. What it all added up to was that *Izvestia*—and obviously the Party—was on the attack against the Ehrenburg memoirs. This was the kind of argument which it was difficult to win.

Izvestia on January 31 selected two more targets—first, the editorial board of the magazine *Yunost* for publishing some poetry by Andrei Voznesensky in the January number, and second, the editorial board of *Novy Mir* for publishing an essay by Alexander Yashin entitled "Wedding in Vologda" which allegedly slandered the author's native village, described in his essay.

On March 7 the leaders of the Party called a new meeting with writers and artists. There was a new Ilyichev speech on literature, a new and quite bitter attack on Ehrenburg, and, most importantly, a new Khrushchev speech. Since this was Khrushchev's first published personal major utterance of length and substance in this controversy it had great importance. It was not an encouraging speech—it seemed more Stalinist than anything the Soviet Party and government leader had uttered since the Hungarian aftermath in 1957. Khrushchev attacked the sculptor Ernst Neizvestny. He dwelt on the whole question of Ehrenburg and "silence" during the Stalin purges —offering a justification of Soviet leaders who had not intervened to stop Stalin. On the one hand, as it emerged from his speech, he and other Soviet leaders of the time had not known of Stalin's own personal involvement in the abuses of the terror and, on the other hand, in seeming contradiction, as it emerged from his account, he had saved some individuals and groups from the terror. He picked some other literary-artistic targets: the motion picture entitled *Zastava Ilicha*, Victor Nekrasov for his account in *Novy Mir* of his trip to the United States in which he found some things to admire in America and other things to criticize in Russia, and also Yevgeny Yevtushenko and his poem "Babi Yar." He delivered a justification of Soviet policy on the Jewish question in this connection. And then he went on to complain that since the publication of Solzhenitsyn's *One Day in the Life of Ivan Denisovich* Soviet magazines and publishing houses had been flooded with manuscripts about concentration camps. It was, he pointed out, a very dangerous and touchy subject.

All in all the Khrushchev speech of March 8, though a very interesting document, represented a clear step backward toward Stalinism in Khrushchev's attitudes on literature.

This meeting at the beginning of March set the stage for a much stepped-up campaign on the literary front: strong criticism of individual works in newspapers and magazines, various meetings at which some writers denounced other writers, and the criticized writers were required to "recant" their mistakes. The whole thing had a very bitter tone.

On March 15 *Pravda* carried a statement from sculptor Ernst Neizvestny which was a public "recantation." On March 29 in the press Andrei Voznesensky and Yevgeny Yevtushenko publicly admitted their errors and promised to do better in the future. On March 30 Alexander Solzhenitsyn's new story, "Matryena's Home," was gently criticized. On the same day Yevgeny Yevtushenko's *Precocious Autobiography*, published originally in Paris, was given the full treatment in *Komsomal Pravda* through the simple device of quoting its more provocatory remarks quite out of context—so as to give Soviet readers the impression, unfairly, that Yevtushenko had written an anti-Soviet booklet, which he had certainly not. Before that on March 22 the Young Communist League head, S. Pavlov, had attacked *Novy Mir* and *Yunost* for publication of allegedly offensive works—including "Oranges from Morocco" by Vasily Aksenov. On April 3 Aksenov, who had been rather constantly under attack, issued his declaration of recantation. Meanwhile, a meeting of the Moscow "artistic intelligentsia," called in late March, heard some quite violent attacks on the "formalists" in art and literature. This was mild, however, compared to the deep bitterness voiced in early April at a meeting of the Russian Union of Writers. It is worth quoting a paragraph from one of the speeches made at this meeting because it illustrates one aspect of the whole controversy.*

Declared S. Baruzdin: "What did we fear? Being voted down by secret ballot? Having labels like 'dogmatist,' 'Stalinist,' etc., pinned on us? Or, last, were we perhaps afraid that our actions might have an impact on our own artistic fortunes, that we might not get into print, that we might be ignored, or that we might be beaten over the head with criticism from the noble standpoint of the 'struggle for quality'?"

The latter part of April saw some kind of a letup in the name-calling that was being so extensively and intensively indulged in by dogmatist writers who were out for revenge. But the general campaign continued without major new developments. As May proceeded preparations were going on intensively for the coming Plenum of the Central Committee called to discuss ideological issues. And it was in May that the first sign of a possible improvement in the literary climate appeared. This came in the form of the publication

* *Literaturnaya Rossiya*, April 5, pp. 3–4.

in the Soviet press of the full text of an interview given by Alexander Tvardovsky, editor still of the controversial *Novy Mir*, to the American correspondent Henry Shapiro.*

Tvardovsky's interview, in gentle language but clear, defended his own original point of view and made clear that *Novy Mir* intended to go ahead with much the same program as in the past. In particular he went so far as to defend one or two of the works which had come under the most bitter attack during this campaign—including Alexander Yashin's essay on "A Wedding in Vologda" which he called "an excellent sketch" which is "full of poetry."

On June 18 the long-awaited Central Committee Plenum was called. The keynote address was given by Ilyichev again. He, however, added little so far as literature was concerned to things he had previously said—and the most important thing he came up with was a proposal that all the creative artists' unions be united in one big union combining graphic artists, composers, writers, etc. This was patently intended to submerge the highly liberal Moscow Writers' Organization and the Union of Soviet Writers in a mass of graphic artists and the like, and thereby establish a basis for a firmer control over writers.

Khrushchev also, of course, addressed the Plenum, but he had little to say about literature, nothing, at any rate, of much importance.

The Plenum ended after adopting a resolution which made the ringing declaration that: "To propagate peaceful coexistence of ideologies is treason to Marxism-Leninism, treachery to the workers' and peasants' cause."

Nothing was done immediately on the Ilyichev proposal for creation of one big union of creative artists.

So far as literature was concerned the Plenum turned out to be pretty much a big nothing. And for a pretty obvious reason.

What had happened was this: As the Plenum had convened the controversy—played up as an ideological controversy—between the Soviet Union and Communist China had broken completely and bitterly into the open. The Plenum, in this circumstance, turned principally into a platform for the delivery of statements mainly aimed at this issue and not at Soviet literature.

There was more to it than even this. From the West an olive branch had been offered—by President Kennedy. It was being looked at with the greatest of interest. The new test-ban treaty was already in the air—and much more. There was in Moscow a more relaxed atmosphere.

Not only this: Some of the Western European communists, in

* *Pravda*, May 12, pp. 4–5.

particular the Italians, had taken a rather negative attitude toward the whole campaign in literature. Much the same reaction had come from some of the more advanced East European communist countries—as, for instance, Poland.

Was there a new policy change in the air back toward liberalism in art? It seemed possible.

Ilya Ehrenburg came out of his seclusion a little later—to make a statement at an international writers' meeting to the effect that Soviet writers ought to be permitted to write experimentally for selected audiences. A few weeks earlier this might have sounded like some kind of treason to the Party line. But it didn't any longer. So rapidly could things shift in the Soviet Union.*

Right after that two other similar developments followed. First, *Novy Mir* published a new story by Alexander Solzhenitsyn entitled "For the Good of the Cause," which was an attack on bureaucracy and disregard of human needs. This story was criticized by the assistant managing editor of the *Literary Gazette* just after it came out—the fact remained that it had appeared.† Second, *Izvestia* on August 18 published on two pages the text of a new poem by Alexander Tvardovsky in which the poet, leader of the liberal camp of Soviet writers and editor-in-chief of the liberal literary journal *Novy Mir,* resurrected his famous wartime hero, Vasily Terkin, in order to put him in the unusual situation of being sent to "that world" only to find that it was run by an omnipotent bureaucracy and a leader who recalls Stalin. It is a satire—and an attack on Stalinism. And Tvardovsky read the poem, the paper announced over the signature of its editor-in-chief, Alexei Adzhubei, to Khrushchev in the presence of leading Russian and foreign writers. The poem is entitled "Terkin in That World."

In the light of these and other developments in the weeks preceding, an experienced American journalist present in Moscow at the time could predict with some assurance that new important novels, poems, and plays were in the offing and that a letup in the big clampdown of early 1963 was under way.‡

4. The View Ahead
And so things seemed to be starting to ease up again—at least temporarily. And perhaps one could conclude by early September

* *The New York Times,* Aug. 14, 1963.
† Henry Tanner in *The New York Times,* Aug. 18, 1963, p. 1, and Theodore Shabad in *The New York Times,* Sept. 1, 1963, p. 7.
‡ Max Frankel in *The New York Times,* Aug. 14, 1963.

1963, keeping one's fingers crossed just in case, that post-Stalin Russia under Nikita Khrushchev's leadership had once more passed through and left behind another literary-political crisis which for some anxious months seemed to be threatening to kill off abruptly the tender and promising beginnings of a Russian literary revival. Hopes for the future of Russian literature could start to rise again.

Of course, only a foolhardy individual would undertake to predict the course of events ahead in this area—so frequent had been the reversals of policy in Russian art and literature during the previous decade. And yet there are, nevertheless, some conclusions which one can reach on the basis of all the recent experience. And perhaps the best starting point for getting to these is to take a look—an analytical look this time—at exactly what did happen during the big clampdown from December 1962 to June 1963, carefully distinguishing in this between noisy rhetoric and awesome-sounding threats and scoldings and actual happenings. It is also necessary to take a look at what did *not* happen.

First the things that did happen:

There was, as we have seen, a determined and vigorous reassertion of Party leadership in art and literature. In the process of this reassertion of Party authority over the arts there was, at the same time, a firm restatement of the fundamental principles of the Party's ideological control system embodied in the slogan of socialist-realism. In this reaffirmation of its right and duty to control, the Party fell back for support on the dogmatist faction among writers and artists —and for a time gave them their much-desired role as the Party's policemen among their fellow creative artists. In this action, though on this occasion they were kept rather carefully under control, there was implicit the threat that this might happen again on a more intense and broader scale if it should become necessary from the Party's point of view. In this connection the Party put into effect a very few but significant administrative measures to "correct" the situation which had developed—and the most important of these was the drastic reorganization of the editorial board of the newspaper, the *Literary Gazette,* involving the replacement of the editor-in-chief by a more conservative figure who acted firmly to curb the liberal tendencies of the paper.

If one examines the campaign of the Party propaganda authorities during the period of the clampdown carefully, one sees that its targets were picked with some care and discrimination as each representing a symbol of things deemed particularly undesirable. Thus, there was the campaign to discredit Ilya Ehrenburg because of his cosmopolitanism, because of his campaign to revive the memories of the Russian literary traditions of the early decades of the century, because of his clarion call for creative freedom, and because of his great influence on the young people and the intelligentsia. Yevgeny Yevtushenko was selected for attack as a symbol of brash and bold youth waging a struggle for uninhibited creativity, because of his popularity, because of his injection of the personal element into writing on a wholesale scale, because of a "dangerous" element of bohemianism in his makeup—and also for his violation of the dictum that Soviet writers must not publish works outside the USSR which have not been deemed suitable for publication inside the USSR. Victor Nekrasov was chosen as a target because he had appeared to make "ideological coexistence" a platform of his work and because he had attacked an essential aspect of the security system. Andrei Voznesensky was attacked because of his great popularity and because he was the most advanced of all the poets in terms of form and style—and was therefore regarded as the symbol of wanton disregard for the realist criteria of Soviet art. Vasily Aksenov was attacked because he, more than anyone else, in his works seemed to be encouraging that youth phenomenon known in Russian parlance as *stilyazhestvo.**

One of the things which happened as the campaign continued was the development of a conscious effort by the Party to inhibit somewhat the rather uncontrolled contacts on a wholesale scale between Russian writers and foreigners which had developed in the most recent period. Thus, for a time, there was a hold-down on trips abroad for writers—among other things Yevtushenko's journey to America was canceled—and there were warnings about meeting foreigners indiscriminately and scoldings of writers for "bad con-

---

* The Russian postwar term *stilyazhestvo,* originally slang but now an integral part of the language, is derived from the term *stilyaga,* usually used in the plural, *stilyagi,* which in turn is derived from the French and English word "style." A contemporary Soviet dictionary gives the following definition of the word *stilyaga:* "A contemptuous name for a person, usually without any ideological or social interests, for whom a striving for exaggeratedly fashionable style of dress and extravagance of manners is characteristic." The Russian *stilyagi* have been compared at various times to American zoot-suiters and, more recently, to American beatniks. As often as not, however, they are merely young people, bored with the clichés and drabness of ordinary life, who are seeking some kind of expression of individuality or romanticism in terms of manner of dress and behavior, often imitating what they consider to be in mode among their Western counterparts in age and psychology—blue jeans, maybe beards, etc. Soviet propaganda attempts deliberately to confuse the various phenomena of juvenile delinquency such as hooliganism, petty crime, speculation, alcoholism, parasitism, etc., with genuine soul-searching, discontent, and protest—and to lump all nonconformist behavior of Soviet young people under the heading of *stilyazhestvo* which is systematically persecuted by the Young Communist League, which frequently works in cooperation with the police in this campaign.

duct" while abroad. As the campaign proceeded there was also a definite effort made to push to the forefront young provincial writers from outside the liberal group in the hopes, evidently, that they would be a counterweight to the liberals. Finally, there was also the campaign sponsored by L. F. Ilyichev to create one big union for the creative artists—in which inevitably the liberal writers, it was obviously hoped by the plan's authors, would be inundated in a conservative mass of dogmatist painters and sculptors. But up to the end of the summer this special project, though advanced formally by the leadership at the Central Committee meeting of the Party in June, did not seem to have got off the ground. It even looked as if it might have been quietly killed.

There were other things which were done as well—but this list covers many of the most important Party moves in the clampdown. Now, what about the things that were *not* done?

For one thing no single writer, so far as is known, was subjected to serious repressive measures of a penal nature.*

None, so far as has yet been reported, was even expelled from the Young Communist League—as several were in 1957—or from the Communist Party—though Khrushchev himself called for expulsion of Victor Nekrasov from the Party. None, so far as has yet been reported, was even expelled, as Pasternak had been in 1958 during the Nobel Prize scandal, from the Writers' Union. Not only this, but a number of the writers involved, including Victor Nekrasov, had dared to violate the established time-honored Party ritual which required that a member accused of sins by the Party must publicly recant and repent those sins in an abject and humble manner. And not even Nekrasov had been hit by the Party lightning that might have been expected—though, of course, there were serious enough difficulties of one kind and another, such as inability for the time being to publish.

Equally significantly throughout the whole turmoil, editor-in-chief of *Novy Mir*, Alexander Tvardovsky, leader of the liberal writ-

---

* There were a number of newspaper reports published in the West to the effect that three Soviet writers who had managed to smuggle antiregime works to the West for publication there had been imprisoned in "insane asylums." Among them, it was reported, was the poet Alexander Yesenin-Volpin, attacked bitterly by Ilyichev in his December speech. A letter to *Pravda* by two of his relatives, sisters of his father, the famous poet Sergei Yesenin, described Yesenin-Volpin as insane—perhaps in order to justify publicly his incarceration in this fashion. Subsequent reports had it that the writers allegedly put in asylums had been later released. These particular cases, whatever the facts in them, seem to have no particular relationship to the big clampdown—except to the extent that the Yesenin-Volpin case was used by Ilyichev as a point of attack in his initial discourse on art and literature delivered on December 17, 1962.

ers and of the most liberal of the Russian literary journals, had kept his job. His entire editorial board remained intact. He was not the only liberal to retain an important post. The editorial board of the magazine for young people, *Yunost,* still had among its members such liberal and much-criticized writers as Yevgeny Yevtushenko and Vasily Aksenov. There were similar situations elsewhere on the literary front.

Interesting works actually never entirely ceased to come out throughout the clampdown. This is not to say that the campaign had no effect at all on the selection of authors and works published by literary journals and publishing houses. Of course it did, particularly after March. But there was still in no sense any drive to push things all the way back, in terms of the sort of material published, to the situation of even a few years before.

And perhaps most indicative of all was the fact that there was a whole large group of the most important and advanced progressive writers left nearly untouched by this campaign of criticism. Among these were all the writers represented in this anthology except Vasily Aksenov. This is not to say that no word of criticism was directed against any one of them in the press, for there was—but it is to say that they were not made major targets of the propaganda barrage laid down by the Party propaganda apparatus in the sense that such writers as Ehrenburg, Yevtushenko, Voznesensky, Nekrasov, Aksenov, Bulat Okudzhava, and others were made such targets.

Take, for example, Yuri Kazakov. He almost never writes anything that can really be styled Party propaganda. He avoids the stereotypes and clichés of socialist-realism. He is almost never "optimistic." On nearly the eve of the big clampdown he published a story entitled "Adam and Eve" * which could have been interpreted, if the authorities had so desired, as a defense of a modern, "formalist" painter and a criticism of the mandarins of the Soviet art world. In late December *Pravda* published his story, "The Easy Life," which could have been interpreted, were there the desire to do so, as a caustic comment on the Soviet way of life. But it got a favorable review in the *Literary Gazette.* Later on, a major literary magazine republished his story entitled "On the Island" which dealt with a deeply personal, emotional theme which seemed to have no relationship at all to "socialist construction." And yet throughout the clampdown Yuri Kazakov, though not immune from criticism, was not the victim of any organized campaign of criticism. The few reviews of his work published in the first months of 1963 expressed divided views—for and against. The same is true of Vladimir

* Available in translation in *Encounter,* April, 1963—translation by Manya Harari.

Tendryakov and of Yuri Nagibin, even though, as can be seen from their stories included in this anthology, they often enough write works which can hardly be called Party propaganda. Each of these two caught a brickbat or so in the course of the campaign for "idea-ness" and "party-ness" in literature. But neither was singled out for special condemnation, and it was clear each of them was going to continue to pursue his own creative course.

Not only did some of the most important prose writers escape persecution during the big clampdown, but so did some of the most advanced of the younger poets. Robert Rozhdestvensky was singled out in one Khrushchev utterance—because he had attacked the dogmatist poet Gribachev and his political pamphlet in verse directed against the young progressive poets which was entitled *No Boys!* Khrushchev advised Rozhdestvensky to learn some lessons from Gribachev. But he was otherwise largely left alone. Such poets as Yevgeny Vinokurov, Bella Akhmadulina, and Boris Slutsky who had close ties with the Yevtushenko-Voznesensky poetry group emerged pretty much unscathed.

It is worth going into this question of who got real scoldings and who did not at such length in order to make the exact boundaries of the whole campaign quite clear.

There is one more thing worth noting about the clampdown, in order to define and analyze its limits. And that is the fact that by and large in the whole first stage of its development, after the initial kickoff on December 2 to early March, Premier Khrushchev allowed the Central Committee secretary in charge of propaganda and ideological matters, Leonid F. Ilyichev, to spearhead the drive insofar as all major public utterances and speeches were concerned. Except for his casual and not particularly connected remarks made at the art exhibit at the Old Riding School in early December, Khrushchev made no addresses or speeches for publication on the art and literature question until his big speech of March 8. Even after this Khrushchev left the public sponsorship of the clampdown campaign to Ilyichev—and it was the latter who made the keynote report at the Central Committee Plenum in June which had been called to consider this subject. What one can deduce from all of this is that Nikita Khrushchev himself may well have preferred to have Party Secretary Ilyichev take the initiative on this issue, withholding his own fire till it seemed to be absolutely required and even then allowing Ilyichev to continue to occupy the driver's seat. There is certainly an implication here that the Premier may well have been anxious not to get his own prestige too deeply involved in this sensitive question.

Now in the light of all of this—the things actually done and the things not done—what are we entitled to conclude?

The most obvious thing about the clampdown is that it served a serious and deliberate warning on the liberals in Russian literature that the Party still has all the plenitude of power, that it can call all the shots in literature and art—and when necessary force obedience to its edicts. It was a warning that whenever the Party feels that its authority in literature and the arts is being challenged or flouted it can be expected to take determined action to reassert its authority. It was a warning that the Party for the present at least will only allow things to go so far in terms of relative freedom of expression for writers—and not further. The clampdown made clear that the Soviet arts and literature are still expected to serve the cause of the building of communism and that there has been no repeal of the fundamental concept of socialist-realism.

Once more this particular clampdown illustrated the close connection between Russian literature and Soviet politics—including both Soviet foreign relations and intraparty politics. It showed once more the fact that official policy toward literature is a direct function of the intensity both of tensions between the Soviet Union and the outside world and also of tensions within the system at home.

It seems to confirm the general rule in literary policy in the years since the death of Stalin of three steps forward and two steps back and then another three steps forward and two back—in other words the jerky, intermittent, often interrupted general trend which leads slowly and seemingly uncertainly toward greater freedom in creative expression. And likewise it seems to illustrate rather vividly some of the present sensitive limits of this general trend.

Perhaps the most important conclusion of all to be reached from a detailed examination of this phenomenon is that *the present Party leadership* under Khrushchev seems to adhere to a steadfast intention to use its great powers still relatively sparingly in the area of literature, to be determined to avoid return to the repressive methods of Stalinism.

The Party is evidently determined to influence the development of Russian literature, one would judge, through the many means available to it which are short of physical repression or persecution of writers. These means include: ultimate control of all publishing houses and periodicals through government ownership, Party policing and the censorship; power to influence directly the monetary remuneration of all writers; power to influence the course of criticism of writers' works and the building up or knockdown of their public reputations; power to hold out as rewards many other things than merely money, such as junkets abroad, prizes, and the many perquisites of fame and popularity.

The most effective weapon, however, which the Party possesses in literature, is well illustrated in the course of the recent clampdown —and this is the imposition of a *collective responsibility* on Soviet writers—which means that a writer who gets out of line causes harm not only to himself but to his fellow writers as well. A writer who stretches his freedom to write beyond the bounds tolerable to the Party thereby brings on *all* writers, and not just himself, a curtailment of the freedom to write. It is difficult for Westerners, unaccustomed to the group cohesiveness of Russian writers, to imagine how strong a coercive force this imposition of collective responsibility really is in Soviet conditions.

No one should underestimate, considering everything, the effectiveness of a campaign like the recent clampdown in influencing the direction of development of literary work. Its effects will certainly be felt for a long time ahead—and many a writer, including younger writers and also many who are well established and talented, will consciously try to adjust to criteria established.

At the same time it seems possible from consideration of some of the writers who were not condemned or severely criticized during the recent clampdown that, for the time being at least, the concept of what is permissible in Soviet literature may have broadened to include a wide range of nonpolitical or apolitical writing, such as that represented in this anthology. And this is, of course, a very encouraging development.

What then is the view ahead for Russian literature in the sixties? The first years of the decade saw, as we have seen, the rapid development of Russian literature, both poetry and prose. Will this now continue—or be resumed—in the wake of the clampdown?

It is too early confidently to answer this question. But perhaps the main lesson of this story is that Russian writers, despite difficulties, are certainly going to continue to try to broaden their possibilities of self-expression, are certainly going to continue to endeavor to produce original and perceptive literary works in all genres despite difficulties, handicaps, and obstacles. After all, one must remember that the relationship between the political authority and the literary community in Russia has *always* been difficult, always uncomfortable, even in the best of times. And Russian writers have managed, when at all possible, to write works of more than transitory interest despite this chronic situation. And now, despite the recent fireworks from December to June 1963, this relationship between the political authority and the literary community is essentially better than it has been for most of the time since the Revolution. For this, to give credit where credit is due, one should mention the role of Nikita Khrushchev who has, despite his irritating vacillations and occasional wrathful explosions, more often smiled on the liberalization of literature than he has frowned at it and on whom much depends for the future.

Russian writers can confidently be expected to take full advantage of whatever new relaxation there is in the atmosphere surrounding their work. And if God and Nikita Khrushchev are willing—perhaps they may succeed in accomplishing much more than their already respectable beginning for this decade.

After all, the sixties have only just begun for Russia. And Russia has some fabulous literary assets: enthusiastic, skilled, and promising young writers and older, experienced, and evidently courageous mentors from the senior generation, and most important of all an eager public.

Where else in the world would 25,000 people or so turn out for an outdoor poetry recitation—as eagerly seeking admittance as if it were the decisive football game for the championship? Where else could a set of literary memoirs cause tremors in a government or a poem fan the flames of national emotion? Where else, indeed, is literature and art a matter of national policy and national concern quite on a par with foreign policy or national economic development?

Yes, Russian writers could write if given a chance. This they had already demonstrated. But would they be permitted to? This is one of the big questions of the decade—and there are many people outside Russia in many different countries as well as many millions inside the Soviet Union waiting anxiously for the answer.

Vasily Aksenov

An Introduction to Vasily Aksenov

Vasily Aksenov (pronounced AK-SYON-OFF, with the accent on the second syllable) entered writing, as did Anton Chekhov, via medicine. He was born in 1932 in Kazan and graduated from his medical institute in Leningrad in 1956.

"I began to write prose when I was in medical school and was a member of a literary club in the Petrograd district of Leningrad," he has recounted.

For four years after completion of medical school he worked as a physician. Initially, he was employed in the Leningrad merchant marine port—inspecting foreign and Soviet ships passing through quarantine and the like. After a time at this assignment he was sent to work at the Voznesensk Hospital in a remote rural lake area difficult of access. The long nights there during the long cold winter gave him plenty of time to work away at his writing.

His literary career began with the publication of his first short stories in the magazine, *Yunost,* in 1959. His subsequent work in writing has been closely connected with this magazine, published for and about young people and often featuring young writers.

As soon as it became apparent that Aksenov was going to be a successful writer he moved to Moscow—continuing for a period his medical work as well as his writing, as a doctor in a Moscow dispensary. By 1960 his writing was taking up so much of his time and energy that he abandoned medicine to become a full-time writer. Since then in the course of collecting materials for his stories and novels he has traveled much throughout the Soviet Union, including the Far East.

Aksenov submitted his first major literary work—a short novel entitled *Colleagues*—to *Yunost* not long after his first stories had appeared.

As Aksenov himself has told: "Valentin Katayev, as editor of *Yunost,* read the manuscript ... He picked to pieces the first third of the book. That part was really very bad. I rewrote it. I'm going to keep the manuscript with Katayev's sharp remarks in the margins for the rest of my life. I am going to keep his favorable comments too."

When *Colleagues* * appeared—in the June and July 1960 issues

---

* This novel is available in English translations: Vasily Aksenov, *Colleagues* (Moscow: Foreign Languages Publishing House), translated by Margaret Wetlin; also in *Soviet Literature Monthly,* No. 4, 1961; also Vasilii Aksenov, *Colleagues,* translated by A. Brown (London, 1962), 240 pp.

of the magazine—it was immediately noticed. Not very surprisingly the story was about three young doctors, two of whom worked, as Aksenov himself had, in the Leningrad merchant marine port, and the third of whom was stationed, as Aksenov himself had been for a time, in a remote village on one of the big lakes in Leningrad Province.

There isn't any question, of course, but that this work contains much autobiographical material out of Aksenov's own experiences. He takes as his principal characters for the story three young doctors —general practitioners like himself—who have just completed their medical school in the mid-fifties in Leningrad.

The adroit combination of vivid and true-to-Soviet-life depiction of young people, forthrightness in expression of political and social views on the part of the novel's hero, and an ending in which all the chief characters find their orientation in life in a positive sense for the Soviet system pleased nearly everyone. The book became popular among readers. It was well received by the critics, who found it refreshing and different—and also by propaganda and press authorities. It was quickly made into a motion picture, and Aksenov found himself a successful author at the age of 28.

In *Colleagues* Vasily Aksenov had already demonstrated some of the marks of his writing style which, while it was his own, bore evidence of Western influences. Aksenov knows very well—and admires, as he has said himself, such Western writers as Hemingway, Faulkner, and Salinger. He has obviously drawn on both Hemingway and Salinger in particular in developing his own writing technique. He has, one might imagine, used Erich Maria Remarque, who has had such great popularity in the present-day Soviet Union, as a model—in particular, his novel *Three Comrades*.

Aksenov speaks—and this is his most obvious characteristic of style—in a colloquial language typical of the more advanced elements of Soviet youth today—replete with contemporary jargon and colorful expressions, often iconoclastic in relation to the clichés of the system and leaving a net impression of a disrespectful and sceptical attitude on the part of the speaker. Obviously, Aksenov has studied the language of these young people in more than a routine way and knows all the innuendoes, wisecracks, and pet expressions of the day. There are many references to things foreign. His phrases are often clipped and exceedingly idiomatic—many are unlikely to be found in a dictionary.

Aksenov then went much further with this same style and technique of writing in his next novel, entitled *Ticket to the Stars*. In it he deals with a younger group—teenagers from Moscow. He picks them from among the "stilyagi" with their beards—in some cases—and bluejeans, their love for "rok'n rol," as they call it, and other items which reflect what they conceive to be the appurtenances of advanced Western youth. This time the group also consists, as in *Colleagues,* of three young men, but a pretty girl is added for good measure. *Ticket to the Stars* * was published in *Yunost* in two installments—in June and July 1961.

Ticket to the Stars quickly won even more enthusiastic reader approval than *Colleagues.* It was regarded, in fact, among Russians as something of a publishing sensation. Its free and easy treatment of the moods of discontent and iconoclasm among the most advanced Russian young people—the so-called "stilyagi" and others who would not accept unquestioningly all the official slogans—was radically new. Aksenov seemed to be saying, in a way, that the much-criticized phenomenon of "stilyazhestvo" was not so much to worry about after all, that it was among the "stilyagi" and those of their general sympathy that perhaps the best spirits and impulses of Russian youth were to be found. Not very surprisingly this raised a great controversy which still continues.

Ticket to the Stars and its author were publicly attacked by the leading Soviet official concerned with press and propaganda, L. F. Ilyichev, now a secretary of the Central Committee in charge of ideological and propaganda activity of the Party, in December 1961. Singled out by Ilyichev along with *Ticket to the Stars* was Victor Rozov's *A B C.* Both works were roundly condemned, the editors of *Yunost* were officially reprimanded for publishing them, and the editor-in-chief of *Yunost,* Valentin Katayev, was fired from his post.

For a time in late 1962 it began to look as if the shadow of official disapproval was off Aksenov. He had cooperated in a redoing of *Ticket to the Stars* for the cinema—since the first version had been rejected. And the film was actually released. Aksenov was added to the *Yunost* editorial board, which could only be regarded as a sign of official esteem and confidence.

Novy Mir for July carried two short stories by Aksenov, entitled "Halfway to the Moon" and "Papa, What Does That Spell?" † In the opinion of this writer these are far and away the artistically most interesting works which Aksenov has yet published. They deal with men more mature and developed than the leading characters in all his short novels—and the stories have a feel of greater maturity themselves. They show very strong influence of American writ-

---

* Available in English translations: Vasili Aksenov, *Ticket to the Stars,* translated by Andrew R. MacAndrew (New York: Signet Books), 176 pp., also Vasilii Aksenov, *A Starry Ticket,* translated by A. Brown (London: Putnam, 1962), 224 pp.
† These are included in this anthology. Another translation into English of "Halfway to the Moon," by Ronald Hingley, can be found in *Encounter,* April 1963.

ing on Aksenov—one is tempted to say of the *New Yorker*. The fact that with them Aksenov for the first time was published in *Novy Mir,* the leading Soviet liberal literary journal of the Soviet Union, showed also that he was aiming for the first time at the adult audience.

The two stories were criticized, severely by some critics—and also praised. M. Chudakova and A. Chudakov, in their article in *Novy Mir* (February 1963) entitled "The Art of the Whole" analyzed "Halfway to the Moon" and took a very positive view. They wrote:

"One is immediately carried away by the completeness of the hero, the vivid manifestation by him of his character and that free attitude of the writer toward his subject which permits Kirpichenko (the hero) to make one after another, as if it were the most commonplace thing in the world, his fantastic plane flights back and forth. At the base of this lies the original effort on the part of the author to find the meaning of new material taken from life, an effort to find meaning which is unfettered by alien literary tradition, an effort which found its own form . . .

". . . in the story, 'Halfway to the Moon,' there is not that feeling of the immobility of phenomena and characters which is so common a fault in short stories. There is in it a sensation of the spaciousness of life which comes to V. Aksenov perhaps more easily than to anyone else among contemporary storytellers."

In December 1962 the big clampdown in literature and art began. It was clear from the start that Aksenov, as one of the most outspoken writers dealing with the sensitive subject of young people, was in a vulnerable position and might well be subjected to an attack. And so it happened—but not all at once.

When Ilyichev, who had criticized Aksenov severely exactly a year before, spoke to young writers setting forth the Party line at the end of December 1962 he complimented Aksenov for assisting in the reworking of his novel, *Ticket to the Stars,* in its film version (entitled *My Younger Brother*). He also mentioned that Aksenov had spoken to the meeting he was addressing and that his statement, like those of several other young writers, held forth the hope that they would endeavor to write "in the spirit of the demands of the Party and the people, to march in step with the times."

But then in another part of his speech Ilyichev devoted a paragraph to the question of young people who, in works of literature, express a spirit of revolt against "high words." He said that mistrust of high words really means mistrust "of our ideals and of the most sacred things in our life." This, of course, seemed to be a direct reference to Aksenov, whose young heroes stood, par excellence, against "high words."

In January 1963 Aksenov's new novel, *Oranges from Morocco,* appeared in *Yunost*. It dealt, much in the same spirit as his previous two novels, with young people—this time with young workers in the Far East.

It was not long before the press reacted to the new Aksenov work. The *Literary Gazette* criticized it very severely in early February—and the real attack on the new work was launched by *Komsomol Pravda* in mid-February.

Declared the youth paper: "In distinction from *Colleagues*, in Aksenov's new story we do not find any of the real complexity of life at all, even though the writer may think it is there."

The *Komsomol Pravda* article continued: "We expected discoveries and turned out to be in the situation of people who were offered stale goods. We hoped Aksenov would go to the Far East to discover both for himself and for us a new hero, but he simply took with him his old acquaintances, in essence, the same young men who were in *Ticket to the Stars,* who during the period that had passed had grown a little older but no wiser."

There were a number of different items of criticism in the *Literary Gazette* article and in *Komsomol Pravda*. The most serious points made were that Aksenov in his new novel had been guilty of bad taste and artistic clumsiness in the use of language and that by holding up to admiration, in his heroes, a certain kind of behavior and speech which was essentially crude and disrespectful of things deserving to be respected, he was in fact offering this as a standard of behavior for Russian young people and deploring idealism in young people.

Aksenov responded to this and other criticism with a formal statement of repentance published in *Pravda* on April 3. In it, among other things, he said:

". . . it would be still more thoughtless of me to believe that one could now restrict oneself merely to an admission of errors. This would not be the writer's way or the communist way. I will never forget Nikita Sergeyevich Khrushchev's stern but kind words to me and his advice at the Kremlin meeting: 'Get to work and show through your labor what you are worth!' "

He said that he had now found that the direction of his future work, the aim of which is service to the people and to the ideals of communism, had become clear to him, that in the future he would try to tell about the life around him, about complex and beautiful life, with full honesty.

This recantation had the effect of taking the edge off the attacks on him. Aksenov thereupon disappeared from view. It was stated in *Izvestia* on May 7 that he was going to Siberia to a construction project.

Meanwhile, the editor-in-chief of *Yunost*, Boris Polevoi, had announced that entry to the pages of his magazine would thenceforth be closed to that category of young people in stories known as the "starry boys."

A little later Aksenov wrote of his plans:

"Right now I'm writing a new novel. Again about young people. I would like in this book to touch upon the inner ties between people, about what hinders them and what helps them to live and work. I think that during this summer I shall finish the story. On my schedule is a satirical play. In September I intend to go to Novosibirsk—to the new Science City—to gather material for a cinema scenario about scientists. I have many projects."

Papa, What Does That Spell?*

A tall man in a bright-colored shirt worn outside his trousers stood in the burning sun. He was staring up into the heavens at a thick cloudy dark-blue sky piling up threateningly over beyond the Ukraina Hotel.

"In Fili it must be pouring already," he thought to himself.

In Fili, of course, everything must have turned to mud. People on a Sunday outing are probably fleeing along ground torn up by bulldozers, hiding in temporary shacks, or beneath the trees, or underneath the kiosk awnings. At the Belorussian Station electric trains are arriving from out there to the West all wet, and dry electric trains from the station are traveling to the West and running into the shower and through it onward, to the further suburban stations—Zhavoronki, Golitsyno, and Zvenigorod where little streams flow down the gullies, where it smells of wet pines, where old white churches stand up on the hills. All of a sudden he wanted to be somewhere out there, to wrap up his little Olga in his jacket, to take her up in his arms and run beneath the rain to the station.

"I just hope it doesn't get as far as the Luzhniki Stadium," he thought to himself.

He himself loved to play soccer beneath the rain when, with the wet ball flying at you like a heavy cannonball, it was no joking matter. You can't lead. You try to pass. You try to play exactly, precisely. The boys all around pant, heavy and wet. There is heavy, hurried work like on a ship in an emergency . . . But up in the stands you can just sit beneath the sun and make up a hat from a newspaper for yourself.

He looked behind him and called:

"Olga!"

The little six-year-old girl was playing hopscotch in the shade of a large apartment house. Hearing her father's voice she ran up to him and took him by the hand. She was an obedient girl. They went under the awning of the summer refreshment parlor appropriately named "Summer." The man studied the storm clouds once more.

"Maybe it will even go past the stadium," he guessed.

The little girl was reading a sign and spelling it out letter by letter.

* Russian title: "Papa, Slozhi!" First published in *Novy Mir*, No. 7 (1962), pp. 98–107.

She said: "T, O, B, R, I, N, G."

Beneath the awning it seemed even hotter than on the street. The flushed faces of the customers, sitting at the outside fence, gleamed in the sun. The little drops of sweat on their faces shone distinctly. It was awful to see people eating hot soup and even being brought crackling *shashlyks*.

"A," the little girl continued to read, "and L, C, O, H ... Papa, what does that spell?"

Her father looked at the sign and read it to himself:

TO BRING ALCOHOLIC DRINKS
TO THE RESTAURANT
IS STRICTLY FORBIDDEN.

"What does it say?" the little girl asked.

"Some nonsense," he laughed.

"Do they really write nonsense with printed letters?" she expressed her doubt.

"It happens."

He went to the distant shady corner where his friends were sitting. They were drinking cold beer. The little girl sat down next to them, a tow-haired little girl in a dark blue sailor's blouse and a neatly pleated skirt, nylon ribbons in her braids, white socks on her feet. She was all in her Sunday best and clean, such an exemplary child, like those depicted on the walls of miniature autobuses in advertisements for canned goods: "Our children know that these canned goods are good." He did not have to pull her along. She did not stare about but went calmly following her papa.

Her papa had been at one time an athlete and the hero of the three nearest streets. When of an evening in spring he returned from training, the children on all those nearby streets went out from gateways and greeted him, and the little girls cast looks full of excitement in his direction. Even the most inveterate skeptics raised their caps respectfully, and the retired lieutenant colonel, Kolomeitsev, who couldn't even imagine life without soccer, dropped in and said:

"I heard you're improving. Improve!"

And he went about in a little gray cap of the kind in which the entire team went around. The second team, replacements for the stars—walked around with that special, loose soccer walk derived not from anything but simply from fatigue. (Only the *pijons* intentionally work up for themselves such a walk.) And he smiled with a soft smile, and everything in him sang from youth and from athletic exhaustion.

This was still before Olga's birth. And she, understandably, knew nothing about this. But for him these last six years had passed as if they were six days. By that time, by the time of her birth, he had already ceased to "improve" but was still playing. In summer he played soccer, and in winter hockey—that was it. From the field to the bench and then to the stands, but just the same—in summer soccer, in winter hockey—six summer seasons and six winter seasons ...

He conducted a two-way discussion with himself: "Well so what? What's so bad about that! The in-between seasons, fall, spring —are periods of training ... And what else do you have? ... Thank you, I have a wife ... A wife? You mean you have a woman in bed ... No, I say I have a wife. A family, you understand? A wife and daughter ... Oh, even a daughter! You even remembered about your little daughter ... Soccer, hockey, hockey, soccer ... Aren't you tired of it? ... Good heavens, is it possible that sport could bore one? And beside that I have the factory ... And hasn't that bored you yet? ... Stop, no one from outside is permitted to enter the factory ... Well, all right ... And so, the factory and football, yes? And beside that your wife and daughter ... So what? I provide for my family well—one and a half thousand a month plus bonuses ... Incidentally, I've made improvements in the production process. I am an innovator. And I have lots of friends too as a matter of fact. And there they sit. Petka Strukov and Ildar, Vladik, Zhenechka, Igor, Petka-Second also—all of them are here. They pushed together two tables. They've already got the place all littered up with crab claws, and there are already puddles on the table. A good gang. All my age ... And how old are you? ... Eh, eh, we're all from 1929! And that means we're all 32."

"What's that, Serega, your little one?" Petka-Second asked.

All looked at the little girl with curiosity.

He sat down on the chair which was set out for him and seated the little girl on his knee. She was uncomfortable, but she sat quietly.

"Sit quietly, Olyus, now you're going to get a candy."

They shoved a mug of beer at him and a plate of crabs, and he ordered lemonade for the little girl and 200 grams of candy. His friends looked at him with enormous curiosity. They were seeing him for the first time with his daughter.

"You see, Alka had a meeting today," he explained to Petka Strukov.

"Sunday?" Igor was surprised.

"They have conferences eternally, those helpers of death," Sergei laughed and added almost guiltily: "And my mother-in-law went visiting—and so I had to ..." He pointed with his eye at the head of the little girl. Her hair was divided in the middle by the thread of her part.

"Drink your beer," said Ildar, "it's cold ..."

Sergei raised his mug, scanned the circle of his friends all the way around and laughed. He bent his head, concealing the warmth. He loved his whole good gang of companions and every one of them individually and knew they also loved him. They loved him somehow especially, probably because at one time among all of them he was the most "improving." He had "improved" right in front of their eyes. He had played for the second team. He had had good physical resources and a strong kick and he was capable at sizing up the field. And he had married by rights the prettiest of their girls.

Sergei clung to his friends. Only among them did he feel himself as he had felt six years before. They all firmly clung to one another and did not admit outsiders. Just as if they were bound together by a secret oath they carried in their tight circle their youthful tastes and customs. They, all of them, dragged together into the unknown future the fragments of time already past . . . The forwards and the guards had married, gone into the reserve, become fans. They had had children, but their children, their wives, and all of their living surroundings were somewhere beyond the invisible boundary line of that male Moscow life in which those who are late run from the subway to the stadium, just as if they were attacking down the field, and there is excitement in the stands, and all of them are intoxicated by that enormous spring feeling of solidarity. They did not understand why their little girls (those very same women fans and women partners at dances) became such bores. Now they were playing on intramural teams, reminiscing over beer, remembering the time they played on the factory varsity teams and how one or another from among them had been invited to play on the second team for the all-stars, and Serega had already played as a replacement and might have become a regular on the all-stars, if it had not been for Alka, his wife. All of the wives—Olka, Ninka, Tamarka—were bores . . .

"Papa, don't break off his head!" said the little girl on his knee. Sergei started and looked into her attentive and strict light-blue eyes, Alka's eyes. He dropped his hand with the red beauty of a crab. This light-blue glance, attentive and strict. Eight years ago it had stopped him: "Take your hands off me and come to me when you are sober." Such a glance. One might, of course, chatter with the boys about the fact of how much the "old woman" bored one, and, perhaps, she really had come to bore one, because of no-no, and all that. And all of a sudden you want to make the acquaintance of one or another of the younger girls born in 1940, some swimmer or gymnast, and you might get acquainted, it might happen, but that look . . .

"And don't tear his legs off of him."

"Why?" he muttered in embarrassment, just as he had then on that other remembered occasion.

"Because he looks like he is alive."

He put the crab down on the table.

"And what should I do with him?"

"Give him to me."

Olya took the crab and wrapped him in her handkerchief.

His friends all roared with laughter.

"Well, some girl you have, Sergei! That's what!"

"Do you love the crab, Olenka?" asked Zyamka who didn't have any children.

"Yes," said the girl. "He moves backwards."

"Oh-ho-ho! Oh-ho-ho!" the neighboring table broke down in laughter. "That's a smart girl! A smart girl!"

"All right, be quiet!" Petka Strukov shouted and the neighboring tables grew silent.

Ildar pulled out the championship schedule and put it on the table, and all bent over the schedule and began to discuss the team, that team, which, according to their calculations, must win the championship, but which for some reason was hovering in the middle of the league. They were fans of this particular team. But they were fans, not in the sense that unknowing fanatics ordinarily are fans—selecting their favorite team according to some kind of incomprehensible considerations. No, it was simply *their* team—this was *The Team* with a capital letter, this was the one which according to their opinion corresponded most of all to the high concept of a "soccer team." In the stands they did not stamp their feet, they did not whistle, and they did not shout "Less vodka!" at players who made errors. They knew how all of this might happen, after all, even the best goalkeeper might miss the ball: the ball was round and the team—it was not a machine, but eleven different lads.

Suddenly from the street, from the white hot day, there entered the restaurant a man in a light-colored jacket and a dark necktie— Vyacheslav Sorokin. He was greeted noisily:

"Greetings, Slava!"

"Welcome home, Slava!"

"Well how is Leningrad, Slava?"

"A city-museum," Sorokin answered curtly and began to shake everyone's hands, missing no one.

"Hello, Olyus!" he said to Sergei's daughter and shook her hand.

"Hello, Uncle Vyacha!" she said.

Sergei thought to himself: "How does she know him? Yes, and she even calls him Vyacha."

They pushed a mug of beer to Sorokin. He drank and told about Leningrad, where he had been at a closely related factory—with a factory delegation—for the exchange of experience.

"Surprising architectural groups, the creations of Rastrelli, Rossi, Kazakov, Kvarengi . . ." he hurriedly set forth.

"He already has succeeded in grabbing off some culture for himself," Sergei thought.

He had also been in Leningrad when he played for the second team, but then he had been a lad in training and hadn't permitted himself very much, he hadn't even succeeded in making anyone's acquaintance.

". . . Doric pillars, Gothic pillars, all kinds of other pillars . . ." Sorokin explained.

"I'm not saying a thing, not a thing," said Sergei and everyone laughed.

Sorokin pretended that he was not offended. With flicks of his fingers he snapped the remains of the crab from the table onto the asphalt below and moved over to look at the schedule. He lit up from Zhenechka's cigarette and said that, in his opinion, the team would lose today.

"It will win," said Sergei.

"But no, Serezha," Sorokin said softly and looked into his eyes. "They aren't going to win today. There are laws of the game, theories, calculations . . ."

"You don't understand the least little thing in the game, Vyacha," Sergei laughed coldly.

"I don't understand?" Sorokin immediately began. "I read books!"

"Books! Boys, listen, Vyacha, our Vyacha, reads books! That's what kind he is, our Vyacha!"

Sorokin immediately took himself in hand and stroked his tender sparse hair. He smiled at Sergei just as if he were sorry for him.

"Yes, I don't like it when they call me Vyacha," his smile seemed to say. "But that's what you're calling me, Sergei, but you're not going to get anywhere with that. The boys aren't going to call me Vyacha, but will call me Slava, or Slavik, just as they used to. Yes, Sergei, you played on the second team, but after all right now you don't play any more. Yes, you married the most beautiful of our girls, but . . ."

Sergei also restrained himself.

"Take it easy," he thought to himself. "Don't forget that you're friends."

Sergei raised his head. The canvas tent was shaking, just as if on top someone plump was lying and rolling from side to side. The refreshment hall was already full to the brim. A gloomy person in a cap sitting at the next table set his mug down heavily on the table, pushed his cap to the rear of his head and said, without addressing anyone:

"I'm here on a trip, you understand? I don't belong here... I have a woman here in Moscow, a woman... In short, I'm living with her, that's all!"

He knocked his fist on the table, pulled his cap forward and grew quiet, evidently for a long while.

Sergei wiped the sweat from his forehead—it had become unbearably hot here. Sorokin bent across the table and whispered to him:

"Serezha, take the girl away from here. Let her play out in the open."

"It's not your business," Sergei whispered to him in answer.

Sorokin sat back and again smiled as if he pitied him. Then he got up and buttoned his jacket.

"Pardon me, boys, I have to go."

"Are you going to the stadium?" Petka asked.

"Unfortunately I can't. I have to study."

"On Sunday?" again Igor was surprised.

"Well what can I do about it? I have an examination coming up."

"What year are you completing now, Slavka," asked Zhenechka.

"The third," answered Sorokin. "Well, so long," he said. "Greetings to everyone!" He waved his clenched hands. "Olyus, take it!" he smiled and reached out a piece of chocolate to the little girl.

"Hey, wait a second," Zhenechka called to him. "We're all going. It's too hot here."

They all got up and went out in a crowd into the white-hot street. The asphalt was elastic beneath their feet, like a sheet of foam rubber. The clouds had not moved. Just as before the sky was dark and threatening over to the West beyond the Ukraina Hotel skyscraper.

"And are you going to the stadium?" Sorokin addressed Sergei in a conciliatory tone.

"What, do you think I'd miss such a soccer game?"

"I don't think anything," wearily said Sorokin.

"Well if you don't think anything, then be silent."

Sorokin ran across the street and got in a bus, and all the others slowly went along the shady side, talking quietly and laughing. Ordinarily they made their way out with noise and racket. Zyamka told jokes. Ildar played on the guitar. But right now there was a small girl among them, and they did not know how to conduct themselves.

"Where are we going?" asked Sergei.

"We're going to walk along slowly to the stadium," said Igor.

"We'll watch the basketball in the small arena a while, the women's semi-finals."

"Papa, can I talk to you for a minute?" said Olya.

Sergei stopped, surprised by the fact that she was talking quite like an adult. His friends went ahead.

"I thought we would be going to the park," said the little girl.

"We are going to the stadium. It's also a park there, you know, trees, kiosks . . ."

"And the merry-go-round?"

"No, they don't have one of those there, but instead . . ."

"I want to go to the park."

"You're not right, Olga," he said restraining himself.

"I don't want to go with those men," she became quite capricious.

"You're not right," he repeated obtusely.

"Mama promised to give me a ride on the merry-go-round."

"Well let Mama give you a ride," Sergei said with irritation and looked around. The fellows were standing on the corner.

Olya's little face frowned.

"She's not to blame she has a meeting."

"Boys!" Sergei shouted. "Go along without me! I will come by game time!" he took Olya by the hand and jerked her: "Let's walk more quickly."

"Meetings, meetings," he thought while walking along, "These eternal meetings. A happy Sunday! What's good about it? Alka is going to get a doctor's degree, then just try to hold on to her. Even now she doesn't consider you worth a cent."

He went along with rapid steps and the girl, hardly keeping up, ran alongside. In her right hand she held the crab wrapped up in the handkerchief. From her little fist, just like the antenna of a small radio receiver, the crab's moustaches stuck out. She ran along merrily and read aloud the letters which she saw:

"C, L, O, T, H . . . Papa!"

"Cloth!" Sergei tossed through his teeth. "Meat!" "Haberdashery!"

"She will have her doctorate and he will be an unsuccessful soccer player whose name is remembered only by the oldest fans in the stands. One hundred people out of 100,000. 'Yes, yes, there was such a person, uh-huh, I remember, he didn't stay long . . .' And who is to blame that he didn't become such a star as, for example, Netto, that he didn't make the trip then, that time, to Syria, that he . . . A respected doctor of philosophy, a learned woman, a beauty . . . Oh, you, beauty . . . For her there's already nothing to talk with him about. But at night they find a common language, and daytimes let her talk with someone else, with Vyacha for example, he'll tell her about Kvarengi and about all the rest and about pillars of different kinds there—he'll tell her everything, set it forth in two seconds . . . You broke the fourth ten-ruble note . . . Ah, so you've begun to talk again? You're now spending the fourth ten rubles. On what? Leave me alone! Sport came to an end, love comes to an end . . . Oh, love! Why shouldn't I find a girl born in 1940, some swimmer or other . . . Oh, I'm not talking about that. Leave me alone! Listen, leave me alone!"

In the park they rode on the merry-go-rounds, sitting next to each other on two dappled gray steeds. Sergei held on to his daughter. She roared, was completely shaken with laughter, put the crab on the horse between its ears.

"And the crab is riding too!" she cried, tossing back her head.

Sergei smiled gloomily. All of a sudden he noticed the chief technologist from his factory. He was standing in line at the merry-go-round and holding a little boy by the hand. He bowed to Sergei and raised his hat. Sergei was jarred by this community with the chief technologist, a man who had become fat and who was boring.

"Your daughter?" shouted the chief technologist.

Through the air floated the words of the song being played on the phonograph as the carousel whirled: "The little box is filled with things—satin and silk and diamond rings . . . ."

"Your son?" shouted Sergei the next time around.

More words from the song: "Pity, oh sweetheart, oh lady love, the young . . ."

The chief technologist nodded several times.

And the song: ". . . Should . . . er!"

"Yes, yes, son!" shouted the chief technologist.

"Well, what records they play on the merry-go-round! No, nevertheless he's a pleasant chap, the chief technologist," Sergei thought to himself.

Olya could not forget for a long time the brilliant whirling on the merry-go-round.

"Papa, papa, let's tell Mama how the crab took a ride!"

"Listen, Olga, how is it that you know Uncle Vyacha?" Sergei asked unexpectedly for himself.

"We meet him often with Mama when we go to work. He is very gay."

"Ah, that's how it is, he, it turns out, is even gay," thought Sergei to himself. "Vyacha—a gay chap. And that means he has begun to play his tricks again. Oh, he's asking for it from me."

He left Olga on the bench and went himself to a telephone booth and began to phone the institute where that wise conference was supposed to be going on. He hoped that the conference was over and then he could take his daughter home, turn her over to Alka, and go himself to the stadium, and spend the whole evening with the boys.

In the receiver lengthy rings resounded for a long time, and finally they were interrupted, and an elderly voice said:

"Hello!"

"Has your wonderful meeting come to an end yet?" asked Sergei.

"What meeting are you talking about?" the receiver muttered indistinctly. "Today is Sunday . . ."

"Is this the Institute?" shouted Sergei.

"Well, of course it is the Institute."

Sergei went out of the telephone booth. The air rose in streams, as if it was melting from the heat. A fat perspiring man in a silk shirt with broad sleeves came along the walk. He waved the flies away wearily. The flies flew stubbornly after him, circled about his head, they evidently liked him.

"Ssooo," thought Sergei to himself. And all of a sudden his legs almost collapsed beneath him from the unexpected fright which was like a blow in the back. He would have run out of the park, but he remembered Olga. She was sitting in the shade on a bench and playing with the crab.

She was repeating to herself the words of a rhyme: "Even crabs, even crabs, are such squabblers. They also move backwards and wiggle their moustaches."

"She's a talented little girl," thought Sergei to himself. "She gets it from her mother."

He took her by the hand and dragged her along. She squealed and showed him the crab.

"Papa, he's such a smart one. He has almost become alive!"

Sergei stopped, tore the crab from her hand, broke it in two and threw it into the bushes.

"You don't play with crabs," he said. "You eat them. They go with beer."

The little girl immediately started to weep in three streams and refused to go further. He picked her up in his arms and ran.

He jumped out of the park. A taxi turned up right at that moment. In the hot airless quiet the Moscow River flashed below, looking like a broad ribbon of silver foil. There opened out ahead another river, of asphalt, a river which was named the Garden Ring along which he was flying, hurrying, pursuing his unhappiness. The little girl was sitting in his arms. She had stopped weeping and was smiling. She was entranced by the speed. In her face there flew letters from notices, signs, posters, advertisements. All the letters which she had learned, and 10,000 others—red, dark blue, green—flew to meet her, all the letters of the eleven planets of the solar system.

"P, J, O, P, J, L, R, J, U, E, J . . . Papa, what does it spell!" She was picking out letters at random as they flashed into her eyes.

"PJOPJLRJUEJ," Sergei tried to pronounce to himself in his head. "Why are there so many J's?" And then he began to think of all of the words which came to his mind which began with the letter J in Russian: thirst, cruelty, heat, women, giraffes, fat, life, yolk, gutter, horror . . . 'Papa, what does it spell!' Just try to find out what it spells at such a speed."

"Your back axle is knocking," he said to the driver and left him a tip of thirty kopecks.

He ran into his apartment house, jumped up the stairway three steps at a time, opened the door and burst into his apartment. It was empty. It was hot. It was clean. Sergei looked about, lit up a cigarette, and this his own two-room apartment seemed to him to be alien, so alien that right this minute there might come out suddenly from another room a complete stranger who had no relationship to anyone in the world. He felt ill and shook his head.

"Maybe there's some kind of a mix-up," he thought with relief and turned on the television set to find out whether the game had begun.

The TV set whistled quietly, and the roar of the stands was heard and by the character of the roar he understood immediately that the warm-up was taking place.

"Maybe she is at Tamarka's or Galina's," he thought to himself.

Descending the stairway, he kept trying to convince himself that she was at Tamarka's or at Galina's, and tried to persuade himself not to phone up. Nevertheless, he went to the pay telephone and phoned. She was not at either Tamarka's nor at Galina's. He came out of the telephone booth. The sun burned his shoulders. Olga was jumping right in the heat of the sun, playing hopscotch again.

She came up to him and took him by the hand.

"Papa, where are we going now?"

"Wherever you want," he answered. "Let's go somewhere."

They went slowly along the sunny side, and then he figured out that they should cross to the other side.

"Why did you tear up the crab?" Olga asked strictly.

"Do you want ice cream?" he asked.

"And you?"

"I would like it."

They went through side streets to the Arbat directly to the cafe. In the cafe it was cold and half-dark. Above the tables along the entire wall there stretched a mirror. Sergei looked into the mirror as he went into the cafe and saw what a red face he had and how large already were the balding areas over his temples. Olga could not be seen in the mirror—she hadn't grown up that far yet.

"You've already had enough, citizen," said the waitress, going past their table.

"Give us ice cream!" he shouted after her.

She approached and saw that the man was by no means drunk. He simply had a red face and his eyes were wandering not from vodka, but from some other causes.

Olya ate her ice cream and dangled her legs. Sergei also ate his, without noticing its taste, feeling only the coldness in his mouth.

Next to them there sat a pair. The young man, who had a hairdo a little like one of those tall Caucasian hats, was trying to convince the girl of something or other, persuading her. The girl looked at him with big round eyes.

"Would you like a turtle, daughter?" asked Sergei.

Olya started and even stretched out her neck.

"What do you mean, a turtle?" she asked carefully.

"A real live turtle. There's a pet store not far away from here. We can go there right now and pick out a first-class turtle."

"Let's go right away!"

They got up and went to the exit. In the hatcheck room they could hear the muffled squeal of the radio announcer and the distant roar from the stadium which sounded like a sea. Sergei wanted to go past without stopping, but he could not restrain himself, and he asked the hatcheck girl how things were going.

The first half had just finished. His team was losing.

They went out onto the Arbat. There weren't many passersby and there weren't even many cars. Everyone on such days was outside the city. Across the street walked a surprisingly tall schoolboy. In an unbuttoned gray tunic, narrow-shouldered, and very lean, handsome, and gay, he seemed to hold the promise of growing up to become an athlete, the center of the all-star basketball team of the whole country. Sergei followed him with his eyes for a long way. It was pleasant to watch how that tall chap walked along, how his handsome, stylishly trimmed head floated along high above the crowd.

In the pet store Olya at first was perplexed. There were birds, dogs—green parakeets, song sparrows, canaries. There were aquariums in which just like metal dust there shone silvery little bits of fish. And finally there was a glassed-in grotto in which there were turtles. The grotto was porous, made from plaster and painted gray. At its bottom, which was covered with grass, lay a multitude of little turtles. They lay crowded against each other and didn't move. They were like a cobblestone pavement. They maintained silence and patiently waited their fate. Maybe they were lying, frigid with terror, having lost faith in their shells, not knowing that they would not be eaten, that they would not be served up with beer, that they would gradually be bought up by gay little children, and they would begin a fairly bearable, though lonely, life. Finally one stuck his little snout out from under his shell, climbed up on top of his neighbor, and moved along on the backs of his immobile sisters. Where he was crawling and why, he probably didn't even know himself, but he kept crawling and crawling and by this token Olya came to like him more than the others.

Papa actually bought this turtle. They pulled him out of the grotto, put him in a cardboard box with holes in it, and pushed some grass into it.

"What does it eat?" Papa asked the saleswoman.

"Grass," said the saleswoman.

"And what should we feed her during the winter?" Papa asked further.

"Hay," answered the clerk.

"That means that I have to go a haying," Papa joked.

"What?" asked the saleswoman.

"That means, that I have to go a haying, I am saying," Papa repeated his joke.

The saleswoman became offended and turned away. When they went out on the street the second half had already begun. They could hear the shouts from almost all of the windows—that was the radio announcer. Olya was carrying the box with the turtle and looking into the holes. It was dark in there. She could hear a weak little rustling.

"Will it live for a long time?" asked Olya.

"They say that they live 300 years," said Sergei.

"And how old is ours, Papa?"

Sergei looked into the box.

"Ours is still young. He's 80 years old. Almost a little boy."

A roar from the nearest window announced the fact that Sergei's team had evened the count.

"And how long will we live?" asked the little girl.

"Who we?"

"Well us—people . . ."

"We live less," laughed Sergei. "Seventy years or a hundred."

Oh, what a fight was going on out there evidently! The radio announcer was shouting as if he were collapsing into a hundred different pieces.

"And what then?" asked Olya.

Sergei stopped and looked at her. She with her dark blue eyes looked at him questioningly, just like Alka. He bought cigarettes in the kiosk and answered her:

"After that, soup with the cat."

Olya laughed. "With the cat! After that, soup with the cat! Papa, and where are we going now?"

"Let's go up to the Lenin Hills," he proposed.

"Let's!"

The sun was sinking behind Moscow University building and in places was piercing it through with its rays. Sergei raised his daughter up and set her on the parapet.

"Oi, how beautiful!" exclaimed the little girl.

Down below an excursion steamer was moving down the river. The shadow of the Lenin Hills divided the river in half. One-half of it was still gleaming in the sun. On the other shore of the river lay the bowl of the large Luzhniki Sports Stadium. The field could not be seen. There were just visible the upper rows of the eastern side, filled to the top with people. The voices of the announcers could be heard but their words could not be distinguished. Further were the park, the walks, and Moscow.

Moscow the boundless, with the sun gleaming on a million windows. There, in Moscow, was his apartment house, his apartment and its 35 square meters. There in Moscow were telephone booths on every corner, in each of which one might learn about danger, in each of which one's heart might beat faster and one's legs bend beneath one, in each of which one might at long last get reassuring news and be relieved. There in Moscow, all of his 32 years were quietly promenading along the streets, hallooing to each other, and not finding each other. There in Moscow, there were plenty of beauties, hundreds of thousands of beauties. There the wise institutes were conducting research work, there people were getting promotions. There lay his calm relaxation at his lathe, there was his factory. There were his relaxation and his alarms, his springtime love which had now come to an end. There lay his youth, which had walked past—like that gay, unbelievably tall schoolboy—in the training halls and stadiums, at school desks and in beer parlors, on dance floors, in entryways, in kisses, to the accompaniment of music in the park . . . And there lay everything which would still happen to him. And what then? After that, soup with the cat.

Sergei held the little girl by her hand and felt how her pulse was beating. He looked at her face from the side, at her turned-up nose, at her open mouth, in which, like pearls, shone her teeth, and all of a sudden it was as if something had happened to him. It became easier, because he thought about the fact that his daughter would grow up, he thought about how she would be eight years old, and then 14, and then 16, 18, 20, how she would go to the pioneer camps and would return from there, how he would teach her to swim, what a stylish young lady she would be, and how she would kiss some *stilyaga* or other in the entryway, how he would shout at her and how they would go together somewhere sometime, maybe to the sea-shore. Maybe to the sea.

Olya moved her finger in the air, writing letters.

"Papa, guess what I am writing."

He watched how above the stadium and over all of Moscow the finger of the little girl was moving.

"I don't know," he said. "I can't understand."

"Oh you! Papa! Look here!" And she began to write the letters on his hand: "O, L, Y, A, P, A, P, A . . ."

A powerful roar, like an explosion, flew up from out of the stadium. Sergei understood that his team had scored the goal.

Halfway to the Moon*

"Would you like some coffee?"

"Why not?"

"Turkish?"

"Huh?"

"Turkish coffee," the waitress sang out triumphantly and sailed past down the aisle.

"Nonsense, just one more skirt!" Kirpichenko consoled himself, chasing her with his eyes.

"Nonsense!" he thought to himself, scowling from his headache. "Only fifty minutes left anyway. They're just about to announce the flight—and you might as well never have seen this city. What a city! Some hick town! Not Moscow! Maybe some people like it, but as for me I couldn't care less. The hell with it! Maybe the next time I'll like it."

The evening before he had lots to drink. Not enough to get really drunk, to pass out, but plenty. Yesterday evening, the evening before too, and the one before that. All because of that snake, Banin, and his darling little sister. They certainly took you for a ride on your own well-earned rubles!

Kirpichenko had run into Banin three days before at the airport in Yuzhny. He hadn't even known their vacations came at the same time. He really didn't have much to do with Banin. At the lumber trust they were always making a big to-do over him, always shouting: "Banin, Banin! Catch up with Banin!" Valery Kirpichenko couldn't care less. Of course, he knew the name and was acquainted with him—the electrician Banin. But in sum total he wasn't much of an impressive personality notwithstanding all the to-do made over him on holidays.

"So that's Banin! There's Banin for you!"

In the lumber camp were fellows who worked no worse than Banin, who could even give him a handicap in all departments. But, after all, with the management it's always the same: it grabs hold of one person and dances around him. There's no cause to envy such chaps. They should be pitied. In Bayukly there was a certain Sinitsyn who also worked on a diesel just as Kirpichenko did. The newspaper reporters discovered him and made a big to-do about him. The fel-

* Russian title: "Na Polputi k Lune," first published in *Novy Mir*, No. 7 (1962), pp. 86–98.

low at first collected his newspaper clippings but soon couldn't stand it any more and took off for Okha. With Banin it was all right. He took it in his stride. He went about neat and bright. He kept himself in line, that little type, kept himself quiet and inconspicuous. Last spring 200 girls from the mainland, seasonal workers, had been brought to the fish cannery. The boys had gotten together to pay them a visit. They climbed up on the truck, hollered, made a racket. They looked: in the rear corner sat Banin, so quietly, not to be seen or heard.

"That Banin ..."

At the airdrome in Yuzhny Banin had thrown himself upon Kirpichenko as if they were the best of friends. Literally gasping with gladness, he howled he was terribly glad, that he had a sister in Khabarovsk, that she had girl friends—swell gals. He began to describe the whole thing in detail and Kirpichenko nearly fainted. After the departure of the girls from the fish combine Valery had seen only two women the whole winter, more exactly two elderly crocodiles—the timekeeper and the cook.

"Oh you, Banin, Banin."

In the airplane Banin had kept shouting at the pilots:

"Hey, you pilots, pile on more coal!"

It was impossible to recognize him, he was such a comedian.

"I should have really given you the works, Banin!"

The house in which Banin's sister lived just barely stuck up above the top of a snowdrift. The humped street was evidently cleaned by special machines, and the piles of snow had not been carried off and almost buried the little bits of houses. The houses lay as if in a trench. In the crackling frosty air light blue pillars of smoke rose above the chimneys. Antennae and poles with birdhouses stuck up at all angles. This was really a village street. Even difficult to believe that just beyond on the hill a trolleybus route ran along the avenue.

Kirpichenko had already gone a little bit off his rocker while still at the airport when he saw a long line of automobiles with green lights and the glass wall of a restaurant through whose frosty patterns glimmered a sedate jazz orchestra. In the *gastronome*—the store for fancy foods, drinks, and delicacies—on the main street he let himself go completely. He pulled out of his pockets green fifty-ruble notes. He shouted with laughter and shoveled up armfuls of canned goods. The gay Banin laughed even more than Kirpichenko but also picked up some cheese and canned goods and then got into a conversation with the head of the section and bought a sausage besides. Banin and Kirpichenko rolled up to the little house in a taxi piled high with all kinds of food and bottles of Chechen-Ingush cognac. One might say they did not arrive at his sister's house with empty hands.

Kirpichenko entered the room—his shaggy cap almost at ceiling level—and dropped the foodstuffs onto the bed covered with a white pique bedspread. He straightened up and right away saw his red, lean, unpleasant face in the mirror.

Larisa, Banin's sister, such a plump little nurse to judge from her appearance, was already unbuttoning his coat and repeating:

"My brother's friends are my friends."

Then she put on her own coat and galoshes and went out somewhere.

Banin went to work with the corkscrew and the knife, and Kirpichenko for a time looked around. The room was decently furnished: a chiffonier with a mirror, a chest of drawers, a radio-phonograph. Over the chest of drawers hung a portrait of Marshal Voroshilov, a prewar picture, without shoulder boards, with his marshal's stars in tabs, and next to it a certificate in a frame: "To a distinguished marksman of the guards for successes in defense and political preparation. Signed: Administration for Labor Camps of the Northeast."

"My father's," Banin explained.

"And what was he, a camp guard?"

"He was and he went," Banin sighed. "He died."

However he was not sad very long—he began to twirl some records. The records were familiar: "Rio-Rita," "Black Sea Seagull," and one in French—three men singing in different voices so magnificently it seemed as if they had traveled the whole wide world over and seen things no one else would ever see.

Larisa returned with her girl friend called Toma and began to put the table in order. She ran back and forth to the kitchen, brought pickles and mushrooms while Toma sat in the corner as if she were made of stone and kept her hands on her knees. How things would work out with her Kirpichenko didn't know. He tried not to look at her and as soon as he took a glance he began to see spots in his eyes and got faint.

Banin exclaimed with nervous joyfulness:

"Our hands are frozen, our feet are chill. Isn't it time to drink our fill! I beg you to sit down at the table, Mesdames et Messieurs."

Kirpichenko was smoking long *papirosy*—Russian cigarettes with long hollow paper mouthpieces—a brand called "Forty years of the Soviet Ukraine." He was smoking and puffing out smoke rings. Larisa was roaring with laughter, trying to catch them on her little finger. The atmosphere in the low-ceilinged room was stuffy.

Kirpichenko's feet grew damp in his felt boots and steam evidently was rising from them. Banin was dancing with Toma. She had not said one word all evening. Banin whispered in her ear and she made a crooked smile with tightly closed mouth. The girl had a well-proportioned figure. From beneath her nylon blouse gleamed rose-colored undergarments. In front of Kirpichenko in dark orange-colored circles, swam walls, the portrait of Voroshilov, the little elephant on the chest of drawers. The smoke rings he was blowing jumped about, and Larisa's finger described signals in the air.

Banin and Toma went into the other room. The lock clicked quietly behind them.

"Ha, ha, ha!" laughed Larisa, "Why didn't you dance, Valery? You should have danced."

The record came to an end and silence fell. Larisa looked at him, squinting her crossed brown eyes. From the neighboring room came the sound of subdued squeals.

"From you, Valery, there's only food and no fun," Larisa giggled, and Kirpichenko suddenly saw she was pushing thirty and that she had been around.

She slipped up to him and whispered:

"Let's dance."

"But I'm wearing felt boots," he said.

"That's all right."

He got up. She put on a record and in the room smelling of tomatoes and Chechen-Ingush cognac the three Frenchmen sang in different voices about the fact they had traveled the wide world over and seen sights such as you would never see.

"Not that one," Kirpichenko said hoarsely.

"Which one?" cried out Larisa. "Just think, he has to have a special record! Putting on airs!"

She was circling around the room. Her skirt was swishing about her legs. Kirpichenko took off the record and put on "Rio-Rita." Then he stepped over to Larisa and seized her by the shoulders.

That's always the way, when fingers slip along your neck in the darkness, it seems as if they are the fingers of the moon, no matter what cheap broad is lying beside you . . . just the same afterwards, when fingers touch your neck—and you should slap her hands—it seems as if . . . Indeed what doesn't it seem, with the moon up high, looking through the frosty glass like a runny egg yolk? But that never ever happens really, and don't you fool yourself into thinking that it ever will. You're already 29, and for all of your disorganized and organized, all of your beautiful, hot, cold life, such as it is, when fingers touch your neck in the darkness, it seems as if . . .

"How old are you?" the woman asked.

"Thirty-two."

"You're a truck driver?"

"Well?"

"Do you make much?"

Valery lit a match and saw her round face with her brown crossed eyes.

"And what's it to you?" He lit up.

The next morning Banin shuffled around the room in warm Chinese-style underwear. He squeezed dill pickles into a glass and threw them, wrinkled and squeezed out, into a saucer. Toma sat in a corner, neat and silent, just as yesterday evening. After breakfast she and Larisa went to work.

"Well, so you had fun? How about it, Valery?" Banin laughed ingratiatingly. "Well all right, so let's go to a movie."

They saw three motion pictures in a row and then went back to the *gastronome* where Kirpichenko really let himself go again: He dragged out of his pocket red ruble notes and piled into Banin's arms cheeses and canned goods.

This went on for three days and three nights in a row and that morning when the girls had left, Banin all of a sudden had put it to him:

"So I guess we're relatives, you and I, Valery?"

Kirpichenko choked on the pickle brine he was drinking.

"Whaatt?"

"What-what!" Banin yelled back. "Are you sleeping with my sister or not? Come on, let's talk about when we're going to have a wedding, or else I'm going to turn you in to the bosses. For immorality, do you understand?"

Kirpichenko hit him on the cheekbone from all the way across the table. Banin flew off into a corner and got up immediately and grabbed hold of a chair.

"You're a bastard!" Kirpichenko growled and renewed his attack. "Marry every cheap broad!"

"Concentration camp scum!" screeched Banin. "Convict!" And he threw the chair at him.

And right then and there Kirpichenko gave it to him. When Banin, grabbing his sheepskin coat, jumped out into the yard, Kirpichenko, his teeth chattering from anger, agitation, and wild loneliness, dragged out his suitcase, threw his duds in it, put on his overcoat and on top of it his sheepskin coat, pulled out of his pocket his photo (dressed in necktie and his very best sports shirt) and quickly wrote: "To Larisa with affectionate memories," put it in Larisa's room on her pillow and left. In the courtyard Banin, spitting and swearing, let loose an angry dog on him. Kirpichenko kicked the dog aside and went on out of the gate.

"Well, how was your coffee?" the waitress asked him.

"Not so bad, it helps," Kirpichenko sighed and stroked her arm.

"Careful there," the waitress smiled.

At that moment they announced his flight.

With lightness in his heart and with strong, long strides Kirpichenko went out onto the airfield to get away farther, farther, farther! There are some years of life one doesn't have a vacation just to hang around in a suffocating hut in the sticks and eat Dutch cheese. There are characters who spend their whole vacation in such shacks, but he was not a fool. He would go to Moscow, would buy three new suits and some shoes in the Central Department Store and then go farther, farther, to the Black Sea. "Seagull, Black Sea seagull, my dream," he hummed to himself. He would eat *chebureki* and wander around in his jacket without an overcoat.

He saw himself at that moment as he looked to others—big, strong, in an overcoat and sheepskin coat over it, in a cap of musk-rat fur, in felt boots. Stepping ahead. One broad with whom he had an affair the previous summer told him he had the face of an Indian chief. And she was chief of a geological expedition, what about that! She was a good one, too, Anna Petrovna, even had a degree. She had written him letters and he had answered: "How do you do, respected Anna Petrovna! Valery Kirpichenko is writing you..."—and all kinds of other stuff and nonsense.

A large crowd of passengers had already gathered at the turn-stile. Not far away Larisa was jumping up and down in her boots. Her face was white and bluish, her lips bright red, her brooch which represented a running deer and which she was wearing on her collar looked terribly stupid.

"Why did you come?" Kirpichenko asked.

Larisa could hardly say it: "To see you off."

"Listen, stop it!" he cut her off with his hand. "So you and your brother worked me over for three days—all right, but don't try to make love out of it..."

Larisa wept and Valery got frightened.

"All right, all right..."

"Yes we worked you over," Larisa babbled. "So we worked you over... Well, all right... I know what you think about me... That's what I am... And so because of that I can't love you, is that it?"

"Cut it out."

"But I will, I will!" Larisa almost shouted. "You, Valya," she moved up close to him, "You're not like the rest..."

"I'm just the same as everyone, only I can..." And Kirpichenko slowly dragged out his lips into a smile.

Larisa turned away and wept still harder. All her pitiful body shook.

"Well, come on, come on..." Kirpichenko was taken aback and stroked her shoulder.

Then the crowd moved out onto the airfield. And Kirpichenko went along, without looking behind, thinking of the fact that he was sorry for Larisa, that she had become no longer a stranger to him but, as a matter of fact, every one of them became no longer a stranger, such was his silly character, but then you forgot them, and everything was normal, normal. Normal—and an end to it.

He stepped along in the crowd of passengers, looking at the enormous airplane waiting for him, gleaming in the sun, and quick, quick he forgot everything—the whole nasty mess of his three-day stay here and those fingers on his neck. He wouldn't fall for that. It was always that way. He would not fall for that. He would not be broken. Some who were not just cheap broads had even come his way. He had had fine women too. Anna Petrovna, the scientist, for example—a really good person. They had all fallen in love with him, and Valery understood this took place not because of his cruelty but for quite a different reason: perhaps, because of his silence, perhaps, because every one of them wanted to become something special for him, because they, evidently, felt in those minutes that he was groping forward like a blind man. But he always said to himself: You can't buy me with those tricks. You can't break me. It's over and that's an end to it. And everything is normal. Normal.

The airplane was frighteningly enormous: It was enormous and heavy like a cruiser. Kirpichenko had not yet flown on such airplanes and at this moment his breath was simply taken away with delight. That's what he loved—technology. He climbed up the high set of steps leading to the plane. The stewardess in a blue suit and cap examined his ticket and told him where his seat was. The seat was in the first salon but there was already some character sitting in it, a bespectacled type in a pie-shaped cap.

"Beat it," Kirpichenko said peacefully and showed the bespectacled character his ticket.

"Couldn't you sit in my seat?" asked the bespectacled character. "I get sick in the rear."

"Beat it, I'm telling you," Kirpichenko barked at him.

"Couldn't you be more polite," the bespectacled type was hurt. For some reason he didn't get up.

Kirpichenko grabbed his cap from off him and threw it into the back of the airplane, in the direction of his rightful seat. In general he showed him where—beat it back there, take your place according to your ticket.

"Citizen, why are you being disorderly?" asked the stewardess.

"Take it easy," said Kirpichenko.

The bespectacled individual in extreme consternation went to look for his cap and Kirpichenko took his rightful seat.

He took off his sheepskin coat and put it at his feet. Consolidated himself, so to speak, in his place.

The passengers came into the airplane one after another. It seemed as if they would never stop. Light music was playing in the plane. Sunny, frosty steam rolled into the hatchway. The stewardesses busily ran up and down the passageway. All of them were in identical dark-blue suits, long-legged, and in high heels. Kirpichenko read the newspaper. About disarmament and about Berlin, about preparation for the championship in Chile, and about the problem of retaining snow on collective farm fields.

An elderly woman, wrapped up in a shawl was sitting by the window, and a rosy-cheeked sailor took the seat next to Kirpichenko. He kept joking:

"Lady, have you made your will?" And he shouted to the stewardess: "Girl, who shall I give my will to?"

It was Kirpichenko's luck to travel with such comedians! Finally, the door of the hatchway was slammed shut and a red sign lit up: "Don't smoke. Fasten your seat belts." And there was something in English, perhaps the same, and perhaps something different. Perhaps, just the opposite: "Please smoke. Don't fasten your seat belts." Kirpichenko did not know English.

A woman's voice came over the loudspeaker system:

"I ask your attention! The commander of the airplane welcomes aboard the passengers of the Soviet liner TU-114. Our airplane-giant is traveling on the route from Khabarovsk to Moscow. The flight will take place at a height of 9,000 meters with a speed of 700 kilometers an hour. The elapsed time will be 8 hours 30 minutes. I thank you for your attention."

And then in English: "Kurly, shurly, lops, drops . . . Senk you."

"That's how it should be done," said Kirpichenko with satisfaction and winked at the sailor. "On the nose."

"And what did you think," said the sailor just as if the airplane were his own personal property, as if he had arranged the whole thing: an announcement in two languages and all kinds of other conveniences.

The airplane was pulled out to the take-off strip. The elderly female sat concentrated. Outside the porthole the airport buildings swam by.

"May I take your overcoat?" asked the stewardess.

It was the same one who had rebuked Kirpichenko. He looked at her and was stupefied. She smiled. Over him hung her smiling face and her dark hair, no, not black, just dark, and it must be, soft, and with a dense exact hairdo just like fur, like mouton, like nylon, like all the treasures of the world. Her fingers touched the fur collar of his sheepskin coat. Such fingers don't exist. No, all of that exists in magazines, and that means not only there, but it just doesn't happen that there is all of that and also such a smile and the voice of the very first woman in the world—that just doesn't happen.

"You understand, she took my sheepskin coat," said Kirpichenko smiling stupidly at the sailor, and the sailor winked at him and said proudly:

"Is the personnel satisfactory? So-so."

She returned and took the woman's sheepskin coat, the sailor's leather coat and Kirpichenko's overcoat. She pressed all the coats at once to her divine body and said:

"Buckle your seat belts, comrades."

The motors roared. The elderly woman at the window shrank in fear and quietly crossed herself. The sailor teased her without mercy, looking all the time out of the corner of his eye to see whether Kirpichenko was laughing. But Kirpichenko was craning his neck, following the girl, that girl, that very girl, as she carried off to somewhere the overcoats and jackets. Then she reappeared with a tray and offered them all candies, and maybe not really candies but gold nuggets, or pills for the heart, and then, with the plane already aloft, she went about to everyone with water, with soft drinks and mineral water, that very same water which flows from the highest and cleanest waterfalls. And then she disappeared.

"Would you like to play cards?" asked the sailor. "We could get a game together."

The red sign went out and Kirpichenko understood he could smoke. He got up and went to the front of the plane, into the small section behind the curtain from which billows of smoke were rolling.

"We are reporting information on the flight," the loud speaker said. "Altitude 9,000 meters, speed 750 kilometers an hour. Temperature of the air outside the ship minus 58 degrees Centigrade. I thank you for your attention."

Below, a long distance away, there flowed past a stony, lifeless country. Kirpichenko shuddered, picturing to himself, how in that icy space over cruel, desert land there floated a metal cigar filled with human warmth, politeness, cigarette smoke, the hollow rumble of conversation and laughter, jokes (tear them off and throw them away) with mineral water, the drops of a waterfall from fertile regions. And he was sitting there and smoking and somewhere in the tail, and maybe in the middle of the plane a woman who does not exist in actual fact, of a kind to whom for you it is a long long ways, as far as to the moon, was walking back and forth.

He began to think about his life and to reminisce. He had never before reminisced. Unless, when he had to say something, he had told some little story or other. But now all of a sudden he thought: "It's the fourth time I have rolled across the whole country and the first time I have paid my own way. What fun!"

Previously all of his trips had been at the expense of the government. In 1939 when Valery was still a very small boy, their whole collective farm—in the Stavropol region—had been resettled in the Far Eastern Maritime Province. It was a long trip. He remembered that trip only a little. Sour milk and sour cabbage soup. His mother doing the wash in the corner of a heated freight car and hanging the laundry outside. It fluttered outside the window, like flags, and then began to rattle and bang because it had frozen from the cold, and he sang the song:

> "The planes are flying high, high, high,
> The pilots are looking at us from the sky . . ."

His mother had died during the war, and his father had "fallen the death of the brave"—perished in the last days of the war—in the Kurile Islands in 1945. In the orphanage Valery finished seven years of school, then went to vocational training and worked in a mine. As the phrase went: "He gave his country coal, small coal, but much . . ." In 1950 he went to do his military service. Again he traveled across the entire country—this time to the Baltic area. In the army he had become a truck driver and after demobilization he and a friend of his had settled down in Novorossisk on the Black Sea. A year later he was picked up by the police. Some scoundrel had stolen spare parts from the garage, but they hadn't spent long on figuring out on whom to pin the blame. They had sent him up as "the person, materially to be held responsible for the loss." He got three years and was sent to a labor camp in Sakhalin. He had spent a year and a half in the prison camp. He had been freed on points, and later they removed his conviction from his record. From then on he had worked in the lumber camp. He liked the work. He earned lots of money. His work was to haul trailers loaded with timber up through the pass and then to come on down on all his brakes. He drank straight alcohol, saw movies, went to the dances in summer at the fish cannery. He lived in a dormitory. He had always lived in dormitories, barracks, camps. Cots, cots, simple two-storied bunks, board beds, in bins ... He had no friends but many acquaintances. He was feared. He was not one to fool with. He didn't stop to consider before giving you a black eye. And at work he was a leader. He loved technology. He remembered the machines on which he had worked as one remembers friends: "Ivan Willys" in the army, and then a tractor, and then a one-and-a-half-ton GAZ, and a "Tatra," and now his present diesel ... In towns, in Yuzhno-Sakhalinsk, in Poronaisk, in Korsakov, he sometimes stopped at a corner and looked into the windows of new apartment houses, at the stylish floor lamps and curtains, and this filled him with alarm. He did not count his years and only recently had come to understand that in a few months he would pass thirty. Take it easy! In Moscow he would buy himself three suits and a green hat and would go south, like some engineer or technician. Sewn in his underdrawers were letters of credit, money—a whole carload. It would be gay in the south. Everything was normal. Normal—and that was all!

He got up and went back to look for her. Where had she gone? Really! The passengers had dry throats and there she was standing and gossiping in English with some kind of a capitalist.

She was chattering, squinting her eyes, smiling with her mouth. Evidently she found it pleasant to chatter in English. The capitalist stood next to her, tall and thin, with a gray crew cut, young in years. His jacket was unbuttoned. From his belt hung a thin gold chain which disappeared into his pocket. He spoke with a roll. His words thundered in his mouth just as if they were knocking against his teeth. We know that kind of conversation!

He: Let's go to San Francisco, darling, and we'll drink whiskey.

She: You are very presumptuous.

He: In banana-lemon Singapore * ... Do you understand?

She: Do you really mean it? When the banana tree bends beneath the wind? *

He: And so we climbed up to the 102nd floor. The jazz orchestra there was knocking out boogie-woogie.

Kirpichenko approached and shouldered the capitalist away. The latter was surprised and said: "Ai em saree," which, of course, meant: "Watch it, boy, you're looking for trouble."

"Take it easy," said Kirpichenko. "Peace—friendship."

He knew politics.

---

* "In banana-lemon Singapore" and "When the banana tree bends beneath the wind" are fragments of lines from the song "Tango Magnolia" from the repertoire of the famous Russian cabaret singer, Alexander Vertinsky. The song is a symbol of tropic exoticism for Russians

The capitalist said something to her over his head, probably: "You choose, me or him, San Francisco or Bayukly."

And she said to him with a smile: "I know this comrade," and, "Leave me, I am a Soviet person."

"What do you want, comrade?" she asked Kirpichenko.

"That," he pointed. "My throat is dry. Could I wet it with something?"

"Let's go," she said, and went ahead like some kind of a nanny goat, as in the cinema, as in a dream. Ah, how he had longed for her while he was smoking there, up in front.

She went ahead like I don't know who and led him into something like a buffet, and maybe to herself at home where there was nobody and where the high sun with peaceful fury shone through the porthole, and maybe, through a window in a new apartment building on the ninth floor. She took a bottle and poured out bubbling water into a glass cup. She raised this little cup, and it caught fire beneath the high sun. And he looked at the girl and he wanted to have her children, but he didn't even picture to himself that it might be possible to do with her what people do when they want to have children. And that was the first time this had ever happened, and he was all of a sudden burning with the unexpected first feeling of happiness.

"What's your name?" he asked with that feeling which he had every time after he had crossed the pass—it was terrifying and everything was behind him.

"Tatyana Viktorovna," she answered. "Tanya."

"And I am Kirpichenko—Valery," he said and reached out his hand. She gave him her fingers and smiled.

"You're an unrestrained comrade."

"Just a trifle," he said blushingly.

For several seconds they looked at each other in silence. She was seized with laughter. She struggled with herself and he also struggled, but all of a sudden he could no longer restrain himself and smiled in such a way as, in all probability, he had never smiled in all his life.

At that moment she was called and she ran down the stairway to the first floor of the plane.

Kirpichenko turned and saw his smiling face in some sort of a mirror: "Some mug you have, Valery," he thought to himself. "Awful. Like a thug. But it seems as if the girl isn't afraid of you. I'm sure she isn't afraid, not a drop."

He went back along the aisle and saw the bespectacled character who had tried before to take over his rightful seat. The bespectacled type was lying back in his armchair with his eyes shut. He had a handsome face, pure marble.

"Listen, friend," Kirpichenko punched him in the shoulder, "do you want to take my seat?"

The bespectacled character opened his eyes and weakly smiled: "Thank you, I'm all right . . ."

Maybe it wasn't the first time that he had flown on such airplanes, that bespectacled type, and took the seat in the first salon in order to watch how the door into the pilot's cabin opens, and watch there the pilots, watch them scratch themselves, smoke, joke, and laugh, read the newspapers, and now and again look at the instruments.

Tanya began to distribute the meal. She also gave Valery a tray and looked at him as at an acquaintance.

"And where do you live, Tanya?" he asked.

And he thought to himself: "Tanya, Ta-Nya, T-A-N-Y-A."

"In Moscow," she answered and left.

Kirpichenko ate and it seemed to him that his steak was thicker than for the rest, that his apple was larger, that she had given him more bread. And then she brought tea.

"So that means you are a Muscovite?" again he asked.

"Uh-huh," she answered smartly and went away.

"It's all for nothing that you're trying so hard, fellow countryman," smirked the sailor. "There's probably a well-dressed little character waiting for her in Moscow."

"Take it easy," said Kirpichenko with an even and broad sensation of his well-being and happiness.

But, after all, such flights do not last forever and it is a characteristic of airplanes to descend from up above, from such great altitudes. And work shifts come to an end, official duties are completed, and they give you back your overcoat, and the thin little fingers bring you your sheepskin coat, and eyes wander somewhere already far away, and everything slowly runs down just like the spring in toys, and everything becomes flat like a page from a magazine. "Aeroflot—your representative during trips by air"—how wonderful—all those manicures, high-heeled slippers, and hairdos.

No, no, no, nothing runs down, nothing becomes flat, although already we are rolling along the ground . . .

Such a rush began and the dark blue stewardess's cap was already somewhere distant . . .

"Don't dally, citizen . . ."

"Let's get a move on, fellow countryman . . ."

"Boys, there she is, and Moscow . . ."

"Moscow, that's something . . ."

"Well, move along with you, really..."

Still not understanding what was taking place with him, Kirpichenko emerged with the sailor from the airplane, descended the stair, and climbed up into an autobus. The autobus rolled along to the airport building and soon the "Soviet liner TU-114, the airplane-giant," the flying fortress of his incomprehensible hopes, had disappeared from sight.

The taxi flew along the broad, broad highway. There was traffic in two lanes. Trucks, vans, dump trucks pressed over to the edge, and passenger cars went at high speed and passed them as if they were standing still. And then the forest came to an end and Kirpichenko and the sailor saw the rosy thousand-eyed apartment blocks of the South-West. The sailor began to fidget and put his hand on Valery's shoulder.

"The capital! Well, how about it, Valery!"

"Listen, is our airplane going to fly back now?" Kirpichenko asked.

"Of course. They'll fly tomorrow."

"With the same crew?"

The sailor whistled derisively.

"Stop it. A wonder indeed—a modern skirt. There are a million in Moscow. Don't be crazy."

"I was simply asking." Kirpichenko murmured.

"Where are you going, boys?" asked the chauffeur.

"Let's go to GUM!" Kirpichenko barked and immediately forgot all about the airplane.

The car was already rolling along the streets of Moscow.

In GUM—the Main Department Store—he quickly bought three suits—dark blue, gray, and brown. He kept on the new brown suit and wrapped his old suit made four years before in a tailor shop in Korsakov into a bundle and left it in a booth in the toilet. The sailor picked out a piece of gabardine cloth for a mackintosh for himself and said he would have it made up in Odessa. Then in the *gastronome* they each drank a bottle of champagne and went on an excursion to the Kremlin. Then they went to the Hotel Natsional to have lunch and ate the devil only knew what—julien—and drank a drink called "KS." There were many girls here looking like Tanya, and maybe Tanya herself came here. Maybe she was sitting with them at a table and pouring out "Narzan" mineral water for him, running to the kitchen and seeing how his steak was being cooked. In any case the capitalist was here. Kirpichenko waved his hand to him, and he stood up and bowed. Then they went out onto the street and each drank still another bottle of champagne. Tanya manifested furious activity on Gorky Street. She jumped from out of trolley busses and ran into stores, promenaded with *pijons* on the other side of the street, and even smiled from out of show windows. Kirpichenko and the sailor, firmly arm-in-arm, went along Gorky Street and smiled. The sailor sang:

"Ma-da-gas-car, my country . . ."

This was the hour when twilight was already thickening but when street lights had not yet gone on. Yes, and at the end of the street, at the edge of the earth, spring was burning. Yes, this was the land of hopes come true. They were surprised that the girls shied away from them.

Later, everywhere there were closed doors, queues, and it wasn't possible to get in anywhere. They thought about the question of a place to spend the night, took a taxi, and went to the airport at Vnukovo. They rented a double room in the airport hotel and only on seeing the white sheets did Kirpichenko understand how tired he was. He pulled his new suit off and threw himself onto the bed.

In an hour the sailor woke him up. He was running about the room, scraping his cheeks with an electric razor called "Sputnik," and chirping, crowing, and gasping:

"Let's go, Valery! I got acquainted with such girls, ah, ah! Get up, let's go and visit them! They live here in the dormitory. It's a sure thing, brother. No difficulties . . . I have a nose for that . . . Get up, get out of bed! Ma-da-gas-car . . ."

"Stop cackling as if you'd laid an egg!" said Kirpichenko, taking a cigarette off the bedstand and lighting up.

"Are you coming or not?" the sailor asked, already at the door.

"Turn out the light," Kirpichenko asked him.

The light went out and the moonlit rectangle of the window was immediately projected onto the wall, intersected by the frames and the rocking shadows of naked branches. It was silent. Somewhere far off a phonograph was playing. Through the wall he could hear: "Who has a six?"—and heard a blow on the table. Then an airplane thundered in to land. Kirpichenko smoked and pictured to himself how she was lying alongside him, how they were lying together, the two of them, already after everything, and how her fingers were stroking his neck. No, that is what this world really is, not make-believe, but actually real, because everything incomprehensible that took place with him in childhood when goose pimples ran along his whole body and in his youth—the Far Eastern rolling knolls imprinted with the rosy fire of the dawn, and the sea in the darkness, and the melting snow, and fatigue after work, and Saturday and Sunday morning—this is she.

"Well, that's the thing," he thought to himself and again he was overcome with an even and broad sensation of well-being and happiness. He was happy that this had happened to him. He feared only one thing, that a century would go by and that he would forget her face and voice.

The sailor came into the room. He undressed and lay down, took a cigarette from off the bedstand, lit up and sadly sang:

"Ma-da-gas-car, my country, here like everywhere the spring is in flower . . . Oh, the devil take it," he said heartily, "Well, what a life! Eternal passage . . ."

"How many years have you been a sailor?" Kirpichenko asked.

"From half a century seven," the sailor answered and again sang:

> "Madagascar across the sea
> Madagascar my own country
> Madagascar of thee I sing
> Madagascar where blooms the spring.
> We're people too
> And we love like you.
> Black is our skin
> But our blood's not thin."

"Write me out the words," Kirpichenko asked him.

They lit the light and the sailor dictated to Valery the words of this entrancing song. Kirpichenko loved such songs very much.

The next day they had their tickets stamped: Kirpichenko for Adler on the Black Sea, the sailor for Odessa. They had their breakfast. Kirpichenko bought a book by Chekhov and the magazine *Ogonyek* in a kiosk.

"Listen," said the sailor, "she really does have a good-looking girl friend. Maybe we could go and see them in Moscow?"

Kirpichenko sat down in an armchair and opened the book.

"No," he said. "You go, just the two of you, and I'm going to sit here and read this politics."

The sailor waved out a naval signal: "Your signal read. Wish you success. Continuing on course."

All day long Kirpichenko hung around the airport, but he didn't see Tanya. In the evening he saw the sailor off for Odessa, well, and they each drank a bottle of champagne, and then he saw the sailor's girl friend to her dormitory, and returned to the airport, went to the ticket window and bought a ticket on the airplane-giant TU-114, Flight No. 901, Moscow to Khabarovsk.

In the airplane it was all just as it had been before. The announcements in two languages and other conveniences, but there was no Tanya. There was another crew. There were girls just as young, just as beautiful, just like Tanya, but nevertheless they were not the first one—Tanya was the first one. All the rest of this breed came after her.

In the morning Kirpichenko was in Khabarovsk and one hour later he again flew to Moscow, already on another airplane. But Tanya was not there either.

And so he flew and kept flying on TU-114 airplanes, at a height of 9,000 meters, at a speed of 750 kilometers an hour. The temperature of the air outside hovered between minus 50 to 60 degrees Centigrade. All the apparatus worked normally.

He already knew by face almost all of the stewardesses on this line and even some of the pilots. He was afraid they might remember him.

He was afraid they might even take him for a spy.

He changed his suits. One trip in the dark blue, another in the brown, a third in the gray.

He opened up his underdrawers and took out the letters of credit and put them into his jacket pocket. The letters of credit grew less and less in number.

Still there was no Tanya.

There was a bright high sun, and the sunrises and the sunsets took place above a snowy cloudy waste. There was a moon and it seemed to be close. It in fact was not so far away.

On occasion he got lost in time and space and stopped changing his watch. Khabarovsk seemed to him to be a suburb of Moscow and Moscow a new district of Khabarovsk.

He read very much. He never in his life had read so much. He never in his life had thought so much.

He never in his life had wept.

He never in his life had taken such a first-class restful vacation.

In Moscow spring had begun. Drops from those very same high and pure waterfalls fell down into his collar. He bought himself a gray scarf in large black checks.

In case of a meeting he had prepared a gift for Tanya—a perfume set, "May First," and a piece of material for a dress.

I met him in the building of Khabarovsk Airport. He was sitting in an armchair, one leg crossed over the other and reading a book by Stanyukovich. On the arm of the armchair hung a string bag, full of oranges. On the cover of the book a clipper flew under hurricane sails.

"Are you a sailor?" he asked me, looking over my leather coat.

"No."

I stared at his surprising face which aroused misgiving and he read a few lines more and again asked:

"Are you sorry you're not a sailor?"

"Of course it's too bad," I said.

"I also regret it," he laughed. "I have a friend who is a sailor. Here he sent me a radiogram from the sea."

He showed me the radiogram.

"Uh-huh," I said.

And he asked me, changing over to the intimate personal pronoun:

"What's your year of birth?"

"Nineteen thirty-two," I answered him.

He was all aglow:

"Listen, you and I are the same age!"

The coincidence was really phenomenal and I shook his hand.

"Maybe you live in Moscow?" he asked.

"You guessed it," I answered. "In Moscow."

"Maybe you have an apartment, yes? A wife, a kid, yes? And the other stuff and nonsense?"

"You guessed it. That's just the way things are."

"Let's go and have our breakfast, what?"

I was all ready to go with him but right at that moment they announced my flight. I was flying to Petropavlovsk. We exchanged addresses and I went off to my plane. I went along the airfield, bending beneath the wind, and I thought to myself: "What a strange chap."

And during that time he looked at his watch, took up his string bag, and went out. He took a taxi and went to the city. He and the taxi driver together just barely found that humped-up village street because he had not remembered its name. The houses on that street were all like one another. In all the courtyards enormous dogs were barking, and he was a little at a loss. Finally, he remembered that particular little house. He got out of the car, hung his string bag with its oranges on the fence, covered it with a newspaper so that passers-by or neighbors should not steal this treasure, and returned to the car.

"Come on, chief, speed it up! I don't want to be late for my plane."

"Where are you flying?" asked the driver.

"To Moscow, to the capital."

Tanya he finally saw two days later at the airport in Khabarovsk, when he was already returning home to Sakhalin, when all of his letters of credit had already come to an end and there remained only several red bills in his pocket. She was in a white fur coat, belted about with a leather strap. She was laughing, eating candies, getting them out of her bag, offering them to the other girls who were also laughing. He immediately lost all his strength and sat down on his suitcase. He watched how Tanya was giving away candies, taking off their wrappings, and how all the other girls were doing exactly the same, and he did not understand why they were all standing in one place, laughing and going nowhere. Then he realized spring had come, that it was now a spring night and that the moon over the airdrome was like an orange, that now at this moment it was not cold, and that one could stand just this way and simply look at the light and laugh and take thought for a moment with a candy in one's mouth . . .

"What are you doing, Kirpichenko?" His Sakhalin acquaintance, Manyevich, touched him on the shoulder. Manyevich was also returning from vacation. "Let's go! They've already announced the flight."

"Manyevich, do you know how many kilometers it is to the moon?" Kirpichenko asked.

"Evidently you must have had too much to drink during your vacation," Manyevich said angrily and went away.

Kirpichenko caught him out on the field.

"You're a young specialist, Manyevich," he said beggingly, looking at Tanya. "You ought to know . . ."

"Well 300,000 maybe," said Manyevich, moving back.

"It's not so far," thought Kirpichenko to himself. "A spitting distance." He looked at Tanya and pictured to himself how he would remember her on the road up to the pass, and on the pass all of a sudden he would forget, he would not be up to that up there, and afterward, at the end of the descent, he would remember her again and from then on he would remember her for the entire evening and night and in the morning he would awaken with thoughts of her.

Then he got up from his suitcase.

Yuri Kazakov

An Introduction to Yuri Kazakov

Serious, sensitive, 36-year-old Yuri Kazakov stands out among the new prose writers of promise in Russia. Already several years ago he achieved recognition among other writers and among critics in the Soviet Union as an outstanding talent, almost in a class by himself. In terms also of the steadfast independence of his creative course to date he is also unique. He has all along in his writing eschewed politics, political themes, and the cult of optimism of socialist-realism as this is generally comprehended. He has so far firmly hewed to a course of keeping all kinds of blatant propaganda out of his writing. Yevtushenko may write encomiums of praise to Fidel Castro —and this may at times serve as a counterweight in the estimation of the Party for other elements in his writing—and conduct—which have been less welcome to powerful elements in the Establishment. Yuri Nagibin, one-time political officer in the army and a veteran war correspondent, finds no inconsistency in combining the writing of delicately perceptive, completely apolitical, short stories with others which are not by any means so delicate and which make some kind of obvious little communist moral or other in their conclusion. Not so with Kazakov. He is as patriotic and as loyal, no doubt, in his acceptance of the communist way of life as any of the other important contemporary Soviet writers—and this can be felt in his works by those who have the sensitivity to perceive it, but he doesn't cram this down the reader's throat or shove it into his face like so many others. This is there, but it is in the background, in the foundation of his works, rather than in their visible superstructure. As a writer he is deeply faithful to the truth of life as he sees it— and one can sense this in his stories. He lets his chips fall where they may—and evidently at the very beginning of his career decided that he was not going to be in any obvious sense, in the Stalinist literary tradition, any "engineer of the human soul."

"I do not think that literature has an immediate and direct effect on the life of a man and on his ethics. As an example you may take many unfair slovenly critics who, of course, have read Tolstoi, Chekhov, and Hemingway—read them without learning a thing. All the same I do believe in the educational power of literature. And I believe that a writer who spends all of his life advocating the goodness, truth, and beauty of man does raise the moral qualities of his contemporaries and successors, those of them, of course, who are willing to read and think over what they have read. How profound are the qualitative changes that take place in human nature under the influence of literature I do not venture to judge. It probably varies with everyone. What is important though, is that the writer should perfect his own moral qualities. Then he will have the right to teach others something." *

This view seems hardly to jibe with the view of Soviet political and propaganda authorities—which sees the chief functions of literature in helping to raise labor productivity, in the inspiring of Soviet citizens to the "storming of the new heights," in the "construction of Communism," and in the depiction of the "grandeur and glory of the new Soviet man."

Yuri Kazakov concerns himself primarily with the inner man rather than the external world of material values. He directs his gaze into the soul of Russians of today rather than at the factories and hydroelectric stations they are building. And when he reports the results, in his stories, he finds in those souls not only glory and grandeur—often in the most unexpected places so far as the standard concepts of orthodox Soviet literary thinking are concerned— but also depths of murk, hopelessness, and evil.

In all these different respects Yuri Kazakov is blazing new literary trails in the Soviet Union for this era. (The only other Russian writer comparable to him in this sense is Alexander Solzhenitsyn, author of *One Day in the Life of Ivan Denisovich* and of three subsequent short stories. These two men, though comparable in this respect, are very different as writers.)

Moreover, he possesses formidable qualities as a writer. He writes tersely and with economy of words. He draws vivid images of Russia and Russians of today. Throughout his short stories—many quite short—looms a stark, somber strength. In many there is a bleak sense of loneliness and alienation of human beings from one another. He has close kinship in this with many Western writers of the period. In this sense he is modern.

He is also modern—for Russia—in orientation as between countryside and city. He writes often about the rural scene, but always one feels the point of view of the author as an inveterate city dweller. Kazakov is no "peasant" writer. He concentrates penetrating insight on the inner world of complicated, contradictory, irrational human beings who, as it happens, are modern-day Russians but who experience joys, sorrows, longings, frustrations which are universal in modern society.

Kazakov, in pursuing such a literary course, has inevitably

---

* Quoted from a reply to a questionnaire distributed by and published in issues of *Voprosy Literatury* in 1962—for English translation of Kazakov's answers see *Soviet Literature Monthly*, No. 12 (1962), p. 135.

brought down on his prematurely balding head a flurry of controversy—getting both criticism and defense.

In early 1959 at the All-Union Congress of Writers Kazakov was attacked severely by Leonid Sobolev, chairman of the Union of Writers of the Russian Republic. Admitting Kazakov's talents, his capacity for acute observation, and a tendency to thoughtfulness not frequently encountered in novels, Sobolev declared that he was not making the most effective use of them: "He has a sense of language . . . A young talent that should follow the right path. But instead he writes about tramps who attempt to corrupt a young girl, about crude and stupid young men who leave their fiancées in the country for the sake of a career in sports in the cities." Sobolev delivered a blunt condemnation of Kazakov's course in writing.

Kazakov's defense was taken up at the same time by one of the most respected senior writers of Russia, prominent in the liberal wing of the Russian writers' controversy in recent years—Konstantin Paustovsky, who answered the question he said was being asked widely in the country—whether there were talented, hard-working writers among the Soviet younger generation—by saying there were. He put Yuri Kazakov's name first on his honor list, saying that his work possesses both depth and clarity: "Its truth and the strength of its ties with the people touch the heart."

A more recent evaluation of Kazakov's work was given in mid-1962 in an essay by V. V. Buznik in the anthology entitled *The Problem of Character in Contemporary Soviet Literature*. Rejecting the thesis of some of Kazakov's more violent literary enemies that he is merely imitative of the Russian classics and actually quite untalented, Buznik nevertheless took him to task for allegedly allowing himself to be distracted from the social content of contemporary life by his desire to be pictorial in his descriptions, by his pursuit of "literary-ness." Buznik concluded his essay on Kazakov with the comment that although in *some* cases he succeeds in establishing a close tie between contemporary life, "typicality" of the conflicts which he describes, and his colorfully drawn figures and perceptively noted particularities, most of his stories lack such a tie. And, therefore, he concluded, although the "author subjectively has striven to be closer to the individual human being, to the spiritual world of individuality, objectively he turned out to be, on the contrary, artificially separated from contemporary life in its concrete, unique essence."

Or as another critic put it: "For example in the creative work of Y. Kazakov social content as such often fades and is entirely extinguished."

What these criticisms come down to is that Kazakov has chosen for himself a broader canvas than the particular special transient political-economic-psychological problems of Soviet life. He wants to deal with life itself. As stated at the beginning of this introduction he eschews politics, political themes, and the cult of optimism. Thus he poses to Soviet critics the really fundamental question with which these critics have always so far, for obvious political reasons, been incapable of dealing objectively—of the role of the writer in human culture.

Despite a generally critical attitude toward Kazakov the scholar Buznik * did give an interesting and generally fair description of Kazakov's writing techniques in his essay:

"The young author's talent is a special one. He attracts with the humanity of his perception of the world. Kazakov scrutinizes with good attention the phenomena of nature and is full of their wise meaning. For him nature is alive ... It's not possible to pass by in silence the fact that just such a natural participation in living life is missing among many contemporary storytellers who incline toward morality-teaching descriptiveness. One need not therefore be surprised that on the background of such works the stories of Kazakov seem almost even to be 'living water.'

"Notable also in Y. Kazakov is the fact that in his best works as, for example, 'The Light Blue and the Green,' 'Arcturus—a Hound,' 'Manka,' he advances an affirmation of feelings which are strong and whole, uncompromising: loyalty to the extent of self-sacrifice, love without self-serving purpose, bravery, goodness. And this particularity also distinguishes him from many other storytellers whose heroes in their majority are distinguished by some kind of stereotyped duality of desires and thoughts, by shyness of emotions, by the petty, workaday reality underlying their feelings.

"And to characterize on the whole of Kazakov's manner of writing it needs to be said that it represents underlined, stressed, pictoriality of imagery, arising from precise vision of details.

"Read over again, if you please, his collection *At the Whistle Stop,* and you will doubtless catch the impression that before your eyes have passed colorfully drawn scenes or film episodes with characteristic incidents, faces, details photographed closeup, instead of stories in which storytelling—the setting forth of events, disclosure of characters in their connections and mutual dependence—stands in the foreground. The chief thing for Kazakov is to show. And he is very skillful at showing. From amazingly exact images and sur-

* V. V. Buznik, "The Art of Communication. (On Quarrels about Artistic Individualization)," Akademiya Nauk SSSR, Institut Russkoi Literatury Pushkinskii Dom, *Problema Kharaktera v Sovremennoi Sovietskoi Literature,* Izdatelstvo Akademii Nauk SSRR (Moscow-Leningrad, 1962), pp. 162–217.

prisingly precise definitions, from the very structure of speech, simple, compressed, transparently clear, there arises the charm of truthfulness to life. It is as if one could actually hear the sounds, smell the odors, see the colors, feel the very 'texture' of life . . . The content of the stories of Kazakov is not so much in the interplay of incident or direct statements of the writer and heroes as in the implication which seeps little by little through eloquent details.

"We hardly ever encounter in him heroes who disclose themselves in their thoughts and judgments, or arguments. He sculpts characters, fixing upon an expressive gesture, a particular manner of conduct and, particularly, external characteristics."

Yuri Kazakov was born in 1927 in Moscow—the son of a worker. He entered initially a technical school for construction engineering, but he gave up this for music. He attended the famous Gnesin Music School in Moscow—studying the cello. He graduated from there in 1951 at the age of 24, and for nearly two years he played in symphony and jazz orchestras. His liking for jazz is expressed in several of his stories—as, for example, in "There Goes a Dog" and also in "Autumn in an Oak Forest." While he was a musician he began writing—and getting his works published.

His first work, he has reported, was a one-act play entitled *The New Lathe* which appeared in 1952 in an anthology.

In 1956 he published a story called "Smoke," which was severely criticized by the paper *Komsomol Pravda*, and Kazakov was accused of "pessimism." In 1957 his first book of short stories appeared, entitled *Teddy*.

From this time on he has published his works more or less continuously. So far his writing has been restricted to just two genres —short stories and a pair or so of travel essays. He has announced that he is working on a novel, but it hasn't appeared yet.

Altogether, including his first book, by late 1963 he had to his credit half a dozen collections of stories in book form—plus a number of individual stories in magazines and even in newspapers.

After Kazakov had begun to publish stories he attended the Gorky Literary Institute in Moscow—graduating from it in 1958. He studied in the seminar of Nikolai Zamoshkin for his entire five-year course at this cradle of contemporary Soviet literary talent.

He loves to travel—and his journeys in Russia, incidentally, have often given him the stage settings for his stories: the arctic, the rural fields and woods of Smolensk Province, the shores of the Oka River near Tarusa, south of Moscow, etc.

Among Kazakov's earlier stories—those published before the sixties—"Manka," "Arcturus—a Hound," "The House Beneath the Precipice," "On the Island," "At the Whistle Stop," and "The Outsider" have been particularly noted by Russian and Western critics and scholars.

Interestingly enough, as recounted in the general introduction to this collection, Yuri Kazakov emerged from the whole furor of early 1963 relatively unscathed. He was not, at any rate, made a principal target of the political and literary critics. If anything he gained in terms of the relative degree of official approval for his work. One of his stories, "The Easy Life," was published in *Pravda* itself in late December—and praised. Another—entitled "I Weep and I Sob"—came out in January in *Ogonyek,* the nearest Soviet equivalent to *Look* or *Life,* a mass-circulation magazine controlled by a relatively conservative editorial board. The story published in *Pravda* got complimentary reviews—and was in fact contrasted favorably in the *Literary Gazette* to works which were then under attack, specifically the two short stories of Vasily Aksenov included in this anthology and Aksenov's latest novel, *Oranges from Morocco.* In August *Ogonyek,* moreover, brought out in one of its literary supplements—for years almost wholly reserved for the more conservative and "dogmatist" writers—a collection of Kazakov's short stories, in an edition of 115,000 copies. Earlier in the year another publication largely controlled by conservatives, *Soviet Literature Monthly,* had carried a story by Kazakov and a sketch of him, indicating he was officially approved for circulation abroad. And meanwhile he was getting notice in America—in *Esquire,* which carried one of his stories in 1962 and four more in 1963, and in *Encounter,* which carried one of his stories in April 1963.*

Declared Kazakov not long ago:

"With trepidation and hope I am now starting an antiwar novel. That, by the way, is an important problem, perhaps the most important one today, and it is painful to think that one might write about it with insufficient strength. How I want to write about it honestly and powerfully!"

---

* In January 1964 a collection of Kazakov short stories was published in the United States: Yuri Kazakov, *Going to Town and Other Stories,* compiled and translated by Gabriella Azrael (Boston: Houghton Mifflin and Co.). This volume which contained 22 stories altogether, well translated and selected, received good reviews in major American publications. Another collection of Kazakov stories has been published in England. Still another has been published in French in France. It seems clear that Yuri Kazakov has established for himself an international literary reputation.

There Goes a Dog *

The glowing summer sunset had long since faded. The empty evening cities, pallid with deathlike glare from fluorescent lamps, had swept past and were left behind. The bus had burst out at long last onto the broad plain of the highway. With a plaintive monotonous buzzing, "zhzhzhzhzhzhzhzh," and with a hum outside its windows, at a constant speed, lilting a little on curves, it was hurtling triumphantly and frighteningly into the darkness, throwing out far and wide the light of its whole array of headlights.

Inside the bus the passengers had first chatted, rustled newspapers and magazines, drunk stealthily straight from their bottles, followed up the drink with a bite or two of something, gone out to smoke, and then begun to settle down, to push back the seats, to stretch out, to turn out the milky white bus lights, and commenced to roll their heads on the bolsters. Then in an hour or so it was all dark and all were asleep in the warm bus with its complicated smells. Only down below along the aisle was there a blue light burning just above the floor. And still further down, beneath the floor, streamed the oily surface of the highway as the wheels whirled madly.

Only Krymov and the woman sitting next to him were not asleep.

Krymov, a Moscow mechanic, was not asleep because he had not been out of Moscow for a long time and was now in a state of suppressed happiness. He was happy because he was on his way for a three-day fishing trip to his own special, secret, personal fishing spot, because down below in the baggage compartment, among many suitcases and bags, amidst a strong aroma of apples, lay his knapsack and fishing rod. He was happy, lastly, because at dawn he was going to disembark at a curve in the highway and walk through a wet meadow to the river where there awaited him the brief and feverish happiness of a fisherman.

He could not sit quietly and turned, following with his eyes something dark and vague which rushed past, stretched out his neck and looked ahead over the shoulder of the driver through the windshield at the distant dullness of the highway.

And the woman next to him for some unknown reason was not sleeping. She sat motionless, with closed eyelashes, biting her red lips, which in the darkness seemed black.

* Russian title: "Von Bezhit Sobaka," published in *Znamya*, No. 9 (1961), pp. 107–13.

One other person was not asleep in the bus—the driver. He was monstrously fat, hairy, all unbuttoned. Through his clothes his body bulged out powerfully, violently. Only his head was small, and his hair was smoothly combed with a straight part and shiny, so that it even gleamed in the darkness. His strong woolly arms, bare to the elbows, lay calmly on the steering wheel. And indeed he was quiet all over, just like a Buddha, as if he knew something which exalted him above all the passengers, above the road and above space. He was in dark shade behind and palely lit up in front by the light of the instruments and by light reflections from the road ahead.

Krymov wanted to smoke, but he didn't want to disturb his neighbor. So instead of getting up to go up ahead he got out a cigarette, bent over, snapped his lighter stealthily, drew in with pleasure, and let out the smoke in a thin little jet, invisible in the dark, directed downward at his feet.

"Do you have a cigarette?" he heard the whisper of his neighbor. "I am desperate for a smoke."

In getting out a cigarette Krymov lightly leaned toward her and looked closely into her face, but saw only a pale spot with dark cavities for the eyes, and lips, and straight shoulder-length hair. He gave her a cigarette and again snapped his lighter. She, just as he had done before, lit up, bent down, protecting the light with her hands, which became semitransparently pink for a second, and then again Krymov could see nothing, only the straight nose, her cheekbones, and her dropped eyelashes.

"Oh, how good!" she said, drawing in and inclining toward him. "Are those *Aromatics?* Thank you—they're strong."

There was a bitter and tender touch of her perfume in the air, and in her whisper there was something strange, not only gratitude but as if she had asked him: "Well, talk with me, let's get to know each other, because I'm so lonely!" And Krymov for one moment felt a surge of that easiness that comes in traveling when one wants to flirt, to make little hints, to speak with an intentionally quivering frankness in one's voice when one wishes, as if by chance, to touch the hand of one's traveling companion and bend over as if looking for something out of the window in order to touch with one's face her hair and see whether she draws away or not...

He started and felt his heart beating. His nostrils quivered. But right away it all went away, pushed into the background by the happiness which awaited him in the morning.

"This is nothing!" he whispered to her, burning already with something different. "This isn't smoking—in a bus or in the workshop. But out there on the river in the morning, you know, when the fish are biting, when all are somewhere off to the side, and all of a sudden there's such a jerk on your line! You pull it out on the shore and take it off the hook, toss it in the grass and oh how it jumps. Then you light up a smoke—and that's really smoking!"

"You're a fisherman?" she whispered.

"I love it!" Krymov drew in and wrinkled his nose with satisfaction. "I'm a mechanic. For months I don't see a river. We have real work—production, a factory. It's not a soft spot—one can't loaf ... Do you know how long it is since I've had a chance to fish? Since May! And now it's July. I work hard—and they pile it on me, too. And so finally they gave me three days off for overtime. Oh, it's all right. I'll have my vacation soon—then I'll get a chance."

"Where are you going?" she asked. And once more in her whisper Krymov sensed something strange, some other question.

"I know a place," he muttered evasively, superstitiously. "And why is it that you aren't asleep? Are you getting off soon?"

"No, I'm going to the end ... You say you have three days? When are you going back?"

"Tuesday."

"Tuesday? Just a minute ... Tuesday ..."

She thought about something for a second and then sighed and asked:

"And why aren't you asleep?"

"I get off at four in the morning."

Krymov pulled up the sleeve of his jacket and looked for a long time at his watch, picking out what time it was.

"Three more hours left," he thought to himself. "And you can't get a decent sleep in that time. It's better not to sleep at all—or else you'll be drowsy when fishing ..."

The driver looked back and again turned back to the road. In his figure there was hesitation. Then he carefully reached out his hand to the radio and turned it on. The radio hissed out and the driver hurriedly turned it down and began to search for a station. He found one station, another, a third. But they all were muttering foreign voices or folk instruments and this, evidently, was not what he wanted. Finally, from out of the noise there rose the weak sound of jazz, and the driver took his hand off the knob. He even smiled with satisfaction and even from behind one could see how his plump cheeks drew back toward his ears.

The music was quiet, monotonous, the same melody endlessly passing from piano to sax, to horn, to electric guitar, and Krymov and his neighbor were still, listening intently, thinking each his and her own thoughts and each slightly moving, swaying to the rhythmic sounds of the bass.

Outside the window once in a long while there hurtled past lonely trucks left for the night on the highway shoulders. It was strange to look at their immobility and loneliness. It was as if something had happened in the world and all the drivers had left, turning on in farewell little lights on the fenders—lights which would burn for a long time until the power in the batteries had gone.

Even less frequently they met, coming from the opposite direction, such long-distance buses as their own. Long before they met, over the horizon, over the swelling of the roadway, there flickered the glow of their light. Then, in the immeasurable distance, there appeared a gleaming point. It approached, grew, became double, triple, and then five powerful headlights below and above could be seen which suddenly were turned off and then turned on again and then off again as both buses slowed down and finally came to a stop. The drivers stuck their heads out of the windows and talked about something for a little while. Smoke rose from the motors and the rays from the headlights pierced it in crooked columns. Then the buses moved off and in another minute rushed into the blackness, the night, each in its own direction.

"Interesting where she is going?" thought Krymov about his neighbor. "And is she married? And why did she start to smoke? Just like that or from grief?"

But right then again he forgot about her, absorbed in the road, in the expectation of dawn, in thoughts about the three days which he would live alongside the river. He wondered whether the tent might not leak and thought that this would be bad if there were rain and whether the bus might not be held up for some reason or other along the way making him late for the early morning fishing . . ."

Happy concern tired him and then his neighbor again occupied his imagination. And now she was silent, her head thrown back on the bolster of the seat and her eyes shut. But whenever he peered ahead at the road or into the window for too long a time and then looked at her it seemed to him every time that her face was as if half turned to him, and that her eyes, undistinguishable in the dark, were watching him from beneath her lashes.

"Who is she?" he thought—but couldn't make up his mind to ask. And he tried to guess, remembering the little she had said and her quiet whisper. Somehow or other he hadn't noticed her during the evening. He hadn't been interested, but now he hoped that she was beautiful.

"Give me a smoke!" she suddenly whispered. "And tell me something . . . What's the use of not saying anything. We're not sleeping anyway!"

Krymov caught a note of irritation in her whisper and was surprised but kept still and gave her a cigarette obediently. "What's there to talk about?" he thought, already a little angry. "She's a strange one!" But he said aloud:

"I keep thinking that you women don't like hunting, fishing, and yet it's really such a big sensation! And you not only don't like it, but somehow you don't even understand it, just as if there were something lacking in you in that sense. Why should that be?"

In the darkness it was visible how she stirred, threw back her hair, and wiped her forehead.

"Hunting is killing and women are mothers. And killing is doubly repulsive to them. You say that it's a delight to see how the fish struggles. To me that's sickening. But I understand you—that is I understand that you hunt and fish not out of cruelty. Tolstoi, for example, suffered much later, after his hunting, recollecting death. And Prishvin also . . ."

"What kind of nonsense is she talking?" Krymov thought dismally and looked at his watch.

"An hour and a half is left!" he said with gladness.

Then his neighbor put out her cigarette, raised the collar of her raincoat, curled up her legs and put her head on its side on the bolster with the back of her head toward Krymov.

"She wanted to sleep," Krymov decided. "So much the better. It's high time. I don't like chatter on the road! How good that I'm not married," he thought to himself unexpectedly. "Otherwise there would be one like this who would discuss killing, deliver lectures . . . One would go crazy!"

But somewhere he had been hurt, and although he thought only about the morning's fishing he didn't feel any longer his former deep, stupendous gladness.

The driver up ahead bent down without taking his eye off the road. He fumbled for something down below, holding the wheel with one hand. Then he straightened up and began to fool with something on his knees, holding, as before, the wheel with only his left hand. Finally, the driver took a bottle in his mouth, tossed it back and took a sip. He sighed, again tossed it up, and sipped. And one could see how his neck and its sides swelled and subsided during his swallows.

"What's he drinking?" thought Krymov. "Could it be beer? No, of course, he's not supposed to while driving . . . Aha! Lemonade! I wish we'd get there more quickly."

And right then he remembered his coffee in his knapsack and the pot, and he wanted coffee.

It began to get noticeably light, but the green on the trees was still dark and only the infrequent little houses which flashed by in the fields startled with their morning whiteness. Krymov's mouth grew dry from smoking. But his mood improved. He forgot his neighbor once and for all and thought only about his secret fishing place, the river, the fog, and looked greedily ahead.

The driver shut off the headlights and the dawn became brighter. It became more and more light with every minute and everything—kilometer posts, advertising boards, road signs, the line of the horizon in the West—was distinctly visible.

The 500th kilometer post went by. The driver turned about and caught the questioning look of Krymov and nodded. In a minute he cut down on the gas and turned off to the right on the shoulder. A sign warned of a sharp curve ahead. A big meadow loomed. And there in the distance, seven hundred meters from the highway the tops of the willows stood out darkly.

The bus, already coasting, rolled ever more slowly, silently, quietly. The treads on the tires no longer hummed but muttered in rhythm. Finally, everything came seemingly completely to a stop, and only the crunching of the sand beneath the wheels told that the bus was still moving its last meter. Everything grew silent. The driver took his hands off the wheel and breathed sweetly with his body bulging out in every direction. He yawned and opened the door. He went out first and banged the baggage compartment below.

"Pardon me!" said Krymov, hurriedly rising and touching his neighbor on her shoulder.

"Oh?" she said in fright. "Already? You've arrived?" If you please, good luck ..."

"The devil!" Krymov replied to himself, with hunter's custom, pushing forward. He jumped out and first of all looked gladly at the meadow and then turned back to the bus. The bus stood there enormous, long, a little dusty, with heated tires and motor and exuded its warmth into the morning chill. The baggage carrier on the right side was open. Krymov went up to it, moved over suitcases and bags, and got his knapsack and found his rod with difficulty. The driver loudly slammed the iron door of the baggage compartment, locked it, and, passing the bus from the front, went off into the woods.

"So this is where your place is!" There was a voice from behind. Krymov looked back and saw his neighbor. She had gotten out of the bus and stood there, tossing her hair behind her and looking at the meadow. She was beautiful and reminded him of a cinema actress, but Krymov was hardly interested in her.

"Well give me another smoke for farewell," she said, coming up to him and smiling shyly. "You are very good! And I have been bothering you all night with my requests ..."

When she lit up her lips and hands shook so that she couldn't hit the end of the cigarette with the flame for a long time. "Why is that?" Krymov was surprised and looked at his knapsack. "I guess I'll have to go along!"

"You are fortunate!" she said, inhaling greedily. "You are going to live in such peace and quiet for three days." She grew silent and listened. She picked a crumb of tobacco off her lips. "The birds are awake. Do you hear? And I have to go to Pskov."

"Shall I go or not?" Krymov wavered without listening to her. But it was already impolite to go off right away. "I'll wait until they leave. He isn't going to park here for an hour," he decided and also lit up.

"Well . . . Yes," he said just to say something.

"You know I've long dreamed of living in a tent. Do you have a tent?" she asked, looking at Krymov from the side. Her face suddenly became sorrowful and the corners of her lips trembled and drooped. "I'm, you see, a Muscovite and it just never worked out so that I could . . ."

"Well . . . yes . . ." Krymov said again without looking at her, shifting from one foot to the other and looking across the empty highway into the woods where the driver had disappeared.

Then she inhaled several times, knitting her brow, held back her breathing, and bit her lip.

Just at this minute from out of the roadside thicket jumped a dog that ran along the highway, cutting across it diagonally. It was wet from the dew. The hair on its belly and paws was curly and drops of dew on its snout and whiskers gleamed like red cranberries in the already crimson eastern light.

"There goes a dog!" said Krymov mechanically, thinking of nothing at all. "There goes a dog!"—slowly he repeated with satisfaction as one sometimes repeats without any meaning a line from a rhyme.

The dog was running actively, purposefully, without looking to the sides. And there was such quiet that they could hear how his claws clicked on the asphalt.

At long last the driver came out of the woods, emerged onto the highway, looked at the running dog, whistled to it—but it didn't turn. The driver went up to the bus and looked at it as if he was seeing it for the first time. His shoes were all wet with dew and there was even dew on his woolly arms. He loudly stamped his feet in order to get rid of the dew and walked around the bus kicking the tires and climbed up inside.

"Well, thank you for the cigarettes!" said the girl and also climbed up on the step.

"Good luck!" muttered Krymov bending down over his knapsack.

The motor roared and the bus pulled away. A dawn-lit, sad face looked out from inside at Krymov in parting, and he weakly waved, unthinkingly smiled, descended the embankment, and went in a straight line to the river.

"There goes a dog! There goes a dog!" he sang to himself silently, walking across the meadow and adapting the words to the rhythm of his steps.

Then he looked with childlike gladness on the sparkling meadow, at the sky. He breathed in to the full limit of his chest expansion, and he had only one concern—that someone else might have gotten there first and taken his place.

Approaching the river he jumped from a small bank down onto the sand and looked jealously. No, there was not one track on the sand. The river was narrow, slow, with pools and reeds, with sand banks. It wound lazily and quietly through meadows.

Krymov quickly unpacked his knapsack, got out the coffee, the pot, and sugar. He scooped up water, gathered up some dry driftwood, and right there on the sand lit up a small bonfire. Then he stuck two forked sticks in the sand, hung the pot on them, and waited.

There were the smells of smoke, wet shore, and from afar hay in the air. Krymov sat down and gloated in his happiness. He hadn't supposed he could be so glad of that morning, of that river, and of the fact he was alone.

"I'll drink my coffee and then cast!" he decided and began to put together his casting rod, noting at the same time all at once with an experienced glance the river and how the fire was burning and the water in the pot which had begun slowly to stir.

"There goes a dog!" he repeated as if it were an incantation. "There goes . . . I'll drink my coffee and then cast!"

On the other side, beneath the reeds, a pike splashed loudly. Krymov shuddered, froze, momentarily sweated and looked at the place. Big circles were expanding in waves.

"No, first I'll cast. There's plenty of time for coffee," he immediately decided, drawing the line through the rings on the rod and fastening to it his favorite lure, the "Baikal," silver with a red feather. Again, but in another place, the pike jumped and right after, next to the shore, a roach gleamed in fright.

"Wait, wait!" thought Krymov in delight. "There goes a dog! Wait . . ." And he set the reel on the rod handle.

The water gurgled in the pot and its foam boiled up and poured over the edge, hissing on the coals. A cloud of steam rose. Krymov looked at the pot, took it off, and licked his dry lips. "The devil! Coffee, I must say, however, that's a real thing," he thought to himself, looking askance at the river and opening the coffee can. He sniffed it and sneezed.

"Ugh! You!" he said aloud and with his rod held between his knees he began to boil his coffee.

The dawn became ever brighter. The colors on the reeds and the water incessantly changed. Mist floated in wisps along the river. The willow leaves shone as if they were lacquered, and by then long since in the reeds, further in the meadow, and close to somewhere in the willow the birds had been making different-toned noises. The first little breeze smelled by then bittersweet with warm forest odor and rustled the reeds . . .

Krymov was happy!

He fished away and gloried in his aloneness. He slept in the tent, but even at night he suddenly awakened not knowing why. He fanned the fire, boiled some coffee, and whistled, waiting for the dawn. During the day he bathed in the warm river, swam over to the other side, waded among the reeds, inhaled the swamp smells, and then again threw himself into the water, washing himself off, and then, having had his fill of bathing, lay in the sun.

Thus he spent two days and two nights and on the third toward evening, tanned, thinned down, light, with two pikes in his knapsack he went out onto the highway, lit a cigarette, and began to wait for the Moscow bus. He sat blissfully and relaxed, legs spread out, leaning back against his knapsack, and looked for the last time at the meadow, at the tops of the willow groves far off where he had been so recently. He imagined in his mind's eye the river beneath those groves and all its quiet turns and thought that this had now become forever a part of his life.

Along the highway trucks dashed, lit red by the sun—milk tank trucks, enormous silver refrigerator trucks, Volga sedans leaning back toward their back axles, and Krymov now with gladness accompanied them with his eyes. He already wanted cities, lights, newspapers, work. And he imagined already how tomorrow in the workshop he would smell the hot oil and how the lathes would whistle, and he remembered all his pals.

And then he remembered weakly how he had disembarked from the bus three days before at the same spot at dawn and his traveling companion of the bus ride—and how her lips and hands shook when she lit up.

"What was wrong with her?" he muttered and all of a sudden his breathing stopped. His face and his chest became covered with prickly heat. He felt suffocated and vile. A sharp longing seized him by the heart.

"Ai, yai, yai!" he muttered, spitting heavily. "Ai, yai, yai. How could I? Well, I am a scum, ai, yai, yai . . . Ah?"

Something big, beautiful, sad stood there over him, over the fields and the river, something wonderful but already renounced. And it had compassion for him and also regret for him.

"Ah, what a son of a bitch I am!" muttered Krymov, breathing in and out quickly, and he wiped himself with his sleeve. "Ai, yai, yai!" And he struck his knee with his fist so hard he started with the pain.

"Kabiasy"*

The club manager, Zhukov, overstayed his visit at the nearby collective farm. It was August. He had come during the day on business. He had gone all about and talked a lot—but it was an unsuccessful trip. Everyone was in a hurry because it was a busy season.

Quite a young chap, Zhukov had worked in the club hardly a year, and he understood his duties still rather vaguely. They had appointed him because he played well on the accordion and had taken an active part in each district sport competition. He still played on the soccer team for his native Zubatovo, though he now lived in Dubki in a little room in the club.

He should have gone home sooner when there was a car going to Dubki. He started to, but then he had changed his mind and paid a visit to a teacher who was an acquaintance. He wanted to talk about the volleyball team and in general about cultural activities. The teacher was out hunting. He should have returned long before but was late for some reason, and Zhukov stayed waiting dolefully. He understood that it was silly and that he should have left.

He sat two hours this way, smoking out the window and chatting uninterestedly with the mistress of the house. He had even dozed off a bit, but voices outside awakened him: they were driving the herd and the women were calling the cows.

Finally, there was no sense in waiting any longer and Zhukov, irritated at his failure, having gulped down for the road some sour kvas which put his teeth on edge, set out for his own collective farm. It was 12 kilometers away.

Zhukov ran into the night watchman, Matvei, on the bridge. Matvei was standing there in a raggedy winter cap and a well-worn sheepskin coat with his feet set wide apart, holding a gun over his elbow. The old man rolled himself a cigarette and looked up from beneath his brows at the passing Zhukov.

"Ah, Matvei!" Zhukov recognized him even though he had seen him only a couple of times. "Are you going hunting too?"

Matvei, without answering, walked along beside him slowly, squinting at his cigarette. He got out his matches and lit up, inhaled several times, and coughed. Then, scratching the flap of the sheepskin coat with his fingernails, he put away his matches and finally said:

"What hunting? I'm guarding the orchard at night. From my blind where I am hidden."

* Russian title: "Kabiasy," published in *Znamya*, No. 9 (1961), pp. 113–18.

Zhukov still had a bad taste in his mouth from the kvas. He spit and then also lit a cigarette.

"Bet you sleep the whole night long," he said absent-mindedly, thinking that he should have gone home earlier when there was a car. And now he had to walk.

"I'd like to all right!" Matvei retorted in a meaningful tone after a moment of silence. "I'd sleep all right but they don't let me..."

"Why? Are they stealing?" Zhukov asked ironically.

"Stealing pooh!" Matvei laughed and all of a sudden walked along more relaxed. He sort of settled down with a backward tilt like a person who had long been confined and had come out at last into open space. He didn't look at Zhukov at all, but kept peering to the sides into the twilit fields.

"Steal, they don't, fellow, but they come..."

"Girls, you mean?" Zhukov asked and laughed, remembering Lyubka and that he would see her tonight.

"Those same ones..." Matvei said indistinctly.

"That's an old man for you! Stretching it out!" Zhukov spat. "Well who?"

"The kabiasy, that's who," Matvei spoke out mysteriously and looked aslant for the first time at Zhukov.

"Well I must say you've got something there," said Zhukov jokingly. "Tell your old woman about that. And what are the *kabiasy?*"

"That kind," Matvei answered gloomily. "You get caught by them, and you'll find out for yourself."

"Devils are they?" Zhukov asked, making a serious face.

Matvei again peered at him.

"That kind," he blurted out vaguely. "Black ones. The ones with green..."

He pulled out of his pockets two copper cartridges and blew the *makhorka* dust from his pocket off them.

"Look there," he said, pointing to the paper wadding in the cartridges.

Zhukov looked and saw crosses scratched on the wadding with pencil.

"Charmed!" Matvei said with satisfaction, hiding the cartridges. "I know how to deal with them!"

"They bother you?" Zhukov asked jokingly, but, catching himself again, made a serious face to show that he believed.

"Not too badly," Matvei answered seriously. "They don't come near my blind. Instead... they come out of the dark one after another and gather under the apple trees. They make noise, they're so little and they stand in a row." Matvei dropped his eyes to the road and moved his hand in front of himself. "They stand there and play songs."

"Songs?" Zhukov couldn't control himself and burst out laughing. "My! Just like in our club—amateur night! What kind of songs?"

"Different ones . . . Sometimes awfully sad. And then sometimes they say: 'Matvei, Matvei! Come here! Come here!' "

"And you?"

"And I give it to them good: oh you!—with such mother oaths . . . Beat it!"

Matvei smiled affectionately.

"And then they begin to come toward my blind and I load up with a charmed cartridge and how I let them have it—bang!"

"Do you hit them?"

"Hit them!" Matvei spoke out contemptuously. "Do you think you can kill an evil spirit? I just chase them away a bit till morning, till the first cock crows."

"Well!" said Zhukov after a little silence and sighed. "It's bad, bad!"

"Whom?" asked Matvei.

"Things are bad with my atheistic propaganda, that's what!" said Zhukov and knitted his brows, looking at Matvei. "So maybe you're telling this nonsense in the village and scaring the girls?" he asked severely, remembering all of a sudden that he was the manager of the club. *"Kabiasy!* You're a *kabias* yourself."

"Whom?" Matvei asked again and his face suddenly became malicious and impressive. "And you're going to walk past the forest?"

"So what? I'll walk past!"

"You're going to walk past, so watch out: lucky if you get home."

Matvei turned away without saying anything and without even saying goodbye and went quickly across the field to the orchard which was dark in the distance. Even his figure seemed embittered.

Left alone on the road Zhukov lit a cigarette and looked about. The twilight shadows were advancing. The sky in the west grew pale. The collective farm behind was no longer visible. There were only some dark roofs among the aspens and a windmill generator.

A birch forest was on the left. It went in steps to the horizon. It was as if someone had blindly drawn strokes from top to bottom on a dark background with a white pencil. First sparsely, further on more thickly, and in the murk the horizon drew a timid light stripe crosswise.

On the left could be seen a lake lying as if it had been welded there, standing motionless on a level with its banks, the only shining thing in all the dark. On the shore of the lake burned a bonfire and smoke wafted from it to the road. Dew was already falling and the smoke was wet.

And on the right in the twilight, meadows and cuts, between the dark capes of the forest, from hillock to hillock marched latticed electric power towers. They were like a file of enormous silent beings thrown to us from other worlds and walking soundlessly with raised arms to the west in the direction of the flaring green star, their homeland.

Zhukov again looked about, still hoping that perhaps a car might come along. Then he strode down the road. He walked on and looked all the time at the bonfire and the lake. There was no one near the fire. There was not even anyone visible on the lake and the lonely fire, seemingly lit for no one and for no reason, produced a strange impression.

Zhukov went along at first uncertainly, smoking, looking back, waiting for a car or a fellow traveler afoot. But there was no one visible either before or behind as far as the horizon itself, and Zhukov finally decided and began walking along at a real pace.

He had gone four kilometers when it became completely dark. Only the road was light, crossed in places by mist. The night was warm. Only when Zhukov moved into the mist patches did he feel a chill. But then he came back out into the warm air and these changes from cold to warm air were pleasant.

"Our people are superstitious!" thought Zhukov. He walked sticking his hands in his pockets, moving his brows and remembering the face of Matvei, how it had become malicious and contemptuous right away when he had laughed at him. "Yes," he thought, "I must, must step up atheistic propaganda. Superstition must be uprooted." And he wanted even more to talk with someone about things cultural, things intellectual.

Then he began to think that it was time for him to move to the city, to enroll in some educational institution for study. And right then he began to imagine how he was directing a chorus, not in a collective farm club where there weren't even curtains, where young people smoked in the hall and laughed across the room at each other, but in Moscow and that his chorus had a hundred persons in it—an academic capella.

As always he felt from such thoughts a glad liveliness and paid no attention to things around him, didn't look at the stars nor at the road, walked along unevenly, compressing and releasing his fists, moving his brows. He began to sing and laugh aloud, not fearing that anyone would see him. He was even glad he was walking alone without companions. It was then that he approached an empty barn near the road and sat down on a beam to rest and smoke.

Once this had been a separate farm, but soon after the establishment of the collective farm the farmhouse had been torn down and only the barn remained. It was open and empty. In it, evidently, there wasn't even a door. It was all dark and askew, and in its innards, deep inside it, there was especially deep darkness.

Zhukov sat there, placing his elbows on his high raised knees, his face to the road, his back to the barn, and smoked. Gradually, he cooled off and thought no more about the conservatory but about Lyubka when he felt he was being looked at from behind.

He understood suddenly that he was sitting alone in the darkness, among empty fields, among mysterious dark spots that could be bushes and could be something other than bushes.

He remembered Matvei, his cruel-prophetic face at the end and the empty, mute lake with the bonfire lit for an unknown reason.

Holding his breath he slowly turned and looked at the barn. Its roof hung in the air and the stars were visible in the gap. But as he was looking, it settled on its frame and behind the barn something ran with audible footfall into the field uttering a suppressed monotonous cry: "Oh! Oh! Oh!"—ever more distant and more quietly. Zhukov's hair stood on end and he jumped out onto the road.

"Well!" he thought awestricken. "I'm a goner!" And he struck off down the road. The air whistled in his ears and in the bushes on both sides of the road something moved, sniffed, breathed on his back with a chill. "I should cross myself!" thought Zhukov, feeling how something was trying to grab him from behind. "Oh Lord God, I am in your hands . . ." And having crossed himself he stopped, already unable to run any farther. And he turned around.

But there was no one on the road nor in the field, and the barn was no longer to be seen. Zhukov wiped himself off with his sleeve without dropping his eyes from the road and said hoarsely, "Ha!" and shuddered, having frightened himself. Then he coughed, listened, and again said, with an effort, so his voice did not tremble: "Ho! Ho! Ei!"

Having caught his breath Zhukov hurriedly walked along, remembering with feverish loneliness how far he still had to go, what black night lay all about, and that the forest about which Matvei had so mysteriously hinted still lay ahead.

The road dropped down to a stream and Zhukov as if in his sleep jumped in enormous leaps across the bridge over the black water and the willow thickets. From beneath the bridge there was a croak, but Zhukov couldn't even decide whether there had really been a sound or whether it just seemed to him as if there had been one. "Well, wait, I'll catch up with you," Zhukov thought with fear of Matvei, while ascending the slope on which, as he knew, the woods began.

The forest commenced with dewiness and damp. Something powerful breathed from its depths, bringing out into the warm field air the odor of rot, mushrooms, water and pines. On the right in the forest hung thick murk. On the left the field was more visible. Up above the stars shone down. The later it got the thicker they were strewn. The heaven, even though it was black, possessed a weak smoky light, and the trees stood out on its background with firm silhouettes.

From the forest murk from some branch or other an owl leaped. With a weak rustle it flew and perched on a branch ahead. Zhukov heard it, but he couldn't see it no matter how hard he tried. He saw only how, crossing off the stars, the branch on which it perched rocked.

Coming up to it Zhukov scared it off again, and it began to fly about in circles, over part of the field and immediately returning into the forest darkness. And now Zhukov saw it. On the horizon, beyond the fields, there still glimmered a remnant of the sunset, even not a remnant but simply a lighter sky, more immaterial there, and the owl, flying past, flashed there each time, a soundless, dark spot.

Looking askance at the owl Zhukov stumbled on a root and cursed it in his mind. He didn't dare to look directly into the forest or behind. And when, nevertheless, he looked ahead on the road a chill ran up and down his spine: up ahead and a little to the left, from the woods across the road there were standing waiting for him the *kabiasy*. They were little, just as Matvei had said. One of them snickered just at that moment and another groaned dolefully with the same sound he had heard just before behind the barn: "Oh-oh ... Oh-oh ..." And a third cried in the voice of a quail:

"Come here! Come here!"

Zhukov clenched his teeth and grew numb. He couldn't even cross himself. His hands wouldn't rise.

"Ahhhhhh!" he hollered through the whole forest, and all of a sudden he saw that they were little fir trees. Trembling like a hunting dog on a point, he took first one step toward them, then another ... Behind the firs something rustled and started rolling with a worried cry into the field.

"A bird!" Zhukov guessed with gladness, resuming his breathing and moving his shoulders beneath his wet shirt. Speedily passing the little fir trees he pulled out a cigarette and started to get out his matches, but realized immediately that if he lit it he would be visible throughout the forest. He didn't know who would see him and he was afraid to think, but he knew that they would.

Zhukov sat down, looked around on all sides, pulled his jacket over his head and thus under his jacket lit up. "I'll go through the fields!" he decided. He could not any longer go through the forest, on the road. And in the fields, though it was awful, it wasn't that bad.

He roared past the nut trees beginning on the edge of the forest and emerged into the open and walked parallel to the forest, bypassing at a distance everything on his path which was dark, incessantly looking to the right. The owl kept on flying, rustling, and squeaking everywhere, and somewhere in the very depth of the forest, among the ravines could be heard something which wasn't quite a cry nor a groan and which lingered long in the air, rolling like an echo through the edge of the woods.

But there the forest ended and again the dusty light road writhed like a snake. Zhukov came out on it and squealing with fright, without looking behind, ran at a full trot, pressing his elbows to his sides like a long-distance runner. He ran and the air screamed in his ears and the forest fell further and further behind till it became a barely noticeable dark ribbon. Zhukov had already decided there was nothing to look at and had begun to rejoice. He had begun, in rhythm with his running pace, to sing something to himself which was monotonous and unnaturally merry: "Tee-ta-ta! Tee-ta-ta!" when suddenly he again pulled back sharply and his eyes grew wide.

What he saw this time was neither tree, nor bird, such as he had already grown used to seeing, but something alive which was moving toward him across his path on a field boundary. It was neither like a man, a cow, nor a horse and had an indefinite look to it. Zhukov already clearly heard the crunching of the tall weeds on the boundary line, a soft hopping, a weak knocking.

"Who is it?" roared a resounding voice.

Zhukov didn't make a sound.

"Are you someone I know? Or not?" the voice asked from the road. Zhukov by now understood that he was being called, that a human being was approaching him, pushing a bicycle, but as before he couldn't answer. He could only breathe.

"Zhukov?" the person guessed without conviction, coming right up to him and staring at him. "That's funny. Why are you so quiet? And I thought who could it be? Do you have matches? Give me a light!"

And now Zhukov recognized Popov from the local Youth Communist League executive committee. Zhukov's hands trembled so that the matches rattled in the box when he gave them to Popov.

"Where are you coming from?" Popov asked him, after getting a light. "I, you see, lost my way. I was going to your place and missed my turn because I was thinking about something else. I finally came out over in Gorki, and then came from that road over here along the boundary ... What's wrong with you?"

"Wait a minute ..." Zhukov said hoarsely, feeling weakness and dizziness. "Wait just a minute ..."

He stood there smiling guiltily and couldn't manage to get control over his weakness. He was sweating profusely and breathing hurriedly. There was a smell of dusty, strong roadside weeds in the air.

"Are you ill?" Popov asked with fright.

Zhukov silently nodded.

"Well, in that case sit down!" Popov said with determination and pushed up the bicycle. "Get on to the handlebars. Well!"

Popov pushed the bicycle in uneven pushes and jumped into its seat, moving strongly from side to side. He blew away the locks of hair which fell into his eyes and rolled off to Dubki. Zhukov sat on the bar. He was uncomfortable and ashamed. He felt how heavy the bicycle was moving along on the dust. Popov was breathing heatedly on his back and knocking against him with his knees.

Almost the whole way both were silent. Finally the lights of the collective farm came into view and Zhukov stirred.

"Stop ..." he said.

"Sit there, just sit there!" Popov answered breathlessly. "It's only a little further. We'll get to the clinic ..."

"No, put on the brakes ..." said Zhukov wrinkling his brows, and stretching out his foot, caught hold of the ground.

Popov braked with relief. They jumped from the bicycle and stood for a while silently without knowing what to talk about. Next to them was a stable. The horses heard the people and grew impatient, tramping with their hooves on the planking. There was a strong and pleasant odor of manure and tar from the stable.

"Give me the matches," Popov said again.

He lit up and wiped the sweat from his face lengthily and with satisfaction. Then he unbuttoned the collar of his shirt entirely.

"Well how do you feel? Are you better?" he asked hopefully.

"Now it's nothing," Zhukov said hurriedly. "I drank some *kvas*. Probably that was it ..."

They walked slowly down the street, listening to the quieting sounds of the big village.

"How are things in the club?" Popov asked.

"So, so ... You know yourself. It's harvest time and people are busy," Zhukov answered absent-mindedly and all of a sudden remembered:

"Have you ever heard the word *kabiasy?*"

"What, what? *Kabiasy?*" Popov thought. "No, I've never heard it. And why do you need to know? For a play?"

"Just something that popped into my mind," Zhukov said evasively.

They came up beside the club and shook hands.

"Take the matches," said Zhukov. "I have some at home."

"Good!" Popov took the matches. "And you drink some milk—it helps a troubled stomach."

He got on his bicycle and rode off to the house of the farm chairman, and Zhukov went along the dark corridors and unlocked the door to his room. After drinking cold tea he smoked, listened to the radio in the darkness, opened the window, and lay down.

He had almost gone to sleep when everything in him turned upside down and, as if from above, from a hill, he saw the nighttime fields, the empty lake, the dark rows of power towers with raised arms, the lonely bonfire, and heard the life which filled these enormous spaces in the deaf night hours.

He began to relive over again his whole journey, all the way, but this time with happiness, with a warm feeling for the night, for the stars, for the smells, for the rustlings and cries of the birds.

He wanted again to talk with someone about cultural things, high things—about eternity, for example. He thought about Lyubka and jumped up from his cot and pattered barefoot across the room. He pulled on his clothes and went out.

Autumn in an Oak Forest[*]

I took the pail to get water from the spring. I was happy that night because she was coming on the night boat. But I knew what happiness was, I knew its inconstancy, and therefore I intentionally took the pail as if I wasn't hoping at all for her arrival, but was simply going after water.

Everything was working out just too well for me that autumn!

Slate black was that late autumn night. I didn't want to go out of the house. But nevertheless I went. It took me a long time to put the candle in the lantern. And when I finally put it in and lit it, the glass fogged up a minute and the weak little spot of light blinked, blinked until at last the candle flamed up and the glass dried out and became transparent.

I intentionally did not put out the light in the house. And the lighted window was easily visible as I was descended along the larch-covered walk to the River Oka. My lantern cast a trembling light ahead and to each side. And I probably looked like a railway switchman. But beneath my boots there rustled tonelessly the piles of maple leaves, wet with the night, and the larch needles which even in the dim light of the lantern were golden. And on naked bushes the barberries glowed.

It is awesome to go afoot all alone with a lantern at night time. All alone you rustle along with your boots. All alone you are lit up and visible. Everything else, hidden, can watch you.

The path steeply descended the slope. The light in the window of my house quickly disappeared. Then even the larch avenue came to an end. There were only disorderly shrubs, oak and fir trees. Against the pail there slapped the last high daisies and the ends of the paws of the fir branches and some kind of bare twigs. And from them, now tonelessly, now ringingly, there resounded: "Boom! Boom!" And it could be heard a long ways away in the silence.

The path became steeper and more winding. Frequently, birch trees appeared. Their white trunks emerged every moment from the murk. Then even the birch trees came to an end. There began to be some stones on the pathway. There was a breath of freshness. And even though beyond the little spot of light from the lantern nothing was visible I felt before me a broad expanse. I had emerged at the river.

[*] Russian title: "Osen v Dubovykh Lesakh," published in *Znamya*, No. 9 (1961), pp. 118–24.

There already I could see a distant buoy on the right. Its red light grew double, reflected in the water. Then I could see the buoy on my own side, much nearer, and it winked gently also, and the river began to stand out.

I went down to the river on the wet grass between the willow bushes to that place where ordinarily the boat stopped——if anyone disembarked on our out-of-the-way side. In the darkness the little spring monotonously gurgled and spluttered. I put down the lantern, went to the spring, scooped out water, drank it down, and wiped myself off with my sleeve. Then I put the wet pail down alongside the lantern and began to look in the direction of the far-away landing.

The boat was already standing near the landing. The red and green lights on its sides were weakly visible. I sat down and lit up a smoke. My hands trembled and were cold. All of a sudden I remembered that if she were not on the boat, and they should notice my lantern, they would think that I wanted to embark and come up to the shore . . . Then I put out the lantern.

Immediately it became dark, but the buoys burned, as if pierced by a needle, across the entire river. There was a resounding silence. At that late hour, truly, I was the only person for many kilometers along the shore. And up above, beyond the oak forest, lay a dark little village. Everyone there long since had gone to sleep, and only in my house on its very edge was there a light burning.

I suddenly pictured her entire long journey to me, how she had come all the way from Archangel, how she had slept or sat beside the window in the railway car and talked with someone. How she, like me, had been thinking all of these days of our meeting. And how she was now descending the Oka River and seeing the shores I had described to her when I had written her to come to me. How she was standing at the rail and how the wind, bearing the odor of damp oak forest, was blowing in her face. And what conversation took place below for all her boat trip, in the warmth, behind the misted glass, and how they explained to her where to get off and where to spend the night if no one were there to meet her.

And then I remembered the North, my wanderings there, and how I had lived with the fishermen and how she and I had gone out into the white arctic night to hunt the sea wolf. The fishermen slept soundly, snoring and moaning in their sleep. And we waited for low tide and went out to sea in a fishing boat. She rowed soundlessly, and I looked down into the depths, into the clumps of seaweeds, looking among them for the outlines of the sea wolf. I quietly drew up the harpoon and thrust its white blade into the back of the head of the sea wolf. Straining, I pulled it out of the water, while, splashing us in the face, it beat fiercely against the harpoon, opened an awful mouth, wound itself into a ring, and straightened out like a spring, like a triton. And then on the bottom of the fishing boat it flapped about for a long time, trembled, and seized whatever came its way in a death grip.

And I remembered all of that year, now happy it was for me, how many stories I had succeeded in writing and still, in all probability, would succeed in writing during the remaining remote, quiet days on that river, there immersed in that nature, already dry and withered and prewinter . . . The night was all around, and my cigarette, when I drew on it, brightly lit my hands and face and boots, but didn't prevent me from seeing the stars—and in that autumn there was such a brilliant multitude of them that their ashy light could be seen. The river, lit by the stars, could be seen, and the trees, and the white stones on the shore, the dark rectangular fields on the hillsides. And in the ravines it was much darker and more fragrant than in the fields.

And I thought right then that the most important thing in life is not how long one lives: thirty, fifty, or eighty years. Because it's always too little anyway. And it's going to be awful to die all the same. But the chief thing is how many such nights there will be for each human being.

The boat had already left the landing. It was so far away still that it was impossible to perceive its movement. It seemed as if it was standing in one place. But it separated from the landing, and this meant that it was moving now upward to me. Soon I could hear the high tone of the diesel engine, and all at once I became frightened that she was not coming, that she was not aboard, and that I was waiting in vain. I saw suddenly the distance and the days she had had to overcome in order to get to me. And I understood how all of this was fragile and uncertain—some kind of plan of mine for a happy life here for the two of us.

"What is it!" I said aloud and rose. I could no longer sit and I began to walk along the shore. "What is it!" I repeated helplessly from time to time and kept looking at the boat, and I thought to myself how dreadful it would be for me—to climb back up all by myself alone with my pail of water and how empty my house would be when I got there. And could it possibly be that we would be unlucky in the end and, after so many days and all our failures, that we should not get together and that everything should turn to dust?

I remembered how I had left the North three months before for home, how she unexpectedly had come into the village from the fishery in order to say farewell to me, how she had stood on the gangway until I took my place in the motorboat in order to go out to the steamer in the distant roadstead, and how she had said over and over the same thing: "Where are you going? You don't understand anything! You don't understand anything! Where are you going?" And I, already in the motorboat, among farewells, among the tears of women, the cries of youths and all kinds of noise, understood that I was doing something childish in going away, and I weakly hoped somehow to correct everything in the future.

The boat was now close and I was no longer walking back and forth but standing on the very edge, on the very bank, above the black water, looking at the boat without taking my eyes off it, squinting and breathing loudly from excitement and hope.

The sound of the motor suddenly became lower. A searchlight gleamed on the deckhouse and a smoky crooked ray searched along the shore, jumping from tree to tree. The boat was looking for a place to land. It kept pulling to the right. The strained ray of the searchlight struck me in the face. I turned away and then looked again. On the upper deck stood a sailor, and he was already opening the side to go below and throw the gangplank across to the shore. And next to him she stood dressed in something light-colored.

The nose of the boat thrust softly and deeply into the shore. The sailor moved the gangplank, helped her descend, and I grabbed her suitcase, took it further away, put it next to the pail and only then slowly turned around. The light of the searchlight blinded me, and no matter how hard I tried I could not really distinguish her clearly. Casting an enormous wavering shadow on the forested slope upward she approached. I wanted to kiss her, but then I thought better of it. I didn't want that in the light of the searchlight. And we simply stood next to each other, protecting ourselves with our hands from the light, and smiled with strain, and began to watch the boat. The boat backed away. The ray of the projector crept sideways and then went out entirely. The diesel below sang out again, and the boat with a long row of windows in its lower cabins all lighted began to depart quickly up the river. We remained by ourselves.

"Well, hello!" I said, embarrassed. She rose up on her tiptoes, seized me hard by the shoulders and kissed me on the eyes.

"Let's go!" I said and coughed. "The devil, it's so dark! Wait a minute, I'll light the lantern . . ."

I lit the lantern and again it fogged up at first and we had to wait until the candle blazed up and the glass dried out and became transparent. And then we walked ahead: I in front with the suitcase and the lantern and she behind with the pail of water.

"Is it too heavy for you?" I asked her after a minute.

"Get along, get along!" she said huskily.

She had always had a husky low voice and as a rule it was hard and strong, and I had for a long time not loved this in her. Because I loved tenderness in women. But at that moment, there, on the shore of the river, at night, when we were going one after the other to the house after so many days of bitterness, parting, letters, and strange, threatening dreams, her voice, and her strong body, and her rough hands, her northern speech, were like the breathing of a bird from far away—wild, gray-feathered, left behind from the autumn flock.

We turned to the right into a ravine along which went a short little road paved by someone unknown at some unknown time— narrow, grown over with nut trees, pines, and mountain ash. We began to rise along it into the darkness, barely lighting our way with the lantern, and above us flowed a narrow river of stars. Along it floated the black branches of the pines, and they, taking turns, covered and discovered the stars.

Hardly catching our breath, we came out to the larch walk and walked along together.

All at once I wanted to tell her everything and show her everything about things here, about the people, about various little events.

"See how it smells!" I said.

"Of wine," she answered, panting lightly from the walk. "I felt it a long way back, on the boat..."

"That's the leaves. And now come here!"

We left our things in the pathway, jumped across a little ditch and went into the bushes, lighting our way with the lantern.

I muttered: "It should be somewhere here..."

"Mushrooms!" she said with astonishment from behind.

Finally, I found what I was looking for. It was white feathers from a young chicken, scattered along the grass, the needles and the yellow leaves.

"Look here," I said and began to light it up. "We have a poultry farm here in the village. The chicks have grown up, and they have begun to let them out—and now a fox comes here every day and sits in the bushes. When the young chickens wander into the forest it catches one and eats it right on the spot."

I pictured to myself that fox with gray hair on its dark snout and licking its chops and huffing in order to blow the down from off its nose.

"It should be killed!" she said.

"I have a gun. We'll walk around the forest together, and, perhaps, we'll succeed."

We returned again to the pathway and went further. The lit window of my house came into view, and I began to think about what would take place when we arrived. I wanted right away to have a drink—and I had some *ryabinovka* all prepared. I had made it myself. It was good to pick berries from the mountain ash in the woods, to bring them home, to crush them in a juicer, so that the yellow foam should flow, and then to strain the juice into a bottle with vodka.

"And back north it's already winter time!" she said as if surprised. "The Dvina River has frozen over and only in the very middle have the ice breakers broken a passage. Everything is white and the passageway through the river ice is black . . . And the steam rises. And when a boat goes along through the black water then the dogs run alongside on the ice next to it. And for some reason they always run in threes."

She spoke the phrase, "in threes," in a northern way, and I pictured to myself the Dvina River and the steamboats and Archangel, and the village on the White Sea, from whence she had come. Tall two-story empty huts, black walls, silence, and isolation.

"Has the ice already appeared in the sea?" I asked.

"It's coming," she said, and she also thought about something, perhaps about what she had left behind there. "I'll have to go back on reindeers if . . ."

She was silent for a time. I waited, listening to her breathing and her steps, and then I asked: "What—if?"

"Nothing," she said particularly huskily and slowly. "If the ice gets worse, that's what!"

Having stamped along the porch we went into the house.

"Uhhh," she said, looking around and taking the kerchief off her head. Always when she was surprised or happy she uttered this low and slow "uhhh." The house was small and old. I had rented it from a Muscovite who lived in it only during the summer. There was almost no furniture—only some old cots, a table, and chairs . . . The walls had been eaten away by a wood-beetle, and they were all sprinkled with white dust. But there was a radio, an electric light, a stove, and several old fat books which I loved to read in the evening.

"Take your coat off!" I said. "Now we'll heat the stove . . ."

And I went out into the courtyard to cut some kindling wood for the stove. But I felt dizzy with happiness. There was a ringing in my head. My hands trembled. I felt weak and wanted to sit down. The stars gleamed small and sharp. "There will be a frost," I thought. "And that means that in the morning all the leaves will fall. Soon winter will begin!"

Down on the Oka there slowly began a singing three-toned whistle which continued for a long while, rolling across the hills. Somewhere down there below was a tug, one of those old steam tugs of which there are no longer very many. The new cutters and the new big tugs whistle short, high, and nasally. Awakened by the whistle, out in the poultry house, several cocks crowed in falsetto . . .

I cut some branches, collected some firewood, and went into the house. She had taken off her overcoat and was standing with her back to me and was leafing over newspapers: she had got something out of her suitcase. She was in a flowered dress. It was tight on her. And if I were to go out with her in Moscow somewhere—to a club—everyone would quietly smile. And yet this, in all probability, was her best dress. And I remembered that ordinarily she went about in slacks, stuffed into the top of her boots, and on top some kind of an old, faded shirt. And there in the North this was wonderful.

I put on the teapot and began to heat up the stove. In the stove there was soon a roar. The branches crackled. It smelled of smoke and firewood.

"This is for you!" she said from behind.

I turned about and saw on the table a salmon. Magnificent, lusterless silver, with a broad dark back, with a lower jaw bent upward. In the house it smelled of fish and sea and a longing for wanderings seized me again.

She was of the sea. She had even been born in the sea on a motorboat in the summertime in a golden night. But she was indifferent to the white Arctic nights. Indeed only visitors see them and go mad from their quiet and loneliness. Only when you are a visitor there, separated from all and seemingly forgotten by all, only then you do not sleep at night and keep thinking, thinking, and saying to yourself: "Well, well! It is nothing, it is simply nighttime, and you are not here forever and what has the night to do with you, let the sun creep along the edge of the sea, sleep, sleep . . ."

And she? She slept soundly at nighttime, at the fisheries behind a calico curtain, because at the dawn she had to get up and row together with the sturdy fishermen, get the fish from out of the traps, and then cook a fish soup and wash the dishes . . . And it had been that way always, every summer, until I had come.

And here now on the Oka River we were drinking *ryabinovka*, eating salmon, and talking, remembering different things. How we went out in the white night to sea to spear sea wolves and how in the storm we pulled in the traps with the fishermen and swallowed bitter water and how we felt sick.

And how we had gone to the lighthouse for bread. And how we had once sat at nighttime in the village library room and, having taken off our shoes and thrown off our quilted jackets, had read all the newspapers and magazines which had come out during the days we had been at the fisheries.

I threw a fur coat with its fur side up on the floor by the stove. We placed the teakettle and candy next to each other, took our cups, and lay on the fur coat, looking alternately at one another and into the rosy fire, at the coals, watching how the little fires ran up and down them. And in order to lie there longer, I stood up from time to time and threw some more branches into the stove, and it began to crackle, and we moved back a bit from the heat.

At two o'clock in the night I got up in the darkness because I couldn't sleep any more. It seemed to me as if, if I were to sleep, she would go away from me somewhere and I would no longer feel her with me. And I wanted her to be with me all the time and I knew she would be. "Take me into your dreams in order that I should always be with you!" I wanted to say. "Because it is impossible to be without you for long." And then I thought that people who leave us, whom we do not meet any more, these people die for us. And we die for them. Strange thoughts come into one's head at nighttime, when one cannot sleep from gladness or from loneliness.

"Are you sleeping?" I asked her quietly.

"No," she replied from the bed. "I feel good. Don't look, I'm going to get dressed . . ."

Then I went into the corner where the radio hung from straps on the wall. I turned it on. Among the crackle and mutter of the announcers I looked for music. I knew that it must be there and I found it. A velvety male voice said something in English, and then there was a pause, and I understood that now they would begin to play.

I trembled because from the very first sound I recognized the melody. When I feel very good or on the other hand bad, I always remember this jazz melody. It is alien to me, but in it there resounds some secret thought, and I cannot understand whether it is sad or glad. I often remembered it when I was away somewhere on a trip, when something gladdened me or, on the other hand, oppressed me.

I hauled the coat over to the radio, and we sat down on it next to each other, embracing each other. All these months in my soul there had lived a feeling of loss, and now I had found everything. And what I had found was even better than I could have supposed.

The bass muttered sentimentally, seeking in the darkness its movement of counterpoint, getting lost in indecisiveness, rising and falling, and this slow movement reminded me of the star-lit heaven. And listening to it, the saxaphone complained about something. Again and again the horn climbed to violent heights. And the piano, from time to time, wandered between them with its apocalyptic chords in fifths. And like a metronome, like time, laying out rhythm in syncopes, the drummer subordinated himself to all the rest with soft empty blows.

"We won't light the light, is that all right?" she said, looking from the floor upward, at the green dial of the radio, at its winking eye.

"All right," I agreed and thought that perhaps I should never have another such night. And I became sad that already three hours had passed. I wanted it to begin all over again, to go out with my lantern and wait, that we should again remember, and that again we should be afraid to say farewell one to another in the darkness.

She got up for a minute for something, looked out the window, and huskily said:

"Snow . . ."

I also got up and looked into the darkness outside the window. There was a snowfall. It was the first real snow of that autumn. I pictured to myself how tomorrow in the morning one could see the mouse tracks around the pile of fresh wood in the forest, and the rabbit tracks near the acacia, which they loved to knaw at nighttime. I remembered my gun. I became joyful, and I was seized with a quiver of delight. God, how wonderful! How glorious it is that there is snow, that she arrived, that we are alone by ourselves, and that we have with us music, our past and our future, which perhaps will be even better than the past, and that tomorrow I will take her to my favorite place, show her the Oka, the fields, the hills, the forest, and the ravines . . . The night was passing and we could still not go to sleep. We talked in whispers and we embraced each other, fearing to lose each other, and again we fired up the stove, looked into its fiery mouth, and the red light baked our faces. We went to sleep at seven in the morning, the windows were already pale blue and light, and we slept for a long time, because no one awakened us in our home.

While we had been sleeping the sun had come up and everything had thawed but then had frozen again. Having had my tea, I took my gun and we went out of the house. It was even painful for a second—such a white winter light struck our eyes, and so clear and sharp was the air. The snow had gone away, but everywhere there remained icy crusts. They were dull and lusterless, semitransparent. From out of the stable arose a fragrant steam. The heifers crowded about and stamped loudly, hollowly, as if on a footway of planking. This was because beneath the upper icy crusts the dung-water had still not frozen. And several of them grazed with enjoyment on the gray winter grain shoots and urinated frequently, raising up their tails and putting their legs wide apart, which were curly at the groin. And where they had wet there appeared emerald spots of wet young rye.

First we went along the road. The ruts were dull surfaced, but under the ice there was clay-filled water, and when our boots broke the crust, there were brown splashes on the ice. And in the forest out from under the ice peered the last, hardly faded dandelions. In the ice could be seen the leaves and pine needles frozen there. The last mushrooms stood there frozen and when we kicked them they broke and rattling along, jumping up and down, rolled along the ice for a long time. The ice beneath our feet settled and crackled and thundered all about: in front of us, behind us and to the side.

The fields on the hillocks were smoky green in the distance and as if sprinkled with flour. The haystacks had turned black. The forest was transparent. It was black and naked. Only there oozed sharply through it a white palisade of birches. The trunks of the aspens were velvety and glossy with green. And, indeed, in some places along the forested hillside there still flowered and burned the last red caps of trees that had not yet shed their leaves. The river was visible through the forest for a long distance and was empty and cold to the view. We went down through a snowy ravine, leaving behind deep, at first dirty, then clean tracks, and began to drink from the spring near a felled aspen. In the immobile pool of the spring blackened maple and oak leaves had dropped compactly to the bottom. And the cut-down aspen smelled bitter and cold, and the open surface of the wood where it had been cut was amber.

"Is it good?" I asked. I looked at her and I was astonished. Her eyes were green.

"It's good!" she said, greedily looking around and licking her lips.

"Is it better than on the White Sea?" I asked her further.

She began again to look at the river and up the slope, and her eyes became still more green.

"Well, the White Sea!" she said indefinitely. "We have ... We have ... But there are oaks here," she interrupted herself. "How is it that you found such a place?"

I was happy, but I also felt strange and fearful: everything had worked out awfully well for me that fall. In order to calm myself, I lit a cigarette and was all in smoke and steam. On the Oka, from the direction of Aleksin, there appeared a tug. It ran swiftly down the stream and made a wave, and we followed it silently with our eyes. From its engine came abundant steam, and streams of water poured out from its side from a hole above the waterline.

When the tug hid behind a curve in the river, holding hands, we began to climb back up the hill among the sparse trees, in the bright forest, in order to look once more at the Oka from up above. We went quietly, silently, as in a white dream, in which we were at long last together.

The Smell of Bread*

I

The telegram arrived New Year's Day. Dusya was in the kitchen and so her husband went to the door. With a hangover, in his undershirt, he yawned irrepressibly, signed for it and tried to think from whom he might be receiving another New Year's greeting. It was in this state, still yawning, that he read that short mournful telegram about the death of Dusya's mother—a 70-year-old woman in a distant village.

"How untimely!" he thought with fright and called to his wife. Dusya did not weep, only became slightly pale, went into the room, smoothed out the tablecloth, and sat down. Her husband looked dully at the unfinished bottle on the table, poured himself a drink, and tossed it down. At that point he thought again and poured one out for Dusya too.

"Drink!" he said. "My God, how my head aches! Oh, oh, oh . . . We'll all be there. What are you going to do—go there?"

Dusya was silent, moved her hand along the tablecloth, and then swallowed the drink down, walked as if she were blind over to the bed, and lay down.

"I don't know," she said a minute later.

Her husband went up to Dusya and stroked her round body.

"Well, all right . . . What are you going to do? What will you do!" He didn't know what else to say, returned to the table, and again poured himself a drink. "Heaven be her kingdom! We'll all be there!"

The whole day long Dusya went about the apartment wilted. Her head ached, and she didn't go out to pay visits to anyone. She wanted to weep, but she somehow had no desire to weep. She was simply sad. Dusya had not seen her mother for fifteen years. She had left the village even before that and almost never recollected anything from her past life. And if she remembered something, more often than not it was something from her early childhood or how she was escorted home from the club when she was a girl.

Dusya began to look over her old photographs and again she could not weep: in all the photographs her mother had an alien and strained face, her eyes were popping out and her heavy dark hands hung down as if she were standing at attention.

* Russian title: "Zapakh Khleba," first published in *Tarusskie Stranitsy, Litera-turno-Khudozhestvenny Sbornik*, Kaluzhskoye Knizhnoye Izdatelstvo (Kaluga, 1961), pp. 76–78.

That night, lying in her bed, Dusya had a long talk with her husband and at the very end of their conversation said:

"I'm not going to go! Why should I go? It's cold there now ... Yes, and all the rubbish there has probably already been hauled off by my kinfolk. We have plenty of kin there. No, I'm not going."

II

The winter passed and Dusya had completely forgotten about her mother. Her husband was doing well. They were living to their own satisfaction and Dusya had become even more round and more beautiful.

But at the beginning of May Dusya received a letter from her nephew, Misha. The letter was written to dictation on a sheet of paper with lines askew. Misha gave greetings from the multitudinous kinfolk and wrote that the house and possessions of his grandmother were whole and complete and that Dusya must come.

"Go!" said the husband. "Go along! Don't spend a lot of time there. Sell everything as fast as you can, whatever there is. Or else others will use it or it will go to the collective farm."

And so Dusya went. It was a long time since she had traveled and it was a lengthy trip. And she succeeded in enjoying the trip to the full. She talked with many different people and made the acquaintance of many.

She had sent a telegram that she was coming, but for some reason no one came to meet her. So she had to go on foot from the station, but even the walk was a satisfaction for Dusya. The road was flat and rolled smooth, and along its sides stretched her native Smolensk fields with light blue coppices on the horizon.

Dusya arrived at her village three hours later, stopped still on a new bridge across the small river, and looked. The village had been considerably built up. White livestock buildings reached out broadly, and it was difficult to recognize it. And these changes were somehow not pleasing to Dusya.

She went along the street, looking sharply at all of those she encountered, trying to guess who they were. But she recognized almost no one, while many recognized her, stopped, and were astonished at how she had matured.

Her sister was glad at Dusya's arrival, wept, and ran to put on the samovar. Dusya began to get the presents she had brought out of her traveling bag. Her sister looked at the presents, wept again, and then embraced Dusya. And Misha sat on the bench and was astonished at why they were weeping.

The sisters sat down to drink tea, and Dusya learned that many of her mother's things had already been taken away by her kinfolk.

The livestock—a pig, three spring lambs, a goat and chickens—the sister had taken for herself. At first Dusya silently resented this, but then she forgot about it, the more so that there was much left, and the main thing was that the house was left. After drinking tea and talking, the sisters went to look at the house.

The kitchen garden had been plowed, and Dusya was surprised. But her sister said the neighbors had plowed it so the earth should not go to seed. And the house seemed to Dusya by no means as large as she had remembered it.

The windows were covered with boards, and there was a lock hanging on the door. The sister for a long time tried to open it. Then Dusya tried, then again her sister, and they both were worn out before they finally did get it open.

In the house it was dark. The light barely filtered through the boards on the windows. The house was damp and had a feel of not having been lived in, but it smelled of bread, a smell which belonged to her childhood, and Dusya's heart beat faster. She went about the room, looking things over, and getting used to the dim light: the ceiling was low and dark-brown. The photographs still hung on the walls, but the ikons, except for one not worth anything, were no longer there. Also missing were the embroideries on the stoves and chests.

Remaining alone by herself, Dusya opened up a chest—it smelled of her mother. In it lay old-fashioned dark skirts, sarafans, and a well-worn sheepskin coat. Dusya pulled all of it out, looked it over, and then once more went over the house, looked into the empty courtyard, and it seemed to her as if sometime a long time ago she had dreamed all this before and that now she was returning into her dream.

III

As soon as they heard about the sale, the neighbors began to come to Dusya. They looked everything over carefully, felt everything, but Dusya did not ask very much for them, and the things were sold quickly.

The chief thing was the house! Dusya asked about prices for houses and was surprised and gladdened at how prices had risen. Three buyers appeared immediately—two from this same village and one from a neighboring village. But Dusya did not sell immediately. She kept worrying that her mother had left behind some hidden money. She searched three days: she knocked on the walls, felt the mattresses, climbed down into the cellar and up into the attic, but she didn't find anything.

Having agreed with the buyer on a price, Dusya went into the district center, had the documents for the sale of the house drawn up and put the money in a savings account. On returning she brought her sister still more gifts and began to get her things together to return to Moscow. In the evening her sister went out to the livestock farm, and Dusya pulled herself together for a visit to her mother's grave. Misha accompanied her.

They went at sunset and walked along the meadow. In some places the dandelions had already popped out in bloom. The grass was tender and green. The day had darkened somewhat during its second half, grown cloudy, but toward the evening the clouds had departed, and only on the horizon in the direction in which Dusya and Misha were walking there still hung a row of ashy rose clouds. They were so distant and so vague that it seemed as if they were standing behind the sun.

A river two kilometers in distance from the village made a sharp loop and it was in this loop, on the high right bank, as if on a peninsula, that the cemetery was located. At one time it had been surrounded by a brick wall, and visitors had to pass through high arched gates. But after the war the bricks from the broken-up wall had been taken away for building, leaving, for some reason, only the gate with the trails into the cemetery running in all directions.

Dusya asked Misha along the way about school, about work payments on the collective farms, about the chairman of the farm, about harvests, and was calm and even-tempered. But then the old cemetery loomed ahead, lit red by the low sun. Along its edges where at one time there had been a fence, where sweetbriar bushes were growing, were the especially old graves which had long since lost the appearance of graves. And next to them there could be seen in the bushes freshly painted little fences with low wooden obelisks— "brother graves"—in other words, the mass graves of Russian soldiers left behind by the war.

Dusya and Misha passed the gates, turned to the right, then to the left—among the birches which were just coming into leaf, among sharply smelling bushes. And Dusya grew ever more pale, and her mouth hung half open.

"Grandmother is over there..." said Misha, and Dusya saw a little mound which had settled, covered by a sparse sharp grass. Through the grass loamy soil was visible. There was a small gray cross, which had not been touched up after the wintertime, and which already stood crookedly.

Dusya became completely pale. And all of a sudden it was just as if a knife had been plunged into her breast, where her heart lay. Such a black longing struck her in the soul that she choked, was all atremble, cried out, fell down, and crawled to the grave on her knees, sobbing out so violently words which came to her from she knew not where that Misha grew frightened.

"Ooohh ..." Dusya moaned low, falling with her face onto the grave, sinking her fingers deeply into the moist earth. "My priceless little mother ... My own beloved little mother ... Ooohhh ... Ah ... Yes, and we shall never see each other again in this world, never, never! How can I live without you, who is going to caress me, who is going to comfort me? Mother, little mother, little mother, what have you done?"

"Aunt Dusya ... Aunt Dusya ...," Misha whimpered from fear and pulled her by the sleeve. And when Dusya, starting to wheeze, began to arch her back upward and beat her head on the grave, Misha ran off to the village.

In an hour, already in deep twilight, they ran from the village to get Dusya. She was lying right there, quite out of her mind, and she could not even weep, she could not even speak a word, she could not think, she only moaned through her tightly closed teeth. Her face was black from the earth and frightening.

They picked her up, rubbed her temples, began to comfort her, to persuade her, led her home, and she understood nothing, looked at all of them with enormous swollen eyes—life seemed to her to be night. When they took her to her sister's house, she collapsed on the bed—she had hardly managed to get there—and she immediately went to sleep.

On the next day having already gathered together all her things for the trip to Moscow, she drank tea with her sister in farewell. She was merry and told about what a wonderful apartment they had in Moscow and what conveniences.

And so she left, gay and calm, having given Misha another ten rubles. About two weeks later her old mother's house was opened up, the floors were washed, things moved in, and new people began to live in it.

To the City[*]

I

Vasily Kamanin was walking along the road of Ozerishche early in the morning. His boots were muddy. His brown neck had been unwashed for a long time. His eyes looked outward cloudily through their yellow whites and downward, from the very eyes themselves, there was a gray bristle on his face. His walk was uneven. His feet slipped in different directions and somehow fell behind his body, which was straining forward. A cold wind was blowing on his back. On both sides lay the dark endless furrows of plowed earth. Between the furrows in spots water gleamed with a lead-like color—the rains had been coming down for a whole week. Along the shoulders of the road the red-brown horse sorrel, spattered with mud, waved in the wind.

The previous evening Vasily Kamanin had had a lot to drink with his son-in-law's father. Today he had a headache. He also had an ache through his whole body—of the kind he only had when the weather was bad. A nasty saliva gathered in his mouth. Vasily spat, raised his heavy head, and looked ahead with melancholy. But before him was only a muddy, rutted road. The haystacks wearily darkened. And to the very horizon there hung over the landscape a low gray heaven without the least little bit of clear space, without any hope for the sun. Vasily dropped his eyes, seeking, as usual, a place which was drier, but then, absorbed in his thoughts, he again walked along without looking where he was stepping, slipping, moving his feet heavily, leaning forward with his lean body.

Vasily Kamanin lived in the village of Mokhavatka in a roomy old hut which stood separately from the rest. Before the war Mokhovatka had been a large village and the Kamanin house had stood in a row with the others. But, in retreating, the Germans had burned down the village. It had all burned to ashes except only the Kamanins' house which by some miracle had remained whole. After the war the village had been rebuilt—but a long ways away from the former village—and Vasily's hut turned out to be beyond its edges. They had proposed to move his hut. He himself had intended to. But somehow or other it never got done. And so he continued living apart.

[*] Russian title: "V Gorod," first published in *Tarusskie Stranitsy, Literaturno-Khudozhestvenny Sbornik*, Kaluzhskoye Knizhnoye Izdatelstvo (Kaluga, 1961), pp. 78-82.

His three daughters, one after the other, had married and gone to live in the city. His hut had grown empty. More and more frequently Vasily hired himself out for work outside the collective farm. He was a good carpenter, he earned a lot, but as the years passed he began to grow bored, to drink, and in his cups he was gloomy and beat his wife.

Vasily had not loved his wife Akulina for a long time. Even before the war somehow or other he had been hired for work on a large construction project, and had worked there for an entire summer, and since that time the thought of moving to the city had never left him.

Every year in the fall, when there wasn't much work, he was seized by melancholy. He became indifferent to everything. He would sprawl for long periods in the barn, with eyes closed, and think about life in the city. He couldn't stand city people. He considered them all parasites. But city life—parks, restaurants, cinema theatres and stadiums—he loved so much that he even dreamed about the city.

Several times he was just about to move to the city and even sold the cow, but Akulina whispered at nighttimes into his ear about the earth, about his kinfolk, about his house and the plot of land surrounding it, about the fact that she would die of homesickness in the city, and he changed his mind and remained.

Everyone in the collective farm knew about his passion for the city and laughed at it.

"Well, so you didn't leave?" they asked him.

"The night cuckoo outcuckoos the daytime cuckoo," he answered in a proverb, gloomily laughing and hiding his anger at his wife.

In the springtime Akulina grew ill. At first they thought she would get well. Akulina began to go to the medical aid office, took home the powders and medicines prescribed, and willingly, with faith in her cure, drank the bitter drugs. But she did not improve. She became, on the contrary, ever sicker. Then she tried secret cures. Old women came frequently to Vasily's home, bringing charmed water in hot water bottles, and brews from roots. But even this didn't help. Akulina's eyes fell inwards, her temples began to sink. Her hair began to fall out. She grew thin, melted, at an improbable speed. People who had seen her healthy not long before, now stopped when they met her, looked at her for a long time, and followed her with their eyes. It became awful to sleep with her: she was so thin and she moaned so much in her sleep. Vasily began to sleep in the barn, out on the fresh hay.

He spent whole days in the fields, worked at the haying, quarreled with the brigadier, and, knitting his large dark brows, thought about his wife, convincing himself ever more firmly that soon she would die. And at evening time he carried home hay, dragged bags with grain which had been given him in advance payment for his work by the collective farm. He came home tired, with a face brown from the sun, sat down on the bench, put his cracking hands on his knees, and looked out from under his brow at his wife.

Akulina, grown very thin, with a violent look in her dark dry eyes, which were still beautiful, served him at the table. Then, leaning against the wall, she breathed with difficulty, opening her black mouth. Abundant perspiration appeared on her face.

"Vasya" she begged. "Take me to the city, for the sake of Jesus Christ! Take me! I'm going to die soon, I think . . . I don't have any strength. I'm all sick, Vasya!"

Vasily in silence gulped down his soup, fearing to look at his wife, to reveal his secret thoughts.

"Take me, Vasya!" Akulina said very quietly and sat on the floor next to the wall. "I can't eat anything. I throw up everything. I can't even take milk any longer . . . We have livestock, Vasya! They have to be looked after, and it's difficult for me—I can only crawl along on all fours . . . I crawl, it's easier for me that way. And inside something is burning, it's burning so much! Take me, let a professor look at me. I don't believe anyone here, and I'm so bad, oi, so bad!"

And so now Vasily was going to Ozerishche to the chairman of the collective farm to ask for a horse for his wife, so he could take her into town, and at the same time in order to ask to be released from the collective farm once and for all.

His mood was bad. His head was aching with his hangover. He was filled with wrath at his wife, at the foreman, and his neighbors. He cursed and he thought how more cleverly to ask the chairman to let him move to the city.

II

Vasily arrived in Ozerishche an hour later and was so tired that his legs were giving way underneath him. The chairman's house was distinguished by its large size, by its porch with pillars, its iron roof, and tall barn, covered not with straw like everyone else's but with shingles. In the orchard beneath the apple trees stood dark beehives. Carefully wiping his boots on the footscraper, Vasily looked out of the corner of his eyes at the hives and thought for the hundredth time: "I should get some bees, a good thing!" But remembering why he had come, he only grunted and, feeling an unaccustomed embarrassment and agitation, opened the door into the dark, cluttered passageway. Inside the house things had not been picked up. It was dirty. It smelled of baked milk and sour cabbage. On the table stood a sewing machine. On the floor lay scraps of materials. On wires from the lamp to the radio receiver hung socks. The master of the house was absent. His wife, Marya, a strong dark-haired woman with a tight rear, was next to the hotly burning stove. She was moving the oven prongs, her legs set far apart, and squatting.

"Hello!" Vasily said gloomily, dragging off his cap. "Where is Danilych?"

"Why do you need him?" just as gloomily, without looking at Vasily, Marya asked.

"Because I have some business."

"He's out in the fields. He went out just as soon as it was light."

"Is he going to be home soon?"

"He said he'd be home for breakfast, but I don't know ..."

"I'll wait then!" said Vasily with determination and sat down heavily on the bench with his face to the stove.

He took out some makhorka and wanted to smoke, but he remembered that Marya did not like people to smoke in her house, and he hid his tobacco pouch. And in fact he didn't even want to smoke. In his body he felt a repulsive weakness. In his head there was noise.

Vasily dropped his head and thought a bit. He thought about the fact that his wife was soon going to die, that it would be necessary to make a coffin, and that it would be better to get some good boards ahead of time. He would have to kill the ram, maybe even two, for the wake. The kinfolk would come all right, they loved to eat ...

Then he began to think about to whom and for how much to sell the house and the rest of the property and where to go. For a while perhaps he could go to Smolensk and stay with his older daughter, and then he would see. He would have money, thank heaven, and he could hunt for some kind of a little house there in the city.

Then he began to try to assemble the most convincing words possible so that the chairman of the farm would not oppose him. In his mind everything came out very neatly, and the chairman could not withstand Vasily's arguments.

"Why did you come?" asked the mistress of the house, putting the oven prongs into the corner and sitting down at the table.

Vasily did not understand at first what he was being asked about because he was so immersed in his thoughts. Blinking, as if half awake, he looked at Marya's red face, at her full lips and her light-blue eyes which were impertinent and slightly bulging.

"My wife is very sick," finally he said. "I have come to ask about a horse. I want to take her to the city. And then also about some other things."

"How old is Akulina?" Marya asked with interest.

"How old?" Vasily thought for a minute. "Well count: I am fifty-five and she is two years younger."

"Ah!" was all that the mistress of the house said.

For a while she was silent, also deeply immersed in thought about something or other, then she bent down to her sewing machine, bit off a thread, selected some material, and a measured even hum filled the hut.

Vasily again shut his eyes. He felt like lying down on the bench, covering himself up from his head down, not to think about anything, and to go to sleep ... The thought that it was necessary to wait for the chairman, to speak and prove that it was impossible for him to remain any longer in the collective farm, and then to walk the dirty road back to Mokhovatka, this filled him with loathing and cold. Between his shoulder blades something jerked, and the skin on his chest and on his arms tightened.

Soon Vasily fell into forgetfulness, no longer hearing the hum of the sewing machine, no longer thinking about anything and started when solid footsteps stamped in the passageway and the master of the house came in.

He was tall and had a small pale face on which, as on the face of a eunuch, grew whitish, hardly noticeable bunches of hair. He had come on horseback and on entering first rubbed his thighs and wrinkled his brows and bent over and looked at something in the window. Vasily also turned and looked: a boy was leading a tall bony colt with a bobbed tail along the fence. The animal's hooves were slipping out from under him in different directions and he was tossing his head back.

"Well how are things?" Marya asked loudly, going up to the hearth and again picking up the stove tongs.

The chairman, still bending over, turned his head to her, and started to say something, but saw Vasily, and, keeping silence instead, extended to him his cold, moist hand. Then he went through the hut, sighed like a person who is very tired, sat down on the bench with his back to the window, and started to pull off his boots.

Having removed his boots, moving the toes of his bare feet, he looked at his wife, and his face gradually took on a sleepy and secret expression. Vasily also watched Marya attentively, how she strained moving about the cast-iron kettles in the oven. He looked at her strong back and involuntarily thought to himself: "The devil! See how smooth!"

"Well, how is everything with you?" asked the chairman. "Are you getting in the hay?"

"We're getting it in," Vasily answered hurriedly, moving his eyes away from Marya. "We're getting it in, but it's not likely that we'll soon be finished . . . The rains came at a bad time. It's very wet. Yes, and there aren't many people to work. They're sitting at home."

"What does the brigadier over there use to think with?" the chairman frowned. "How many times was he told to get the hay in! So they waited for the rain! Just wait, I'll catch up with that brigadier yet!"

The chairman looked at his wife and sighed again. Vasily coughed and fidgeted on the bench.

"Will it be soon?" asked the chairman of his wife.

"It will be ready right away," Marya said indistinctly.

Vasily remained in suspense. The master of the house did not ask why he had come, and it was awkward for him to begin to speak first of his request. All of the words which he had thought up while he sat in expectation had suddenly disappeared, and again Vasily felt that he was quite sick and that the chief thing at this particular minute—was to get over his hangover and lie down and go to sleep.

"We looked at the field in Bukatina," said the chairman and came to life, "with a correspondent from the regional newspaper. The flax is going to be excellent. He promised to write about our girls."

Without turning around, he reached behind on the windowsill for a newspaper which was lying there, tore off a piece of paper, stretched out his right leg, got some makhorka out of his pocket, and lit up a smoke.

"Well!" Vasily pretended to be surprised and also lit a smoke in a hurry. "They'll write! That's their business—to write . . ."

"Smoking things up," Marya said with a frown and, slamming the door, went out into the courtyard.

"Why do you want to see me? What's your business?" asked the chairman, giving a wink in the wake of his wife and smiling at Vasily.

Vasily picked up his feet and seated himself more solidly and bent his head.

"My wife is badly ill," he began. "I want to take her to the city. The road has gone to pieces. The trucks don't go at all. Couldn't you give me a horse, Danilych?"

"A horse?" the chairman groaned, scratched his head. "And what, hasn't she been at the medical aid office?"

"She was there, only I think she needs an operation."

"Well all right! Today it's too late, but tomorrow I'll tell them to give you one. You can go in the morning."

"And I don't feel so good myself either for some reason . . ." Vasily began again, making a sad face. "Why don't you drop in and see me some time?" he interrupted himself all of a sudden, remembering that one does not begin such business without preparation. "I have some home brew. My daughter sent a package from the city—sugar. We could have a drink together. The home brew is good. My wife brewed it the other day, it's not bad at all. There's bacon fat too. The pig weighed eight poods . . . You should drop in!"

"Maybe I can drop in," said the chairman, smiling.

"And I, Danilych," Vasily who was gladdened at the reaction, went on, "Have decided to say goodbye to the collective farm for good."

"What do you mean, say goodbye?" the chairman stopped smiling.

"Well here's how it is," said Vasily, gathering determination and lifting his eyebrows. "Here's how it is—I don't want to work here any more. My wife is ill. My daughters are writing me, inviting me to come and stay with them . . . Why should I stay here! Then I have long since wanted to leave . . . The old chairman let me go, ask whoever you like. Let others work, but I've had enough of it. I can work as a carpenter in the city at any time. And what's there for me to do here?"

"How do you mean what!" the chairman examined Vasily, as if he were seeing him for the first time. "Does that mean that you've forgotten about what was said at the management meeting?"

"What's the management to me . . ."

"Just a minute, don't you 'what' me! So there's no work? In the fall we have to build a new barn—and what does that mean to you? Then we have to rebuild the club, and that's not work for you? And then we have to put in hot beds—and isn't that work?"

"All that's true, but let others do it. And don't hold me here. I'm going to leave anyway. I know my rights."

"You know them? And do you also know there are not enough people in the collective farm?"

"That doesn't concern me. That's your problem to see that no one runs away from the collective farm. One doesn't run away from something that's good. And as for me, I want maybe to live a little. I'm not an old man with 100 years behind him who wants to lie on the stove. And what do I have from the collective farm? Do I have comfort and conveniences from the collective farm? There isn't even any place to have a drink."

"Don't tell me you're living poorly!" the chairman stooped

voraciously and his face began to grow yellow. "Are you trying to tell me that you're dying from overwork on the collective farm?"

"Don't you jump on me!" said Vasily and moved his brows. "Don't you threaten me! Whatever I own I earned with my own hard work. From your collective farm one can't even get snow in the winter time."

"So ... Let others work, let others struggle, and you want to go to the city?"

"My wife is dying over yonder," Vasily's head was ringing and his breathing was momentarily interrupted. "I have to take her to the city? How is that?"

"We're going to give you a horse," the chairman got up.

"So you're not going to let me go, that means?" Vasily asked, also getting up.

"You evidently have heaped up a lot of money?"

"My money the devil wouldn't be able to pile up on a stove," Vasily confirmed seriously.

"Well known!" the chairman loudly breathed. "Piling up money as a workman on the side. So you build us a barn, and a club, and hotbeds, and then we'll see."

"A barn? And you don't want this?" Vasily made an indecent gesture.

The chairman turned to the window.

"Our conversation is finished. Run along with you! You know the party's decree. You're illiterate? That's all. We'll call you into the management and talk to you there!"

"All right," Vasily pulled his cap down over his eyes. "All right, you know what you can do with your mother ... We'll see! We can find a noose for your neck too!"

Slamming the door, he tumbled out into the passageway, and thundered off the porch. Snorting through his nose with hurt, gritting his teeth discolored with tobacco smoke, he quickly went out into the street, frightening the chickens who had found a place for themselves along the fence.

"What a talk ..." he muttered, wiping his perspiring face. "It's all clear—without a half-liter of vodka no conversation!"

And all the whole way home he regretted that he had come to see the chairman of the collective farm without a half-liter.

III

On the next day in the early morning, after a drink of home brew, Vasily went to the farm stable and returned half an hour later on a horse. Tying the horse to the porch, he took hay from the barn, piled it up on the cart and spread it out, thought a bit, tossed some to the horse too and went into the house. The evening before he had already decided to slaughter the ram: it was market day in the city today, and the ram had already been coughing for two weeks. Instructing Akulina to get her things together, he took a long narrow German bayonet and went out into the courtyard. The ram, black, big, and old, with a white spot on his neck, he was hardly able to pull out of the barn: the ram did not want to come, put down his heels, and trembled.

"So you feel what's coming?" muttered Vasily and smiled with an evil smile. Catching his breath a bit Vasily grabbed hold of the warm curled horn. The ram looked with transparent eyes at the open door.

"Well, say your prayers!" said Vasily. He threw the ram down on his side, put his knee on the soft flank and gripped his snout with his hand. The ram kicked out and slipped out from under his knee. Vasily, breathing hoarsely, again pressed him down beneath himself and pushed his head backwards, stretching his throat with its white curly-haired spot. Then, clenching his teeth, he took measure and with even excessive force cut at the right spot.

The ram shuddered and became flabby beneath his knee. From the broadly opened wound burst thickly almost black blood, flowing out on the straw and the manure, making spots on Vasily's hand.

There was a slight tremble through the body of the ram. The eyes which had previously looked at the light, squinted, and became cloudy. The calf which had sniffed from out of its corner with curiosity began suddenly to breathe heavily and knocked several times against the wall.

Vasily got up, threw down the bayonet, carefully dragged out his tobacco pouch and began to make himself a cigarette with his bloody fingers. He quickly wet the paper with spit and did not take his eyes off the ram.

The ram began to jerk, to stretch out, his eyes were completely shut. His back legs jerked again more strongly, and his whole body after a minute beat strong and in measure, his legs kicked out gaily as if he were running, kicking up straw and clumps of chicken manure.

Waiting until the ram grew quiet, Vasily hung him up on a crossbar and began quickly and skillfully to remove his skin, cutting into the dull gray membranes and cutting off the tendons in the legs.

Having opened up the stomach, from out of which there breathed steam, he removed the hot liver, cut off a piece for himself and chewed it up with a crunch, spotting his lips and chin with blood.

Akulina came out on the porch, dressed cleanly, a knot of clothes in her hand. In the knot was a change of underwear in case she should be kept in the hospital. Crawling up onto the cart somehow or other, she covered herself with a raincoat and began to wait for Vasily, looking with longing and love at the dark fields and the river below, looking at them as if she were saying goodbye to them forever, goodbye to her home and her village.

A little later Vasily came out of the barn, holding as if it were a child the carcass of the ram, already cut in pieces and wrapped in a bag.

Putting the carcass in the front part of the cart, he went to give fodder to the livestock and to lock the house. And Akulina all of a sudden smelled the sweet odor of the fresh slaughter. She used to love this smell. It had always hung over the hut on days before holidays. But now she felt ill from it and covered her mouth and nose with her scarf ends.

Vasily, once more gulping down home brew and locking the house, emerged, putting a belt on himself on the porch. In the morning he had shaved and washed, put on a new shirt, and now he looked younger and gay.

"Vasya!" said Akulina. "Look at how beautiful it all is . . . I suppose I'm going to die in the city. I'm sorry to say goodbye to it all. My heart hurts . . ." Vasily also looked about the fields with their dark haystacks and with the black cloud wedges, the little river which was dark from the rain, the roofs of the village, spat and said nothing.

Then he untied and bridled the horse, which jerked strongly and broke its lip. He smoothed out once more the hay in the cart, sat down, and set forth. The frightened horse took off with a quick step. The cart began to sway in the broad ruts.

Akulina sat in the rear, compressing her shoulders, holding her bosom, looking with longing eyes at the hut from both sides, at the birch trees and the mountain ash trees with their already ripening saffron-red clusters of berries.

She looked and she remembered all her life on the collective farm: her youth, her marriage, her children, loving all of it even more strongly and more sharply, knowing that perhaps she would never again see her native places and those close to her. Her tears rolled down her sunken cheeks. One thing she desired: to die at home, in her native village, and to be buried in her own cemetery.

The women who happened to be on the street at this moment stopped and, watching her in silence, bowed to her. Akulina smiled through her tears, wore a strained ashamed little smile and also bowed—willingly, low, almost touching the edges of the cart with her head.

Vasily kept urging on the horse. His red face was strained with expectation and gladness. He thought about how, having put his wife in a hospital, he would go to the market, sell the ram, go pay a visit to his kinfolk, and then would go to the railway station restaurant.

He would sit there and drink light wine, looking through the window at the passing trains. He would be waited on by waitresses in white aprons and headdresses. There would be an orchestra playing. There would be the smell of food and the smoke of good cigarettes.

And once there, after talking it over with his kinfolk, he would decide how to proceed further. How he should work it cleverly so as to get out of the collective farm and sell the farmhouse and all of the household property for the best price he could get, and move to the city.

Victor Rozov

An Introduction to Victor Rozov

It is now a century since Ivan Turgenev wrote *Fathers and Sons* dramatizing the conflict between the younger and elder generations of the Russia of his day. Victor Rozov, a short, somewhat bald, energetic, and productive playwright in his mid-forties, has become perhaps the most successful contemporary Russian dramatist by his skill and frankness in treating the conflict between the older and younger generations of present-day Russia. Rozov specializes in writing plays for and about young people which are also well-attended by adults. During the season of 1960–61 as many as four plays by Rozov were being performed in Moscow theaters alone—and there were many other productions of his plays on stage in the provinces. The royalties rolled in and he became wealthy—but Rozov remained a modest, unassuming, sympathetic person absorbed in his all-consuming subject of young people. He worked long hours with young would-be dramatists at the Gorky Literary Institute where he had studied in his own time himself and where he heads the Theater Section. He took an active part in the young people's literary journal of the Union of Soviet Writers, *Yunost,* where he is a member of the editorial board. He worked with the talented young people at Moscow's most exciting theater, the Sovremmenik or Contemporary of which he is the artistic director. He was a busy man—spending every available moment among Russian boys and girls and young men and young women. And his own direct personal knowledge of what interests, concerns, and moves young Russians is reflected in the trueness to life of the images of young Russians presented in his dramas.

The conflict between the younger and the older generation is an eternal theme of life and literature. Sometimes, however, it becomes more sharp than at other times. This was so in the sixties and seventies of the last century in Russia. In a period when the serfs were at last being liberated and the Russian social and state structure was at last being "liberalized" after the ignominious end of a long period of bleak, severe repression directed by a reactionary, bigoted sovereign, the gap in outlook between conservative "fathers," uneasy at the pace of reform imposed from above, and radical, revolutionary "sons"—who under the influence of Western European and Russian social thinking, found the tempo of change too slow and the extent of changes too little—was very great. The "sons" held their "fathers" in contempt and the "fathers" were unable to understand their "sons." It was of this that Turgenev wrote.

Nowadays too the conflict between "fathers" and "sons" in Russia is deep-set. The "fathers" were, many of them, indoctrinated under Stalin, and many of them in different ways are still addicted to dictatorial, high-handed methods, though it is also they who exposed, of their own will, some evils of the Stalin epoch. The "fathers" are men who bore the cruel sacrifices of pellmell industrialization and agricultural collectivization. The "fathers" bore the sacrifices of World War II. The "fathers" expect to be respected and obeyed for their sacrifices—but the Russian "sons" of today have their own view. They have been told so much about "sacrifice" and "duty" they are sick of hearing "high" words. Brought up in days when as children they were taught to worship Stalin as a god they suffered a particularly keen disillusionment when it turned out Stalin was guilty of horrible crimes. If the "fathers" are impressed with accomplishments of Soviet society the "sons" are more impressed with imperfections and faults. Born too late to take part in the war they are tired of hearing endlessly about the "heroism" of those who did.

Here in this conflict between the generations is rich dramatic material. More than any other writer of the period Rozov has used it successfully for stage and screen.

It is also material full of social dynamite. In outspokenness about failings of their parents Russian youngsters today often get over into what could be viewed as sacrilege to the system. The problem of a Soviet dramatist who, like Rozov, is himself a convinced communist and who, as a practical matter, must never let his work become a diatribe against the Soviet Establishment is a very difficult one.

The Soviet political authority, of course, denies steadfastly that there is any "fathers and sons" problem whatsoever in the Soviet Union today. Attacks on writers who claimed to find such a "fathers and sons" conflict were a main theme of the recent clampdown in Soviet literature and art from December 1962 on.

If Victor Rozov escaped any kind of severe attack during that most recent clampdown—even though in December 1961 he had been subjected to vigorous official censure for his cinema scenario *A B C* in its original version—it was certainly because, as a general rule, while Rozov has gone further than almost any other writer in the outspoken expression of the attitudes and moods of Russian young people he has also managed with great skill to combine this with a handling of his plots in such a way that in the end the erstwhile perhaps errant young people are brought back effectively into the communist fold.

The American scholar, Gene Sosin, visited Rozov at his apartment in Moscow two years ago and has given an interesting report on his visit in a magazine article.*

Wrote Sosin: "I spoke briefly with Rozov in his new apartment not far from the Dynamo Sports Stadium on the outskirts of Moscow. Rozov is most famous in the West as the writer of the Cannes Festival prize-winning film, 'The Cranes Are Flying.' He is equally famous inside the USSR as a playwright, holding the undisputed place as the top dramatist for children and adolescents. (His play, *In Search of Happiness*, first written for the juvenile stage, is now also playing in the adult theater.) Rozov probably earns at least 30,000 rubles for every play, plus a cut (about 5 per cent) of the box office receipts of every performance (this is the usual procedure with established dramatists). Thus he is comfortably situated—and his apartment shows it...

"Rozov is not a well man; he had a serious heart attack last year and even in late April he was still weak; he planned to return the following week to the hospital to stay there for a while. He is about 45, warm, direct, good-humoured and sensitive. He said that he preferred writing for children because he felt that he was helping to shape their personalities, where writing for adults was less likely to have such a lasting effect. He was interested in Tennessee Williams and I was able to tell him about *Sweet Bird of Youth* which I had seen just before leaving for Moscow. He also listened to Frida Anatolievna's description of *Cat on a Hot Tin Roof* (she was very familiar with the plot) and expressed his amazement that a playwright should be so preoccupied with abnormal people. I said that perhaps Williams found them more interesting to write about than average people, but Rozov said he thought such an interest was pathological. His curiosity made me feel, though, that he would not turn down an opportunity to see Williams' plays."

Rozov's own plays are a far cry from those of Tennessee Williams.

One example, dating from the mid-1950's is the comedy entitled *In Good Time* which deals with Russian young people who are at that critical point in their lives at which their entire future is being decided by examinations for entrance to institutions of higher education. Those who cannot get admitted face the problem of what to do with themselves. Some do not want to go to work in factories and the like—and there lies a further problem. Mothers and fathers are as involved as their sons and daughters in the admissions furor. And there are young people and parents who prefer "back door"

* Gene Sosin, "Talks with Soviet Writers," *Survey, a Journal of Soviet and East European Studies*, No. 36 (April–June 1961), pp. 7–8.

methods—personal pull—to the honest path of taking the examinations and allowing one's fate to stand or fall on them alone.

Rozov's *The Cranes Are Flying* was based on his play, *The Immortals,* which is quite distinct from *In Good Time.*

The Immortals deals with the impact of World War II on a
Russian family of the intelligentsia, that of the fifty-seven-year-old
physician, Fedor Ivanovich Borozdin. Concentrating its action entirely on the rear, including Moscow and a city in the East, it tells
of the heroism of those at the front through the doings and sayings
of those far from the front. It shows the pathos of the war deftly
and adroitly, and it demonstrates how the war brought out both
bravery and cowardice in those subjected to its trials.

Rozov's play *In Search of Happiness* was written primarily for
young audiences. It was performed in the repertoire of the Central
Childrens' Theater and received a prize in 1957 in the All-Russian
Competition for the best full-length Soviet play. It contains much
that is typical of Rozov's treatment of Russian young people and
their problems.

One of Rozov's latest plays is entitled *Before Dinner*—published in the January 1963 issue of the Soviet magazine *Teatr.* In
this drama he sticks to his accustomed theme of Soviet youth—and
to the family setting so familiar to Soviet theatergoers. This time his
hero is Grigori Nedelin, a student. Again the play is concerned with
the feelings and problems of a group of young people. A conflict
develops when there appears in the home a relative involved in the
abuses of Stalin's personality cult—who during the course of the play
sees his mistakes and undertakes to reorient himself in the light of
the new demands of Soviet life. Alongside him there also appears an
unreconstructed Stalinist who dreams of a return of the old scheme
of rule by terror—and he, of course, is the villain. *Before Dinner* is
one more appeal by Rozov for respect for Soviet young people.

This play was severely criticized by at least one Soviet critic—
I. Vishnevskaya—in an article generally quite sympathetic and favorable to Rozov in *Teatr* for June 1963. The faults Vishnevskaya
finds are several. The most significant of them is the absence of
public or social concerns in the young people in the play, an alienation from and lack of interest in public affairs. Vishnevskaya considers that the play's characters are too entirely absorbed in their
own private and personal concerns.

She writes: "While demanding respect for young people, for the
new generation, in the play *Before Dinner* the dramatist himself ex-
cludes them from the area of sharp ideological conflict, leaving all
their interests solely in ethical, moral, and emotional areas. Why is
there nothing for the young heroes of the year 1962 which is beyond

the windows of their own hearts, of their apartments, of their feelings? The conflicts of the adults in the play exist separately from the happiness and sufferings of the youth."

Vishnevskaya also claims that Rozov's characters in the play do not come alive in the way his young people in many of his previous plays did come alive.

And she makes the quite serious point that Rozov is repeating himself, that in *Before Dinner* he has failed to keep pace with the times, that while, in his depiction of young Russians a few years ago he was outstanding in his freshness and originality, nowadays the times themselves, and other dramatists too, have caught up with him while he has not been advancing.

"And therefore," she writes, "the comedy, *Before Dinner,* which is written with great skill, which possesses an excellent sense of humor and a pure moral atmosphere, nevertheless, in great degree, is a repeat play in which there are all the characters seen before in Rozov —the papas and mamas, the good old elder brothers, and the petit-bourgeois neighbor women, the sly girls, and the boys with their good deeds. In this play there did not take place an artistic discovery—the situations and characters have been fully exploited in preceding plays."

The critic, who obviously likes Rozov and his work and has great faith in him, then, however, goes on to conclude he will do better next time:

"All the plans of the writer, all his concerns, are connected with the affairs and the concerns of young people. Nothing of youth's big and noisy life gets past the dramatist. He knows what young people argue about at Young Communist League meetings and about what lovers talk on the embankments of Moscow River. He has a sensitive touch for the severe, ascetic inner world of young scientists and the jolly ringing strength of young lyric poets. And given all of this the image of the new young hero will inevitably come to life in Victor Rozov's next play."

Rozov himself has revealed the subject of his newest drama. He wrote in *Pravda* of June 16, 1963:

"Right now I am working on a play for the Sovremmenik Theater. Its chief characters will be young people who are doing good work at their factory and who in addition are studying in schools for working youth.

"I very much want to write a play which is both sincere and better."

ABC–A Cinema Scenario for Reading.*

A heavy freight train thunders across the steppes. The train is carrying construction materials: beams, boards, stones and machinery. Several of the freight cars are empty.

On the rear platform of the last car with a little green flag in his hand stands a young lad in railwayman's uniform. He is handsome and quite young. A small station flies past. Some people wave to the lad. He looks past them with an unseeing eye. Children wave their little hands at him, but he does not see them. A girl in the fields waves her handkerchief at him, but he doesn't look. Past him fly the fields, woods, villages, cities, construction projects—he doesn't see anything. He is deep in his own thoughts.

The train slows down. The signal shows a red light.

The train stops at the Moscow Marshaling Yards.

The boy and the engineer, crossing the railway tracks, go to the dispatcher's office.

In the dispatcher's office the engineer signs in.

DISPATCHER (to the boy). Well, Fedorov, how does this work suit you? Do you like it?

VOLODYA. I'm quitting. (And he leaves the dispatcher's office.)

The boy goes into the city. He seats himself in a bus.

He goes into the entry of an apartment house in the new Southwest District of Moscow. He goes up in the elevator. He presses a doorbell. No one opens the door for him. He takes a key out of his pocket and opens it. He goes through the rooms and looks about to see whether there is anyone at home. There is no one. He notices on the table a note: "Volodya: Your father and I have gone to a motion picture. Wait for us. There is something to eat for you in the kitchen. Mother."

He crumples up the note in his fist. He goes to the kitchen. At the table everything is ready for him. He looks into the icebox—there is also food there. He opens the waste-disposal chute door and throws the note down it. He goes into his own room —all the furnishings in it are quite modest: dumbbells lie on the floor, a tennis racket hangs on the wall in clamps. He goes to the window and looks with a sad gaze at Moscow. He thinks about something. He goes into the bathroom.

* Russian title: *A B V D G*, first published in the magazine *Yunost*, No. 9 (Sept. 1961).

156

He is again in his own room. He is changing his clothes—putting on a good suit. He looks at himself in the mirror, but evidently even in his new appearance he is still dissatisfied with himself. He goes out.

The Scene Changes.

Gorky Street at evening time—noisy and crowded. Among the crowd of those walking about are Volodya and a girl.

GIRL. I was lonely without you. How about you?

VOLODYA. I am always lonely.

GIRL. Vovka, tell me, what are you thinking about all the time, thinking, thinking?

VOLODYA. I have brains—so I think.

GIRL. I also have brains.

VOLODYA. You don't have those perplexities.

GIRL. Thank God.

VOLODYA. For certain.

GIRL. One can go crazy.

VOLODYA. Not excluded.

GIRL. But tell me, about what?

VOLODYA (half serious). About the fact the world is imperfect, uncompleted.

GIRL. So what! What's it to you!

VOLODYA. You want it to whirl about in that state?

GIRL. A fact.

VOLODYA (with sadness). So let it! (The girl takes a photograph of herself out of her purse.)

GIRL. Shall I give it to you?

VOLODYA (indifferently). Of course. (He takes the photograph and puts it in his jacket pocket.)

GIRL. Vovka, don't try to act as if you are better than others: people don't like it when others think they're better than them. I've noticed.

VOLODYA. So I'll be not the tops but the bottom. Is that what you want?

GIRL. The bottom—that's too much.

VOLODYA. I don't want to be average!

They approach a cafe: Dance music is heard from it. Volodya opens the door and lets the girl through ahead of him.

The Scene Changes.

At home at Volodya's apartment. It is very late. The light in the windows has been dimmed. His father sits in an armchair and reads. His mother goes about the room from one corner to another.

FATHER. Go to bed, Olga. It's already half past one.

MOTHER. I don't think we can make our trip, Kostya. We can't leave him alone. He'll go completely to pieces.

FATHER. Yes, indeed, I guess we can't make the trip.

MOTHER. Kostya, what can we do with him?

FATHER (puts aside his book, and in general it is clear that his thoughts were not occupied by the book). I don't know myself. He has everything. There is nothing for him to strive for. And so he goes mad. Just remember our own youth . . .

MOTHER. No, Kostya, no! All people must live free from material dependence.

FATHER (in a rage). And I say to you: Yes, we are to blame for everything—both you and I!

There can be heard the slamming of a door in the vestibule. Steps along the parquet floor. It is Volodya, going to his room.

FATHER. Vladimir!

VOLODYA'S VOICE. What?

FATHER. Come here.

VOLODYA'S VOICE. I am going to bed.

The father gets up from his chair, and goes to his son's room. The mother also goes to Volodya's room.

FATHER. You might at least say hello . . .

MOTHER. He probably thought we were asleep.

VOLODYA. How do you do!

FATHER. Do you consider it normal that we should be waiting for you till two o'clock in the morning?

VOLODYA. No, you should have been asleep long ago.

FATHER. Look here, Vladimir . . .

VOLODYA. Papa, can I ask you one favor?

FATHER. Yes.

VOLODYA. Please don't talk with me. I'm in a very bad mood as it is.

FATHER (shouts). What is so "bad"? What?

MOTHER (to the father). Wait a while, Kostya. (To her son.) Right up to the last year in school—the 10th grade—you got very good marks, especially in physics.

VOLODYA. Only because you were the teacher in it . . . I would have been ashamed in front of the rest of my friends. They might have thought I was getting decent marks because of pull: So I worked hard and learned everything by heart.

MOTHER. It's not true. I can always distinguish a talented pupil from one who pretends to be . . . Perhaps it's saying too much, but I

think you are very talented . . . That's a rare thing, Volodya . . .
Why did you drop everything?

VOLODYA. It's repulsive to be a physicist.

MOTHER. Why don't I think so then?

VOLODYA. And why do I have to think like you?

FATHER. Don't you dare talk that way to your mother!

VOLODYA. I don't want to be a physicist because I don't like science.

MOTHER. Why?

VOLODYA. Because people invent color television and tape recorders.
They are ready to discover the secrets of protein and to fly to
the moon. But from all this they don't become either more
honest or happier.

FATHER. Just see what nonsense he has in his head! You finished ten
years of school and you owe . . .

VOLODYA. I don't owe anybody anything! I didn't even get into this
world before I began to hear: "You owe, owe, owe!" I don't
owe anybody anything!

FATHER (in a rage). I know why you are like this! Your mother and
I forever strained our muscles, our brains, and did everything
for you . . . And so your muscles are flabby, lazy, weak!

VOLODYA (jumps up). So why did you do it? Did I ask you to?

FATHER (without listening). You don't want to take up anything in
life—either bad or good.

VOLODYA. Not true. I love everything good. And you are satisfied with
both good and bad! You are used to it!

FATHER (not listening). You and those like you come to everything
when it is all ready. And you discuss it, condemn it, and only
make wry faces!

VOLODYA (laughs). Ready for what? For what . . . You so love to read
the newspapers . . . Just what is it that is all ready, finished in
the world? You are probably referring to this apartment which
you just recently received, to meals . . . a piece of bread . . . You
think in very narrow terms—that's what.

MOTHER. Don't you dare to talk that way, Volodya! You were born
in 1942. Your father received the news of your birth on the
front near Rostov. They drank to your birth in a wet foxhole!
For you! You were going on four when your father returned.
That was the first time he had seen you . . . And he told me that
it was you who brought him out of the war alive, because all
the time he thought about you! He had you. He had you!

VOLODYA. I don't love sentimentality, mother.

FATHER. Don't you dare to tell him anything! Don't you dare! He's
an unfeeling beast, a jackass!

VOLODYA. Well, the circus has begun again!

FATHER (to the mother). Do you hear that! Do you hear that!

VOLODYA. In the end all your arguments come down to bad language.

> *A heavy pause.*

MOTHER. Why don't you respect us, Vova?

> *Volodya is silent.*

MOTHER. Why?

> *Volodya is still silent.*

MOTHER. Don't you want to answer?

> *Volodya is still silent.*

VOLODYA. And now can I go to sleep?

MOTHER. Lie down. And remember, Vova. There is only one road to the truth and there are as many roads as you please to error.

VOLODYA. Maybe that's also not a truth, mother.

> *Volodya is asleep. The door opens quietly. His mother enters. She goes up to Volodya. She listens to his breathing. She sits down beside him. She looks at him. She pats him on the head and all of a sudden she sees two little teardrops roll from Volodya's eyes down his cheeks. She understands that Volodya is not asleep. She is disturbed. She stands up and quietly goes out of the room.*
>
> *Sunday morning in the same apartment. Volodya's parents are having their breakfast. Volodya comes out of his room and after saying "Good morning," sits down at the table. His mother pours him out tea.*

VOLODYA. If you please, I would like to have coffee instead.

MOTHER. All right. (She goes into the kitchen. Father and son do not say anything for a while.)

FATHER. How are things at work?

VOLODYA. I already quit my job on the railroad.

FATHER. Again you don't like it? What's wrong?

VOLODYA. I don't know.

FATHER. Where are you going now?

VOLODYA. I haven't decided yet.

> *His mother comes in and serves him coffee. They breakfast in silence.*

FATHER. Again he's quit work.

MOTHER. Maybe you would like to go with us to Essentuki?

VOLODYA. I don't like the people at resorts.

MOTHER. It's not a matter of a resort—your father and I have to take a cure.

FATHER. He needs a cure too.

VOLODYA. Mineral waters aren't going to help me.

FATHER. What you need is a sniff of life.

VOLODYA. I am sniffing it. (His father wants to say something but Volodya interrupts him.) Let's not continue our argument of yesterday, papa. Are you afraid to leave me all by myself? (Pause. Volodya understands he was not wrong.) Yes, I can see I really stick in your throats ... (Again a pause.) I wouldn't mind myself taking off for wherever I feel like ... Yes! Don't we have some kind of kinfolk somewhere out in the sticks?

FATHER. In the first place, not in the sticks, but out beyond the Urals. And in the second place, not *some* kind of kinfolk, but your own uncle, my own brother ...

VOLODYA. I wouldn't mind going to visit him. Well?

FATHER. I'm not against it. It wouldn't be a bad thing. Vasily was a famous partisan.

VOLODYA. You know, for me all authorities are relative.

MOTHER. You're cynical, Vladimir.

VOLODYA. You would want me to say what I don't think.

MOTHER. No, that would be still worse. What I would like is for you to think otherwise.

VOLODYA. Wait a while. Probably with time I'll be broken.

MOTHER. We don't want you to "be broken."

VOLODYA. All are ...

MOTHER. You are hinting at us? But take into consideration: we grew up in a more complicated time. It's easier for you. It's much easier for you.

VOLODYA. I don't think so. But don't worry. I will go away.

The Scene Changes.

> *A very small provincial town.*

> *Volodya's uncle and Volodya are walking from the station to the town. The uncle is carrying a handsome, large suitcase for his nephew. Volodya is carrying a small weekend bag. They walk around puddles. They jump over ditches. Clinging to the fence, they skirt piles of earth in places where construction work is under way.*

> *Volodya is dressed quite elegantly. The few passersby look at him with interest. Some curious people even stick their heads out of their windows to see him. His uncle, doffing his cap, exchanges greetings with almost every person he meets. Evidently he knows everyone in this town and everyone knows him. The uncle and his nephew walk around a pile of sand.*

UNCLE (as if apologizing for the disorder). That's the new Collective Farmer Hostelry. It will have 42 cots ... There will be two stories ... (And he exchanges greetings, evidently with the construction superintendent.)

UNCLE. How is everything?

ZAKHARYCH. We're getting along. (He looks at Volodya.)

UNCLE (again as if apologizing, but this time to Zakharych). And I was just at the station to meet my nephew ...

They go along further.

UNCLE (feeling he has to say something). Our city is small, not Moscow, not Karaganda, but it has prospects ... And right here there used to be a smithy. Now it's being equipped as a machine shop ...

VOLODYA. And have you lived in this city for a long time?

UNCLE. All my life ... Except, of course, when I was in the war—subtract four years. Well, and now and then I am sent on business trips ... And your father was born here, in this same house in which I live right now. I suppose you'll enjoy finding out about your father's childhood, what?

But Volodya doesn't answer. He is deep in his own thoughts. And evidently these thoughts are calm, undisturbed.

UNCLE. The nursery school here was opened during the last May holidays ... (He sees a woman on the porch of the nursery school.) How do you do, Tatyana Semyenovna!

TATYANA SEMYENOVNA. How do you do, Vasily Nikolayevich!

UNCLE. How is everything?

TATYANA SEMYENOVNA (pointing to the herd of children). Busy!

She looks at Volodya.

UNCLE. This is my nephew, from Moscow, Vladimir ... My brother's son ... (And he walks briskly ahead. They are silent.) This is a bath that is being built.

VOLODYA. How many washtubs?

UNCLE. Washtubs I don't know, but twig brooms there will be ... Birch ones ...

VOLODYA (laughs). Uncle, well indeed! It turns out you are alive after all!

UNCLE (drily). And you, my boy, are a pig.

VOLODYA (sadly). That I know.

And again they walk along in silence. The only sound is the squelching of their shoes in the mud.

A volleyball court is next to the house in which Volodya's uncle and his family live. Girls and boys are playing volleyball. Among those playing is Sima.

Anna Ilinichna looks out the window of the house.

ANNA ILINICHNA. Serafima, that's not nice. Come into the house this minute. They're coming right away.

SIMA (without breaking off the game). I'm not coming. So what! So a spoiled brat is coming! You said yourselves he should be taken in hand. And now you have organized a whole welcome! (She hits the ball.)

The uncle and Volodya approach the house.

UNCLE. That's your cousin—the towhead, in the green dress . . .

VOLODYA. Uncle, take this for a minute . . .

He throws off his jacket and gives it to his uncle. He runs out onto the volleyball court and with all his might hits the ball straight at Sima. He hits it so hard that Sima falls down. Volodya runs up to her, lifts her up, and kisses her on her lips. He kisses her in fun, like a brother.

SIMA (completely taken aback, in confusion). What are you doing? Are you crazy?

VOLODYA. As if you've never been kissed?

He laughs. Sima throws herself on him and begins to beat him with her fists on his back and shoulders. Volodya laughs. Sima sees her father, who is also laughing, and finally understands that this is her cousin, Vladimir.

UNCLE. Give it to him! Let him get acquainted with us. (He goes up closer.) So you've gotten acquainted. (To Volodya.) Her name is Serafima—Sima, in other words. And those are her friends. They just finished school. Get acquainted . . . (To the boys.) This is my nephew, Serafima's cousin, Vladimir. (Volodya says hello to all of them. The boys and girls look at him, not without curiosity.) Let's go into the house and annihilate some of Anna Ilinichna's pies! (To Volodya.) Now you can wash and clean up from your trip . . .

The uncle's home.

Sima and Volodya are on the back porch in the courtyard. Volodya takes his large suitcase and puts it on the step. He looks about at the beautiful landscape.

VOLODYA. What beauty!

SIMA. Beautiful enough.

VOLODYA. Yes, but if one lives here a month, one would want to hang himself from boredom with that beauty!

Sima leads Volodya to the wash-hand-stand. She shows it to him.

SIMA. The water is here. There is the dipper. And there is the soap. Here's a towel. There's no bathroom.

VOLODYA (taking his linen out of his suitcase). I sympathize with you.

He gets out the things he needs. He goes to the wash-hand-stand which hangs from a cord.

VOLODYA. How am I to deal with this latest development of modern technology?

Sima rocks the wash-hand-stand and water pours out.

VOLODYA. How lovely! Well, let's go back to the old folks!

He takes off his shirt. Sima feels herself awkward, embarrassed, and goes out.

Sima changes her clothes in her own room. Family and group of young people all sit at the table, on which are the samovar and Russian pies.

VOLODYA. I can't believe my eyes . . . like stage scenery! (He laughs. He really is in an excellent mood.)

UNCLE. What's the news from Moscow?

VOLODYA. No news as always.

UNCLE. You don't say . . . We know from the newspapers, yes and from the radio: there is reconstruction going on there . . .

VOLODYA. That's the way it has been ever since I can remember. It's always going on, going on, and on . . .

UNCLE. So you finished school last year?

VOLODYA. Yes.

UNCLE. Are you working?

VOLODYA. I'm trying . . . I've already left two jobs.

UNCLE. You're fastidious?

VOLODYA. Possibly. I myself don't understand.

UNCLE. Take hold of some one thing and stick to it.

VOLODYA. It doesn't stick. I tried.

UNCLE. Take hold of yourself.

VOLODYA. How?

UNCLE. Well, this way . . . (He clenches his fists as if to shake himself up a bit—he makes a kind of a movement people make in order to show: take yourself in hand, straighten up!) This way!

VOLODYA (repeats the gesture). I even tried such gestures. They don't help.

UNCLE. Work, brother, work! Work—it ennobles a human being.

VOLODYA. Possibly.

UNCLE. It's not I, brother, who said that—but Gorky.

VOLODYA. And you believe him?

UNCLE. Whom? Gorky?

VOLODYA. Yes, Aleksei Maksimovich . . .

UNCLE. Don't joke, brother, about such things.

MITYA. He just doesn't want to work. He wants to go into the university right away.

UNCLE. Well, well, Mitya! Fight with the Muscovite. You're a lad of principles.

VOLODYA. Mitya, that's the worst of it all, that I don't even want to go to the university!

MITYA. That's interesting. And who are you going to live off of?

VOLODYA. Mama and papa!

MITYA. And that suits you?

VOLODYA. Completely. It's simply wonderful! And everything is clear to you in life?

MITYA (he also becomes arrogant). Yes. Everything!

VOLODYA. God! How happy you are!

UNCLE. No, nevertheless, you tell us whether you have some desires, some dreams? What would you like to do, you know, something remarkable, unusual? What?

VOLODYA. My daydreams, uncle, are the most wonderful! Well, for example, to destroy all the self-satisfied asses, thieves, careerists, bootlickers, opportunists, hypocritical little souls on the earth . . .

UNCLE. It's not a bad business, brother, but not so easy . . .

VOLODYA. And sometimes I think it's simply impossible! And so I think maybe the whole earth should be blown to hell! Destroy the whole thing in one sweep! Let's begin it all over again from the beginning, from one-celled beings. Maybe those others will be lucky!

UNCLE. What I'm afraid of, Vladimir, is that in wrath and in a fit of temper you can do worse than those against whom you protest . . .

VOLODYA. Comrades, my mama and papa taught me everything. The best teachers of Moscow tried—so to speak, the leading lights of pedagogy! And it did no good. So don't take the trouble. The coefficient of efficiency will be equal to zero, I swear! I warn you! I have long since learned by heart all of those basic truths—A, and B, and C, and D . . . They are stuck in my teeth and I am sick of them . . . For heaven sakes, let me rest from them . . .

MITYA. Rest from what?

SECOND BOY. He's so tired, the poor little chap!

FIRST GIRL. Just think, what a V.I.P. has come! An unrecognized genius!

VOLODYA (beginning to be angry). Goodness! Help! I surrender! (He raises his arms.)

UNCLE (he begins to become angry). Don't make a clown of yourself. Your father and your mother write in a letter that we should make a human being out of you . . .

VOLODYA (taken aback). They wrote that to you?

UNCLE. Yes . . . And we are going to try . . .

VOLODYA (stunned). Make a human being out of me? That means I am not a human being? Good! You are going to make a human being out of me . . . According to your image and the likes of you! You, my dear dullness and mediocrity!

BOYS. You should be ashamed! Disgrace! What kind of a way to act is that!

Volodya jumps up from behind a table and knocks a piece of pie to the floor.

UNCLE. Pick it up!

VOLODYA. Just think—I knocked the consecrated bread onto the floor! Heavens alive! What a misfortune! Sacrilege! You earned it with sweat, with labor, on the virgin land!

ANNA ILINICHNA. I baked it for your arrival, Vovochka!

VOICES. Hooligan! *Stilyaga!* He should be sent up! Scum!

UNCLE. Now look here, my half-baked philosopher, it's not for nothing that I was the chief of a partisan detachment and that I have eleven decorations . . .

VOLODYA. You're going to beat me?

ANNA ILINICHNA (to her husband). Vasya! (She is really frightened for her husband.)

VOLODYA (loudly and coldly). What time does the train leave for Moscow from your two-bit town?

A pause. All are silent.

VOLODYA (continues). So I got acquainted with you. I'm pleased. Everywhere it's one and the same thing! Hell! (He wants to take his suitcase, but Sima grabs hold of the handle.) Let me go! (He tears away the suitcase and from out of it there scatter shirts, neckties, money, socks, underwear, and a bottle of liquor . . .)

Volodya is ashamed. Everyone sees his personal things.

FIRST BOY. Carrying liquor!

VOLODYA. It was a gift for my uncle, stupid! (He kicks about all his belongings.) So what, I can travel light. Adieu, my happy people! (He opens the door with a kick and runs out onto the street.) *Pause.*

FIRST BOY. He won't go away! He won't go away without money . . . He'll come back crawling! We'll work him over!

UNCLE. Serafima! Catch him! Bring him back! Do you hear!

Sima grabs her jacket and hurls herself out of the door.

UNCLE. How bad that I exploded . . . Blurted out about my decorations . . . A bad show . . .

ANNA ILINICHNA. We all started to yell . . . And when people yell no good comes of it.

The Scene Changes.
    The railway station.

Two clangs of the railway bell. The train is ready for departure. It's a small station with a plank platform and a very few people seeing the train off. A drizzling rain.

VOICE ON THE LOUDSPEAKER: Citizen passengers! Train Number 72 from Khabarovsk to Moscow will depart in five minutes. Will those who are not passengers please leave the train immediately?

Volodya runs across the station square swiftly. He runs through the station. He is on the platform. He grabs hold of the handrails of the first railway car to which he comes. The conductor stops him and does not allow him to go into the car.

CONDUCTOR. Your ticket, citizen.

VOLODYA. I have a ticket. I have a ticket. (He tries to get up onto the railway car platform.)

CONDUCTOR (stopping Volodya). Show it to me.

VOLODYA. I didn't have a chance to buy it . . . I will buy it at the next station.

CONDUCTOR. You can't, citizen, it's not permitted. (Volodya pulls money from his jacket pocket and shows it to the conductor.)

VOLODYA. There, you see, I can pay . . . (He tries to charm her into letting him by.) Please, my girl, we can reach an agreement . . . I need it very much . . .

CONDUCTOR. What kind of outrage is that! What kind of a girl am I to you! I have a youngest child who is older than you. He is finishing an institute . . . And you want to "come to an agreement" with me . . . What does that mean . . . Do you want to bribe me? Yes? Get off!

The train leaves the station. The conductor tries to tear Volodya's hand off the handbars.

VOLODYA. Don't touch my hand! (He wants to force his way into the car. The citizen who is standing on the railway car platform loses his temper.)

CITIZEN. You should be ashamed of yourself, you good-for-nothing!

The citizen throws Volodya off from the bottom step by main strength. His money flies out of his hand. Volodya flies onto the wet boards of the platform and slides along them on his entire body. The people on the platform watch this scene and even gasp. Several run to help Volodya, but he pushes them away rudely.

Dirty, disheveled, with a face frenzied with wrath and humiliation, he runs vainly after the train which is picking up speed.

Somewhere behind the people and the fences, parallel to him, Sima is running.

Volodya is already running along the ties behind the train which is going ever farther and farther away from him.

Sima is also running along the railway right-of-way, chasing Volodya.

SIMA. Voval

Volodya continues running without turning.

SIMA. Voval

Volodya is running without turning about.

SIMA. Voval

Volodya does not hear her and continues to run.

They both dash along the ties, and it is as if they are running a race or as if they had gone crazy. Sima makes a desperate effort and catches up with Volodya. She grabs him by the hand. Volodya stops, stands still, and does not even understand who is in front of him. He breathes with a gasp. His eyes are burning. He looks as if a snake were just about to jump out of his mouth.

VOLODYA. All right! All right! I'll show them!

SIMA. Whom?

VOLODYA. I'll show them! They want to make a human being out of me! I'll walk all the way home afoot, on my hands and feet, on all fours ... But I'll show them! I'll show them!

He wants to go. Sima tries to hold him back. He pushes her away sharply. It's just as if he hadn't even seen her. He shoves her away as if she were some inanimate object.

The train has long since disappeared in the distance, but Volodya, seized with fury, walks swiftly along the ties. Sima runs behind him. Volodya's face is cold and vicious. He is walking with an even, energetic rhythm. The city is already out of sight. All about lie forests, fields, villages in the distance ...

SIMA (out of breath, shouting). There's a train coming from behind! A train! Get off the track!

Volodya without turning around gets off the track onto the shoulder alongside and continues at the same speed. A heavy freight train, loaded with machinery, thunders past ...

Just as rapidly Volodya continues his course further along the ties. Sima is behind him and has a hard time keeping up. It is clear that both he and she are tired.

The landscape has already changed ... Evidently, they have already gone a long distance. Ahead can be seen a flag station.

SIMA. That is Shchukino ... The through train stops at it only for one minute—and only the one going to Vladivistock ... Do you have money for your ticket?

Volodya is silent.

SIMA. Do you have money for your ticket? Or was all of it in your suitcase?

Volodya does not answer.

SIMA. I have three rubles. (She pulls out of her jacket pocket a three-ruble note and waves it at him.) We can go back, on the local train ... They leave here often. It costs 50 kopecks ... I was at the peat-diggings in Shchukino for a whole month ...

They approach the flag station. Volodya is tired. He sits down on a beam lying not far from the railway track. Sima sits down beside him ...

SIMA. My father, of course, got angry with you, but just the same he is worried about you ... And about me also ... It's all right, we can get home by dinnertime ... I will buy the tickets ...

Sima goes for tickets. Volodya sits on the beams, his arms around his knees. He looks down at the ground. The noise of the train can be heard. Sima runs back. The locomotive whistles.

SIMA. A train! Let's go ...

Volodya does not move.

SIMA. You don't even have to think about it twice ... When you get back everything will work out. You'll see. I know my father. You did say things that hurt him ... (Volodya makes some kind of an indefinite movement.) Well, I'm not going to try to talk you into anything, I won't! In the worst case you'll take your money and leave ... Tomorrow ... You can't spend the night here ... (The whistle comes closer.) It's coming!

Volodya gets up, goes to the train. They go up to the railway cars.

SIMA. We can get in any car ... Get into that one there. It's almost empty ... In 20 minutes we'll be home ...

Volodya walks along.

SIMA (continuing). Get on! Get on! It's moving ... (She climbs up on the first step and reaches out her hand to Volodya.) Come on, come on ... (The train moves. Volodya walks past. Sima jumps down from the steps and follows him. They go in one direction and the train goes in the other.)

SIMA (she shouts, almost weeping). Volodya! Volodya!

The train has disappeared. Volodya goes ahead and Sima behind.

SIMA. Are you really going to walk on foot all the way to Moscow? You're crazy, that's the truth!

The Scene Changes.

It gets dark. A freight train thunders past. Volodya walks more slowly than before but in rhythm. Sima already has as much as she can do just to drag along behind him. She falls behind and breaks a heel.

SIMA. Volodya, wait for me! I broke a heel! Wait for me! I can't... (She jumps after Volodya. She is almost weeping.) Volodya, please wait! (She sobs.)

Volodya stops all of a sudden and turns about sharply on Sima.

VOLODYA (spitefully). Why did you attach yourself to me? Well? Why are you trailing along behind me? Well, why don't you say something?

SIMA. Do you think I thought you... I, quite by accident... Papa told me...

VOLODYA. So go on back to your papa.

He goes ahead. He turns back. Sima is still following him.

VOLODYA. What did I tell you? Go back!

SIMA. You've gone out of your head! Where can I go alone? At night ... I am afraid...

VOLODYA (threateningly). Go home, I'm telling you!

He makes a motion in the direction of Sima. Sima runs away.

VOLODYA. If you come after me—look out! You hear!

He goes ahead. In a little while he turns around. Sima is still there. They stand there one facing the other like two enemies.

VOLODYA. What are you doing, mocking me? Ugh! You should be sitting at home and blowing on tea from your samovar together with your boring friends... Everything's so wonderful for you in this world, so unrebellious! Go play your baby games! Well, beat it, get out! Do you hear me?

They stand silently. Sima remains at a respectful distance from him. She moves clumsily. Her one leg is shorter than the other—her heel is in her hand.

VOLODYA (continues). Just remember one thing. Whether you are behind me or not doesn't interest me. Don't make any claims for politeness. You all have the same way: You drive a person to madness and then you yourselves exclaim: "Oh, what a rude boy!" I am a rude boy, do you understand!

He goes ahead. Sima follows him. Volodya once more turns about, but he says nothing.

It begins to drizzle. Sima is barefoot. She is carrying her shoes in her hand.

On one side there can be seen the roofs of a brickworks and piles of bricks.

The rain begins to rage. Volodya turns off the railway right-of-way and goes along a path to the brickworks.

SIMA. Where are you going?

Volodya does not answer. He shelters himself from the rain under the roof of a brick dryer. Sima stands not far from him.

SIMA. What are they thinking at home . . . Ai, yai, yai, yai, yai! I'm hungry . .

VOLODYA. At the first station you're going to cast off for home. Do you understand?

SIMA. And you?

VOLODYA. That doesn't concern you.

A pause. The rain pours.

SIMA. I understand you. Right now you're irritated. And you feel as if you were all alone on the whole earth. Alone, alone, all alone! I also feel that way sometimes. Sometimes all of a sudden I become sad, so sad! It's as if no one needs you . . . I even cry . . . I sob, I sob, and then it's so sweet in my soul . . . And I feel so sorry, sorry for myself . . .

VOLODYA. Stop muttering, silly!

Sima is hurt. Pause. The rain beats on the roof. Sima sucks her finger.

SIMA. I think I have a splinter in my finger. Look at it, please.

She reaches out her hand to Volodya's face. Volodya beats Sima's hand.

VOLODYA. Leave me alone, do you hear!

Sima is hurt again. Volodya thinks with concentration. Sima tries to put the heel on her shoe.

SIMA (shyly). Couldn't you fix it, Vova?

Volodya is silent. Then Sima shyly reaches out to him her spoiled shoe.

SIMA. Look at it . .

Volodya grabs her shoe and with all his might flings it over the pile of bricks somewhere into the bushes. Sima starts to run after her shoe, but Volodya by this time is running out underneath the pouring rain. Sima, fearing to lose Volodya, dashes after him. Volodya runs to a barn, opens the door, goes in and Sima follows him.

In the barn there are pigs, chickens. It's dry, there's a smell of hay, of manure . . . The chickens cluck with alarm and the pigs grunt . . . Volodya drops down on a pile of hay in the corner. Sima climbs up into the hayloft.

All of a sudden Volodya gets up and goes to the door.

SIMA (with alarm, quietly, in a whisper). Where are you going?

VOLODYA (also in a whisper, since they are in someone else's barn). You just come after me and you'll see.

SIMA (understanding). Oh! Will you come back?

VOLODYA. Yes.

SIMA. You give me your word of honor?

> *But Volodya does not answer. He goes out. Sima waits with alarm. Yet she is ashamed to look out the door. Volodya comes back.*

SIMA. I am going to run out for a moment too ... (She goes out.)

> *Volodya again lies down in the corner on the hay. His face is upward. His eyes are tired but hard. Sima returns.*

SIMA. I also looked for my shoe. I didn't find it. (She climbs back up on the hayloft.) What is my father thinking now? They're going to go crazy before we return tomorrow. Ai, yai! What have I done! And they're also, of course, worried about you ... Vova! Are you there, Vova! Are you sleeping?

> *Quiet. We do not know whether Volodya is asleep or not. Quiet. In the distance there is the whistle of a passing train.*
>
> *The morning. It's light in the barn. The chickens are wandering about. The pigs are champing. Sima awakes. She looks on the face of the sleeping Volodya. He, evidently, feels her insistent look and opens his eyes, but at this moment the door of the barn opens and a farm woman comes in. She is a young woman of twenty-four. She gives fodder to the piglets, feed to the chickens, gathers the eggs from the nests. Behind her enters a young man, her husband. He unbuttons his shirt on the way.*

WOMAN (laughing). So why are you following me into the pigsty!

MAN. I love you. We're married for three months and I still can't believe it ... I love you ...

> *He embraces her. He kisses her with passion. So it seems. Both laugh happily.*

SHE. Let me go!

HE. Just a minute ...

SHE. Do you love me?

HE. I love ...

SHE. And I ... also ... very much ...

> *He kisses her face, her neck, her breast, her shoulders.*

SHE. Let me go ... Don't squeeze me ... Grisha, we're going to have a little one ...

HE (stunned). What do you say!

SHE. The doctor said so ...

HE (triumphantly). But no ... Is it true? A boy?

SHE. Do you think I know?

HE. A boy ... Vaska! Vaska it will be! Vaska! My darling! You are my beloved love!

He again embraces her but tenderly, tenderly. They laugh. They kiss with a long kiss.

SHE. Go and eat. It's your shift soon ... Now look here, don't tell one soul. See to it!

HE. I understand. A secret!

They laugh quietly and happily for a long time. They go out.

Volodya hears this conversation. He gets up, brushes the hay off himself. Sima mechanically puts on one shoe and looks for the other and then remembers. Nevertheless she takes the one shoe along. They descend.

They walk through the courtyard of a poultry farm, past tubs with water which stand beneath a drainpipe. It is an early clear morning after the rain. The tubs are full of water and the water reflects the sky above and the faces of Volodya and Sima who want to wash themselves. Volodya and Sima, scooping up water, wash. During this time the collective farm woman who was in the barn walks past them. Volodya and Sima drop their eyes. They are silent and look at one another out of the corners of their eyes. Volodya wipes himself off with his handkerchief. All of a sudden Sima notices something on the bottom of a tub.

SIMA. Look here, look here! (She puts her hand into the tub up to her very shoulder and pulls out her shoe without a heel. She looks it over.) It's too bad! Those are my very best—they were bought for graduation—I only put them on once ... (Turning away, she wipes off her face and her hands with the edge of her skirt.) Shall we go back? Or to the siding 12 kilometers further?

Volodya, without uttering one word, as if Sima were not there with him, goes ahead.

And again Volodya and Sima walk along the tracks. They encounter a trackwalker who is checking the tracks. His face is cut across by a scar.

TRACKMAN. Where are you going, young people?

SIMA. We got left behind by our train. From the Moscow train ... We stopped in a field. He (pointing at Volodya) got out of the car to pick flowers for me and I went after him, and the train went away ... We ran, but what was the use! It went away ...

TRACKMAN. You foolish children! A train is a material object—it doesn't wait. You've been pattering along for a long while?

SIMA. Since yesterday evening!

TRACKMAN. Goodness! What a thing! Are you hungry?

SIMA. Very.

TRACKMAN. Come to my house, I'll feed you. Maybe I can call ahead for you . . . And I have been inspecting the tracks here. Pretty soon it will be the 42nd kilometer. Where are you from?

SIMA. Muscovites.

TRACKMAN. Eh! Such important people! (To Volodya.) And why are you so sad?

VOLODYA. On the contrary, I am very joyful.

TRACKMAN. Adventure!

SIMA (to Volodya). Let's go in . . . We can rest a bit . . . (Very quietly.) Maybe they'll feed us . . .

Volodya doesn't answer, but it is clear that he agrees to go to the trackman's house. They approach the railwayman's booth. They see the trackman's wife and his son, age 10.

TRACKMAN. Marusia, welcome our unfortunate guests. They missed the Moscow train. I'm going to call ahead for them. And while I do you put something to eat on the table. Sit down, young friends. What are you? Boy friend, girl friend? Pardon my immodest question.

SIMA. Brother and sister.

TRACKMAN. So that's what it is. (He says this with some kind of an unconvinced intonation.)

SIMA. Word of honor.

TRACKMAN. Perhaps you are. How is everything in Moscow?

SIMA. Everything is just as it's always been . . . Excellent.

TRACKMAN (to Volodya). Listen, here's what you can tell me right away. You in Moscow know the real truth. Will there be a war or not?

WIFE. Well, you certainly found what to talk about! How boring can you be!

VOLODYA. What have you to be afraid of? Your booth is out at the end of nowhere. The bombs aren't going to fall on you.

TRACKMAN. Crazy! I'm not asking for my own sake. I, so to speak, think in general terms, for all of humanity.

VOLODYA. Well, and humanity is behaving itself so badly that perhaps it ought to be punished a little bit.

WIFE. Shall I put on the teakettle?

TRACKMAN. After all, I'm asking a question, not joking.

VOLODYA. I'm being serious too.

The mistress of the house sets the table. The little boy watches from out of the corner.

TRACKMAN (sullen). So that's the way it stands! It sounds as if you were sort of not against . . .

VOLODYA. No one is going to ask me.

TRACKMAN. And if they asked?

VOLODYA. They don't ask.

TRACKMAN. But nevertheless?

VOLODYA. I don't care.

TRACKMAN (all wilted). So that's the way it is!

WIFE. Eat, dear guests!

TRACKMAN. No, you wait with your food! (He strikes his fist on the table.)

WIFE. So you've let yourself go! (To Volodya and Sima.) He was shell-shocked in the war, in a tank ... He lost his first wife with his little children in Gomel. Little Lenya and I are his second family ... (To her husband.) The young man is simply chattering, wagging his tongue ... Well, why don't you say something? (To Volodya and Sima.) Now he's going to shut up. I already know. You eat, don't pay any attention.

The trackman gets up, takes his signal flag off the wall, and goes to the door. The little boy, Lenya, looks spitefully at Volodya and runs after his father. Volodya and Sima sit at the table alone.

WIFE. Eat.

VOLODYA (gets up). Thank you. (He goes to the door and Sima follows him.)

The Scene Changes.

Beside the track stand the trackman and Lenya with a green flag, giving the train the green signal. The train approaches with thunder ... The thunder is stronger ... A hellish noise ... The boy holds the green flag ... The thunder disappears ... The train has gone past. Volodya and Sima walk along the ties. The little boy leans over, picks up a stone and throws it at Volodya ... He hits him in the back ... Volodya screws up his face with pain and turns about ... The little boy runs away ...

SIMA. Why did you talk with him that way?

VOLODYA. And why does he ask those silly questions! So tell me right now: If I should give up my life, permit myself to be cut into 100,000 little pieces and then there would be no war, I would say: please do it ... I won't even make a little noise ... If you please! Take me! That's where the whole stupidity of the situation lies: Not one human being can do anything ... There isn't any blockhouse which one can throw one's self against, with all of one's body, in order to save the situation. There isn't any! The only thing everyone does is to guess, tell fortunes, read the tea leaves, lay out the cards: will it happen or not ... (All of a sudden.) It's enough of your trailing along behind me! I've decided you're going to get a ticket—and go home. Do you understand?

SIMA. And you?

VOLODYA. Give me your money.

SIMA. Take it. (She gives him her money.)

VOLODYA. I'll buy the ticket myself.

The Scene Changes.
> *The junction.*
> *A multitude of railway lines going in different directions. On one side stands a suburban train. Volodya and Sima are on the tracks. Wind.*

VOLODYA (giving Sima the ticket). Get along with you! Here are three kopecks of small change for you. (He gives her the change.)

SIMA. Are you ashamed to return? Yes? You said awful things at my home. Terrible things! But I think it was really just from spite, from anger . . . Yes? Sometimes I do the same thing. When I get angry I say such nonsense in wrath to my father or my mother, foolishly . . . And I understood from the first glance that you are good . . .

VOLODYA. Will you stop jabbering?

SIMA. Oh you! Good luck! Are you really going on foot?

VOLODYA. It's not your business.

SIMA. You'll die.

VOLODYA. So what? Would that be so bad?

> *Sima goes up to the train and gets into the car. Volodya stands there thoughtfully. Sima sits down on the bench in an almost empty car and also thinks. Her face is inspired, perhaps, and her eyes are even moist. A railway trackman walks past Volodya.*

VOLODYA. Where does this railway go?

TRACKMAN. To Klintsy.

VOLODYA. And that one?

TRACKMAN. To Yeremino.

VOLODYA. And that one?

TRACKMAN. Where do you want to go?

VOLODYA. To Moscow.

TRACKMAN. You go on the local train to Khobotov. The Moscow train stops there, but not here . . .

VOLODYA. And which is the track to Moscow?

TRACKMAN (not understanding). That one there. (He points.) And where are you from?

> *Volodya does not answer and walks forward. The trackman follows him with his eyes.*
> *Sima is in the car. The train starts. Sima can't stand it any longer and looks out the window. Through the dusty window of the railroad car she sees the lonely figure of Volodya walking*

along the tracks. The train picks up speed. Sima all of a sudden jumps up, runs, and jumps off the lower step.

Volodya walks alone, deep in his thoughts. His cheeks are deeply sunken, probably both from walking and from hunger. All of a sudden he hears behind him the crunch of pebbles. He turns around. He sees Sima. He stops. And all of a sudden he dashes at her with a clear desire to beat her off. Sima runs away from him to one side. They run. Volodya throws sticks at Sima. Both are tired and barely, barely able to run—there is emotion but no strength.

They sit down on the shoulder: one on one side, the other on the other side. There is a train. When it has passed Sima sees that Volodya has disappeared. She is frightened. She gets up and looks for him. She goes over onto the other side. And all of a sudden he jumps out from behind a shelter and grabs Sima.

VOLODYA. Well?

Sima shrinks, fearing that he is going to give her a beating. He shakes her. But he doesn't himself know what to do with her.

VOLODYA (ominously). You're going to get aboard a train and go away —do you understand?

SIMA (shyly). Yes.

VOLODYA. Give me your word.

SIMA. Word of honor.

Volodya, not letting go of Sima, leads her along the ties like a caught beast.

The Scene Changes.

On the highway which goes along beside the railway right-of-way, there stands a truck loaded to the top. The driver is fixing something, and has the hood raised. Sima and Volodya walk fast.

VOLODYA. Hey, friend, wouldn't you drop us at the station?

DRIVER. I'd drop you off, old friend, but I only have one seat.

VOLODYA. That's all I need.

DRIVER. I thought you were with the young lady.

VOLODYA. The young lady is going in the other direction.

DRIVER. Then get in!

Volodya climbs into the cabin. Sima loses her head. The driver slams down the hood.

SIMA (to Volodya). What are you doing! Where are you going! And I?

The driver gets into the cabin.

SIMA. Comrade driver, don't take him, don't you dare!

VOLODYA (to the driver). Go ahead!

The driver steps on the gas and the motor roars.

SIMA (in desperation). That's my husband . . . He is leaving me . . . We have a child . . .

DRIVER (to Volodya). What's it all about?

VOLODYA. She's lying, lying. Don't listen to her—just go ahead!

SIMA. You'll catch it where it matters, you'll see! I will remember the license plate . . . You'll hear from this . . .

VOLODYA. Get going, friend, get going! She's . . .

DRIVER. No, friend, you'd better get out.

VOLODYA. It's not true . . . she's lying.

SIMA. He's lying, he!

DRIVER. The devil with both of you, the devil with you. Work it out yourselves. Get down, I'm telling you! Just get mixed up with such as you . . . Get down, I'm telling you—there's no time! (He pushes Volodya. Volodya unwillingly gets out. The truck goes ahead. Sima and Volodya look at each other.)

VOLODYA. You'll remember this!

SIMA. I'm not going to let you forget it either. (Volodya's betrayal really has hurt her.) Give me my money for my ticket. I'm going home.

   Volodya does not answer. He stops at the edge of the road, waiting for another car.

SIMA. I'm telling you: please, give me my money for the ticket.

VOLODYA (angrily). I have no money!

SIMA. What do you mean "no"?

VOLODYA. This is how! (He empties his pockets.)

SIMA (she didn't expect that). And I'm dying of hunger.

VOLODYA. And I?

The Scene Changes.

   Volodya and Sima rest, sitting on the edge of an excavation near the railway. Both are silent. Trucks scurry back and forth in the excavation, coming in unloaded and going out loaded. It's a sand pit. Sima once more tries to put the heel back on her shoe.

VOLODYA. What are you puffing about? Give it here!

   Sima readily gives him her shoes. Volodya tears the heel off the other shoe. Sima doesn't even get a chance to exclaim.

VOLODYA (handing the shoes to Sima). There you are! The latest style!

SIMA. But what am I going to do with them that way?

VOLODYA. You just set your mind at rest with sayings: "Clothes don't make the man," "Poverty is no sin." And all the rest. Get along with you!

SIMA (she tries on her shoes, walks up and down in them). Well, you know, not so bad! (Again she sits down not far away from Volodya.) I calculated in my head: if you go to Moscow on foot it's going to take a half a year ... I want to eat.

VOLODYA (he takes his jacket off). Take it, sell it.

He takes his things out of the pockets of his jacket: his key, his notebook, his fountain pen, his wallet—and puts everything in the pocket of his trousers. From out of his wallet falls a photo of the same girl he saw in Moscow.

SIMA (looking at it). Who is that?

Volodya picks up the photograph with intentional carelessness.

SIMA. Ah! You're taking it nevertheless.

VOLODYA. So what does your provincial significant tone signify?

Sima is silent.

VOLODYA. You females are all trash. You are worth exactly one kopeck. This one is simply prettier than others. I am carrying it in order to laugh at. (He snaps his fingers at the photo.)

All of a sudden Sima with all her strength pushes Volodya and he flies into the excavation, raising up clouds of sand. He drops the photograph. Sima picks up the photograph, looks at it. Then she wipes off the dust and puts it into the pocket of her own jacket. Volodya clambers up out of the excavation. He points his finger at his head, signifying that Sima is not normal. He looks for the photograph.

VOLODYA. Where is it?

SIMA. It's not here.

VOLODYA (understanding where the photo is). I'll tell her in Moscow —and she'll be surprised!

He gives Sima the jacket.

VOLODYA. Go ahead, sell it, for heaven's sake! And really, we should eat. Let's go and sell it at the station.

The Scene Changes.

The station market. Little booths built of boards at which all kinds of things are for sale—broiled chicken, dill pickles, milk, eggs, entrails, etc.

Because the express train has just arrived very many people are at the market.

Volodya and Sima offer the jacket for sale. A group of suspicious types surrounds them and examines the jacket.

FIRST. Oh, ho! It's a nice little thing.

SECOND. Trash.

THIRD. It's worth something!

The jacket goes from hand to hand among the curious. A complete ring of people has surrounded Volodya and Sima. The jacket floats ever farther away. Volodya tries to get to it. He pushes the crowd. There's a whistle of the locomotive. All run to the train. In a second the market is completely empty. Only Volodya and Sima stand in the center of it. The jacket has disappeared forever.

From out of the windows of the railway cars hands wave at them: departing women and children.

Sima and Volodya, gloomy, leave the market.

Sima searches her pockets.

SIMA. Look, three kopecks! Let's go to a bakery.

They walk along the street of the little town to a bakery.

VOLODYA. Are you in love with someone?

SIMA. Are you crazy!

VOLODYA. There's no such thing as love—remember that once and for all. And don't be a sentimental little fool. If you have a yearning for someone—get yourself in hand. Your accessibility sticks in my throat.

SIMA. I myself despise those who run about ... Even if I like someone he will never know about it. I just won't show it ... I won't make one step after him ... And have you ever loved someone?

VOLODYA. I'm telling you: there's no such thing as love, there is only reproduction.

SIMA. Tfoo! Filth! And you remember there in the barn?

VOLODYA. One out of a million.

SIMA. Maybe two?

VOLODYA. No, I don't admit two.

The Scene Changes.

Volodya and Sima are in the bakery. There's a smell of bread. Volodya cannot tear his eyes away from the window. The bread smell intoxicates him. He sees a five ruble note sticking out of the purse of the woman who is next to him. It sticks there very appealingly. Temptation.

VOLODYA. Citizeness, you are losing your money. (He points at the 5-ruble note.)

The woman counts the money in her purse and looks at Volodya suspiciously. Sima is standing in line at the cashier's window, holding in her hand 3 kopecks. Some citizen pushes her accidently. Sima drops the coin.

SIMA. Pardon me. (She turns around to the people in the line and begins to look for the 3-kopeck piece.)

Volodya goes up to Sima.

VOLODYA. What happened?

SIMA. I dropped it.

> *Both look for the coin on the floor. They look carefully for a long time, but in vain. They straighten up.*

VOLODYA. You crow!

> *Tears rain from Sima's eyes. She leaves the store.*

The Scene Changes.

> *Volodya and Sima are on a little side street of the small town. On the corner of the side street there is a bread stall at which a little boy is buying bread. Sima stops at the fence of a courtyard.*

SIMA (cries). Hello! Hello! (No one answers her.) You wait here, I will go in and find out. Maybe there's some work here. (She goes into the courtyard through the gate. Volodya waits.)

> *During this time the little boy runs across the side street from the bread stall. He has purchased rye bread and rolls. The trimmings from the bread have fallen into the dust. The little boy disappears around the corner. Volodya sees how a piece of bread has fallen. He looks about to make sure no one is looking. And, having decided, he quickly runs to the fallen piece of bread, picks it up, breaks it into two pieces, sticks one of them in his pocket, and hiding behind the corner of the house, quickly, quickly begins to eat the bread, spitting out the sand which crunches on his teeth. Having eaten his piece, he returns to his previous place.*

> *Sima comes out of the gate.*

> *The mistress of the house appears from behind the fence.*

HOUSEWIFE. You should be ashamed! You're young and healthy and you act as if you were a pauper! Lost all sense of shame! People are going to the virgin lands, to all kinds of construction projects, but not her! Go to the factory construction project. There's enough work there.

SIMA. What factory?

HOUSEWIFE. The chemical combine! As if you don't know? (She sees Volodya.) And she even has a boy friend with her. Well, what can one do with them! That's what's happening to our youth! Tfu! (She disappears behind the fence.)

> *Volodya takes out of his pocket the piece of bread and gives it to Sima.*

VOLODYA. There, swallow that.

SIMA. Where did that come from?

VOLODYA. I found it.

SIMA (gladly). Well what do you say! And you?

VOLODYA. I have already regaled myself.

> *Sima eats the bread.*
>
> *Out from behind a neighboring fence an old man sticks his head. He is not so very decrepit. He had heard the conversation of Volodya and Sima with the woman.*

OLD MAN. Semyenovna gives you speeches. And you want food—not lectures ... Come on in, kids, I'll feed you.

SIMA. We don't want it for nothing ... For work ... We would do something.

OLD MAN. Well, let it be so, you can saw some firewood for me ... You don't want to do it for nothing. I understand ... Pride ... For nothing, of course, is not good ...

> *The old man motions Volodya and Sima to the gate. Behind the gate there is a fierce dog.*

OLD MAN. Wait just a minute, I will chain Nero. It's impossible to live without dogs nowadays ...

> *He calls the dog, takes it away, and returns.*

OLD MAN. Come in, my guests. She's a vicious one, that Semyenovna. Noisy. Bad ...

> *The old man takes Sima and Volodya into the courtyard, leads them to the saw-buck, on which and next to which there lie several very substantial logs. He brings out a two-handed crosscut saw.*

OLD MAN. You go to work there for the time being! And I'll cook up something to eat ... I'll boil up some potatoes, and get some dill pickles ... What we have I'll give you ...

> *The old man goes out. Sima and Volodya saw the logs.*

SIMA. I wish he'd fed us first.

VOLODYA. Be patient, don't humiliate yourself.

> *They saw away.*

SIMA. Where did you learn that?

VOLODYA. Just think, electronic controls.

SIMA. Did you go from school to work on collective farms? Yes?

> *Volodya does not answer.*
>
> *They saw away. Evidently the logs are either oak logs or simply wet. It's hard sawing.*

SIMA. Let's catch our breath. (They stop.)

SIMA. You have become thin ... Let's go home. My father will forgive you ...

VOLODYA. Much I need his pardon ... Let's saw ...

> *He jerks the saw with bitterness. Anger gives him strength.*

SIMA. My father wants only good for you ...

VOLODYA. And I don't want good! I want evil! Clear?

SIMA. What demon has gotten into you!

VOLODYA. Yes, a demon.

SIMA. And you're so happy about it! Just think, maybe a real demon? It would be too good for you! You haven't grown up yet to a demon.

They saw away.

The old man comes out, and looks at them, repeating: "Once more! Once more!" The log finally is mastered.

OLD MAN. So that's how you do it—one, two and ready! That's what youth, strength, means! The potatoes are boiling . . . they're my own, crumbly . . . Do you like them with butter or with sour cream?

SIMA. It's all the same!

OLD MAN. I'll even get some pickled mushrooms. I love pickled mushrooms—with garlic, with currant leaves. Crunchy! My own . . . Here's what, my dear guests, while the potatoes are cooking why don't you saw away at that one? Why is it lying there all alone like an orphan . . . (He points at a log like the one they just sawed which is lying there.) Come on, give it to it—one, two and ready! (He helps them carry the log to the sawbuck. They raise it with difficulty up onto the sawbuck.) That's how! There you go! Log, you've lived your life! Zhzhik! And I will go and look to see whether the potatoes aren't ready.

He goes out.

VOLODYA. One could cook the saw in this length of time.

Sima and Volodya again go to work sawing. Sweat pours off both of them. They are very tired. Finally the log drops in two. The old man comes out.

OLD MAN. That's how—already done! I would groan and groan over it—and what does it take you? Exercise is satisfaction. Somewhere there's a little stick lying around here. Come on, kids help me . . . (He takes them up to a beam, lying alongside the fence.) It's been lying here a long time. I'm afraid it's going to begin to rot . . . One, two, three! All at once. We've raised it! (They drag the beam to the sawbuck. They put it on the sawbuck.) You don't have to saw it into small pieces, cut it into four parts. So be it. And I will go to my root cellar for the mushrooms. (He goes out.)

Sima and Volodya take up the saw. Sima has tears in her eyes. Volodya sees this.

VOLODYA. Hey, uncle!

OLD MAN. What, son?

VOLODYA. My sister is tired. You and I will saw . . .

OLD MAN. But I am going for the mushrooms . . .

VOLODYA. The devil with the mushrooms, we can eat without them . . . Come on, take ahold . . .

The old man takes the saw. Volodya begins to saw with

particular frenzy. The old man seems to fall into rhythm, but begins quickly to lose his breath.

OLD MAN. Slower, son, slower . . . Don't hurry . . .

VOLODYA. There's no use waiting, uncle. Come on, come on, faster . . .

They saw. Volodya clenches his teeth but keeps time. He exhausts the old man.

OLD MAN (giving up). Well, the devil with it . . . Let it lie there . . . Let's go into the house.

The old man's house is well-furnished and provided but he does not take his guests into his rooms but into the kitchen. Through the open doors his "chambers" can be seen.

OLD MAN. Let's sit down here in the kitchen . . . Why should we tramp up the living room . . . True?

VOLODYA. Let's go into the kitchen.

On the table there are potatoes in their skins, bread, cut into thick chunks, vegetable oil in a bottle . . . Volodya and Sima eat . . .

VOLODYA. Uncle, and where is the sour cream?

OLD MAN. What sour cream, my dear?

VOLODYA. You said.

OLD MAN. I just asked that in order to find out your taste.

VOLODYA. Bring it!

The old man is frightened.

OLD MAN. I don't know whether there is any.

VOLODYA. There is, I know.

The old man gives them the sour cream. Sima and Volodya eat. Volodya out of spite pours out all of the sour cream. They eat everything on the table and put the bread in their pockets. They go out of the courtyard. The old man runs out and lets his dog loose, but the gate has already slammed behind them. The dog barks and the old man yells behind them.

OLD MAN. *Stilyagi!*

The Scene Changes.

Sima and Volodya are on the steep embankment of a river. Volodya is lying with his face up toward the sky. Sima is sitting.

SIMA. Vovo, look how beautiful . . .

VOLODYA. I am not interested in the world, but in my place in the world.

SIMA. You have much ambition.

VOLODYA. And you?

SIMA. Not a drop.

VOLODYA. Well, so you're an insect! Without ambition a human being is a cockroach. You're a cockroach and a nonentity!

SIMA. I'm going to slap your physiognomy.

VOLODYA (laughs). Ah ha! So you've come to life. The next time don't talk nonsense. I cannot bear it when people talk about themselves: "I am not ambitious!" "I am not interested in money!" "I do not want glory!" All people are ambitious. All want money. All dream of glory. All people—are people. And they should stop pretending.

He runs to the river, takes off his clothing, and Sima also runs in order to bathe.

SIMA. Turn the other way.

VOLODYA. What airs you're putting on!

Both plunge into the water. They swim, racing against each other, and performing all kinds of stunts in front of each other.

VOLODYA. Well, provincial, it turns out that you can do a few things.

They race in the water.

VOLODYA. Are you planning on going to an institute in Moscow?

SIMA. They wouldn't admit me.

VOLODYA. You just learn to race in the water. Get yourself a good sports rating. Then they'll take you. It's infallible. Where do you want to go?

SIMA. Philology. And you?

VOLODYA. Nowhere. I'm a boy without any calling.

They get out onto the shore. They sit down on the sand.

SIMA. My father, no doubt, has by now called out the militia for us. They're looking for us!

VOLODYA. He's suffering. He's from a prehistoric breed.

Sima all of a sudden slaps Volodya in the face.

VOLODYA. Haven't you had enough arguments?

SIMA. You know very well that I am their adopted daughter. You might have just a little bit of tact.

Volodya goes into the bushes to wring out his underpants. Sima goes in the other direction. They come out from their shelters, carrying their wet things, and hang them on the bushes. Sima sits down again on the sand. Volodya goes up to her.

VOLODYA. I swear that I did not know that you were adopted. Is that a fact?

SIMA. My father found me in the forests of Pinsk in 1944, when he was commanding a partisan detachment ... They say I was not a year old ...

VOLODYA. To whom do you belong?

SIMA. We do not know ... We've made so many inquiries, everywhere we could think ...

VOLODYA. What's your name?

SIMA. What do you mean?

VOLODYA. No, I asked: how were you named when you were born?

SIMA. How could I know?

VOLODYA. Just a minute, just a minute! So you could be Zina? Galya? Vera? Tonya? Fekla? Lena? Ulyana? So? Well, tell me, who are you?

SIMA. Leave me alone, if you please!

VOLODYA. You are no one! Do you understand that! You are not you! You are a secret, a riddle! How lovely!

SIMA. Oh, so now you've had something to eat and you're having a good time. Oh you! Ordinarily people when they learn I am an orphan begin to pity me, and you . . .

VOLODYA. Pity? You? For what? It's just a plain fact that all the people in the world are boring and dull! Listen! And perhaps you are a Ukrainian? A Belorussian? . . . And maybe you are a German? In 1944 they were retreating, and they left you behind . . . Yes! Yes! You are without name, without fatherland, without nationality! You are simply a human being! (*He laughs.*)

SIMA. I am Russian.

VOLODYA. How could you know?

SIMA. Everyone decided that.

VOLODYA. They decided! People think they have to decide everything. That soothes them, permits them to avoid being alarmed. They put a period at the end of something and it's all finished! And I think, on the contrary, that everything is more interesting when there is uncertainty, only a series of dots . . . When I know that people, in essence, know nothing, I become happy! It is so lovely! True, Louisa?

SIMA. Let's go to the chemical factory. We have to earn a little bit of money.

VOLODYA. Let's go, Nastya! We have to work because in the center of a human being is a belly. It's humiliating for a thinking being, but . . . it's a real thing!

They take their clothes which by now have dried out. They go off in different directions into the bushes to dress again.

The Scene Changes.

Volodya and Sima walk along the road to the construction project. Along the road which crosses a highway a tow-haired lad of 18 or 19 with a mandolin in his hands joins them. For a while all three walk along in silence.

The lad takes from his pocket a pack of expensive cigarettes and offers one to Volodya.

PALCHIKOV (the lad). Smoke away.

VOLODYA. I don't smoke.

PALCHIKOV. You gave it up?

VOLODYA. I haven't begun yet.

SIMA. What expensive ones they are!

PALCHIKOV (he is flattered). And I love to spend my money on nothing! I just got some prize money—200 rubles—and I sent them all right away to my mother—in one fell swoop... Why do you think? For laughs! So now she's running around there and informing all of Taganka! "My Vovka, oh, my Vovka, oh!"

SIMA. You're from Moscow?

PALCHIKOV. I'm a refugee.

SIMA. A refugee?

PALCHIKOV. Ugh! I think in ways one is not supposed to! I ran away from home when I was sixteen... I was a fool, of course. I took a loaf of bread, and a box of sugar from the kitchen, and ran away in the clothes I was in! They explained to me later that this is what is known as false romanticism... but I didn't know then... Are you by any chance going to the construction project?

SIMA. Yes.

PALCHIKOV. You want to get a job?

SIMA. Yes.

PALCHIKOV. And why don't you have any baggage?

SIMA. It was stolen from us while we were traveling.

PALCHIKOV. Well, what do you know! What parasites! Everything?

SIMA. Uh, huh! They even took his jacket.

PALCHIKOV (to Volodya). Don't be sad, we'll equip you... And what's your speciality?

SIMA. We don't have any yet.

PALCHIKOV. Do you want to get yourself a work record?

SIMA. No, we want to earn some money so we can go on... We are travelers...

PALCHIKOV. It's too bad that you're not going to be with us for long. We need hands... I'll arrange it for you. I know everyone there. My name is Vladimir Palchikov. Have you heard of me?

SIMA. No.

PALCHIKOV. They broadcasted about me on the local radio...

SIMA. His name is also Vladimir, and mine is Sima.

PALCHIKOV (to Volodya). So we're namesakes.

SIMA. I'll walk between you—I'm making a wish.

PALCHIKOV (plays on his mandolin). And I was at the wedding of a friend of mine. He's a driver. He works here with us and lives over there. (He points at the village.) I also love to travel— that's why I ran away then and I went to one construction project and then to this one ... But for some reason I don't have any more time to move about ... But I'll travel still ... I want to go to Africa ... to look at the giraffes in the wilds ... and at the ostriches ... Have you read that they run fast ... And they're probably beautiful ... Maybe I'll still go. Nowadays many are going ...

VOLODYA. In Africa nowadays they are testing atom bombs. Your ostriches are running around with their heads broken. There's nowhere to hide.

PALCHIKOV. Yes ... A vile thing ...

VOLODYA. And you have prehistoric tastes ... Nowadays all are talking about going to the moon ..

PALCHIKOV. I know ... Only I don't want to go to the moon ... What's there: rocks, cold, dead nature ... I like it better here.

SIMA. Where, here?

PALCHIKOV. On the earth.

VOLODYA. What's there interesting here?

PALCHIKOV. Everything!

VOLODYA. Evidently you're a merry chap ...

PALCHIKOV. And you, I see, are in a really bad mood because of the fact that they stole your stuff? It's all right. We'll equip you. You'll get something to eat and your world outlook will change right away. I know from experience.

VOLODYA. I once was both well-fed and well-dressed ...

They see a bus at the stop in the distance.

PALCHIKOV. The bus is waiting! Let's run! It goes from the station to the construction project!

All three run behind the bus. But the bus moves off and disappears. They stop at the bus stop.

PALCHIKOV. We missed it ... Now it will be a while before another comes and we have another six kilometers to tramp ... We'll wait. Our trucks are bringing sand along the road here. They'll pick us up. There's a sand pit over there. They'll drop us off at the construction project. We wouldn't want to wear out our feet.

SIMA. We don't have any money for the bus.

PALCHIKOV. So what! (He pulls money out of his pocket.) Here they are, the sinners!

They stand at the crossing and wait for trucks.

SIMA. And what is your work?

PALCHIKOV. A steeplejack.

SIMA. Ugh! How awful!

PALCHIKOV. Why not! The main thing is not to think ... Maksimych told us when we were learning: "When you work don't dream about anything besides your work. The most dangerous thing is to think about the fact that you can fall, be killed ... If such a thought gets into your head—you're not a worker for the heights. Get down onto the earth. Change your profession ..."

SIMA. Well, you have a belt ...

PALCHIKOV. Well, very few work with belts ... It's worse with belts: Hook and unhook all the time ... You can't earn so much that way ... We're used to it!

VOLODYA. And I would be sure to think.

SIMA. Why?

VOLODYA. Simply in order to find out: am I daring or not?

Palchikov looks at his gold watch on his wrist.

PALCHIKOV. My shift goes on at two o'clock. Here come some of our chaps. They'll pick us up.

Trucks loaded with sand approach. Palchikov raises his hand. One of the trucks stops. On the sand eight boys and girls are already sitting. With shouts of "Palchikov! That's Palchikov!" "Come here Palchikov!" they greet their common favorite with gladness. Out of the cabin climbs a man of middle age. He also says hello to Palchikov.

UNCLE IVAN. I'm going to the city. I'll return by morning. (He leaves.)

PALCHIKOV (calling after him). Uncle Ivan! (He goes up to Uncle Ivan.) Buy me some of my cigarettes and some pastry. (He gives him money. He jumps into the truck.)

Palchikov, Volodya, and Sima are sitting in the truck on the sand together with all the rest. They are on their way.

FIRST YOUTH. Palchikov, let's have a song!

All make a big noise. Palchikov strikes up his mandolin. They sing a song in chorus. Volodya looks askance, disapprovingly, at the whole thing. He is shocked by it all. Some chap slaps him on the shoulder without ceremony.

SECOND YOUTH. Come on, you, sing. What are you keeping to yourself for?

Volodya only scowls the more. He shrinks back. The trucks go out onto the main highway along which long lines of trucks are traveling. The nearness to a big construction works makes itself felt. The songs ring out.

The Scene Changes.

Volodya and Sima shovel rubble with shovels onto a wheelbarrow. Evidently they have been working for a long time. All about work goes on. This is the large construction works for a chemical factory.

VOLODYA. Your father and Maksim Gorky are right: labor ennobles a human being. (*He wipes off the sweat, and tosses several shovelfuls more into the barrel.*)

SIMA. Someone must pick up.

VOLODYA. I have my own theory about the word "must."

SIMA. You despise people who engage in simple physical labor?

VOLODYA. Don't be a cretin. Such primitive things should be done by machines.

SIMA. Till everything is mechanized, someone must. Why not you?

VOLODYA. Listen, scholar, maybe I want to rise by myself above the universal rubble—so others should not suffer.

The foreman walks past Volodya and Sima.

FOREMAN. Students, I'll arrange sleeping quarters for you in the dormitories. Come to me after work is over. I am on the seventh sector. My name is Sapunov.

SIMA. I guess we'll have to stay till morning. We won't be able to get to the station before dark.

VOLODYA. All right, we'll suffer a bit.

At this moment somewhere in the background evidently something has happened. People run. The construction cranes stop. All is in confusion. The foreman also runs there. Sima and Volodya look. A person runs from the spot.

SIMA. What happened?

MAN. A man was killed.

The Scene Changes.

The men's dormitory. This is a long neat barracks. Evening. Almost everyone is asleep. Volodya and the maid come in. They walk between the rows of cots. They come to two empty cots. Eyes are fixed on the maid.

YOUTH. What is the news?

MAID. There still isn't any.

YOUTH. And where is Sapunov?

MAID. He's still there.

She hands Volodya his linen.

MAID. Take it and make your bed.

YOUTH. Why are you turning over his cot to this one, as if he were dead?

MAID. He has to stay in the hospital anyway and this one is here temporarily. There isn't anywhere else for him to sleep. (*To Volodya.*) See to it that you don't touch anything that belongs to someone else. (*She goes out.*)

Volodya sits down on the edge of the cot. He looks at the mandolin hanging above the cot and the picture with giraffes and ostriches. He makes the bed. Under the pillow he discovers the expensive cigarettes and a pack of letters, tied about with a thread. He puts them on the stand.

Next to Volodya a young chap is studying mathematics.

YOUTH. Take yourself a cigarette.

VOLODYA. Can I?

YOUTH. He always offers. He never refuses. With him it's just as if his things belong to everyone.

Volodya offers him the pack. He takes a cigarette himself. He rolls it for a long time in his fingers. He lights up. It seems as if he wants, together with the smoke, to draw in the truth.

VOLODYA. Will he live?

YOUTH. A fact.

VOLODYA. What are you studying?

YOUTH. Mathematics. Things are not so good with my education ... I am going to evening school.

VOLODYA. Why?

YOUTH. Then to the institute.

VOLODYA. And why to the institute?

YOUTH. Beat it! (He puts his nose in the book and is surrounded by tobacco smoke.)

Sapunov enters. All eyes are on him.

SAPUNOV. He died. (He goes up to his own cot which is next to that of Volodya. He notices Volodya.) They already put somebody there! The devil take them! They don't even allow it to get cold! (To Volodya.) Nothing against you, but in general. (He sits down on his cot. All look at him. Sapunov jumps up all of a sudden and in a frenzy but quietly exclaims.) Who was it, who was it, who permitted them to work without belts! Big shots! Loudmouths! Braggarts! Boasters, conceited jackasses, roosters, empty-heads!!! (All are silent.) If I ever see it again I'm going to go up there myself and throw whoever I see doing it to the devil's mother ... With whom are you playing at toys —with the one who hasn't got any nose! He's the one who catches such fools as you ... Now they're going to drag the plant safety measures through the courts—but you should all be tried! Boasting and bragging in front of each other! And you found what with! (And all of a sudden he almost yelled.) You killed Palchikov! (He grabs his head with his hands and throws himself on his cot. Then he gets a mug from his stand and pours in some water, gets some sausage, butter, and cuts himself off a piece of sausage.)

VOLODYA. I'm only here temporarily. Don't worry.

SAPUNOV. And why should I worry. You can stay here forever.

VOLODYA. No, I'm going away in the morning.

SAPUNOV. That's your own business. (All of a sudden he sweeps up the already prepared food and shoves it into the stand.) I can't. He stands there in front of my eyes. (He gets up, and goes out of the barracks with determination.)

> *Volodya notices the pack of cigarettes lying on the table. He turns away in order not to think about anything and he sees on the wall the pictures with the giraffes and drops his head down . . . And then he sees Palchikov's shoes peering out from underneath the cot . . . He jumps up. He goes to the exit.*
>
> *Sapunov is standing out there in the street. Volodya goes out of the barracks.*

SAPUNOV. Why did you go out?

VOLODYA. I can't sleep.

> *They are silent.*

VOLODYA. Where did he fall from?

SAPUNOV. There (he points).

> *The camera is on the scaffolding at which Sapunov is pointing. It climbs upwards—higher, higher, higher. And at the very top there is a piece of construction. On this piece of construction there can be seen a belt which was left by Palchikov. The camera goes higher above the construction into the black emptiness of the heavens.*
>
> *Sapunov and Volodya are at the barracks. Sapunov is smoking. Volodya is leaning against the wooden wall and looking into the distance.*

SAPUNOV. I wish I could sleep . . . It's going to be a difficult shift tomorrow. (To Volodya.) Let's go!

> *But Volodya doesn't answer and thinks his own thoughts.*
>
> *Sapunov goes out. Volodya goes, but not into the barracks, but to the place from which Palchikov fell. He approaches the scaffolding. He begins to climb up on the scaffolding, scrambling upwards, ever higher, higher and higher. He climbs for a long time, tenaciously, with effort. Finally he is on an immense height, like a circus acrobat. He walks out on a beam which sticks out ahead. He leans over, picks up the belt which is hanging across the beam, and throws it downwards. He stands on the very end and quietly whispers: "I can fall . . . I can fall . . ."*
>
> *Volodya stands on the edge. Clouds swim swiftly. The wind whistles. Music begins in the whistle of the wind . . . And on the background of the sweeping clouds ostriches run along the wavy sand of the desert . . . It's impossible to understand whether they are running or floating in the air . . . Palms and pyramids flash past, towers, minarets, caravans of camels and masses of*

Arab horsemen with spears in their hands . . . Everything which might appear to a childish, pure imagination. And in all of this the ostriches run, run, run . . . There appears the laughing face of Palchikov. He watches the ostriches and his laughter passes over into childish delight and triumph. The music rises. The ostriches run faster and faster and the triumph of Palchikov reaches an extreme. But in the music there begins the roar of a flying airplane, an evil roar. It grows and grows swiftly. We see a bomb flying over the desert and the huts. Explosion! The head of Palchikov flying from somewhere above to the ground. His face expresses more wonder than horror . . .

Everything disappears. The clouds fly by.

The Scene Changes.

Morning. In the dormitory all are asleep. Uncle Ivan comes in—the one whom we saw at the crossing. He is a little intoxicated.

UNCLE IVAN (in a whisper, smiling). The builders of Communism are asleep! (He goes up to the cot where Volodya lies. He puts the cigarettes, pastry and small change on the stand beside the bed. He looks at the sleeping Volodya and all of a sudden understands that it is not Palchikov. He looks again and stares to be sure whether or not he was mistaken. There is already no intoxication in his eyes. Just bewilderment.)

The Scene Changes.

Volodya and Sima are walking away from the construction project. Work is going on at top speed at the project. Volodya for a second stops, turns his head and looks upwards. On the same place from which Palchikov fell someone else is working.

SIMA. Are you afraid?

VOLODYA. Of what?

SIMA. He didn't fall because of you.

Volodya is quiet.

SIMA. He is not that kind of a person . . . He couldn't think . . . You didn't cause a reaction in him . . . You don't cause any reaction in me . . .

VOLODYA. Shut up, Agrafena.

Pause.

VOLODYA. Where did you get those shoes?

SIMA. A girl in the barracks gave them to me.

Sima and Volodya are standing in the railway station and looking at the schedule of trains. They are counting their money.

SIMA. Where are you going?

VOLODYA. I still haven't decided. I can get as far as Komarino.

SIMA. And then?

VOLODYA. And then wherever my eyes look. Buy yourself a ticket for home immediately, do you understand? Don't be a fool.

SIMA. Yes and let me buy your ticket too.

VOLODYA (gives her money). See to it that you don't lose it.

SIMA. The ticket windows are still closed.

VOLODYA. Let's go get a bite. (He counts his small change.)

Volodya and Sima are in the hall of the station restaurant. They are sitting at a table and having a snack. At the next table a woman is eating something which she has brought with her from home and drinking tea. In the corner a man of indefinite years is drinking vodka. In front of him on the table there is a carafe and some things to eat. He is already a little bit intoxicated. He looks at Volodya and Sima, picks up his carafe and his food and goes over to their table.

TRAVELING OFFICIAL. Do you have a place for me?

SIMA (dissatisfied). Please.

The Traveling Official doesn't even pay any attention to the fact that the young people are clearly unhappy about his arrival. He sits down at their table.

TRAVELING OFFICIAL. I do not love loneliness! A human being is a social animal, true? (He points at the carafe.) Let's empty it together, what say? How about it, young lady?

SIMA. I do not drink.

TRAVELING OFFICIAL. Smart girl. (To Volodya.) Well, how about your keeping me company? (He pours out for himself and for Volodya.)

TRAVELING OFFICIAL. I am lonely for people. It's already two months that I've been traveling to collective farms. "Poultry Procurement Administration!" Have you ever heard of such an organization? What is there in the Soviet Union that we don't have! All kinds of everything! So I am "Poultry Procurement Administration" for our territory ... I love to chat with people whom I meet on the way ... Freely, without responsibility, so to speak ... (He clinks his glass with that of Volodya.) To your health! (He drinks it down.) And what's wrong with you? Are you being disdainful? Is that it? Come on, brother, don't disdain to have a drink with an ordinary human being ... An ordinary human being ... that is strength. That, brother, is everything! You can't tear yourself away from him ... He, brother, is building communism, that ordinary person!

VOLODYA. So go ahead and build it, build it, and have a bit to eat for yourself.

TRAVELING OFFICIAL. Are you one of those who criticizes everything, is that it?

VOLODYA. One of those very same ones.

TRAVELING OFFICIAL. Aha! To tell the truth, brother, I'm also bitter ... A dog's life! It's true. You, after all, are contemporary, proud! You have imagination ... concepts! But we can't. In our time one couldn't be proud. It wasn't permitted ... Not a chance for relaxation. And even now I do what they tell me to. So if they tell me: "You must destroy all ducks, chickens and geese in our territory!" So I will go about and I will explain: "Destroy every bird to the very last!" Likewise if they say: Breed 1,000 for each person! Chickens for meat? Chickens for meat! Chickens for eggs? Chickens for eggs! I am a manageable person.

SIMA. Why are you saying, uncle, things that you shouldn't?

The Traveling Official stares at Sima.

TRAVELING OFFICIAL. And you, young lady, understand me right ... What I am saying is this: Once our appropriate organizations decide on a definite course of action that means that this is where the very truth is. It's very very heart of it ... The future! One must not then permit oneself to have any doubts ... None! You have to be honest, conscientious.

SIMA (to Volodya). I'm going to take a look to see whether the ticket window is open. (She goes out.)

TRAVELING OFFICIAL. And I see that there's a difference between you and her. She, evidently, is from among those who have ideology.

VOLODYA. And you, uncle, I see are from among those who sputter and wheeze.

TRAVELING OFFICIAL (spitefully). And you? (He stares at Volodya with his drunk eyes.) You think you're so congenial!

VOLODYA. What's it to you?

TRAVELING OFFICIAL. Women! They're all foul! One's just as bad as the other! So I just spent three days in a collective farm with one of the broads there—so plump, succulent ...

The woman sitting nearby jumps up.

WOMAN. And you, you bastard! What are you going to do, undress in front of this young man? Why are you pouring out on him all your soul slops? (To Volodya.) Spit on him! From such as him run to the ends of the earth! They're like an infection, a plague. They corrupt, destroy, stand in the way ... (To the Traveling Official.) Go to your own table! Scat, you rot! Why are you hanging around?

The Traveling Official takes his things and goes into the corner. The girl duty officer for the station walks past.

WOMAN. Is the bus going to be here soon, Comrade Chief?

DUTY OFFICER. It's now loading.

WOMAN. Goodness! (She gathers up her things from the table. To Volodya.) My son is working here on this construction project. I came here to see him. He doesn't expect me, I dare say. He doesn't know ... I haven't seen him for a long, a very long time ... I was lonely for him! (She takes her things and quickly leaves the building. Volodya sits there as if frozen. He understands or, more correctly, feels with all his being that this is Palchikov's mother.)

TRAVELING OFFICIAL (from out of his corner). I hope you're late, old crab!

VOLODYA (in wrath). Shut up, beast! (He grabs a dill pickle from the plate left behind by the Traveling Official and throws it at him and runs out after the woman. He sees she is hurrying to get into the bus.)

VOLODYA. Citizeness! Citizeness!

WOMAN (turning around but still moving). Good luck, my dear! Take care of your soul! Your soul!

She climbs into the bus. Volodya runs after her but the bus, emitting a cloud of smoke, moves off. The woman laughs, waves her hand at Volodya. The bus disappears ... Volodya stands in a cloud of dust and gasoline smoke.

Sima is at a window sending a telegram. She writes: "Accompanying the lunatic to Moscow. Sima." She hands the telegram in at the window. The telegraph girl takes the blank, mechanically counts the number of words, and all of a sudden understands their content. She looks at Sima. She sticks her head out the window. She looks about to see the lunatic.

TELEGRAPH GIRL. Where is he?

SIMA. Who?

The telegraph girl points at the telegram.

SIMA. He's sitting in the restaurant.

TELEGRAPH GIRL. Alone?

SIMA. Alone.

The telegraph girl quickly takes the telegram and hurries to shut her window tight.

Sima buys tickets at the railway ticket window.

SIMA. Two to Komarino.

Two cardboard tickets fly out of the window.

The Scene Changes.

Right away a hurtling train. A coach completely full of people. Sima and Volodya are sitting on a bench. It's late. Only the nightlight is on. Sima and Volodya are dozing. The dozing and the dark make it appear as if they were sitting embracing one another, embracing each other sweetly, cozily, like two puppies. Sima opens her eyes. She sees that Volodya has embraced her, and this she likes very much. She again shuts her eyes. In a moment Volodya opens his eyes. He sees that he holds Sima in his arms and that Sima has pressed herself up to him. Evidently he likes it too. He shuts his eyes tightly.

Morning light pours into the window of the railway car. It's already not nearly so crowded. There are free seats. Volodya carefully moves away from Sima, and leans her against the wall of the railway car, and goes out of the car. Sima senses all of this. When Volodya goes out she pulls her jacket more tightly about herself. At this moment she by chance feels the photograph in the pocket. She takes it out. She looks at the face of the girl whom she has never met and quietly throws it out the half-open window. She watches how the photo whirls off into the wind and disappears. Sima again takes her former position. Volodya comes in. Sima acts as if she has just awakened.

SIMA. I don't even remember how I went to sleep yesterday.

VOLODYA. Me too.

SIMA. And where did you sleep?

VOLODYA. On the next bench.

Sima knows that he has told a lie and is very pleased. A citizen walks past.

SIMA. Will Komarino be soon?

CITIZEN. If you go in this direction, then never ... We passed it two hours ago. (He goes out.)

VOLODYA. Why should we worry about that: Isn't it all the same where we get out?

SIMA. True! I would like to ride and ride and ride ...

VOICE. Citizens, get your tickets ready ...

Two conductors enter the car. One of them is very old and the other is about thirty.

Sima and Volodya are in confusion. They begin to look for a place where they can hide. They even look into the coal box on the car's platform. They begin to go from car to car. They are in a hurry. They are in a fright. Volodya catches his pocket of his trousers on the door handle on one of the passages from car to car. He pulls away and tears his trousers badly so that his underpants and bare leg can be seen. He is taken aback, but there's no time to wait: he has to hide. Holding his torn trousers tightly with his hand, he goes further.

SIMA. Quicker, quicker!

> *They find themselves in a full car. Laughter, noise, talk, songs. In the next car also.*

SIMA. Wait a minute. I know. (And she turns to a young chap nearby.) What kind of people are these?

YOUTH. Can't you see for yourself? We're going off to the virgin lands.

SIMA (quietly to Volodya). Let's stay here: they probably have one ticket for the whole group. No one will notice.

> *Volodya and Sima move in among a group of young people who are in a circle, singing a song. The song evidently is an improvisation of those who are singing—joking, silly, but everyone is very merry because of it. The conductors enter. Sima and Volodya, so as not to seem strangers, began to sing together with all the rest. Sima—happily loud. Volodya—gloomily, very embarrassed. The conductors go through the car without asking for tickets.*

YOUNG CONDUCTOR. Greetings, virgin lands passengers!

> *But no one answers. In the general hubbub evidently no one heard what he said. Coming up to Volodya one of the conductors slaps him on the shoulder: "Let me past, eagle!"*

> *The conductors pass by. Volodya and Sima look for a place to sit down. Finally they find one—in the first compartment from the platform which is often occupied by the conductors. They have just arranged themselves there when the conductors return and come right up to Volodya and Sima. Volodya and Sima jump up.*

OLD CONDUCTOR. Sit down, sit down, you don't hinder.

> *Volodya and Sima sit down and look fearfully at the conductors. The conductors also sit down on the bench.*

YOUNG CONDUCTOR (to Volodya). So you're going to the virgin lands?

SIMA. Yes.

YOUNG CONDUCTOR. From where do you come?

SIMA (quickly). From Omsk.

YOUNG CONDUCTOR. And your parents let you come? They weren't against it?

SIMA. No, they were happy.

YOUNG CONDUCTOR. Conscientious! You're responding to the appeal?

SIMA. To the appeal.

OLD CONDUCTOR. And I am making my last trip this time.

> *He is thoughtful. All are silent. At the end of the car a happy, happy song.*

OLD CONDUCTOR. I'm sixty-three... My eyesight is bad and I have high blood pressure, of course... I'm short of breath also... so I'm going to live on my pension... (Again silence.)

YOUNG CONDUCTOR. Do you envy them, the young people?

OLD CONDUCTOR (after thinking). No, we also plowed our own virgin land. We had it! There are things to remember!

YOUNG CONDUCTOR. That's true, Nikolai Alekseyevich. Every generation has its own virgin land to plow.

OLD CONDUCTOR. Certainly... And now I don't sleep so very well any more... Oh, it's from nothing to do. Different thoughts pop into my head... Why, for example, did I live? Didn't I spoil my life? Don't I want to live it all over again from the beginning, in some other way, so to speak? No, I don't want to. Of course, every person has his own virgin land to plow from his very day of birth. And he spends all his life plowing it... And he digs up the stumps and he picks out the stones and he drags away the boulders and prays for rain and waits for the sun... And plows and plows and plows... And then at his end he looks to see what kind of a harvest he has gathered in... So then I think to myself: It's clear that all of humanity from the very day of its appearance on the earth, from the beginning of its development, in other words, has been plowing some kind of mysterious Universal Eternal Virgin Land. From birth to birth, from generation to generation...

VOLODYA (who is all ears). And why is that, grandfather?

OLD CONDUCTOR. What do you mean "why"?

VOLODYA. Why does a human being plow this Universal Eternal Virgin Land?

OLD CONDUCTOR. He must.

VOLODYA (he starts). Must? Why?

OLD CONDUCTOR. For perfection, dear...

> By this time the entire car is in an uproar. Shouts are heard: "We've arrived!" "Get together your things!", "We're coming to the station!" There appear suitcases, knapsacks, packages.
>
> The station. The new arrivals are met by an orchestra. The station is all in posters, slogans. The young people pour out of the car like peas. They greet those who have come to meet them. Flowers are brought to present to someone.
>
> Volodya and Sima are in the midst of this uproar, the shouts, the music. The current has carried them together with the rest. Volodya even inadvertently receives a bouquet.
>
> All of the new arrivals move out onto the station square where a meeting is taking place. There, on the square, stand rows of trucks which have been provided with benches. They are for the arrivals.

*Volodya and Sima try to make their way out of the crowd
but it's impossible.*

SIMA (to Volodya in the crowd). Maybe we should go with the rest.
We have to earn money anyway!

VOLODYA (pointing at his torn clothing). Right away! That's all I
need. (He wrathfully makes his way out of the crowd. Sima
follows him.)

SIMA. We'll get a needle and thread and we can sew it up.

VOLODYA. Leave me alone! (He tries to break out of the crowd with
new strength.)

*While they are making their way out of the crowd a speech
can be heard from the platform in front.*

ORATOR'S VOICE. Dear friends! Young men and women! You, young
enthusiasts for our great deeds, who have come here today...

*Volodya and Sima manage to make their way to a small
building next to the station. A lad, listening to the speech, sees
Volodya.*

YOUTH. Did you forget something in the car?

Volodya does not answer, and makes his way further.

ORATOR'S VOICE. I greet you, dear comrades I bid you welcome! We
wish you success and happy labor for the benefit of our fatherland.

*Commands are heard. The youths form groups. All of them
run to the trucks. And a minute later Volodya and Sima who have
pushed their way against the current, are alone on the square.
The line of cars disappears in the distance.*

*Volodya has in his hand a completely wilted bouquet. He
carries it mechanically and at this moment throws it onto the
ground. He goes behind the warehouse, looks over his torn
trousers. He stands there and thinks.*

SIMA. Well, let's go.

VOLODYA. Where?

SIMA. Somewhere.

VOLODYA. Looking like this? (One has to note that during the period
of their journey Volodya and Sima have become quite tattered.)

SIMA. Well, are we going to sit all our lives behind this barn?

Volodya doesn't answer.

SIMA. Wait just a minute, I'm going to get a needle and thread.

*Volodya and Sima sit on boxes. Sima is finishing mending
the trousers. She bites off the thread.*

SIMA. Well, what next?

VOLODYA (he walks up and down, looking at his trousers). Not so
bad. Looking like this I wouldn't mind walking on Gorky Street!

Ah hah! They would shout at me again: "You should be ashamed!" "Oh!", "Ah!"

SIMA. We have to think of something, Volodya. I want to eat . . . And in general.

VOLODYA. Listen here, Kapitolina, have you ever kissed anybody?

SIMA. How can you say that? What silliness all of a sudden . . .

VOLODYA. It's very serious! Have you ever kissed anyone? Tell me.

SIMA. Leave me alone!

VOLODYA. I have to know for the clarification of a purely philosophical question!

SIMA. You're a silly fool.

VOLODYA. So that means no. If you had kissed someone, you would have said quickly: "No! No! What do you mean!" (And he turns to a railwayman walking by.) Uncle, wouldn't there be some work at the station?

RAILWAYMAN. And aren't you one of those going to the virgin lands?

VOLODYA. Why should I? I'm not that conscientious yet!

RAILWAYMAN. I think I have some work. Here's what, wise guy, go and look for Andrei Danylich. He's in charge of that. (He goes on further.)

VOLODYA. Andrei Danylich, save us! We're coming.

Volodya is loading packages which he is carrying from the building next to the station, putting them on a cart, and pulling it to a truck.

The Scene Changes.
Volodya is in the office of Andrei Danylich.

ANDREI DANYLICH. Sign the receipt. (He gives him the paper and a pen.) Here's what, my friend, sign for ten rubles.

VOLODYA. For ten?

ANDREI DANYLICH. You worked very well. You will receive seven rubles.

Volodya signs the receipt and gives it to Andrei Danylich.

ANDREI DANYLICH. What did you write? I told you to sign for ten rubles.

VOLODYA. You said seven.

ANDREI DANYLICH. You're a blockhead! We agreed for five, yes?

VOLODYA. Yes.

ANDREI DANYLICH. And I am giving you seven.

VOLODYA. Seven.

ANDREI DANYLICH. And you sign for ten. You understand?

VOLODYA (understanding). I understand.

He again signs the receipt. Andrei Danylich reads.

ANDREI DANYLICH. What did you write?

VOLODYA. Give me five and that's all.

ANDREI DANYLICH. Three rubles you're going to receive . . . No, two and a half . . . I'm sick of you . . . Sign, rat!

VOLODYA. Don't you dare talk that way!

ANDREI DANYLICH. Just think! All kinds of rabble hang around! So you ran away, I dare say, from the virgin lands . . . Or you swiped something from somebody . . . And you even dragged along a tomato with yourself, good for nothing . . .

VOLODYA (rage pours into his brain, and eyes). You're a thief! You're a thief!

ANDREI DANYLICH. So that's what, you cursed parasite! (He shouts.) Demin! Demin!

A husky driver runs in.

VOLODYA (he continues to shout). You're a thief! Thief!

Sima runs in. She was evidently nearby.

ANDREI DANYLICH. Demin, grab hold of him, the skunk!

DEMIN. I don't have the time, Andrei Danylich. I'm taking the mail to the factory.

ANDREI DANYLICH. They won't die there without your mail! I tell you take hold of him!

Demin goes up to Volodya, takes him by the arms. Andrei Danylich yells into the telephone: "Militia! Militia!" But evidently they don't answer.

ANDREI DANYLICH (to Demin). Can you imagine it! We agreed with him for five rubles. And now he wants ten from me. He screeches. (To Volodya.) You're going to catch it—for insults! Demin, you'll be a witness!

SIMA. Let him go, let him go!

VOLODYA. Here's a thief, a cheat! People are going to the virgin lands, and here is a thief! He tried to persuade me when we were alone to sign a receipt for ten rubles . . .

ANDREI DANYLICH. Dog! You yourself demanded ten rubles . . . And then you signed for seven and pushed it at me . . . (He waves at the receipt.) I'll see that you get it, skunk! (To Demin.) Hold him! I'll run here to our station militia. (He goes out quickly.)

SIMA. It's not true . . . Volodya couldn't do it . . . He dragged packages . . . earned wages . . . We had to . . .

DEMIN (he lets Volodya go). Come on, you better get out of here right away or else he's going to get you into some kind of a mess. They'll put you in jail.

SIMA. Let's go, Vova, let's go!

VOLODYA. He can't do it. He can't do it.

DEMIN. You better get out of here while there's still time. Get into my truck. I'll take you to the factory. You'll get as much work as you want.

Volodya makes a movement of protest.

DEMIN. I'm telling you, get along with you: I'm wishing you good!

VOLODYA (to Sima). You see, you see?

Sima pushes Volodya by main force out of the building.

The truck with packages and mail raises a cloud of dust along the rural road. Volodya and Sima sit in the back on packages. Because of the roaring of the truck we do not hear their words, but we see how Volodya is saying something very emotionally to Sima, waving his fists. Evidently he is still angry at Andrei Danylich.

Volodya and Sima stand at the gates on which there is pasted an announcement: "We need: 1. Apprentice blast furnace operators. 2. Steel construction workers. 3. Steel founders. 4. Accounting clerks. 5. Economists. 6. Cook. 7. Miscellaneous workers.

Volodya and Sima read the notice.

Volodya and Sima are in the office of the personnel department. A short man leafs over some papers and turning to a young man sitting on the side with a newspaper in his hands, says:

"Right now, Pavel, right now."

And then he speaks to Sima and Volodya:

"There is no work. I said: No!"

SIMA. Why do you then have a notice hanging on your gate?

PERSONNEL OFFICER. It's not for you.

SIMA. For decoration?

PERSONNEL OFFICER. For those who are serious. And not for those who are looking for seasonal work . . . They have to earn a little money! Here we are building the future, building the future and they want—to earn a little bit! You've found a "quick drink parlor." You can work here but you can't use this place as a place to earn a little bit, is that clear?

Sima and Volodya go to the door.

PERSONNEL OFFICER. Idiots! You are going past your own happiness . . . We need workers right up to here. (He passes the edge of his hand along his throat.) But serious ones . . . I'll provide you with dormitory space. I'll find a place for you in the correspondence course for construction technicians or in an institute. I'll help you . . . I know that you have no training or experience and it's all the same to me that you are crazy. I'll provide your transportation . . . (Turning to Pavel.) Incidentally, Pavel, you should be thinking about studying. You have a clear head, don't you?

PAVEL (laughing). I don't have the time, Ilya Petrovich. What I have is all I want.

PERSONNEL OFFICER (to Volodya and Sima). Well, what do you say? Will you stay? How about it?

VOLODYA. No.

PERSONNEL OFFICER. Well, so go on past! Come on, trot on out of the building. Don't hang around here . . . There are all kinds around these days!

PAVEL (he speaks calmly, quietly). Spit on them, Ilya Petrovich. Why do you wear out your nerves without any result? Listen here, you aristocrats! You say that you don't have enough to get to Moscow . . . (He reaches briskly into his pocket, gets out his wallet and from a pack of money he takes a note, and puts his wallet back.) Here you are, take it! Get along home to your incubators . . .

VOLODYA (calmly, directly). Too little. That's only enough for tickets . . . We have to eat . . .

PAVEL. That kind of arithmetic they know . . . (Again he gets out his billfold and pulls out another bill.) Here, I'm adding another ten . . .

VOLODYA (absolutely sincerely). It's not enough . . . I just can't eat whatever comes my way. I have to go to the dining car. I have to have wine to drink . . .

PERSONNEL OFFICER. Pavel, hit him on the nose . . .

PAVEL. You're right, Ilya Petrovich, right. Don't pay any attention . . . (To Volodya.) How much do you need? What's your name?

VOLODYA. Sidor.

PAVEL. How much do you need, Sidor?

VOLODYA. And how much will you give?

PAVEL. You're a strange one! You tell me, how much you need?

VOLODYA. No! You show me yourself the entire radius of the breadth of your character . . . Maybe you'll give a whole hundred . . . What about it?

PAVEL. Aha! I understand. (He hides his money in his billfold.) Ilya Petrovich, let me have him. My worker, Makhov, is sick. And Sokolov is asking for permission to move to the rolling mill . . .

PERSONNEL OFFICER. And what are you going to do with this fly-by-night? What's the use from him?

PAVEL. Well, let him hang around for a while. Then, after all, I'll find someone or other.

PERSONNEL OFFICER. You're being capricious! He won't go to work with you! They're too delicate. (To Volodya.) Well, will you work as an apprentice blast furnace operator?

SIMA. What do you do there?

PAVEL. He'll see.

VOLODYA. Good God! How much you want to frighten me—poor, rotten member of the intelligentsia, mama's boy, *stilyaga* and nihilist! My hair simply stands on end ...

PAVEL (to Volodya). Come along, we'll find you some work clothes.

Sima and Volodya leave the office.

PERSONNEL OFFICER. Why are you taking on that good-for-nothing? You're going to wreck the whole tempo of your work.

PAVEL. That's all right. We'll handle it ... We'll give him an injection against whooping cough ... He won't cough again for his whole life long ... (He leaves.)

Volodya and Sima stand at the porch. Before them stretches an enormous factory. Part of it has still not been completed. Pavel approaches.

VOLODYA. Where are we to go?

PAVEL (he doesn't answer, but shouts at two girls going past). Galya! Tamara!

The girls approach.

PAVEL. Tamara, do you think you could find some kind of a job for the girl?

TAMARA. Come on, come on, she's needed very much. We'll put her in the restaurant—she can be a waitress or wash dishes. They need extra hands there very badly.

PAVEL. And you, Galochka, show the young man the factory. Explain to him in detail what, how, why. He, you see, is burning with enthusiasm. He wants to put his brick into the common building. So let him do it with knowledge in order that he should not forget why he put it there, where he put it. And then take him off to the fourth blast furnace. (To Volodya.) Are there any questions?

VOLODYA. Unfortunately, everything is all clear.

SIMA. Where are we going to meet, Vova?

VOLODYA (all of a sudden confused). I don't know.

TAMARA. After the shift we'll look for him, he isn't going to get lost.

SIMA (she runs up to Volodya of a sudden and whispers to him in his ear). Maybe you should ask for something to eat first?

VOLODYA. You just let out a squeak about that! Go along with you!

Tamara goes out with Sima. Pavel sits down on his motorcycle and leaves. Galya takes Volodya through the territory of the factory. Past them there rumble railway trains, loaded with ore, completed products—rails and pipes—and also ladles with liquid metal and slag, gondolas with coke.

Galya is a little bit of a towheaded girl, almost an adolescent to judge by her appearance. She has a thin little voice like

*the fluttering of a bird. She gets a real delight out of everything
she shows Volodya in the factory. Everything she says is for her
gladness and poesy. Her little voice rings without ever being
silent. She not only wants to inject Volodya with her enthusiasm, but also simply to enjoy herself once more from what she
sees, what she is speaking about . . . She almost shouts, since she
has to make herself heard over the roar, thunder, whistle, hissing,
that fills this giant factory.*

GALYA. This is Open Hearth Section Number Two. You, so to speak,
will work at the blast furnace and produce pig iron . . . It's also
interesting . . . Part of the pig iron here in the factory is sent
outside, and part for further processing, to the steel smelting
sections . . . Right here, in fact, is the Bessemer Section . . . Right
there they blow through the pig iron in converters and burn out
part of the carbon . . . You probably know all that yourself—
how they make steel from pig iron? Yes? (Volodya does not answer and, evidently, is not listening to Galya at all, but watching with interest everything about him, and, as always, is deeply
immersed in thought.) And that is where they pour the slag . . .
You can't go close . . . If any remnants of the pig iron should
get in there, there could be an explosion . . . Yes! Yes! I saw . . .
(The ladles slowly tip. The slag pours out into the pool. Clouds
of steam, white and thick like cotton, surround Galya and
Volodya. Through the cloud there can be heard the laughter
of Galya and her shout.) Do you see?

*When the cloud has disappeared we see Volodya and Galya
next to a let-down barrier.*

GALYA. Those are the forms into which the steel is poured . . . And
that ore which looks like dust is being taken to the Agglomerate
Factory where it is going to be made into cakes . . . And there are
two windows—that's the laboratory—I work there now . . . We
came here as a whole class . . . When we finished last year they
sent us here . . . The first thing we did was to complete the
building of the rolling mill for sheet steel . . . it was only a little
while ago that it was put into operation—there you can just
see it . . . And now we've all been sent in different directions.
Here, you know, there aren't any limits . . . We come from
Abakan . . . We arrived together with our physics teacher, Nikolai Lvovich . . . Now do you understand how badly the country
needs metal? The steel industry is the basis of bases, get this . . .

*Volodya stops still for a minute. Galya also stops still. They
look at one another. Volodya puts his hand on Galya's forehead,
and touches it.*

VOLODYA. Continue.

Galya blushes, she is embarrassed.

GALYA. Of course you know all of that without me ... but do you understand that when I studied it—it was completely different than now ... Let's go to the fourth blast furnace.

And so they already climb along a steep and narrow steel stairway, like a stepladder ... A work crew of blast furnace workers comes down from the opposite direction. They evidently have just finished their shift—all of them are tired, black like Negroes, and on their clothing metal dust glistens. Volodya steps aside in order to make way and looks at those coming towards him, but no one from among the blast furnace workers even looks at him.

GALYA. Now the foreman will give you some instructions. You will make his acquaintance ... and tomorrow you will begin.

The office of the control room of the blast furnace. A table. A telephone is on it. There is one iron chair. Two walls are in panels on which there are innumerable instruments. There hangs a poster: "Let's reduce the cost of production of pig iron by ten kopecks more than the plan."

Pavel's gang is gathered together—five men. Volodya is in a new thick woolen suit—trousers and a jacket. In his hands a felt hat with brims.

FOREMAN (to Volodya). Get acquainted.

Volodya hesitates for one second, not knowing how to carry out this simple ritual. At long last he approaches each one and, shaking hands, gives his last name:

VOLODYA. Fedorov!

The boys look at him not without curiosity.

The next gang of blast furnace workers comes into the office.

PAVEL. Let's go!

And Pavel's gang go out the door, one after another, to the smelting yard.

The smelting yard. The smelting is taking place. The metal flows along the ditches, sparks fly up over the pig iron, which falls into the ladles which stand on the railway tracks. There is an ocean of fire, smoke and flying stars. In Volodya's hand there is an enormous, heavy crowbar. The work gang works in rhythm, intensely. All of a sudden Volodya notes there is confusion. A small piece of coke has stopped up the pig iron outlet.

PAVEL (shouts). Pick!

Two apprentices run to the long steel rods lying nearby, grab one of them—this is the pick—and hurry to the pig iron outlet. Volodya also grabs ahold of the pick and helps to carry it. They drive the pick into the outlet. They hit with intensity, furiously. Their faces are black and it is as if they were thickly greased with vaseline. The face of Volodya. The end of the pick is heated to white heat and bends into a spiral. Pavel again shouts: "Pick!"

Again the apprentices rush for a pick, carry it. Again, with still greater fury and force, they drive it into the outlet. And again the pick is heated to red heat. But just one more movement and the path for the pig iron is open. The metal pours out, the building is lighted as if by the sun. The smoke tears up underneath the arched roof. Sparks fly upward.

Volodya works. Evidently he hardly can stand on his feet. He breathes heatedly, frequently, but in his eyes there is desperate stubbornness. He is waging a battle for his own worthiness, for his honor.

Volodya rushes to the "spade" in order to raise it and to let the slag into the next bucket, but in doing this almost steps with his foot into the molten mass. Pavel pulls him away by the hand just in time.

PAVEL. Watch out. Mistakes like that don't happen twice. (And he himself raises the "spade.")

Pavel goes to the end.

PAVEL (shouts). Cannon!

And the "cannon" moves itself up to the pig iron outlet. From two hoses water pours onto the nose of the "cannon" in order that it should not burn up. Volodya holds one of the hoses. His hands shake as if he were in a fever—it's from strain. Water touching the liquid metal is transformed with a whistle into steam and white clouds fill the entire building. White steam, black smoke, golden sparks, crimson reflections of the flame. The "cannon" shuts the outlet—and there is immediately darkness and quiet in the building.

Volodya wanted to catch his breath but already from the depths of the foundry yard a bridge crane moves up to the blast furnace. All rush to pick up scrap.

The first smelting is finished. The ditches are prepared for the second smelting and Volodya leaves the building. He stands on a narrow steel passage—a small bridge. It unites the blast furnaces. With his hands he holds onto the railing. He is very tired. The bridge is covered with black dust. And whether from that or from fatigue—and maybe also from his inner state his face has become something completely new, different.

Pavel comes up.

Pavel feels out Volodya with a glance: how, so to speak,

do you feel? Volodya tries to look independent and not tired.

PAVEL. So nevertheless you held out.

VOLODYA. And what did you think, that I was going to cry?

PAVEL. Did you like it?

VOLODYA. Unusual. But it doesn't demand any special strain of brain cells.

PAVEL. Of course. For this kind of work you don't need higher education.

VOLODYA. And for yours?

PAVEL (silence). What do you want to become?

VOLODYA. A physicist. And you?

PAVEL. Are you going to eat?

VOLODYA. No.

PAVEL. Do you have food with you?

Pavel notices that a little stream of blood is flowing from beneath the hand with which Volodya is holding the rail. Volodya understands this look of Pavel and carelessly sticks his hand in his pocket, drops one foot on the other—the full pose of a fop.

PAVEL. Go and sit down somewhere. Your legs are shaking. Sit down otherwise you aren't going to make it for the second smelting. Pavel goes out. Volodya sits down on the steps of the stairway.

In the restaurant. Sima is washing dishes. Through the window, from which the plates are being handed, she sees Pavel. She asks her next door neighbor to replace her and approaches Pavel.

SIMA (to Pavel). And where is Volodya?

Pavel secretly motions Sima to come to him. Sima comes closer. Pavel quietly leads Sima to the buffet. He has gathered sandwiches and even candy.

PAVEL. Here's what ... Your friend is resting there and thinking about something ... Take it to him. (He gives her the food.) Wait just a second! Don't tell him that I sent you ... He's a psychotic ... If he doesn't eat he won't last out the shift. He'll wreck the daily plan. And there won't be any wages for anybody ... Do you understand? Well, in one word, you tell him a little fib. You women know how to do that. (He pushes Sima in the back and goes to the table to eat.)

Sima and Volodya sit on the stairway.

SIMA. I asked for an advance on my wages—and they gave it to me.

VOLODYA. Pavel see you?

SIMA. He's eating. He told me that you are here. Eat! (She lays out food on the newspaper in front of him. Volodya wants to take a sandwich but his hands are shaking and the sandwich falls through the steps downward to the earth . . . Volodya takes a second, raises it to his mouth, but his fingers tremble and a second sandwich, without getting to his mouth, falls. Sima takes a sandwich and puts it up to his mouth. He obediently bites and eats . . .)

SIMA (as if she didn't notice this situation, continuing to feed Volodya). Can you imagine? My father thinks that you and I are already approaching Moscow. Your parents think that you are our guest—isn't that a laugh! Yes! (She laughs.) Tomorrow morning we'll get into a train—and in one direction or the other. It's true! It's enough!

A tall lad from Pavel's gang passes by.

YOUTH. Finish the rest period: the second smelting is coming up soon.

Volodya even trembles, stands up with difficulty, goes up the stairway. Sima watches him with fright. She catches up with him.

SIMA. Maybe you should give it up? It's not necessary?

VOLODYA (tonelessly, but absolutely with determination). Beat it!

He continues to climb the stairs. Sima follows him with her eyes. When Volodya has disappeared behind the doors, Sima quickly runs upwards, half opens the door and looks through the crack. From the smelting yard there is a whistle, thunder, roar. The glassed walls are lit with light and Sima sees how the first flow of molten lava falls into the ladle standing below. Sima slams the door and with wide-open eyes runs down the stairway. The noise, the whistle, the thunder grow in her ears. She dashes through the factory yard and the thundering sounds pursue her.

Sima runs into the restaurant building, slams the door, and the noise breaks off. At a table four steel workers are sitting and they are laughing in a friendly way about something. Sima looks at them and doesn't understand a thing.

The shift is finished. The youths, the members of Pavel's gang, separate in the courtyard. Volodya stands in the courtyard alone. Pavel comes up to him.

They stand at the board of honor where the photographs of the best workers are pasted.

PAVEL. Let's go to the dormitory.

VOLODYA. I am not going to go there.

PAVEL. Where do you want to go?

VOLODYA. I'll walk about.

PAVEL. You don't want to show yourself among people in such a state!

VOLODYA. You guessed.

PAVEL. Yes and if I were in your place I also would want to catch my breath somewhere by myself.

VOLODYA. Is that your picture? (He points at the picture on the honor board.)

PAVEL. Well, yes, it's mine.

VOLODYA. You should be in the institute.

PAVEL. My mother is sick and my brother and sister are going to school. I'll make out.

VOLODYA. I understand.

PAVEL. Shall we go?

VOLODYA. You go alone.

Pavel goes out. Volodya goes through the factory yard. Some of those coming from the other directions look at him, at his slight stagger, and say: "Already succeeded in getting a load on!" There is a light rain.

Volodya goes into some kind of a shed. Under a sloping roof he lies down on his back. He lies, spread out, his arms extended broadly, and looks upward. He is thinking.

Evening. Sima is looking for Volodya. She runs from barracks to barracks under the rain, from dormitory to dormitory, looks into windows, seeking insistently, vigilantly. Behind the windows the life of the barracks is going on: in some places they are dining, in some places chatting, and in some places there is even music, dances, song.

But Volodya can't be found anywhere.

Sima begins to look for him on the factory territory. She is wet through, chilled, pitiful, trembling. She seeks and seeks!

And all of a sudden she runs into Volodya. At the first moment it seems to her that he is dead. She throws herself upon him, sits next to him on the earth. She sees that Volodya is sleeping soundly. She looks at him for a long time. She looks all around. And then she kisses Volodya on his lips with a long long kiss. She makes a pillow for Volodya from a rag lying nearby. She covers him with canvas. She sits silently. Then she gets up and, covering herself from the rain with a piece of plywood, which she raises over her head, runs to her own dormitory.

Early morning. Volodya goes to the house where Sima lives. There is much noise.

VOLODYA (addressing the girl). Sima Fedorova? Does she live here?

FIRST GIRL. Is that the new one? She got sick.

VOLODYA. How is it that she got sick?

FIRST GIRL. Like people get sick: she is in bed and sick, her temperature is three above normal. She caught cold, evidently.

SECOND GIRL (seeing Volodya). Well, what a beauty appeared in the early morning! Girls, where's he from?

The girls look Volodya over.

SECOND GIRL. To whom does he belong? To whom?

THIRD GIRL. Come this evening to the dance. You probably can put on some stylish dances. What say?

Volodya, not listening to the girls, goes through the room to Sima.

Next to Sima there is a girl who gives Sima a pill. Sima is lying in the bed. Her yesterday's clothing is drying at the window. On the windowsill stand her shoes. At the sight of Volodya Sima hides her thin little shoulders underneath the blanket. Volodya takes a chair and brings it up to the bed. From another room can be heard the merry laughter of girls.

VOLODYA. What is this that you've thought up?

SIMA. I don't know.

VOLODYA. Well, that's already also . . .

SIMA. Yes.

VOLODYA. What's wrong with you?

SIMA. I don't know.

VOLODYA. And what aches?

SIMA. Nothing aches . . . just my throat a little bit . . .

VOLODYA. Well, show it to me . . . (Sima opens her mouth, Volodya looks into it.)

VOLODYA. I don't see anything. You have beautiful teeth. And what a funny little tongue you have in the back of your mouth. Why do people have a little tongue there? Do you know?

SIMA. No.

They sit silent.

VOLODYA. How dark! Has the doctor been here yet?

SIMA. The girls ran to get her . . . She will come.

VOLODYA. Did you eat anything?

SIMA. No, I don't want anything.

VOLODYA. You need something. I'll buy it.

SIMA. I don't want anything. Later. (She looks insistently at Volodya.)

VOLODYA. We have to go.

SIMA. I know.

VOLODYA. Well and what?

SIMA. You go out, I'll dress . . .

A woman doctor comes in.

DOCTOR. Are you Fedorova?

SIMA. That's me.

DOCTOR (Putting her medicine case on the table and opening it. She does everything very exactly, businesslike, almost like a machine.) Ah, so you want to be on the sick list, darling . . . Oh, we don't like to work, oh, we don't like it! (She wipes her hand with alcohol.)

VOLODYA (not understanding the joke). I think that you, before saying that ...

DOCTOR. And you get out of here, if you please. (Volodya is confused.)
Go on out, go on out, you ought to know without being told!
Volodya turns and goes out.

DOCTOR (coming up to Sima). So you can talk with the boys from the
very morning, but how about work ... (She takes Sima's hand,
listens to her pulse, and all of a sudden becomes quite caressing.)
What happened to you, darling? Come on now, show me.
*Volodya goes on out and waits at the porch of the little
house, to see the doctor when she comes out. The doctor comes
out.*

VOLODYA. Doctor!

DOCTOR. Well, what do you want?

VOLODYA. I wouldn't even ask you after you were so sharp with me ...

DOCTOR. Well, come on now, come on, come on without lyrical dis-
gressions. In Gogol they were all right but with you they aren't
going to come out.

VOLODYA. Would it be possible today for her to go away on the
train?

DOCTOR. It is impossible and even very much impossible. Look here,
don't play the fool. And where are you from? Why is it that I
haven't seen you here even once?

VOLODYA. And you know everybody?

DOCTOR. Everybody! (She points at people walking past, at drivers,
etc.) That's Stepanov. That's Popolzukhin. That's Gorbachev
on the truck, and that's Silkin who is walking this way. That's
Kashkin ... and what's your name?

VOLODYA. Fedorov.

DOCTOR. Her husband?

VOLODYA. Heavens, no!

DOCTOR. Why are you so dumbfounded, as if you weren't a man?
Her brother?

VOLODYA. That's a complicated situation ...

DOCTOR. Oh! How I don't love these complicated situations! Where
are you working?

VOLODYA. At the fourth blast furnace.

DOCTOR. Come over to my office and I will give you a tetanus shot.
And then you'll tell me all about it. (She goes out.)
Volodya goes in to see Sima. He enters the room.

VOLODYA. How is it?

SIMA. Not so bad, I caught cold. I'll get up right away and dress.

VOLODYA. Lie there ... Funny ...

SIMA. You won't go away ... By yourself?

VOLODYA. Indeed right now is the best time to get rid of you ... I'll give you one day ... At the most two.

SIMA (smiling). And you are going to go there to work again?

VOLODYA. Well, so what?

SIMA. It's hard.

VOLODYA. Just think? (All of a sudden he takes Sima's hand and awkwardly, caressingly, presses it.) Look here, get well! (And he goes out.)

> *Volodya goes to the blast furnace where he worked yester-*
> *day. There Pavel and the foreman are quarreling about some-*
> *thing.*

FOREMAN. Well, I don't have anybody right now, no! Do you understand?

PAVEL. So what am I supposed to do, go to bed? (He sees Volodya.) Well, what did you forget?

VOLODYA. I'm staying here for a pair of days. You aren't against it?

FOREMAN (to Volodya). All right, all right! (To Pavel.) I'll get you someone in a couple of days! (He goes out.)

PAVEL. What happened all of a sudden?

VOLODYA. I wanted to help you out. I do have to even accounts with you.

PAVEL. What are you talking about?

VOLODYA. You sent me sandwiches with Serafima!

PAVEL. Chatterbox!

VOLODYA. No, she lied as always ... But I understood from where they came ...

> *Whistle. Work begins.*
> *After the end of the shift Volodya goes to see Sima. From*
> *far away he sees that at the little house where Sima lives there*
> *stands an ambulance. Volodya, sensing something amiss, runs.*
> *They carry Sima out of the doors on a stretcher.*
> *Volodya wants to go up closer to the stretcher but they chase*
> *him away.*

MEDICAL ORDERLY. Well, what are you looking at, haven't you ever seen sick people? (Volodya runs around to the other side. He is pushed away by a girl.)

GIRL. Where are you pushing, where are you pushing? Go away!

> *They push the stretcher into the car and Volodya cannot*
> *even see Sima's face.*
> *The doors slam. The machine moves away. The girls sepa-*
> *rate. Volodya stands alone right under the window on which*
> *Sima's shoes are drying. Volodya feels a sharp pang of loneli-*
> *ness. He cannot understand where to go, what to do.*
> *Evening. Volodya sits on his cot, and sews a button to his*

shirt. On one side two youths are studying, books, notebooks in front of them.

VOLODYA. In our school from the seventh grade onward we organized an astro-physical group. I was the chairman ... Right up to the tenth class itself ... The most outstanding scientists came to talk to us ... Professors, academicians ... In science what is surprising is not what we already know, but what one can learn ... (And he directs himself to a youth.) What are you doing—the ninth class?

SHAPKIN. He only wants clean studies. He's too lazy to work. It's too hard!

VOLODYA. Shapkin, don't think that it's easier to move your brain cells than your muscles. (And again he directs himself to the young man.) Well, show it to me ... (He takes the textbook. He holds it in his hands. Tenderly.) Congratulations, old chap! (He opens the pages.) Comedy! Listen, don't you have some textbook or books more complicated than this? What about it? I would snap off a pair of problems! How about it?

YOUTH. No.

VOLODYA (becoming excited). After all, I solved the problems for the second year of university, yes, yes! Honestly! Sometimes even for the third! And those. (He points at the textbook.) I can do in my head ... Listen, I'll shut my eyes and you pick a problem for me which is from among the more complicated ones. At the end, leaf over to the end....

The young man reads the problem aloud. Volodya, eyes shut, with enjoyment, solves it, pronouncing the solution aloud. The solution of the problem goes clearly, consecutively. Some of the youths and adults sitting nearby pay attention and look at Volodya as if he were a magician. However, Volodya does not succeed in completing the solution since the door is pushed open and a girl runs in.

GIRL. Fedorov!

VOLODYA (He opens his eyes as if he were coming back to consciousness.) What?

GIRL. Your wife is dying!

Volodya doesn't understand right away what he has been told. Then he jumps up and rushes out the door.

The hospital. Late in the evening. Quiet. The completely perplexed Volodya sits tensely on a chair. The door slams. Volodya trembles, turns about. But it is a nurse. Volodya calls to her ...

VOLODYA. Nurse!

NURSE. What do you want?

VOLODYA. Can I ask you for a sheet of paper and a pencil?

NURSE. Right away.

> *She goes into the office and comes out. She gives Volodya a paper and pencil. Volodya sits down at a small table and writes feverishly. From the door where the patients' rooms are the doctor comes out. She goes up to Volodya, stands near him, but Volodya, not seeing her, writes. Finally he feels the presence of a person and jumps up.*

VOLODYA. Hello!

DOCTOR. Well, why did you jump up? Sit down, sit down! Hello. (She sits Volodya down and then sits down in front of him on a chair.) The girls from the barracks told you?

VOLODYA. Yes. They said that my wife is dying.

DOCTOR. About "wife"—that's exactly what I told them to say. I don't like it when there's indefiniteness. But as for "dying" that they made up all by themselves. Nevertheless Sima is in a critical condition. It's nothing to fool with. I called you.

VOLODYA. You?

DOCTOR. I.

VOLODYA (all of a sudden). She is not dead.

DOCTOR. Not so fast, not so fast. Sit down. I asked her whether we shouldn't send her parents a telegram, so as to inform them, so that they would not be worried. She answered somehow indefinitely. It's as if she were afraid of her father. She mentioned you for some reason. In a word, she's hesitating . . . Should we send a telegram or not?

VOLODYA. And what do you think?

DOCTOR. We should.

VOLODYA. Can she die?

DOCTOR. Quiet, quiet!

> *Pause.*

VOLODYA. Yes, yes . . . send it. I'll run to the station right now . . . Her father was a famous partisan. He has eleven decorations . . . He thinks . . . He will help . . . Right now I'll . . . Doctor, give her this letter, let her read it, immediately, right away . . .

DOCTOR. Not so fast, she can't read.

VOLODYA (waiting a second). You read it to her . . .

DOCTOR. She won't hear it . . .

VOLODYA. Why?

DOCTOR. She is unconscious, Volodya.

> *Pause. Volodya realizes what he has just heard.*

VOLODYA. Doctor, here's what: you sit next to her and quietly, quietly read it into her ear . . . quietly, quietly. She'll hear it, I swear she will, she'll hear! It's important, it's very important . . . Please, consider it silly, but do it. I ask you . . . quiet . . . quiet . . . Every word . . . All right?

DOCTOR. Well, all right, all right . . . I . . . (She takes the letter from Volodya . . . Volodya goes out of the hospital. Pavel stands on the porch. He came on a motorcycle. Volodya, not noticing Pavel, walks by.)

PAVEL. Where are you going?

VOLODYA. To the station, to send a telegram.

PAVEL. Sit down here, I'll take you there.

VOLODYA. All right.

Both sit down on the motorcycle and go away.

The hospital room where Sima is lying. Sima's eyes are shut. Her face shines. She breathes heavily and often. There is a light from a small table lamp. It is dark all around. The doctor sits down at the cot. The doctor's face can hardly be seen in the gloom. She listens to Sima's breathing. The doctor takes out the sheets of Volodya's letter from the pocket of her robe. She puts them on her knee under a light. At that moment there is the noise of a motorcycle dashing by. The doctor quietly and clearly begins to read the letter:

"Sima, my dear Simka! I never wrote such letters and I would not write it for anything if you were healthy . . . I do not believe in any letters, nor in any words, nor in any other expressions of feeling, because all of that is a shell and never expresses the essence of the matter, but only makes it smaller. And although I know that you understand everything without words, nevertheless I for some reason am worried and must pronounce these trite words which say nothing—'I love you!' But much more than I love you! You are a human being, you are interesting and a special person! You are a kind of person whom I have never before seen . . . You are amusing and more stupid than I can believe, but indeed from all of this I am in some kind of a completely insane delight when I see you or think about you. And it costs me unbelievable efforts to control myself in order that no one in the world should see this. If you die maybe I will kill myself. I don't know exactly, I still haven't decided, but if I decide to then I really will. I think that you understand me very well and see all my good sides and bad. Can it really be that no one sees that if there is anyone that suffers from my faults it is in the first place and most of all myself? Do you think it is easy for me to be such a one? But how am I to blame, that I am such? But I am such! And I don't want to be something else. Listen, I don't want to! And I will hate what I consider hateful, and love what I like. Do you understand? Simka, in general,

you are the same kind too! Without you it's very difficult for me now although there are people here who are interesting. Among other things, Pavel promises to put me in the job of a regular blast furnace worker. Of course, not now, but, I think, I will master it. Curious, don't you think? How do you think about that? And if the smelting is successful then all will say that I am working for the increase in pig iron production for the country. But in fact, I'm simply doing this in your honor . . . And they'll even say that I have become re-educated, re-indoctrinated, although in my opinion it's not me but others who should be re-educated and re-indoctrinated . . . But the chief thing is that I, it turns out, want to study! I want to study, do you hear? I will study well, you will see! You'll simply exclaim when you see how I study! The world must be better than it is . . . And we will try . . . What do you think? You must get well! We must live . . . You hear, I write "we" because I can decide . . . I love you, Simka! In the silly human language there are no words and I cannot think them up right here, in the midst of things, but I love you, love you, love you . . .

The roar of the motorcycle becomes louder and we see Volodya and Pavel dashing down the highway. They arrive at the station. Volodya jumps from the motorcycle while it is still running and swiftly runs into the building of the station.

The doctor continues to read the letter: "I love you, I love you . . ."

She is silent. She looks at Sima. Sima breathes more evenly. The nurse, who heard the letter, also looks at Sima, listening to her breathing.

NURSE. Could she really have heard?

DOCTOR. Quiet! Give her some more camphor.

NURSE (looking at Sima). Happy!

The Scene Changes.

The doctor and Uncle Vasily stand near the hospital. Uncle Vasily has a suitcase in his hand.

DOCTOR. Membraneous pneumonia on both sides is nothing to fool with . . .

UNCLE. So, today I can't see her.

DOCTOR. Not today. Tomorrow, perhaps.

UNCLE. That means that there's still a danger?

DOCTOR. There still is.

UNCLE. And where is that scoundrel working, don't you know?

DOCTOR. I know. "The scoundrel" is working at the fourth blast furnace.

UNCLE. I am going to show him right now, that bastard!

*He walks briskly in the direction of the fourth blast furnace.
Uncle stands near the blast furnace. From the stairway Volodya
runs to him—black, in perspiration. His uncle doesn't even recognize him.*

Volodya throws himself on his uncle.

VOLODYA. Hello, Uncle Vasya! (He shakes his uncle's hand.) Were
you there to see Sima?

UNCLE (still not understanding how to conduct himself with his relative). Yes.

VOLODYA. How is she?

UNCLE. Maybe they'll let me in to see her tomorrow.

VOLODYA. Ah, ha! It means she's better . . . I was there this morning
and the doctor didn't tell me . . . (He takes his uncle's suitcase.)
Let's go to the restaurant. You probably are hungry from your
journey .

*They move off to the restaurant. Uncle walks next to
Volodya. From the side they look at each other. They go along
the courtyard, walking around the construction materials which
are lying there, letting trucks go by, and trains. They walk along
in silence.*

VOLODYA. That's the sheet metal rolling mill. They finished it not
long ago. (He sees someone.) Greetings, Genadii! How's everything?

GENADII. Normal . . .

Again they walk along in silence.

VOLODYA. That's the Bessemer Section. (Again he sees someone.)
Hello, Galochka!

GALYA. Greetings, Vova!

VOLODYA. That's a laboratory assistant . . . I know her . . .

Again they walk along in silence.

UNCLE. Your parents are insane with worry. I just sent them a telegram. I got a letter from them. (He gets a letter out of his
pocket.) Here, read about their sufferings.

VOLODYA. It's not necessary. (He pushes the letter away.)

UNCLE. You're not brave enough?

VOLODYA. You like to torture. (He takes the letter and puts it in his
pocket.)

UNCLE. I brought your money.

VOLODYA. What money? Ah! That! That's good: it's necessary to buy
Sima some clothing. We have a store which is not so bad.

Again they walk along silently.

VOLODYA (laughs). That, incidentally, is a bath. With all the necessary equipment. I think that you ought to stay at our dormitory. I will ask Pavel. He'll arrange it.

UNCLE. Who is that?

VOLODYA. Pavel? He's a friend. You're not against it?

UNCLE. No.

> *Volodya, Uncle, Pavel are in the store. Before them on the counter there are dresses, sweaters, even stockings. Volodya picks out shoes for Sima. He points out the most expensive ones.*

VOLODYA (to the saleswoman). Those!

> *A vestibule in the hospital.*
>
> *Volodya and his uncle are waiting for Sima to come out of the hospital. The nurse has taken from them a rather large pack of clothing and gone into the room. Volodya and his uncle sedately sit on chairs. Volodya puts on the table flowers which he has been holding.*

UNCLE. I see that you have learned a lot during this time. You have begun to understand . . . You've become different . . .

VOLODYA. Uncle, when people say something like that to me for some reason or other I begin to get sick to my stomach.

> *His uncle turns crimson with wrath and since he can't shout loudly—because of the hospital, he whispers furiously.*

UNCLE. You still have in you that evil demon!

VOLODYA (joyfully). Without the demon, Uncle, in my opinion, it's not worth living in general: one can't take life seriously!

UNCLE. You don't have very much respect for your elders.

VOLODYA. Why? You are a pleasant old chap . . .

UNCLE (again growing crimson). And as for you, you're a snake and I can never understand whether you're saying something pleasant or nasty to me.

VOLODYA. Pleasant, Uncle Vasya, pleasant!

UNCLE. So so! (They are silent.) This evening so, we're going to go home.

VOLODYA. We're going.

> *Sima comes out. She is in a new dress, new shoes, and she looks well dressed and, as often happens with people after illness, younger and inspired. She has become something different. More quivering. She kisses the uncle. The uncle embraces her tightly, tightly, and holds her for a long time, pressing her to himself. He loves her very much. There are almost tears in his eyes. Volodya stands on one side. Sima approaches him and reaches out her hand.*

SIMA. Hello.

VOLODYA (very carelessly presses her hand). Greetings, sick list!

SIMA (apologizing). Well, that's the way it happened . . . I'm sure it was very difficult for you . . .

VOLODYA (carelessly). So what! Well, I must be going. (He remembers something.) One minute. (He takes the flowers, which are lying on the table. He looks for someone with his eyes. He finds what he is looking for. He goes. He goes up to the doctor.)

VOLODYA. These are for you ... from Uncle ...

DOCTOR. Maybe they're from you?

VOLODYA. In general, as you please ...

DOCTOR. Listen here, I read your crazy letter aloud but I didn't give it to her. Here it is ... (She takes out the sheet of the letter.) Give it to her yourself ...

VOLODYA (taking the letter). Nonsense! (He tears up the letter into small pieces and throws it into a wastebasket.)

DOCTOR. You're so rich!

Volodya, Sima and the uncle leave the hospital.

UNCLE. We will make the evening train.

VOLODYA (not knowing how to begin). Here's what I have decided: you go, the two of you.

UNCLE. And you?

VOLODYA. I have to stay here for a while ... I have one piece of business. It's nonsense, of course ... But nevertheless I have lost a whole lot of time in vain ... Another pair of weeks ... All right?

UNCLE (he looks insistently at Volodya). Yes, you're a curious little beast! Serafima! (He looks at Sima, but understands everything. He is silent. He bursts out.) Well, at least you two can take me to the station to see me off?

VOLODYA. Well, of course.

UNCLE. I wish I'd never laid eyes on you!

All three leave.

The Scene Changes.

> *The blast furnace section. Volodya is working at the pig iron outlet in place of the veteran blast furnace worker. He is concentrated, excited. The last preparations are being made for the smelting. Sima watches from far away in hiding. The foreman watches. The apprentice blast furnace workers watch, not without curiosity. Pavel attentively watches Volodya's actions.*
> *The needles of the instruments flutter.*
> *Pause.*

VOLODYA (in a firm voice but with emotion). Open the pig iron outlet!

> *He pierces the outlet.*
> *A flood of metal pours out and lights up the building. The light is ever brighter, brighter and brighter. A cloud of smoke bursts upwards. Sparks fly like fireworks. Everything is in move-*

ment. Sima's eyes, Pavel's face. Volodya's figure in full length.
The smelting has begun!

The Scene Changes.

A railway track. Volodya and Sima walk along the ties. They
are walking almost in the same way that they had walked along
before. They are dressed in the same way that young people
dress nowadays—quite fashionably. Quite far away there is
barely visible the junction to which they are walking. Volodya
is whistling some kind of a dance melody.

SIMA. What is that you are whistling?

VOLODYA. A fashionable dance. Do you know how to dance?

SIMA. No, of course not.

VOLODYA. I will teach you, without fail! You'll gasp!

SIMA. You tell me: are we going to go to Moscow or to my home?

VOLODYA. That doesn't decide the matter, Yevdokiya! What's important is to have in one's head one's own ostriches.

SIMA. What?

VOLODYA. And, maybe, having lived for a hundred years, to die without even seeing them. Do you understand?

SIMA. Does this dress suit me?

VOLODYA (stopping). Listen, shall I tell you why you insisted on accompanying me?

SIMA. When was that?

VOLODYA. Well, when I was running away from you . . .

SIMA. Why?

VOLODYA. Should I tell you?

SIMA. If you please.

VOLODYA. Because you . . . me!

SIMA. You're a fool, that's what you are!

VOLODYA. Aha! You're afraid!

SIMA. God, how silly you are, how repulsive you are! (She runs quickly
ahead. Volodya follows her. Sima turns around. Her face is burning with indignation, shame, desperation.) Don't you dare follow me! Do you hear? I despise you! You are repulsive! Do you
hear! You're a toad! (Again she goes quickly.)

VOLODYA (catching up with her). Wait!

SIMA (stopping). What did I tell you?

VOLODYA (he laughs). You're afraid of the truth!

SIMA. You're a *stilyaga!* You've got a rich imagination! The only
thing you can do is to tell lies, to lie! Don't follow me, do you
hear?

She runs along the ties. And Volodya follows her.

VOLODYA. Yelena! Tonya! Irina! Vera! Anastasya!

The junction is already close. Sima's dress streams out be-hind as she runs. Volodya keeps up with her. There is a very distant train whistle. Ahead the arms of the semaphores rise.

THE END

Yuri Nagibin

An Introduction to Yuri Nagibin

Yuri Markovich Nagibin was born in 1920 and grew up in Moscow. His family was from among the Russian intelligentsia and lived in the "Chistye Prudy" district of the capital—close by the Chief City Postoffice. Nagibin graduated from a Moscow secondary school and from 1939 to 1941 studied at the scenario faculty of the State Cinematography Institute.

Nagibin has written a great deal about his own childhood and youth in such stories as "There Were Four of Us," "On the Raft," "The Old Turtle," and in his series of stories recently published under the title of *Chistye Prudy*.*

One of Nagibin's most recent books of short stories published in the Soviet Union contains a fairly complete biographical account and evaluation of his work in an appendix by V. Dorofeyev—and it is worth quoting from this Soviet essay at some length.†

Writes Dorofeyev: "A particularly strong influence on the bringing up of the young writer was exercised by his mother. She aroused in him interest in reading, indoctrinated him in good literary taste and from his very childhood awakened love for his native language and literature. It is not for nothing that the lyrical image of the mother, as the nearest and dearest person, often emerges in Nagibin's works.

"From the very first days of the War of the Fatherland Nagibin sought to get to the front. A medical commission found him unsuitable for military service—however he insisted and from the beginning of 1942 to October 1943 he was in the ranks of the army, at the Volkhov, then the Voronezh front, as a political worker. As a result of shell shock Nagibin was demobilized from the army, but even after this he did not leave the front, and from the end of 1943 to 1945 worked as a military correspondent of the newspaper *Trud*. At the end of the war when his literary gifts were already clear Nagibin left the paper and became a professional writer.

"The commencement of Nagibin's literary work goes back to 1939. His first story entitled 'The Double Error' was published in 1940 in one of the March numbers of *Ogonek*. Subsequently, Nagibin

---

* "Chistye Prudy"—his native district in Moscow—can be translated as "Clear Ponds." The series includes the stories: "For a Whole Lifetime," "The Generous Gift," "The Bicycle," "The Torpedo Boat," "I Study Languages," "Zhenya Rumyantseva," and "Twenty Years Afterwards." They were published in the journal *Znamya*, No. 1 (1961).
† Yuri Nagibin, *Rannei Vesnoi; Rasskazy* (Moscow, 1961), pp. 458–60.

prepared for publication a collection of his early literary efforts, but the Great War of the Fatherland interrupted all his previous plans and served as a beginning of a new stage in his life and literary work.

"Nagibin belongs to the generation of Soviet writers who found their creative destiny in the years of the war. Severe reality of the front, difficult effort and the soldier's duty became for this generation the first and indelible university of life. The frontline newspaper and the radio broadcast for soldiers were their first literary tribune.

"In the army, carrying out the demanding duties of a political worker, Nagibin at the same time worked intensely as a writer. He wrote journalistic reports from the front, essays and stories from army life. In 1943 the publishing house 'Sovietsky Pisatel' issued his first collection of stories under the characteristic title *Man From the Front.**

"And when nowadays one reads over again this unassuming publication which is in a literary sense far from without defects one inevitably remembers the words of Lev Tolstoi: 'During certain years the writer can even in some degree sacrifice polish of form; and if merely his attitude to what he is describing is clearly and strongly apparent then his work can attain its purpose.'

"A distinctive trait of the stories of Nagibin of that time is their factual truth to life. In their majority these are frontline stories which exude heroism and bravery. In his subsequent collections such as *Big Heart* (1944), *The Kernel of Life* (1948), and others, Nagibin continues incessantly, and from various sides, to work over the theme of the war, deepening the content and perfecting the form of his stories. And it is very clearly felt when one reads these works, one after another, that the young writer is stubbornly seeking himself, is seeking his own treatment of the complex war theme, is seeking the treatment of near and dear subjects and themes, lines and colors, which correspond to his experience and creative inclination.

"In the war stories and essays of Nagibin one rarely encounters, for example, battle scenes, and as he goes along they completely disappear. Evidently, the picture of mass fighting in general is not his cup of tea. The varied mutual relationships of people on the front, however, are something different for him. Through them there penetrates the psychology of the Soviet person, his moral aspect, the daily heroism of his self-sacrificing war feat. In such cases Nagibin's talent flowers and he writes excellent stories on small and large scale, such as 'Radiosoldier,' 'The Translator,' 'The Path to the Front Areas,' and others.

---

* Nagibin's stories from the front were translated into English and published under the title *Each for All* (New York and London, 1945), 68 pp.

"One of the most remarkable and most typical stories of Nagibin is 'Struggle for Altitude.' This story was written recently and up to the present it is, in my opinion, the peak of everything created by Nagibin. In this story there are combined with surprising harmony deep social content, the most important idea of the overriding significance of the Communist Party approach to any matter whatsoever, and concrete, precise, clear imagery clothing this idea with living artistic flesh of characters and pictures.

"In reading the wartime, the 'peacetime' and the 'childhood' works of Nagibin you evidently will notice one of their traits: in his works there are no sharply gripping plots nor fascinating subjects. There are not described in them any outstanding events which are attractive merely by the fact that they are outstanding. As a rule in his stories Nagibin uses with emphasis workaday events—the conflicts of people in one or another vitally important business ('Struggle for Altitude'), a happening during a hunt ('The Last Hunt,' 'The Nighttime Guest,' and others), meetings along the highways ('In Early Spring,' 'The Crutches,' etc.), and the like.

"However, the writer so attentively looks inside and considers these daily occurrences and then as a rule with such inspiration tells little stories about his everyday heroes that in the course of the telling of the story its 'workaday' character seems to retreat to the back of the stage and before the reader there arises in its firm outlines the real life of people in all of its actual many-faceted and many-colored nature—simultaneously big and small, complex and simple."

As can be seen from this contemporary Russian evaluation of Nagibin and description of his career he has been more or less continuously writing his short stories ever since the age of nineteen—in 1939—and by now, in his early forties, he has a very large number of individual stories and half a dozen or so collections of stories in book form to his credit (and also several cinema scenarios). Three collections—all scanty and not containing any of his best work—have been translated and published in English, including the very brief group of war stories previously mentioned and also a collection called *The Pipe* and another entitled *Dreams.** Nagibin got considerably more notice among Westerners for his two short stories included in the famous collection published in 1956 and entitled *Literary Moscow*. This almanac, which included some outstanding works by leading Russian writers of the older and the younger generations, was all in all a bitter attack on Stalinism and bureaucracy published in the wake of the exposure of Stalin's misdoings at the

---

* Yuri Nagibin, *The Pipe: Stories,* translated by V. Shneerson (Moscow, 1958), 110 pp. And also Yuri Nagibin, *Dreams (Short Stories),* translated by R. Daglish, *et al.* (Moscow, 1958).

Twentieth Communist Party Congress by Nikita Khrushchev. *Literary Moscow* fell under attack from the Party almost as soon as it appeared, and by his participation in it Nagibin, known previously chiefly for his war stories, achieved prominence at home and abroad as one of the more outspoken younger Russian authors.

The more blunt of Nagibin's two stories from *Literary Moscow* is entitled "A Light in the Window." * It is a brief vignette about a rest home whose proprietor maintains the best, most spacious quarters in his establishment always clean, neat and ready in case "he" should come. Who "he" is the reader is left to guess—whether it means the minister of the particular ministry to which the rest home was attached, the local Party secretary, or even perhaps Stalin himself. At any rate the Stalin symbol, of course, immediately comes to mind. Even when newlyweds came and there was no place to put them, "his" quarters remained untouched. The proprietor refused to permit anyone else inside except only Nastya, the maid, who cleans there scrupulously and with almost religious reverence. Nastya waits and waits for "him" to appear. But "he" never comes, and the quarters remain unused year after year. But as time passes and "he" does not come, Nastya feels more and more disappointed. And her disappointment eventually becomes rage. And finally she can bear it no longer. And so it was that one night when he returns to the rest home late at night Vasily Petrovich, the director, sees a light in the window of the sacred quarters. And when he goes to see who it is thus sacrilegiously violating his orders that no one should enter there he finds Nastya and the yardman, Stepan, and Stepan's two children inside the special apartment watching television. He shouts at them and drives them out, and they calmly walk past him, departing with dignity, not saying a word. And Vasily Petrovich falls silent, and inside he senses finally "a feeling of unbearable disgust for himself."

The element of protest which appears in "A Light in the Window" is not, however, a constant theme of Nagibin, though it does recur now and then. Even in the case of this story one has to remember that the "protest" was one well after the event—a protest against the "personality cult" made in 1956 three years after Stalin's death and at a time when it was already "Party line" to decry and condemn the "personality cult." Much more often than they protest against elements of the regime, Nagibin's stories contain aspects—sometimes delicately brought out and sometimes blunt—of propaganda. Nagibin, after all, was a professional propagandist in his work

* In *Bitter Harvest*, edited by Edmund Stillman, translated by Elizabeth Marbury (New York, 1959), pp. 166–74.

during the war both as a political officer at the front and as a front-line correspondent. And this has left obviously a lasting imprint on his outlook. At the same time Nagibin has also written many stories which contain not the slightest element of obvious propaganda and which deal with the inner life of complex Russian human beings with great perception, understanding and sympathy. And it is among these nonpolitical stories that one finds his more interesting work.

Nagibin's favorite setting for his stories about Russians is the Meshchera country, located southeast of Moscow at a distance of 150 miles or so, in what was before the revolution the northern part of old Ryazan Province. The Meshchera country is wild, wooded, and swampy, with lakes and marshes which abound in game birds. It has long been a beloved hunting area for the more hardy Muscovites—and many of the local Meshchera inhabitants have made their livings from hunting and from guiding hunters and fishermen. Nagibin obviously knows this district and its lakes, its game and its local characters, as if it were his own home. One of Nagibin's best stories of the hunters of the Meshchera country is entitled "The Last Hunt."

One of Nagibin's favorite subjects is love—and in his stories he skillfully shows different sides of this familiar human emotion.

To date, in more than two full decades of active professional writing, Yuri Nagibin has clung closely to the short story as his chosen literary form. He has at least one novel—a war story entitled *Pavlik* —to his credit, but it seems likely that he will continue to write mostly short stories.

Generally speaking, Yuri Nagibin was not criticized severely during the big clampdown in literature from December 1962 to June 1963, not, at any rate, for his own literary work. However, he did catch a brickbat thrown his way by L. F. Ilyichev, Central Committee secretary, who in his speech of December 26, 1962, to young writers, said that in an article in the *Literary Gazette* in which he had defended the abstract sculptor, Ernst Neizvestny, Nagibin had taken "a very dubious viewpoint."

It is also noteworthy that Nagibin was not among the writers who got up to attack bitterly, as some did, other Russian progressive writers during this clampdown. Nagibin is a loyal supporter of the Party—and also can be counted as belonging to the liberal or progressive group of Soviet writers. His personal associations are closest with the young liberal writers and poets. He is, for instance, married to Bella Akhmadulina, talented and beautiful poetess who was Yevgeny Yevtushenko's first wife.

Not long ago he was asked in a questionnaire sent out by a Soviet magazine the following question:

"Should it be considered necessary for a writer's own personal life to correspond to what he advocates in his works?"

Nagibin replied: "A writer must be kind and love his fellow men. But we cannot expect him to be an angel. For it is not angels who write books."

Chetunov, Son of Chetunov*

As always Sergei Chetunov awoke because it was hard to breathe. Every morning in the desert began with a sensation of stifling heaviness. This meant the sun had begun to warm the canvas side of the tent near his folding cot. He was a newcomer and had been given the worst place. It would be another several minutes more until the sun reached his tent companions, Moryagin and Struchkov—so both were still sound asleep.

Chetunov's first motion was to seize his canteen. But the canteen, as usual, was empty. Several warmish drops fell on his lower lip and dissolved in the dryness of his mouth, leaving on his teeth the crunch of grains of sand. From the dry swallow his throat smarted.

Chetunov reached up and unbuttoned the flap of the skylight, letting in the aroma of air which was warm but fresher than that in the tent. And a thin little ray of the sun, like an incandescent wire, stretched from the skylight to Moryagin's table. The ray dripped gold on an empty champagne bottle from whose throat a candle-end stuck out. It dissolved in rainbow patches of light along the red leather of the mountain boots which also stood on the table and lit up in two silver buttons the jutting eyes of a lizard covered by a glass jar.

"A lizard! What's it doing there?" Chetunov thought to himself squeamishly, watching how the light-colored skin on the throat of the breathing lizard was being pulled in and puffed out with difficulty, with trembling jerks. "It's going to die!" he stepped toward Moryagin's table in order to let the lizard out, but accidentally touched the table and something rang out. Moryagin raised his red sweaty face over his pillow.

"What is it?" he growled out in a hoarse voice which had not yet been cleared out

"There's a lizard..." Chetunov muttered, embarrassed for some reason.

"It's for my son. Don't touch it!" Moryagin turned on his other side and immediately went back to sleep.

"What a type!" Chetunov thought to himself while making his way out of the tent along the small stairway cut into the clay. (The tent was dug into the earth up to half of its height.) "It should be

* Russian title: "Chetunov, Syn Chetunova," published in Yuri Nagibin, *Rannei Vesnoi, Rasskazy*, Gosudarstvennoye Izdatelstvo, Khudozhestvennoi Literatury (Moskva, 1961), pp. 168–97.

put to sleep with ether. How he shouted at me: 'Don't touch it!' I should have taken and let the lizard out or else forced Moryagin to put it to sleep!"

But in the depth of his soul Chetunov knew that he would not do that and that Moryagin knew that Chetunov wouldn't do it. "People easily guess the tactfulness of someone else. They have found out by now that I am not a troublemaker. But today is my day and not yours, Comrade Moryagin!" And with that Chetunov smiled and immediately fell into a good mood.

He stood near the edge of the *takyr*—a big, flat, clay plate or plain of Central Asia tens of square kilometers in size. Cut across in all directions by a multitude of thin cracks, smooth, firm, whitish, or almost white, the soil of the *takyr* reminded one of a parquet floor. Down along the nearest edge of the *takyr* a row of tents extended half dug into the earth. Several trucks and a portable drilling rig and two tractors stood there.

And further stretched the desert—endless yellow expanses of sand. On the edge of the *takyr* the sand was strewn with angular chunks of clay, blown by the wind from the *takyr* and burned by the sun to the strength of tile, just as if a gigantic load of clay pitchers had been smashed there into smithereens.

The naked landscape, picked to the bone by the sun and the wind, roused a kind of lonely, uncozy feeling in Chetunov. But today Chetunov noticed that the weary sight of the *takyr* did not cause in him the customary unpleasant feeling. He remembered the words of the pilot who had brought him here from Ashkhabad: "An excellent natural flying field." And it was as if the *takyr* would turn out to be a not-so-bad takeoff field for him, Chetunov.

Thinking about his good luck, Chetunov could no longer hold back the flight of his imagination. He thought about it while washing his mouth out with the murky water which came from the barrel and smelled of clay. He thought about it while annihilating one more can of the mackerel of which he was so tired. He thought about it while equipping himself for his trip. In actual fact it couldn't be called just a piece of good luck. For after all a piece of good luck is something which is a matter of chance. And Chetunov had gone to his success with conscious, determined effort.

Sergei Chetunov, the son of a famous geologist, Academician Sergei Pavlovich Chetunov, from his earliest childhood had known that he would not have the same kind of life as others.

Playing with his playmates of his own age the favorite game of childhood, "What are you going to be?" he never hesitated among the possible attractive professions—from composer to deep-sea diver. He always said one and the same thing, simply and with conviction:

"I shall be a famous geologist." There had never been any doubts on this score, neither for him himself nor his family. Indeed, what else could Chetunov, the son of Chetunov, be? There was no need for him to search, to make a mistake in the determination of his course. And he didn't experience either that sudden falling in love with science which a person experiences who once and for all has suddenly discovered his true calling. He could not even say when he had fallen in love with geology. It seemed to him he had loved it always, like his mother, father, the nursemaid, as he had loved everything of his own, everything associated with home and family and inseparable from the familiar beloved world of childhood.

To bear the name of Chetunov was not only a benefit: it carried with it heavy obligation. Sergei Chetunov studied well. He was a leader in school and in the institute, but this surprised no one, just as if that was the way it should be. And Chetunov felt himself under the obligation of always astonishing people. He did not have the right to be the same as everyone else. After all, he was the son of Chetunov. He supposed he was not like everyone else when, renouncing his advanced graduate work, renouncing Moscow, renouncing calm and certain work under the sponsorship of Professor Markov, a pupil of his father, he volunteered to go out to the desert. He saw that all those around him—fellow students, professors, ordinary acquaintances—esteemed his deed. And that gave him the courage without which it would have been difficult to leave his home.

But once he had arrived at the expedition site, somehow he had disappeared into a milieu in which the same concerns and burdens fell to the share of each. For each there was the same flaming sun and the same warmish water, yellow from clay. Here he became again the same as everyone else and therefore desired desperately to stand out from the group, to show he was the one and only, unique, Chetunov, son of Chetunov.

But instead from the beginning he committed stupidities and had to win even the right to be like everyone else. Chetunov could still not remember his blunder without a feeling of shame.

Chetunov knew the most important thing in the desert is water. Drinking water was brought on airplanes. During his first days before taking a swallow he looked carefully to see how much was left in his canteen. He did this secretly, fearing lest others should notice. Then he became convinced that the ration of water per day was fully sufficient and stopped worrying about water. But then he observed that his comrades, "veterans of the desert," were enduring thirst with difficulty. On occasion they asked each other whether or not the airplane with water had arrived. They cast at Chetunov thirsty looks when he drank from his canteen. Chetunov laughed inside himself at this lack of restraint and even said to Moryagin, in whom he had sensed right away a petty person and with whom he was therefore not so much on guard as with the others:

"You should acquire your own personal irrigation director."

"It's easy for you to talk nonsense!" Moryagin snapped back. "You have a full canteen and we've had no water for more than a day."

It turned out that the chief drilling rig was threatened with a stoppage because of lack of water and that the expedition members had decided to sacrifice their drinking water. An exception had been made only for Chetunov because he was a newcomer. And although Chetunov, in the depths of his soul, considered this just, he went to the chief and made a big speech of it. This was his second mistake.

The chief of the expedition, elderly, handsome, with sharp, characteristic features of face, who had something of a tiger in himself, and who possessed powerful, broad gestures, produced on Chetunov the impression of an adult who was sitting at a table for toys. The chief had experienced a sharp reverse in his life: he had occupied a high post in the ministry before being demoted to chief of a small geophysical expedition. Chetunov felt that after this it ought to be awkward for a person to look into the eyes of those about him. But this man not only looked. He drilled into the person with whom he was speaking with his light-gray, shining, caressing-threatening eyes which were deeply hid under his firm forehead bone.

The chief listened to the passionate speech of Chetunov with a calm, even bored look. He yawned broadly and said:

"So what did you make so much noise about? So you want to suffer like everyone else? Please yourself!"

He immediately gave the order not to give Chetunov water, without putting any value whatsoever on the noble act of the young specialist.

Happily water was brought the next day. But Chetunov had drawn his own conclusions. He immediately became modest and very soon became just like everyone else. He taught himself to get along without water when it was necessary but also to be frank and open about his thirst. He taught himself to be sometimes silent and sometimes communicative in accordance with the general mood. He taught himself to drink warm champagne out of the dipper which had a tinny taste and was impossibly repulsive. And to spit out the sediment in a long stream. And Chetunov at the same time persistently sought an opportunity to stand out from his environment. With the chief he had to watch himself carefully: the chief did not like show-offs. Therefore, Chetunov did everything to avoid manifestation of empty enthusiasm. He didn't push himself forward. At production conferences he was silent. But the whole time he remembered his purpose. He was helped in some measure by luck, which always comes to the aid of the person who seeks it intensely. It was not in vain that his father had said to him: "In science luck is one of the forms of conformity with law." During his very first days with the expedition Chetunov had discovered on Moryagin's table a soiled, ruffled map. Chetunov from his childhood had had a passion for maps. Looking it over he became convinced that on the map there was depicted a section of the work of their expedition.

"Where did you get this?" Chetunov asked.

"Over there alongside of us archeologists are working. And I asked them for a piece of blueprint," Moryagin answered. "It's my tablecloth."

Chetunov asked him for the map, and during his spare time he studied it. The map was very carefully drawn up. It gave Chetunov a complete picture of the piece of desert in which he was living and working. And even then vaguely—like some kind of a distant opportunity—one particular thought flashed through his mind, to be even more exact the premonition of a thought. And soon this thought emerged from the secrets of his consciousness as a precise and quite original idea.

For a more definite interpretation of the seismic data of the expedition it was necessary to know the physical traits of the strata which lay at the depth of at least the first reflecting horizon, in other words, at 200 to 300 meters from the surface. For this purpose the drillers had begun to drill three deep wells. But the work was conducted poorly. At times it was stopped by accidents, at times by lack of water. During a month they had drilled in total only a few tens of meters. The chief had called a meeting with the participation of the drill foremen and the workers.

It was stifling and smoky from home-rolled and other cigarettes. The monotonous, impotent words, "We must recognize with all objectivity . . . We must decisively struggle for increase in productivity . . . ," crept into Chetunov's ears.

Incidentally now and then, there were businesslike proposals, but so-so, small change. The senior foreman proposed seeking artesian water in the neighborhood. The chief engineer proposed to try to get new equipment . . . The chief was silent, leaving it up to people to speak out, but Chetunov saw that the bluish whites of his eyes were swelled with blood, and after each statement he moved his jaws strangely, showing his large yellow teeth.

"How good it would be to get up and astonish everyone with some kind of a brilliant idea!" Chetunov thought to himself. And right then and there he remembered the map. He remembered it with extraordinary exactitude, just as if he had only just that moment examined it. A strange shiver—the premonition of discovery—permeated his body notwithstanding the hundred degree temperature. Chetunov unnoticeably sought his way out of the tent and ran off for the map. Indeed, everything was just as he had remembered it: there was that depression and its depth was shown—300 meters. A good map, an excellent map!

When Chetunov returned to the tent where the meeting was being held Struchkov was saying something, and the chief was impatiently moving his jaws. But at that moment Struchkov stopped talking, lifted his hands for some reason, and sat down in his place.

"Permit me!" Chetunov said ringingly, the color leaving his face.

Heads turned about at one and the same time like spheres on axles. The narrow pupils of the chief pierced Chetunov.

"Well, all right, let's listen to geology."

Having begun to speak, Chetunov during the first seconds did not hear his own voice, and nevertheless knew that he was speaking with conviction and firmness. He began with the fact that in the desert among the sands there are locations where there come to the surface deposits of a more ancient age and immediately he gave a list of all of the strata into which these ancient deposits are divided. At this point he already heard himself and he was pleased with the sound of his voice. Intentionally, he was using those special names of strata with which textbooks in geology are full. And seeing bewilderment on the faces of the audience he thought to himself: "That's all right, get used to the language of genuine science."

"Couldn't you be more clear, comrade geologist, and closer to actual business," the chief said impatiently.

"I am speaking in the language of my science," Chetunov answered just as sharply. He was convinced that he was playing a sure game and could permit himself this. "Indeed I am not a geophysicist but only a geologist, but I will undertake to get you samples of the deposits you need, and larger ones than those you can get here from drilling."

Chetunov could judge of the impression which he had made by the fact that everything was immediately quiet. Without hurrying he got out of his pocket the map and laid it out on the table, moving to one side the tobacco pouch and the pipe of the chief.

"Right here, a hundred kilometers from the area of our work there is located the deep depression Kara-Shor. Its steep sides, up to 300 meters in height, are composed of contemporary and tertiary deposits, but in their lower parts there are exposed also deeper deposits of older age. And I could bring to you from there samples of the deposits which interest you which are lying at the same depth, and give you the thickness of the individual strata ..." The slightly excited, triumphant information with which Chetunov finished his statement fell into a cold silence. And he expected an explosion. "They simply didn't understand me," thought Chetunov of the geophysicists with embarrassment and disappointment.

"So, so!" with gleaming eyes, pronounced the chief. "And then we can test these samples for density, magnetism, conductivity, and then we can introduce the data which we have learned into our calculations of depth. How much time do you need?" he asked Chetunov already with a different, businesslike sharpness.

"One day if you will give me an airplane," Chetunov answered him in the same tone.

"Decided!" the chief clapped his hand on the table, got up and, surveying the meeting with a look which had become gay, said: "A real Chetunov!"

With this phrase he immediately assigned to Chetunov his proper place. Yes, from this moment he had ceased to be one of those young specialists, pitiful in their lack of experience, among whom as it would seem he had been numbered. He had become Chetunov, son of Chetunov.

Approaching the tent of the chief, Chetunov with a pleasant feeling of liberation remembered his former shyness before this person.

"Yes, yes, come in please!" sounded from out of the tent the low, powerful voice.

Chetunov entered. The chief stood in the center of the tent, with his short, strong legs, dressed in expensive generals' boots set widely apart. He was wearing britches of light gray gabardine and a silk shirt as white as snow. "He is dressed as if he were waiting every minute to be called to Moscow," Chetunov noted to himself, involuntarily giving way to his previous unpleasant feelings. But this passing thought only slipped through his consciousness, without reflecting itself on the feeling of friendliness which was aroused in Chetunov now at this moment by the figure of the chief—short, heavy-set, leaning forward, with pepper and salt hair exactly like the fur of a silver fox, and his astonishing tender and threatening eyes.

"Sit down, Chetunov!"

"Thank you." Chetunov answered, but he remained standing.

"What is it, you're impatient!" said the chief. His quick and tenacious look seemed to draw Chetunov into the depth of the small, narrow pupils. Chetunov understood that he had been evaluated, weighed, examined in his canvas shirt with its two small pockets, his loose canvas trousers, his mountain boots, and his broad belt with its canteen.

"The map?" asked the chief.

Chetunov clapped his hand on his map case with its transparent celluloid side.

"So you're in a marching mood!" said the chief, paying tribute for a second time to Chetunov's family name. He got up from behind his desk. "Well, I wish you success! There's one condition: no risks."

"No risks!"

They exchanged firm handclasps.

Chetunov walked with a light step out of the tent to where the airplane was waiting for him. Already the entire camp was awake. Rumbling with empty drums, a truck dashed by in the same direction as Chetunov. Behind its thick tires rose pillars of dust. The wind blowing from below transformed the pillars into little whirlwinds. The little whirlwinds merged into long banks, and Chetunov knew that if the wind did not die down in an hour or two the camp would be covered with a yellow layer of dust.

Moryagin came out of the tent and, lazily stretching, went up to the water barrel. Behind him Struchkov put in an appearance in a linen suit and a white felt hat. Stooped as usual he made his way to the drilling rig. And at other tents morning life was on the move: people were washing, shaving, opening canned goods. Chetunov watched all of these busy people and suddenly with astonishing clarity he pictured to himself that he was not like them, that he would always be able to rise above circumstances. It was not for nothing today when they were beginning their customary day, distinguished in no way from other days, that he, Chetunov, though he was the youngest employee here, was awaited by an airplane, awaited by an interesting, big, special assignment.

And the airplane and the pilot in actual fact were already awaiting Chetunov. The airplane was old, a plane which had seen many sights, with darkened metal parts and a fuselage of indefinite color. The pilot, Kozitsyn, was slightly acquainted with Chetunov, and like his airplane he was desert-worn: with burned-out hair, brows, and eyelashes, with a face tanned from sunburn almost into black.

Kozitsyn's glance was open, but somehow too insistent and appraising. Chetunov did not like it. "He is looking me over as if I were a counterfeit coin," he thought to himself.

"So shall we fly?" said Kozitsyn, and laughed just as if it had been a successful joke.

"Evidently so!" Chetunov confirmed with an intentionally foolish tone.

"As a rule in the desert we are supposed to fly in pairs," Kozitsyn continued. "But my companion pilot is busy carrying water." And again he laughed.

"Why is he saying all of that?" thought Chetunov. "Is he testing me out?"

But this light feeling of unfriendliness which he felt toward the pilot convinced him somehow that he could rely on Kozitsyn. The wrathful roar of the motor, the powerful gust of wind from the propellers which cooled his face in a pleasant way, the sensation of earth falling swiftly behind gave Chetunov's soul a lift. He felt himself strong and clean, prepared for a feat.

The airplane speedily gathered altitude. Soon the enormous *takyr* was transformed into a spot of dirt on a gray, corrugated, endless expanse of the desert. Chetunov was by no means disappointed in his life here. He was indifferent toward his tent companions, but right now there grew in him a feeling as if he was leaving a little piece of the world which held for him a certain amount of warmth.

Down below there flowed past a yellowish-gray mirror-like surface with sparse rows of dunes covered with desert bushes in some places. The edges of the desert seemed to bend upward, and it was as if the airplane was hanging up above a gigantic saucer. In this way a little less than an hour passed, and suddenly Chetunov saw beneath the wing of the airplane a lake, surrounded by steep, precipitous sides and covered with a blindingly white, even bluish, snow. At that moment the lake stood on end—the airplane sharply turned to descend, and Chetunov understood that this false lake was the salt marsh Kara-Shor.

Chetunov greedily looked down, but no matter how he tried to convince himself that it was a salt marsh the white concentration appeared to be the icy, snowy surface of a real lake. Nothing looked so hostile to life as this gigantic hole with steep sides like a dead crater of the moon. And for the first time the feeling rose in Chetunov: it would be good if all this were already behind him.

But Kozitsyn landed the plane not far from the edge of the salt marsh.

"It's a strange name for this salt marsh—Kara-Shor," said Chetunov, climbing out of the airplane behind Kozitsyn. "From up above it seems to be snow-white and not black at all."

"In this case evidently the word 'Kara' must be understood as meaning not 'black' but 'bad' or 'fatal,'" Kozitsyn explained calmly. "It is indeed a fatal place: clay and salt. Just try to land down below on that salt marsh. You'll go up to your wings in it. And it's interesting, Comrade Chetunov, how was it formed, that hole? An earthquake?"

"No," Chetunov answered readily. "There is no question of an earthquake there. Of course the movement of the earth's core played its own role, but in general it is supposed that such craters are formed by the dissolving of limestones by water. First there are formed small craters, and then they are combined into larger craters and deepened."

"And where is the water from?"

"In ancient times there was a sea here. All the visible space was covered by a sea ..." Chetunov all of a sudden wanted to share with this simple and curious lad all of his knowledge of the desert. He, who in general did not like "explanatory" conversations, discovered in himself a surprising desire for popularization. "What am I chattering about?" he thought in the very same minute. "Is it that I am trying to stretch out the time?" He repeated already without any enthusiasm: "Yes, a sea ... Well, that's enough, I have to get to work."

"Shall I help you?" Kozitsyn proposed.

"There isn't any help needed there ... You better see to it that your airplane is not blown away by the wind!"

Chetunov said this in a joking way, wishing to show Kozitsyn that he was not at all fearful of the work lying ahead. But the pilot took him quite seriously.

"Now and then it happens. But don't you worry, I noticed some big rocks over there and I will tie it down with a cable. There isn't a wind which could take it then."

"That would be all I needed," Chetunov thought in passing. And pulling his cap down further on his head he marched in the direction of the cliff.

Several times he turned about and waved to Kozitsyn. But then he thought that this could make an impression that he was timid, and he compelled himself not to look behind. When, after having gone on a good distance, he nevertheless turned about, Kozitsyn was no longer visible. The airplane alone, like a small beetle, was dark against the sand. And soon even the airplane disappeared as if it had been sucked down into the sand and Chetunov remained alone.

A feeling of sadness and triumph seized his heart. He saw himself as if from above—a small, fearless figure, stubbornly overcoming the dead burning distance. There was something unusually poetical in the fact that the son of Academician Chetunov, Chetunov junior, like a young warrior who had taken up the arms from the hands of his old father, had entered into a duel with the unknown.

He went up to a crevice which, turning and bending, wound deeply downward to the very bottom of the salt marsh. At first the incline was rather gentle and consisted of clay. But further down below the deposits became more dense. They stood out ahead as gray, greenish and red steps of a gigantic stairway. (Probably marls or limestone.) "What was it his father had written: 'Dear to the heart of every geologist is the beautiful nakedness of deposits.' Just as if it were about a woman!" Chetunov laughed to himself. "But as a matter of fact, women had interested his father very little. He had had only one love—geology. Probably that's the way it should be with every big scientist. And am I such a person or not?"

But it was unpleasant to think about this, and Chetunov turned to another subject. And so he would encounter something unusual —some small thing which would tell nothing to a less vigilant eye. But he would see that small detail, and as a result there would be a new and brilliant theory of the origin of these gigantic karst depressions. At first there would be a brief report in newspapers whose significance would be understood only by a small elite. Then there would be a report before a scientific society, a dissertation—a thin little notebook like Einstein's memorandum. But for it he would be awarded his doctor's degree . . .

Comforting himself with such thoughts, Chetunov was busy enough. He got from out of his knapsack his notebook, his hammer, and his metal tape measure. He adjusted his knapsack on his back so that it should not hinder him from working and slowly continued to descend. Simultaneously, he conducted measurement of the thicknesses of the strata, he made a drawing and brief description of all of the layers which he passed. He decided to collect samples on his way back when he would be fully acquainted with the cross sections.

The sun which was rising high into the heavens burned ever more strong and already after an hour of intense work Chetunov felt that his entire shirt had become salty with sweat and harsh surfaced like a tarpaulin and that his head beneath his cap was wet and hot. There was not the least little shelter from the burning sun, only at the bottom of the highest steps were there narrow ribbons of shade.

Chetunov felt for his canteen and found it beneath his hand. How small and light it was. "No," he ordered himself severely and immediately began to feel a very strong thirst. How strange! Just one minute before he had not wanted to drink at all. But all he had to do was to think about water in order to feel immediately a repulsive, gnawing feeling. "No, I will not drink," he strictly and simply said to himself and understood with gladness that he could restrain himself. This gave him a new feeling of self-respect. He could be severe with himself, merciless toward his weaknesses. It was not in vain that his father had said that without these qualities it was impossible to become a real geologist-explorer! But once this was so, once he had verified himself, tried himself out, then there was nothing to be feared from taking one swallow. When there appeared the real necessity of limiting himself he would be able to go without water entirely. He unscrewed the top of the canteen and took a deep swallow: the water was cool and freshened Chetunov very much.

Now he went to work with new energy. The descent became ever more difficult, but this taste of risk was pleasant to his strong, skillful, young body. The simple work pleased Chetunov. Yes, this was ordinary work such as hundreds of geologists were carrying out every day with danger for their lives. But it was this fact itself which made it beautiful. Chetunov found poetry no longer in a happenchance easy stroke of luck, but in the realization and consciousness that he was one of those thousands of unknown, modest laborers. Yes, he would be a geologist-explorer in the ranks. Tanned, worn by the wind, baked through by the sun, he would unnoticeably proceed along his life path. Only a few persons close to him would know the real value of the simple feat of his life. And only in his old age, near the end, would he make his enormous experience a contribution to science, and the very best, sad, late glory would brighten the last days of his life . . . Chetunov wiped his eyes with the sleeve of his jacket. He was on a steep ledge above five meters high. With difficulty, assisting himself with hands and legs, he let himself down from this ledge and, already sitting down below, thought to himself: "It was stupid to refuse Kozitsyn's help. It would have been much easier to let myself down on a rope. Again this is my pride, my desire to do everything myself. No, I must crush in myself once and for all all those petty cheap feelings. To be simple and strong—that is the line of my life . . ."

Judging by his measurements he had descended already more than 200 meters. That meant he must be closer to the bottom of the depression than to its top. Chetunov looked upward and involuntary fright pierced his heart: from here the wall down which he had descended appeared to be vertical. "How am I going to get back up? And with a full knapsack? Well, it's early to think about that, I was able to descend and I will be able to get back up," he comforted himself.

Chetunov continued his slow and dangerous way. Every meter of descent led him ever more deeply and deeply into the geological past of the earth. The varicolored strata of marls and ribbed limestones, the sharp edges of which scratched his hands, had been formed millions of years ago when there was located here a shallow but broad sea of the Cretaceous Period. Sitting down to rest on one of the ledges, Chetunov began to examine the strata persistently.

Just as if he were leafing over heavy pages he read the ancient chronicle of the earth. Thus, he searched downward with his eyes to the very bottom, where palely, like death, gleamed the smooth salt surface.

Further on the descent became even more difficult. The dense limestones of gray and rose color went downward in almost perpendicular steps. Grasping with his scratched-up hands the least little ledges and clinging with his whole body to the limestones which had powdered him from his head to his feet with a rosy dust, Chetunov slowly but stubbornly continued his descent. At times the thought, "And how am I going to get back up," stung his mind. But Chetunov chased it away, absorbed in one desire: to finish this exhausting descent, to stretch out his body, and the main thing—to drink water. This last became his strongest wish, but right then he warded off pampering himself. One swallow would not quench his thirst, and he had to use his water with calculation. Who knew how much longer he would spend in the salt marsh?

In those seconds when he tore his glance away from the wall and looked upward the sun beat into his eyes with blinding white arrows. The stones also became heated and breathed into his face with the heat of a locomotive boiler. Finally, his foot touched uncertainly an even surface. Chetunov put his other foot onto the surface and, hesitating just a bit, removed his hands from the boulder which he had been holding on to. Yes, he stood firmly on the firm bottom of the salt marsh, and his descent of 300 meters was behind.

The surface of the salt marsh which was blindingly white, smooth, and level seen from above near at hand turned out to be divided into a multitude of small and large polygons. But these polygons were not hard like armor as on the *takyr*, but were, instead, pliable, like asphalt heated by the sun. The layer of salt turned out to be extremely thin. Through it there shone dark wet clay from which there arose a stuffy little steaminess.

"An uncozy spot," Chetunov laughed to himself weakly and involuntarily directed his look upward, where at an awful height swirled in a golden dust the edge of the overhanging, unclimbable wall. Yes, unclimbable, now there wasn't the least doubt of that. And once that was so, he had to seek a more gentle rise. But was there any?

"There is. It cannot be that there is not!" Chetunov said aloud to himself and was frightened at his own voice which resounded strangely in the death-like stillness of the salt marsh. And right after this fright, short like a jerk came a real, serious fear.

He didn't even want to rest. His body again became impatient. Chetunov drank several swallows of the warmed-up water from his canteen and quickly walked along the base of the wall. Passing by a small cape, jutting out into the salt marsh, he saw that from here all along till they disappeared in the distance rose cliffs which were just the same, almost vertical, consisting of layers of strata without a single crack or crevice. It wasn't even worth considering climbing these walls without the help of ropes and wedges. "It looks as if I have fallen into a trap," Chetunov thought to himself and smiled wanly with his dried lips.

Now the working enthusiasm experienced during descent, had disappeared without a trace, giving way to alarmed concern. "Maybe I am not going in the right direction? Maybe the cliffs become less steep not to the east but to the west?" And though for such a supposition there wasn't any basis at all, he seized on it as a truth and quickly walked backward.

There he passed the place of his descent and walking along more than a kilometer remembered all of a sudden that he had promised the geophysicists to make a complete description of the cross section. How was that to be now? After all, in another place where he would make his ascent the cross section would turn out to be different than the place in which he had made his measurements. There would be a mix-up! But, looking intensely at the craggy shores of the "dead lake" Chetunov saw that the varicolored layers of deposits for the whole extent which he could take in with his eyes, lay strictly horizontally, neither changing color nor thickness and therefore also their composition. The conclusion would be that wherever he took his samples he could always show on the diagram of the cross section made by him the strata from which this sample had been taken. That's what marine deposits mean!

But right then a new thought of alarm quenched the short satisfaction of this little discovery. "If that is so and these layers are everywhere similar in their thickness and composition, that means that down along this entire enormous depression they create just exactly the same unclimbable cliffs. Wherever I go before me there will be the same overhanging walls!"

What should he do? He could not even let Kozitsyn know his situation: because of the overhanging cliff Kozitsyn was not in a position to see how Chetunov, fallen into a difficult situation, was wandering about the bottom of the salt marsh. Should he try to go out closer to the center of the salt marsh? It was dangerous: Kozitsyn had said that out there it's a real swamp.

Relax, calm down! After all he wasn't going to perish really when right near was an airplane, when the expedition base was within one hour's flight time. What nonsense this was—this was all nervousness. He must think out the situation and make up a plan for action . . .

"Here's what: I will walk along the edge and seek a gentle incline. If that doesn't succeed I will return to the place where I descended and try to get up there. If that doesn't work out then somehow or other I will get out into the center of the depression and give a trouble signal. I will wave my shirt if necessary for six hours in a row. If even this doesn't help I will simply wait. Kozitsyn finally, seeing that I have not returned, will certainly start to look for me. He's a reliable chap, he isn't going to abandon a human being in misfortune. At the very worst, Kozitsyn will have to fly to the base for help. Well, so I will spend the night in the salt marsh. That's not a catastrophe either."

But as a counterweight to these sober thoughts, his helpful and vivid imagination pictured to him outrageous images of death. He would have a sunstroke, be sucked in by a clay swamp, the wind would damage the plane. He remembered that a lizard, deprived of the possibility of moving, perishes under such a sun in a few minutes. A human being, of course, has more endurance. If he were to collapse the agony would not last less than three or four hours. "In the desert everything happens!" beat in his brain. He drove these thoughts from himself, fearing the weakness which even before he suspected vaguely in himself in which he nevertheless did not believe.

In order to force these thoughts out he began to think about something else: about those who were involuntarily to blame for his misfortune. It was not for nothing that it had always seemed to him as if his father had left something out in telling about his journeys. Indeed, not only his father—but all of those famous explorers who consciously or subconsciously hid the shameful and petty things that they certainly had had to experience during their journeys. Indeed, and who would want to speak of his own weakness when the deed was already done?

Chetunov found a certain sort of strange satisfaction in these malicious and unjust thoughts just as if ahead of time he wanted to justify himself in some kind of an evil extreme to which he would go, even though he himself still would not know what extreme this might be.

The sun—a white-hot, almost colorless sphere—stood at its zenith. And every time Chetunov looked at it—for some reason he had ceased to believe his watch—he had to shut his eyes several seconds. And then before him rose a blood-red shroud with a light blue radiant hole in its middle, like a bullet hole in glass. His mouth was enveloped with sticky saliva. The skin on his face and arms smarted and itched from sunburn, from the extremely small particles of salty and limestone dust. The immobile hot air surrounded all his body in a suffocating cocoon.

The desert possesses a strange trait: it replaces its emptiness and soundlessness with a throng of hallucinations which pursue the lonely traveler. Before Chetunov's eyes rose unsteady, momentarily disappearing, contours of high white buildings. His ear would catch the sound of strange delicate music or the peal of a bell heated by the sun. And then he could hear what sounded like the bubbling of water and at that moment he wanted to drink even more. Several times he took his canteen. Its faded sheath of cloth was so hot that it burned his hand. Finally, he carefully wrapped the canteen in a bag for rock samples and hid it in his knapsack.

From these various movements which seemed to him to be so touching there arose an inexpressible pity for himself. He slowly made his way ahead and, at his side, along the gray cracked clay slithered his pale, transparent, emaciated shadow. It seemed to him as if the sun were penetrating his body just as if it were glass, that his shadow was becoming smaller and smaller, that it was becoming more pale and in just a moment would disappear entirely. "I'm going to suffer the fate of poor little Peter Shlemiel, the boy who lost his shadow," thought Chetunov to himself and immediately remembered his father's library where hour after hour he had sat looking at books. How comfortable and relaxed it was then for him to dream of future feats and discoveries, of a bright, unusual life!

"I am not a coward in the ordinary sense of the word," thought Chetunov as he walked along a semicircular projection which hid from him the distant view of the depression. "I am not afraid of dying for the sake of some kind of a great accomplishment. But to die in this stinking hole, to die, without having done anything, to carry away with myself an entire unrealized world! Well, let me be nothing, but it's not as if I were from among those who pass through life without leaving a trace. If this time I come out of it whole I am going to write such a book about the desert as no one has ever written before. This book cannot, must not perish..."

He got to the extremity of the cape, and before his weary eyes exactly the same kind of tiringly severe monotonous picture stretched out: an overhanging multi-layered cliff and beneath it, disappearing into the distance, the gleaming smooth surface of the salt marsh. Only in the deep blue mirage of the distance did the wall turn somewhere, and there, near the very turn, were dark outlines of what appeared to be crevices. Fearing disappointment Chetunov sighed heavily and in his thoughts calculated the distance: eight or ten kilometers, not less.

"Even if I succeed in making my way out of here I am going to get to the airplane only after dark. And by that time Kozitsyn will decide I have had an accident and will have flown to the camp for help. One way or another I am going to have to spend the night in the desert without food and without even one swallow of water." But he thought of all of this in order to weaken shock if it should turn out that even those distant crevices would not help him to make his way up to the surface.

And again he walked along the craggy shore of the dead lake. Sometimes his boots slipped in different directions on the slippery clay. Sometimes they clicked on hard fragments which had fallen from above. Thirst caused his throat to smart and enveloped his mouth with a rough film, and he didn't even have saliva to remove that repulsive film. And he tried not to think about the fact that in his canteen there were left perhaps only several drops.

Only after three hours and more did Chetunov reach the first crevice. There was a gnawing pain in the muscles of his fatigued trembling legs. There was an ache in his swollen head.

For the last hundreds of meters Chetunov moved along as if unconscious. Now and then he stopped and helplessly looked about himself as if he were seeking something. "No, no," he whispered. "I'll get there and then I'll have a drink . . . Then I'll have a drink. I'll drink water, water . . ."

And then he got there and sat down on a stone. Without even looking at the crevice which promised him freedom he took out his canteen with trembling hands, unscrewed its top and put his lips to its neck. He didn't even notice the first gulp. He didn't feel the taste of water. But the second he swallowed slowly as if it were the finest of wine. And the third he held in his mouth until the moisture disappeared by itself. He wanted to take one more swallow but the canteen was empty . . .

Laboriously, he got onto his feet. He walked to the foot of the narrow steep crevice, which ran upwards in complicated twists and turns. Here, as if he remembered something, he took off his knapsack, put in it all of his equipment, threw it over his back and began to scramble up the gentle stone slope. At the height of 10 meters his path was barred by an overhanging light bluish gray cliff of limestone. Chetunov let himself down on a narrow projection. He sat entirely immobile, with his eyes shut, and didn't think about anything, didn't feel anything except an awful fatigue of spirit. Then somehow the thought lazily fluttered: "After all there is still another crevice."

He didn't even get up to descend but impotently slipped downward, scratching his elbows and his waist. From a distance it appeared that the second crevice was right next to the first. In actual fact they were separated by a good kilometer and Chetunov took not much less than an hour to cover this kilometer. The second crevice was much broader than the first. It reminded him of the one along which he had descended into the salt marsh. And although Chetunov had already succeeded in discovering how deceitful these crevices were he shouted loudly as if in defiance of someone who was holding him a prisoner in this cursed stone sack:

"I'll get out!"

Without difficulty he overcame the first meters up, but further the rise became more steep and the soles of his boots slipped. Chetunov quickly took off his shoes. The heated stones painfully burned the soles of his feet through his thin woolen socks but in return his feet acquired the tenacity of hands and he became suddenly all light. Chetunov laughed, gladdened by this new lightness. And all of a sudden his gladness was replaced by fright. He felt the emptiness of his knapsack on his shoulders.

"And the samples?"

Absorbed with one striving—to get out of the depression—he had forgotten about them. "Oh no," he said to himself. "The devil with the samples. Could I possibly make my way up with a full knapsack?"

There flashed in his memory the sharp, characteristic face of the chief. How small, tiny, this person appeared to be from here! Could he, Chetunov, really seriously take him into account? Chetunov hoarsely laughed. But, thinking of the chief, he involuntarily with ever greater precision recalled in his memory the chief's appearance: his bobtailed, strong figure leaning forward, his short authoritative gesture, his threatening-tender eyes. And against his will this image again acquired for him a strange power. In order to free himself from it Chetunov thought with anger: "A good chief! Sent an inexperienced person to a nearly sure death and didn't even wrinkle his brow! And what am I for him, what for him is our entire expedition? A springboard for a new career. Well, I don't want to make a sacrifice of myself. Let him find fools."

But a feeling of liberation did not come. And Chetunov compelled himself to think of something else. The years would pass. Perhaps, not even so many years. Again he would be in Moscow, in his customary domestic warmth, comfortable and well-provided, and he would remember his present misfortunes which from a great distance would appear to be small and amusing. And, warmed by this imagined warmth of the future, he immediately thought up a joke for the occasion: "I didn't turn out to be a desert explorer."

Away from this fatal pit, from the desert, from this miserable sun, from these demanding, merciless people! But, strange to say: his movements became more slow and weary, as if there lay on his shoulders some invisible burden. Somewhere in the very depth of his being there was moving about the repulsive sensation that he would never manage to escape this accursed desert. Of course, physically sooner or later he would get out of it, but it would drag itself behind him to Moscow, to the home of his parents, even into the heart of his mother. Himself he could manage to deal with everything shameful and foul that he would carry away from here. But for those about him he would be soiled forever.

"Oh, the hell with you all!" Chetunov moaned in a deathlike weariness and let himself down on a stone platform.

With the greatest of exactitude he was seized by a feeling that a multitude of invisible beings had grabbed ahold of him and were not allowing him to make his way to freedom. Vaguely he distinguished among them his comrades among the students, the professors with whom he had studied, and those two or three women with whom he had been intimate, and then with complete clarity his mother and father. For some reason they all needed to have him perish in this accursed oven! Well, after all, his father was not accustomed even to take pity on himself. He had worn himself to shreds over life like an old whip. But his mother, his mother—and she was there together with everyone else!

"Well if they had only brought me up as they should have!" he impotently cried out in the face of his parents. Spasms of weeping painfully seized his throat, but there were no tears because the sun had dried him out so thoroughly. It seemed to him as if he were swallowing rough stones. Is it really true that there is in the world no one with whom one can be oneself? A person who would love one, not as one is imagined, but as one is in fact. Indeed, even his mother—now he was convinced of this—loved him as she imagined him. How wonderfully miraculous it would be to find a woman who knew everything about him, even the most pitiful, the most secret things, and loved him not less because she knew his other, high, valuable essence! All of a sudden he so clearly pictured to himself this beautiful woman with a generous heart, good, intelligent and endlessly devoted, that for a moment it seemed to him as if she were there, alongside him. But the moment flashed by and all about was the same: stones, heat, emptiness. Chetunov got up and submissively, desperately, impotently slid downward.

At the foot of the slope he took off his knapsack, got out his hammer, and, making a wry face with disgust, knocked out in the very lowest part of the cliff a piece of white limestone. He cut into it a number and made a note on his diagram. He did exactly the same thing when he had risen 15 meters and crossed a strata of red limestone. It became ever more difficult to scramble upward, but Chetunov stubbornly hammered out samples and put them in the bag until his heart stopped with a sudden twitch of fatigue. He let himself down on the stones, wiped the dirty sweat from his face, and saw that he was hanging above an abyss. Tens of pulses all at once loudly beat in his body but that was only the automatic reaction of his body to danger.

"So I will fall," thought Chetunov to himself, "what of it!" He got up, feeling the chasm a few inches from his heel, and began to cut out a piece of rosy-white limestone. The small sharp-angled projections did not submit to the blow of his hammer, and he succeeded in chipping off only two little bits of pieces. Then, obeying the same maliciously joyful feeling, Chetunov got out his chisel and went to work to cut out one of the large projections. And then he again climbed upward. The heat singed his face, blinded his eyes. His dry mouth did not want to take in the hot dusty air. His heavy bag dragged him backward. And Chetunov stubbornly, meter after meter, overcame the steepest and most narrow part of the rise. The instinct of self-preservation led him like an intelligent guide, told him where to put his foot, which projection to hold on to, where to crawl and where to go at full height, where boldly to jump, where to run hardly touching with the ends of his toes the unreliable moving earth. It seemed as if his brain was taking no part in this struggle for life. And just as automatically Chetunov hammered off, marked, and put in his bag the samples. And when he finally stepped up on level ground he felt neither surprise nor joy, as if all the time he had been convinced that this is the way it must be. He only felt a death-like fatigue. His scratched up, torn, pierced feet ached. His heavily loaded knapsack pulled him down towards the earth.

Taking off his knapsack, Chetunov crawled on his belly up to the very edge of the precipice and began listlessly to look from above on the awful path which he had just climbed. Not far from the place where he lay the salt marsh depression with a narrow throat united itself with another depression which went off to the very horizon. And Chetunov, who remembered well the map of Moryagin noted in it one incorrectness: on the map the throat of the depression looked quite short. In reality it was a half kilometer long, stone corridor. Probably it was because of this mistake that the archeologists had given the "blueprint" to Moryagin.

This mistake of someone else encouraged Chetunov. He rose up and began to massage the calves of his legs which had become numb. All of a sudden he heard the roar of an airplane. The plane went so low over the edge of the depression that Chetunov involuntarily bent down. Kozitsyn had nevertheless found him! This was an unexpected success, but Chetunov felt not gladness but rather regret. He didn't want to meet Kozitsyn right at this moment, to feel on himself his insistent, penetrating look.

"He's certainly going to ask why I am barefoot," Chetunov thought to himself, watching the airplane which was taxiing up to him. He was so angered that he had to give an account of his actions to someone that he hardly heard Kozitsyn's first words. The pilot was pleased with something—truly at the fact that he had so skillfully sought him out, but his gladness irritated Chetunov.

"And where are your boots?"

"I took them off. You see I didn't like their style," Chetunov muttered through his teeth.

Kozitsyn rounded his brows. He looked on Chetunov with a mixed feeling of pity and curiosity. It was not the first time he had seen how people went out into the great test of the desert, and he knew how difficult this test was for many of them. More than once he had carried off to distant corners of the desert self-confident lads, gleaming with boldness and innocence. And then he had met them as people who had quieted down and become modest. But he was not embarrassed by such a change, for he knew that this is the way in which maturity comes, that the beaten-down state of mind would pass, be forgotten, and manliness and a new knowledge of oneself would remain forever.

But he was not pleased with this one ... He was not pleased by his torn-to-pieces appearance, his dirty feet in tattered socks, his shamelessly white ununiformed appearance ("like a deserter," Kozitsyn thought to himself). He was also not pleased by the empty look of Chetunov, which at the same time seemed to be bearing a grudge, and the fact that he had met him with silence. Or maybe he had had a very bad time and had found out about himself too much of the unexpected?

"Evidently you had a salty time in the salt marsh?" the pilot asked and without waiting for an answer added: "Do you want to drink?"

"To drink ..." Chetunov reacted absent-mindedly. He all the time was expecting something from Kozitsyn, although he didn't himself know what. This was like a premonition of danger. But having heard twice the words, "drink," pronounced first by the pilot and then by himself, mechanically he took hold of his canteen. Only after noticing the surprised look of the pilot he realized that his canteen was empty and wanted to take his hand away. But right then something bubbled in the canteen. Not believing himself, Chetunov raised its throat to his lips and several hot drops fell on his tongue. He himself could not comprehend from where these drops had come.

"You had some water left?"

Chetunov noticed first the astonished intonation in the voice of the pilot and then the meaning of the question reached him. And the answer was born lightly and simply just as if Chetunov had prepared it ahead of time:

"I had to restrain myself: necessary reserve."

This unexpected lie gave him a bearing. And when Kozitsyn brought the thermos from the airplane and, holding it with both his hands, respectfully offered it to Chetunov, Chetunov thought to himself: "Ah, now he is really beginning to respect me."

And Kozitsyn had in fact begun to respect Chetunov. He was a simple and manly person, and it was easier for him to see in others what was good and strong than what was low and bad. And when he raised from the ground the knapsack heavily loaded with samples he had a feeling of guilt before this torn, worn-out human being who had done well his difficult work. And irrelevantly, wishing to hide his embarrassment, he began to tell Chetunov about a certain driver who had gotten lost in the sand. Deciding that he would not be able to get out the chauffeur had written on the backside of the truck with a brush: "Farewell, Mama! Farewell, wife." And the next morning when he was found from the air he was very ashamed . . .

"I'm telling this in order to make the point," Kozitsyn added, feeling that his story sounded rather awkward, "that with us a human being is never left in misfortune."

He stole a look at Chetunov, but the latter had on his face only polite and impersonal attention. Chetunov in actual fact both listened and did not listen to Kozitsyn. From the very minute when he had ceased being afraid he felt inside himself a strange, previously unknown emptiness, as if he had been burned out just like that desert.

And then later sitting in the airplane, Chetunov suddenly remembered the story which had been told by the pilot and thought to himself: "It was of his own choosing that the driver showed his weakness. And I am the only one who knows what happened inside me."

He savored this thought for a long time, but it did not give him any relief.

"Maybe it's even good that I feel so bad right now!" thought Chetunov. Who can say how character is created in human beings? But the emptiness inside him did not permit itself to be expressed in words and Chetunov stopped thinking. For a time he looked at the back of Kozitsyn's head. The round head of the pilot in its leather helmet recalled a football. Finally, Chetunov, unnoticeably for himself, went to sleep and did not awaken even when the landing took place. Kozitsyn ran off and brought back a pail of water, footcloths, a fresh shirt, and only after this did he nudge Chetunov.

"Thank you ... Thank you ... " Chetunov muttered, clambering out of the airplane.

The day's events immediately floated into his consciousness, but his recollections lost their former caustic bite. With him at the university had studied a student, a participant of World War II. He had under his very heart a fragment of a shell which had not been taken out during the operation. The student said that the shell fragment didn't hinder him although he always felt it there. And only when he made careless, sharp movements, the fragment revealed its presence with a sharp pain.

"That's the same way it will be with this," thought Chetunov. "And let the pain remind me of itself. It must not pass for me without trace. But I am alive and I want to live."

With pleasure he poured cold water on himself, washed his feet, and after wrapping them in the dry footcloths brought by Kozitsyn, pulled on his boots. Combing himself in front of a small round little mirror he examined his darkened, dried-out, and therefore more precise and expressive face with satisfaction. And then he said to Kozitsyn with enthusiasm:

"I am going to report to the chief. I will return the shirt and the other things tomorrow ... "

But, approaching the tent of the chief, he suddenly felt irritation against this sleek, well-groomed, self-confident person who for some reason commanded his respect, and who never could value as its worth what he, Chetunov, had done, because the noble half-truth of the sufferings of Chetunov did not interest him in the least. "So, did you fulfill the assignment?" Chetunov in his thought mimicked him.

And right then, whether from an unconscious desire to reward himself for what had really taken place but about which he could not speak, or perhaps from a desire to surprise the chief, or because on the map the area which he had crossed with such torture seemed to him quite tiny, but in any case Chetunov decided on a small, quite harmless lie. Pointing out on the map the area which he had investigated, Chetunov with a careless movement of his finger crossed also part of the second depression.

"Ah, so you also were in the second depression?" said the chief.

"Yes," Chetunov nodded and a little hurriedly added: "the map right there is not quite exact: in actual fact the throat takes the form of a long corridor."

"So, so, very interesting," approvingly said the chief. "So, let's be exact: you went here from this point to the end of the depression, then passed the throat and investigated the second depression up to this point. Is that so?" he took the pencil and with a light line noted the real and the imagined course of Chetunov.

Chetunov had a nasty feeling: this hardly noticeable line seemed to make permanent his lie. "And why did he catch ahold of the second depression? One might think that the whole matter was in that."

"So, and why did you again return to the first depression?" meticulously questioned the chief.

"Because it was necessary," Chetunov answered rudely and impatiently.

He continued his report which now and then was interrupted by questions of the chief. And the further he went the shorter, more abrupt became Chetunov's answers. He suddenly got the feeling that the chief was catching him at something. "Maybe he feels that I am not saying everything? Maybe in my answers there are some errors which are unnoticeable to me? And just why did I lie about the second depression? Everything would have been all right anyway!"

Chetunov's mood spoiled more and more but the chief acted as if he did not notice this. Questioning everything to the very end, he said to Chetunov many flattering words, adding that there would be a special order declaring gratitude. All this did not touch Chetunov in the least. He caught himself with a strange feeling: it appeared to him as if he was being praised not for what he had really done but for the alleged examination of the second depression. And although this was untrue, all of a sudden he convinced himself that he had so-to-speak not carried out the main task. A chance lie had somehow strangely destroyed the value of his work in his own eyes.

When Chetunov left the tent of the chief it was already evening. The sunset spread out across the heavens in green, orange and crimson ribbons. The gray *takyr* reddened, and in these twilight colors the surrounding expanses no longer seemed so nude and unwelcoming.

He was completely worn out and he wanted to go to bed, not

so much for the sake of sleep, but to escape from that long, torturing reality, to get away from himself. But he did not make up his mind to go to his tent. He did not want to see anyone. There would be questions. They would compel him to drink in honor of his "battle baptism" and right then he would certainly go to pieces: his nerves were under too great a strain.

He went away from the tent, out to where in the light-blue mist of the advancing shadows the thin skeletons of the drilling rigs were black. Along the way he encountered a pile of old boxes. He went behind the boxes and lay down on the pleasantly warm earth which retained the heat of the day. Rosy bands of clouds wove in the heaven a complex pattern and suddenly began quickly, visibly, to melt.

Chetunov knew that he had to think over the events of the day, take certain decisions, but his tired brain gave birth only to one brief thought: if everything turns out all right, I will live in a different way. He immediately went to sleep as if he had fallen into a dark cellar.

"Sergei Sergeyevich! Sergei Sergeich!"

Chetunov through his sleep recognized the high, childish voice of the assistant to the drilling foreman, Savushkin. He opened his eyes and was surprised at the night which surrounded him. Low above him hung the heaven strewn with great stars. The round face of Savushkin seemed to be green, like a mermaid.

"Sergei Sergeich!" Savushkin called desperately. "Wake up! I've run off my legs looking for you and finally found you. The chief is asking for you."

There was a painful stab in his heart which broke its rhythm. The ends of his fingers smarted just as if they had been in a frost.

"What's the urgency?" dragging out his words in order to gain time, Chetunov asked and slowly rose. "Is there someone with the chief?"

"There are there those . . . How are they called? . . . The archeologists have come. I heard in passing that they had discovered some kind of a grave monument a hundred kilometers from us . . ."

"So that's what!" thought Chetunov, marching alongside Savushkin. His heart beat so strongly that he moved away from Savushkin, fearing that the latter would hear it. "Everything is clear —it's the second depression! Otherwise there would be no reason for the chief to seek me out so urgently. Be calm, be calm!" He repeated over and over again to himself, trying to take possession of the thoughts which bore forward in striving jumps to the final misfortune. "Evidently they have investigated the second depression and found there an ancient cemetery. Well, so what, I might have been there when they were not there. But a grave monument! I could not but see those cursed grave monuments! Oh, if I only knew how they looked!"

Chetunov tried in vain to imagine them. He saw something entirely different: the bloodshot, wrathful, and amused eyes of the chief, the maliciously glad smile on the face of his comrades and he himself, pitiful, perplexed, mumbling stupid, impotent words. He moaned so loudly that Savushkin stopped for a minute and looked at him in bewilderment. "My tooth, my tooth is aching," Chetunov muttered, taking hold of his cheek.

"Do you want me to get iodine for you?"

"Yes, yes . . . afterward . . ."

Chetunov looked behind himself as if he were being hunted down. In the weak nighttime light the turtle-like armor of the *takyr* shown palely. And all around for thousands of kilometers stretched the desert. But this boundless breadth was the same kind of a dungeon: there was nowhere to run, nowhere to hide . . .

Everything that took place later Chetunov perceived as if through a fever. He saw everything, heard everything, answered questions and, it would seem, comprehensibly. But at the same time he was not certain what was real and what was part of a nightmare from among the things that seemed to be taking place around him.

Everything was close, tangible but at the same time awfully distant, like a locomotive whistle in the night.

When he went in he was met by laughter and loud joking shouts. "And now it begins," Chetunov noted to himself, feeling his mouth stretching out into a strained, unnatural smile, from which his cheeks were in pain. Then he was introduced to some strange people. One of them had long, ostrich-like legs in narrow white trousers, a small disheveled head, a narrow little beard. The other was young —just a little bit older than Chetunov himself, with a round face and terribly shy. All the time he blushed without cause, casting his eyes downward. The elder possessed a thick, roaring bass which deafened Chetunov completely. In this roar Chetunov heard his family name all the time, and time passed before he realized that the talk concerned not him but his father. Then, jerking himself by bunches of his soft gray hairs, this strange person roared out something about grave monuments and again named his father. The round face of the young man was covered with a blush, and the chief laughed and clapped his heavy hands on Chetunov's back.

And Chetunov finally understood that the discovery of these archeologists confirmed some kind of a hypothesis of his father who loved to stick his nose into other peoples' fields. Then he began in a tortured way to realize in what measure this must make his situation better and immediately the chief spoke of him, of his expedition of today and said something good, nice, because both archeologists were very satisfied. The younger one, smiling at Chetunov, blushed happily, and the elder thundered: "That's why he's a Chetunov, the devil take him!" It became clear that the discovery of the archeologists had no relation to the second depression. All this had taken place in a completely different place, and all of Chetunov's tortures had been for nothing. He was so sad about it all that he almost wept, and the chief again and again slapped him on the shoulder and then caressed him and advised him to rest.

And then everything disappeared. Chetunov stood alone in the empty night and the wind which had become chilly whipped across his sweaty face like a wet rag.

"What a fool I am," clenching his fingers, thought Chetunov. "To imagine that grave monuments could be located inside a karst crater! Such a stupidity would not come to the mind of even a school child. No, I must take myself in hand. Otherwise the devil knows what's going to happen to me. Tomorrow I will begin a new life..."

He so clearly pictured to himself this new life that he wanted impatiently for tomorrow to come. He already saw himself quite different, direct, honest in every word, in every movement of his soul, decisive, knowing neither fear nor hesitation, what a totally perfect being...

Pushing aside the canvas door of his tent, Chetunov entered. The night light burned. Struchkov's bed was empty—probably as usual he was absent at the drilling. And Moryagin was asleep, his face shoved down into his pillow, puffing heavily. On the table, under the bell-glass, in the same awful suffocating atmosphere which he himself had experienced that very day, the lizard was dying. "Why didn't I let it go this morning? Weakness, indecisiveness, with such petty things everything begins!" Chetunov looked at Moryagin's loose face, rumpled by the pillow, stepped up to the table and with a sharp movement knocked over the jar. Falling on its edge the jar rang out but didn't break. Moryagin smacked his lips as if he was kissing the pillow and continued sleeping. The lizard remained immobile. The night light played on its shiny lacquer-like skin and was reflected coldly and palely in the beads of its eyes. It was dead.

Chetunov staggered as if from a blow in the chest, fell flat on his bed, and wept.

A Man and a Road*

Powerful corrugated tires devoured the road. The five-ton truck with a tall container rising in the rear left behind on the snow-covered surface of the dirt road not just a tire track but a whole mess of brown porridge. One could think that it was trying to leave things in such a state that no one else would be able to travel this route after it. On level stretches it angrily threw up chunks of snow and gravel, plowing the roadbed down to its soft clay foundation. On inclines upward it broke off with a roar whole pieces of the roadway—oily chunks of clay slid off into the ditch. On downward inclines, whistling and hissing with its pneumatic brakes, it skimmed the surface from the road entirely. At times it rolled swiftly ahead. At times it hardly crept along, with its motor roaring. At times it impotently slipped downhill. And every change in its motion had its effect on the long-suffering body of the road. But the truck was not concerned with this. The goggle eyes of its headlights were pointed ahead into the distance covered with early November dusk. It moved forward, an outsider, a stranger to everything: a stranger to the forest, a stranger to the fields, a stranger to the little villages with the roofs of their huts pressed down beneath the snow, a stranger to the frozen river and the old waterwheel covered with a glassy beard of icicles. It was absorbed in its distant purpose, with its roar, its howl, and its gnashing of teeth, with its suffocating, bitter stink—it even carried with it its own atmosphere, moving in a thick bluish cloud.

And no one was concerned with it either: neither the forest, the fields, the village, the river, nor the waterwheel. Except once in a while with a choking bark a dog dashed at its wheels, or a small boy on one skate chased along trying to grab hold of a fender, or, hearing from far away the heart-rending blast of the horn, a farm drayman, without turning around, moved his sledge off to the side of the road. There were no other cars going in either direction—it was late and it was Saturday night—and there was no one with whom the truck could exchange blinks of its headlights and trade horn signals.

It was growing dark swiftly. The lights were going on in huts.

* Russian title: "Chelovek i Doroga," published in the author's *Rannei Vesnoi, Rasskazy,* Gosudarstvennoye Izdatelstvo Khudozhestvonnoi Literatury (Moskva, 1961), pp. 399–418. This story, dated 1958 by the author, was also published in *Znamya,* No. 12 (December 1958). It was the title story in the Nagibin collection entitled *Chelovek i Dogora,* Sovietsky Pisatel (Moskva, 1958), 250 pp.

Sparse street lights were lit on village streets. The moon was up in the heaven. Alongside the truck rose an enormous ugly coal-black shadow. The shadow crept along the snow, clambered into villages, slid along the walls of huts. Sometimes it moved ahead of the truck, sometimes evenly with it, sometimes it fell behind.

But the enormous powerful truck, wrathful in its struggle with the road, was only a dead tin box by itself. It was someone else's will, someone else's animation, which endowed it with noisy, hot life, with stubbornness and inexhaustibility. In its cabin, holding his feet in well-worn kersey boots on the pedals, and his hands on the crossbars of the steering wheel, looking forward into the distance with bloodshot red eyes, sat a thin lad, twenty-four years old with broad flat chest and dark rings of hair sticking to his forehead, dirty with oil. His army hat with earflaps and without its little red star insignia was back on his head. His cotton-padded jacket was open. In the truck cabin it was warm from the motor and his cotton-padded trousers had slid down a bit, exposing a ribbon of swarthy young body between his belt and his shirt.

Driver of the First Category, Bychkov, was deathly tired. He was working for the second shift in a row without sleep or rest. He had traveled in this truck almost six hundred miles along bad, torn-up roads with heavy, awkward loads. Worst of all his back was tired because he felt every load on his back as if he were carrying it himself. A slope upward—and he seemed to be pulled by his neck and shoulder blades backwards. A slope downward—and it was as if a whole house was piled up on him. There was nothing to breathe. When he braked the truck—it was as if someone were angrily shoving a knee into the small of his back. From this load his back, his ribs, and his entire chest ached. In the big container in the back of the truck there was a transformer which was urgently needed at the most distant and the most backward sector. This was a load with an inclination to tip. Not only on turns but with every movement of the wheel it inclined the truck to one side, threatening to tip it into the ditch. And Bychkov involuntarily braced his body in the other direction so that his ribs cracked and his vertebrae, as they were shifting, crunched.

He wished the devil would take both the transformer and the Fourth Sector where there was always an emergency, where there was always something that they lacked and where everything was demanded urgently, in extremity. He also wished the devil would take Truck Transport Chief Kosachev who had pushed him into this trip. And he wished the devil would take him, himself, for agreeing to make the trip when it was not he who was supposed to go at all but Panyutin. With hurt and bitterness Bychkov remembered once more how Kosachev had wound him around his little finger. That morning Panyutin, who was not so young, almost forty, had taken his wife home from the maternity hospital, where she had given birth to twins. In a tizzy from his late fatherhood, he somehow or other managed to dilly-dally for half a shift and then had gotten permission to leave. Hardly had he left when there was a call to carry the transformer to the Fourth Sector. Kosachev had immediately turned to Bychkov: help! Of course he had flatly refused. Panyutin and his twins were no concern of his. Panyutin was supposed to work—so he should work. And as for him, he had done his share and now he was going to go off to guzzle beer. But Kosachev was clever and always knew how to get around a person: "I, of course, could compel him. But those married chaps are not so very reliable. It's a dangerous road at nighttime. The load is difficult and he has his family on his mind. If he were only to get stuck that wouldn't be so bad, but what if he wrecks the transformer? No, I need an unencumbered person, and I can't trust this to someone who's listening for the yelling of his children!" The Truck Transport chief knew that Bychkov had something against married people—and he played on this. Bychkov wanted to prove to Panyutin, even though he was a husband and a father and the head of a family, that he, Bychkov, a bachelor, with neither house nor home, was nevertheless worth more than Panyutin. And so now pay the piper! And the main thing was that now it was already clear that Kosachev had freed Panyutin from that cursed trip only out of respect for his fatherhood. Yes, and also because, perhaps, he was looking out for him: the road was really a mess, especially on the rise up to the Fourth Sector, and what a load it really was! It was one thing if Panyutin, the head of a family, should perish, and another if it were he, Bychkov, a bachelor. They would write Bychkov off as expendable—and that would be that. From that his mood became even more bitter and vicious, and his thoughts as usual turned to what had wrecked his life. True, it was always with him, that thought never left him, neither on the highway nor when he was drinking nor at nighttime when he was sleeping. It even came to him in his dreams. But sometimes it dozed as a calm, accustomed burden at the depths of his soul, and then again suddenly with unbearable force it tore at his heart and his brain.

Aleksei Bychkov himself couldn't have said when he fell in love with Tosya. When had he begun to love his mother? He had always loved her—from the very time he felt a heart in himself. And so it had been with Tosya. They had always been together, from earliest childhood—on the streets, at the river, in the cutover glades of the forest full of sweet-smelling wild strawberries, during recesses at the school. And whenever they had been separated then they immediately began to look for each other. The whole village considered them engaged. The years went past and Aleksei and Tosya became engaged no longer in make-believe but in truth. When he went to the army for his service he did not ask Tosya to remember him and wait for him. He simply kissed her on her full, cool lips, looked into her eyes, pressed her hand and left, the most calm of all those whose lot it was to be separated.

During all of the four years Aleksei served in the army he received punctually from Tosya letters and photographs.

Her face changed little with the years. It became only more round, cleaner and smoother. Her light-colored, calm eyes looked more directly and openly. And he himself could not have said why toward the end of the third year of separation from her he was seized by a burning melancholy. In vain he sought the answer to the riddle in Tosya's photographs and letters. Her rounded face breathed the very same imperturbable calm. Her stare was just as direct. And her letters were all just as short, simple, and full of greetings from relatives, friends and acquaintances. Moved by a vague feeling of uneasiness he had his photograph taken and on the back of the picture wrote verses he had heard somewhere:

> "If we should never meet again
> If fate should part our ways—
> Then here for you is my stolid face—
> So remember me all of your days."

In answer the usual, calm and short letter arrived and Bychkov did not know whether to be glad or sad that Tosya had not reacted to his alarmed challenge.

He served out his service. And in a new, spic and span uniform with the shoulder board of a sergeant, with the insignia of a distinguished tankman on his chest, in leather military boots pushed together in pleats like the bellows of an accordion, in a forage cap with a black border which sat crookedly on his curly hair, in a white celluloid collarband which gleamed like a newly minted coin, he returned to his native village. And there he learned that Tosya a year before had married the district agronomist. His mother had persuaded her son's former fiancée to hide from him the truth and to write him as before letters and send photographs as if nothing had happened. "Otherwise there will be a misfortune," the old woman had said to her. "Army service is strict and Aleksei without a doubt is going to do something which will be his undoing." Bychkov was still astonished at the unusual insight of his mother: how had she sensed in him, a quiet, modest, uncomplicated lad, a secret store of destructive forces? Perhaps in his blind loyalty to his girl friend, his once and for all chosen, there gleamed through to her the guarantee of a storm hidden in him.

Something broke in Aleksei. He began to drink and while drunk once went to beat up the agronomist. But seeing the not-so-young, thin-bodied man with spectacles on his long, emaciated nose, with lean, sucked-in cheeks, he could not find a decent place on him to sink his fist sweetly. He once ran into Tosya—she was then living in a neighboring village—and there flashed through his brain the thought: "I'll knock her down!" And again his wrath was spent to no purpose. Beneath Tosya's arms, crossed on her breast, bare to the elbow, and strong and tender, he saw a small rounded stomach—she was going to be a mother in the near future. She also looked at him, swarthy, pale, curly, with dark, shining eyes clear with pain, and said, perhaps with surprise, and perhaps as if regretting something: "So that's how it is with you!" And she quietly walked past.

He couldn't get along in the village, yes and he didn't want to destroy himself while his mother watched. For a year now he had been wandering about Russia. In the Crimea he had driven vacationers along the winding mountain roads in a small rattling bus, but the merry, happy, unconcerned people were not to his taste. He had been at a construction project on the Volga River, where he had drowned himself in work and vodka. He liked it better there, but he got there late. The construction project came to an end. He was wafted off to the Altai, to the Virgin Land, and even to the Far East. But no matter where he wandered he did not get away from himself. For half a year he had now been here, in the cold Lake Lagoda district, at a construction project for a high-voltage line, and his fancy had been caught by the gloomy calm of these localities, the dark fir forests, the deserted, lonely highways, the tall straight pine trees standing by themselves with their dolefully whining tips, the cold reserve of the old inhabitants, and the unassuming simplicity of his comrades at work.

He was not at all any longer that modest, neat lad who had returned from the army. Though something built up over years is not destroyed easily, it is not said for nothing that small drops can wear away stone. Well, he was not made of stone, and there were more than just drops to wear him away. Aleksei learned to spend hours in a smoky smelly drinking den where a blind accordionist, with eyes which looked as if a bird had pecked them out from their deep dark sockets, incessantly and unenthusiastically played such songs as "On the Burial Mounds of Manchuria," "The Waves of the Danube," and—especially for Aleksei in return for a three-ruble note in his dry tenacious paw—his favorite, "The Blue Kerchief." He learned to drink vodka without then following it with something to eat. He learned to get together with and to quarrel bitterly with people whom he was seeing for the first and last time in his life. With the girls he learned to put his hands into action before words. He learned not to think about either the present or future—it was only about the past he had not learned how not to think. He was not bothered at all by the fact that certain of his neighbors in their living quarters kept away from him, that the more decent and stricter among the girls didn't want to have anything to do with him, that Truck Transport Chief Kosachev hardly hid his contempt for him and kept him at work only because he was "daring": he always was willing to undertake to get through—and he got through —where others shirked. On the long roads of the construction project as it happened, he found himself suitable friends, men like himself who had withdrawn from life. True, he didn't need them much, and they did not make his great loneliness disappear. He didn't even aspire to this. He loved his orphanhood. He loved the long, empty road with its burdens and fatigue. And right at that minute, out of wrath at Kosachev, at Panyutin and himself, he was not honest with himself to the very end. Somewhere in the depths he even was glad for this unexpected and difficult trip. He loved to work himself to complete fatigue. Forgetfulness from work weariness he preferred even to forgetfulness from liquor . . .

The needle of the speedometer hovered near the number twenty —kilometers per hour. At this speed he would hardly manage to make it to the Fourth Sector for another three hours. He had already gotten past the point where he wanted to rest and even the metronome-like waving of the windshield wiper, which was washing the sticky sleet off of the windshield, was no longer rocking him to sleep as it had at the beginning of his trip.

The moon hid behind clouds and space was cut off on both sides of the road. Ahead, where the light from the headlights came to an end, the road rested up against a black wall of the night, and it seemed as if the machine would smash itself to pieces against this pitch-dark hard blackness. But the wall did not permit itself to be approached. It moved away ever further and further, and the road grew behind it, as if it were born of the light of the headlights. Now and then from out of black nonexistence on the side of the road there sometimes jumped a bush, sometimes a tree, sometimes an old, half-rotten milepost, and, having existed for a moment, disappeared.

The green paw of a fir branch, covered with frozen round little drops, hung over the road and shimmered in rainbow-colored iridescence, but suddenly was quenched and, dark, massive, and heavy, whipped the windshield, sprinkled the glassy fragments of ice on the hood, and bent back. The truck entered the forest and, hurrying past tree trunks and branches, moved along a forest corridor. The branches scraped the body and the door of the cab, scratched the roof, beat against the wheels. Into the measured, accustomed drone of the motor, which seemed to the driver to be quietude itself, the noise of outside life broke in impertinently and stubbornly. His face was covered with disappointment. Guarding his loneliness and his lack of participation in everything which was outside the windows of his cabin, he stepped on the gas and, when the needle of the speedometer jumped up, shifted into fifth speed. The machine began to sway. The violated equilibrium reacted in his body with an additional ache. But the rustle of the branches grew quiet. All of the sounds of the outside became smaller and more frequent, and he had almost gotten back his quietude.

Finally, the forest was behind. Bychkov reduced speed, and the motion of the truck became once more strained and even. Then through growing pressure on his back he felt that the road was imperceptibly going downhill. The yellow rays of his headlights grew light-blue and narrowed. Fog hovered in them. He changed the headlights to the lower beam, as if he were picking it up from beneath the front wheels of the truck. The fog hovered from the very earth, and the deep furrows, hillocks, and ruts of the torn-up dirt road, wrapped in a bluish wavering smoke, seemed to be living waves of a river. On both shores of this river, toward the truck, there ran white stone posts which were like dwarf human beings. The fog began to swirl up even more densely, and a real river, invisible behind it, cast beneath the wheels of the truck hollowly and softly the settling planks of a wooden bridge. The trunk mounted a hillock and burst out of the fog into clean velvet darkness. Ahead, the lights of a village began.

Bychkov shifted the beam of his headlights, and a long ray of silver flowed into the dark window of a nearby hut.

Notwithstanding the cold, windy, uncozy evening, which was not even freezing but chilly and shivery as frequently happens in the juncture between fall and winter, the young people were out enjoying themselves. There were dances going on right in the middle of the street. The noise of the motor drowned out the music. The murk hid the accordionist from Bychkov's eyes. And these couples swirling about to unheard music were strange to him—as if he saw them in a dream. Picked from out of the darkness by the headlights it was as if they had not noticed there was rolling down upon them the immense mass of the truck. They kept whirling and whirling as if they were disembodied spirits through which the truck could pass as through a fog. Bychkov pressed on the horn and the loud, long, cheerless sound cut through the night. The couples unwillingly parted. Some of them even fluttered out from under the very wheels of the truck when Bychkov no longer could see them beneath the straight line of the hood. But none of them stopped dancing. Not one of them broke off the free-flowing, spellbound circling.

"They're crazy!" Bychkov laughed to himself. He stretched out his body, yawned with a crunch, and remembered that underneath his seat there was lying an unopened half-pint of vodka. He was pleased by this even though he didn't want to drink right at that moment. It simply was pleasant to know that it was lying there, cold and slippery. Well, so let it lie there for the time being. He got out from his pocket a rumpled pack of "Priboi" cigarettes, shook it, and pulled one out with his teeth. He spun his lighter and lit up.

The truck came to the outskirts of the village, and on the right side of the road there flashed past the figure of a woman with her hand raised. In essence it was only that white hand, precisely outlined in the blackness of the night, which Bychkov succeeded in seeing. He braked his truck sharply, but he dragged along for a good ten meters more. Time passed while the woman caught up with the truck.

"Will you give me a ride, comrade driver?" he heard a voice out of breath.

Bychkov stuck his head out of the cabin. It was dark but nevertheless he immediately saw that it was a young woman, twenty-five years old, no more. His glance as usual ran from top downward, feeling and sizing up the locks of light-colored hair which came out from under the kerchief on her head and which were all in snowflakes grown icy from the wind and cold. He saw her clean round face and her tight bosom pressed in by her jacket of foalskin leather. In an unpleasant voice he said:

"Get in!"

When the woman climbed up on the high step, having thrown ahead of her into the cabin two tightly filled string bags tied in a knot, he saw a round knee bound in a silk stocking and a high black rubber boot. How do you like that! All dressed up!

The woman finally seated herself, arranged her string bags at her feet, and sighed happily:

"Well I certainly am lucky! I had already lost hope of getting to the Fourth Sector now!"And all of a sudden she caught herself with fright. "And you are going to the Fourth?"

"The very place."

Now Bychkov has guessed the cause of his unpleasant feeling toward this woman whom he had never met: somehow or other she reminded him in an indefinable way of Tosya. There was neither in the features of her face nor in her figure any likeness. Tosya was taller, thinner, dark-haired, large-eyed, large-mouthed. And this woman had more chin to her, was shorter and stronger in build. Her features were smaller and sharper: her nose and mouth were small, she had little bright eyes, light-colored hair. Indeed, only the calm roundness of the oval of the face itself was common to both of them. But it was not a matter of that. From this woman there immediately breathed on him Tosya's definiteness and coolness which excluded intimacy. The fact that she did not even look at him while she was settling herself in the cabin, that in her words and gestures there was not even a glimmer of any playfulness, natural in the acquaintance of a young woman with a young man, even in that careless lack of ceremony with which she had lifted her foot onto the step, there peered through an independent character—and at the same time one narrow and shallow—Tosya's character ... He set the truck in motion. The woman raised herself up a bit and straightened out her skirt so as not to wrinkle it. On her round, calm face was expressed the customary satisfaction of a traveler who has finally come to believe he is moving toward his goal.

Bychkov waited for her to ask him about something, just something at least: where do you come from, perhaps, or when are we going to get to the Fourth Sector. But the woman was silent and did not even look in his direction. And in that also there was something of Tosya, something of Tosya's miserliness of soul. Not for nothing was it, that during childhood and youth she was entirely satisfied with his friendship—she didn't even acquire any girl friends.

"Do you live at the Fourth Sector?" Bychkov asked.

"Aha!" she nodded, not turning her head.

"Are you a native here?"

"No, we are from Tikhvin."

"And how did you come here?"

"Like everyone else—I was hired."

"Are you married?"

The woman shook her head in the negative.

"And are you going with someone?"—passing over to the intimate personal pronoun—Bychkov asked.

"That's all I need! I didn't come here in order to go out."

And in these words of hers there wasn't any playfulness, nor any hint of flirting.

"So why did you come?" Bychkov asked.

"For the same reason as everyone else," she said in a stubborn voice.

"To make some money maybe?"

The woman did not answer, but Bychkov understood that he had guessed correctly. And he felt his superiority over this neat, well-dressed woman who knew her price: he was very little interested in wages.

"You're saving up for a dowry?" he laughed.

"Maybe for a dowry," she answered with a challenge.

"And where do you work?"

"In the store."

"Well, that way you'll quickly save up money," said Bychkov.

She did not respond, looking calmly and without movement straight ahead.

Bychkov tried to picture her future husband. He drew a portrait of him something like Tosya's agronomist: not so young, weak, a thin-bodied type in spectacles. For some reason just such strong and independent girls, seriously building a life for themselves, love to take as husbands reliable, educated men from the cities. "Indeed, she wouldn't marry such a simple, modest lad as me," thought Bychkov to himself, forgetting that long since he had ceased being both simple and modest. As a matter of fact he was looking at himself at this moment with the eyes of his fellow traveler who didn't know anything about his present bad life and notoriety. And he wanted most keenly to get even with that agronomist who eternally stood on his path, that furtive, insinuating type of person who looked as if butter would not melt in his mouth and who took the best girls away from the real spirited lads.

"Well, a beauty like you can find a taker without a dowry!" he said. And removing his hand from the wheel he took hold of the woman's cotton-quilted shoulder.

With a quick movement, just as if she had expected exactly that, she knocked off his hand. He grabbed her under the elbow and pulled her to him. She jerked away and when he repeated the attempt she took his fingers and, bending them backward quite painfully, she got his hand off her and put it back on the wheel.

"You're a hard one to get rid of!" she said without any particular offense intended. "What is it, are you drunk?"

"No!" Bychkov laughed. "It's good that you reminded me!"

Braking the truck, he bent over, and found in his wiping cloth the half-pint which was as cold as a piece of ice. He got it out, and, hitting the bottom on his knee, knocked out the cork.

"How about a drink?"

The woman fastidiously shrugged her shoulders.

"I don't even take the nasty stuff in my mouth."

"As you please!"

Contrary to his expectation, the vodka for some reason didn't flow of itself. And, after having made two big swallows, Bychkov pulled the throat of the bottle out of his mouth. Although the vodka seemed not very tasty, pleasant warmth flowed through his body and his head not only did not grow foggy but on the contrary became clearer, and his feelings which had grown dull from fatigue acquired their daytime sharpness. Through the customary stink of lubricating and fuel oil he smelled the pungent odor of fur acquiring heat and the aroma perhaps of perfume, perhaps of eau de cologne, in a mixture with fragrant powder. And again something moved inside Bychkov. He shoved his right hand behind the woman's back and tried to embrace her.

"Let me go! Do you hear!" she exclaimed sharply.

"Enough putting on airs!" Bychkov said with disappointment.

"What do you want?" asked the woman, turning towards him for the first time. And it was strange. Even when she was angry her face kept its immobility—so closely did it fit the smooth, young skin. All of her wrath was concentrated in her eyes—small, bright, shining.

Bychkov didn't know what he wanted. He was too worn-out and tired to desire anything really. As a matter of fact he did want one thing—for a moment to feel himself the master of the situation, to feel that on him, Bychkov, depended the fate of his old and ancient enemy and his happy opponent. If it had happened that way he himself would have left her alone in peace. Not to use power is by all means more sweet than to use it. But the stubborn resistance of the woman aroused anger in him. He again pulled her with force by the shoulder.

"Let me go! I'm not that kind! Let me go! I'll get out!"

"Don't make a noise," he said calmly. "If you do I'll drop you off right here."

"Drop me off! I myself am not going any further with you!"

Bychkov stopped the machine, bent across the knee of the woman and opened the door. Into the cabin there blew the sharp, piercing cold.

"Get down," Bychkov said without looking at her.

The woman sniffed with her little nose, shifted her string bags, and did not move from her place.

"Well are you going to get down!" Bychkov said lazily.

"You won't pester me?" she said all of a sudden, leaning over toward him and looking at him with a begging look in her eyes. "You won't, darling?"

"So you've already become sweet!" Bychkov laughed to himself. "I won't fall for that!"

He turned down the light, got out his portable repair lamp and climbed down out of the truck. He was surrounded by cold and darkness on all sides. Yes, it wouldn't be so pleasant right now to be left alone on the road. Pushing up the top of the hood, he checked the oil level, took off the cap of the radiator from which with a whistle and hiss hot gray steam shot up, and verified that the water had not boiled away. With his heel he punched the tires which were as firm as stones. Getting down on his knees, he pulled at the cables which held the container in place. And then he returned to his seat.

The woman sat there with pouting lips. And once more her clean round face, her neat, smart clothing aroused in Bychkov rage and irritation. Her smooth cheeks, her locks of hair darkened from the snow which had melted on them, her young, tight bosom, her strong legs with round knees were not for him. Just as other dark locks of hair, another round face with firm dimples on the cheeks, another strong, untried body had turned out to be not for him. Bychkov got out a cigarette, began to roll it in his fingers, and broke it in two. Tossing the cigarette out the window he pulled out another and lit up. The smoke from the unloosened tobacco drew poorly and did not penetrate to his soul. Bychkov threw out this cigarette also.

"Shall we go?" the woman said quietly and impatiently.

Bychkov put his hand on her knee. The woman did not stir. Then he put the gear in second speed and the truck, trembling in all its powerful length, moved. Speeding up, Bychkov shifted successively to third, fourth, and finally to fifth speed. After this he returned his hand to the woman's knee. Fumbling on the metal clasp of her garter, his hand slipped further, and Bychkov felt beneath his fingers the living body. The woman sat, her face turned to the side window, just as if she did not notice his touch. Bychkov ran his hand lightly along the woman's leg, cold, tender, defenseless. And impossibly aching tenderness and pity whipped his heart. He slowly pulled his hand back, very quietly and carefully, as if he feared to offend the woman with this movement. He trembled, again caught his fingers on the metal clasp, and, heaving a sigh of relief, finally got his hand free. He put his hand on the wheel and immediately took it off. On the hand, just like a second skin stuck to his skin, in a light chill there was retained the forbidden contact and from his hand in a current there passed through the entire being of Bychkov an embarrassed feeling of shame, pity, repentance, and incomprehensible, inexplicable gladness.

"Don't be afraid..." he pronounced hoarsely and with difficulty. "I'm not that kind..." He did not know how to define himself and he did not finish the phrase.

The woman looked straight before herself on the freezing, windshield, puffing out her pouting lips and quickly blinking her light-colored barbed eyelashes.

"It's true, I'm not that kind," Bychkov repeated. "Life hurt me, people hurt me . . ."

The woman was silent.

"Well, can you understand me?" said Bychkov longingly, looking into her eyes. "I did it out of foolishness, out of hurt!"

"I didn't do anything to hurt you," she finally blurted out.

"Yes, it wasn't you who hurt me!" and with heat, in confusion, he began to tell her what he had never told anyone ever, neither sober nor drunk: about his love, about the betrayal, about the pain, which had broken his soul.

She did not interrupt him with one word, but her lips remained just as pouting and her face frozen. She did not forgive him the insult, and Bychkov, understanding how unfairly, indecently he had offended her, wanted her only to let him speak his piece to the end. Then she would understand that he was not a lost person, that he had a living soul, and she would forgive him.

"For a whole year and a half now I have been knocking about the whole wide white world, and I can't find myself a place in it . . . When I look at myself I want to vomit . . . And, after all, I love a home, I love a family, I love children . . . If I find someone to stick to with my heart, I'll give everything in order that things should be good for the one I love . . ."

He spoke, and with every word he felt more strongly that this silent, modest, clean woman, the first to whom he had entrusted his deceived heart, was becoming to him ever more necessary and closer. And the miserly "aha!" with which she now and then confirmed that she was listening aroused warmth in his heart.

Already, her similarity to Tosya did not hinder him. On the contrary it was as if that former Tosya had taken on a new form, had merged with this woman, dissolved in her.

Vaguely guessing behind the quiet, modestly reserved appearance of his traveling companion a firm practical sobriety which he found pleasing as a counterweight to his own present shameful lack of roots, Bychkov said:

"I'm not chasing money—but even so I earn more than 1500 a month. And with my way of life I don't even use half of it. I send my mother every month 1000. She, the poor thing, is not glad about the money—she weeps over it. She writes me: 'I don't need anything from you. I have my house, my garden, and farm animals, and I earn money myself. Indeed, I also have my daughter with me.' My mother is just waiting for me to have my own home so that she can rock her grandchildren to sleep. And I, to tell the truth, am not afraid of any kind of work if there were only someone for whom I was doing it..."

Bychkov shyly looked at his traveling companion. She was sitting just as straight, immovable, strict, and sedate as before. But evidently something had relaxed inside her. In her face there had appeared calmness. Her lips pouted no longer and were evenly and softly rosy between her two dark dimples. Growing glad at this awakened confidence, Bychkov quietly said:

"You ask anyone about me. And everyone will say: he's a heavy drinker and this and that and the other thing. But you won't hear anyone call me lazy or a bad worker. And in my opinion if a person hasn't grown cold toward work it's not too late to put him on the right road. How do you think about that?" he asked her with hope.

The woman did not answer. Bychkov waited and quietly looked her in the face. Quiet, even, deep breathing emerged from her half-open small mouth, and her eyes, covered with their short lids with the light-colored needles of her eyelashes seemed to be tightly closed. She was sleeping. This did not even hurt Bychkov. On the contrary it touched him as a new sign of confidence. She was not afraid of him. It was as if she were entrusting herself to him. It meant that what he had said had reached her heart. And in this trusting, defenseless sleep he imagined a silent answer to the question which he had not asked directly. And then from out of the very depths of his being emerged the tender, hot, burning, reliable, sacred word.

"Wife!" he pronounced with his lips alone. "Wife!"

A lonely tear burned his cheek. He was embarrassed, laughed, and wiped his cheek on his shoulder.

It was as if peas were striking the windshield like buckshot. The truck was driving into rain. It often happened this way at this season—during one day one would travel from winter to fall, and from fall to winter. Driven by the wind the streams of rain flew toward the truck like dark short arrows. The hood was covered with little bits of fountains. The wind howled underneath the iron of the fenders and cold, penetrating threads interwove with the heat coming from the motor. Bychkov pulled off his cotton jacket and carefully, trying not to touch her, wound it about the woman's legs.

The wet wind blew through all the chinks, but the hot, fast coursing of his blood defended Bychkov from the cold. He heard the weak breathing of the sleeping woman, and in him sang out the feeling of a traveler who after long wandering has returned to his native home. And like the traveler returning from afar he could not talk enough. Let it be that the sound of his voice would not get through to the woman. Just the same she would hear him as if with an inner ear. And Bychkov talked and talked about the past, about the present, about the future, about his longing for a near and dear person, about how he had been saved by this meeting . . .

Suddenly Bychkov grew quiet and moved up toward the glass. Through the rain mixed with snow he saw on the road the dark figure of a man. He pressed with his finger on the horn and right away drew back, fearing the sharp sound of the horn might awaken his traveling companion. The man on the road awkwardly waved his hands and shouted something. Bychkov blinked his headlights for the man to get out of the way and, when the man jumped off to the side, he dashed past without lowering his speed. "The seat is taken, dear comrade!" he said aloud, as if the man might have been able to hear him.

The Fourth Sector began ahead away up above with a scattering of electric lights. It stretched out on the knoll of a hill, beyond the river. Bychkov went out on the ice with heavy momentum and felt beneath his wheels a strange, unstable, elastic softness. Where he had come from the rivers were firmly shackled in ice. Across them there extended well-traveled snow roads. But only the devil knew what was here—some kind of half liquid mash. But there was only one way out for Bychkov: to dash forward. If he were to stop he would get stuck forever. Then it would be impossible to pull him out. Besides from the river to the peak of the hill where the Fourth Sector was located there was a steep roadway, and the truck needed the momentum.

The headlights revealed the danger in good time: their beams rested against a steep rise of the road and flowed along a wet fleshy clay which during the course of a full day had been poured on and was steeped in rain. In essence there was no road. It had been completely washed away by the water. Instead, between deep ditches there was a red ribbon which was furrowed by deep ruts full of water along which flowed little streams. He decided momentarily . . . Bychkov shifted speed and, panting, took upon himself the heavy inertia of the load and, heavily, in second speed, crept upward.

At first it looked as if everything was going to be all right. The truck trembled and leaned to one side—in another second it would tip over—and buried its nose in a pothole. It scooped up mud and muddy water, but stubbornly mastered the incline. Then Bychkov felt that the rear end of the machine was slipping, that it was slowly and irrevocably being dragged to one side and downward. And it was not even a matter of slippage of the rear wheels, but the road itself slipped out, dragging the truck behind it.

It was flowing out from under the wheels, pulling them toward the ditch. The truck was going sideways like a dog on a village street.

And Bychkov could counterpose to all of this only smooth, unhurried, and incessant movement forward. He did not dare either to step on the gas nor to change speed—it would be death. It was impossible even to stop. He would have been implacably dragged downward. He could fight the road only with restraint and iron patience, with even unchanging effort, and that was devilishly difficult because every muscle, every nerve, demanded an outburst, a sharp, willful drive forward, the blow of a warrior. "It's impossible!" he repeated to himself, evenly and weakly pressing the accelerator with the toe of his boot and lightly turning the wheel in the direction of the truck's slippage. His foot on the pedal seemed to have grown numb. The calf of his leg which seemed to have turned to wood, felt as if it was seized by a cramp. But he did not surrender to that deceitful pain. His leg was avenging itself on him for the fact that he did not permit it to press with all its force on the accelerator, to let loose the unnecessary, and at this very moment fatal, power of the motor . . .

And the woman slept, leaning against the corner of the cabin. She had entirely entrusted herself to him and it would be better to die than to deceive her faith. Ahead, Bychkov saw a stretch of brown, dead grass. If he could just make it there, then the wheels would find support. There, only the last, strongest jerk ahead would be needed—and the truck would overcome the rise.

His wet palms slipped on the wheel. Acrid sweat tormented his eyes and he blinked it onto his cheekbones. Warm drops flowed along his cheeks and made his parched mouth salty. The seething rainwater of the ditch was just two or three meters away, and all of a sudden Bychkov felt that the wheels had "grabbed" the road. He stepped on the gas sharply, freeing all the strength which had been frozen in his foot. The truck trembled, jerked ahead and seemed to leap to the crest of the rise. Ahead of him to the settlement itself opened a roadway broken up into thick folds and gleaming puddles —a reliable road on in.

Bychkov wiped his face with the bottom of his shirt and licked his salty lips. Every nerve fiber, every muscle was twisted in a gnawing, drawn-out ache as if he had carried the truck with all its freight on his own back.

He looked across at his traveling companion. She was sweetly sleeping, knowing nothing of his duel with the road. And that was the way it should be: he was guarding her rest and her sleep. Everything difficult, burdensome, which a human being might meet on the way he was taking on himself. He had a strong back. He could carry any load, overcome any slope, just so long as she was next to him.

The settlement was still awake. In many homes and barracks light was gleaming. It was gleaming also over the entrance door and in the broad windows of the store at which Bychkov stopped his truck. The woman had not awakened when the truck was struggling in torment with the road. But the sudden stop immediately drove sleep away. With a shiver she roused herself, wiped her eyes with the back of her hand, yawned, and began to look for her string bags. Beneath her hand there fell Bychkov's cotton jacket. She put it on the seat. Having found her string bags she moved them to the edge of the cabin, awkwardly, with two hands, opened the door and jumped out onto the ground. Then she took down her string bags. Leaning across the seat, Bychkov with a smile followed her movements, which though somewhat awkward because she had just been roused from a sleep were nevertheless strong and determined.

"And what's going to be with us now?" he asked with tenderness in expectation.

The woman handed him something, and Bychkov wanted to take this something from her small fist and already had touched it with his fingers when all of a sudden he understood that it was money. Just as if he had been burned he jerked back his hand, and the two five-ruble notes which had been rolled into a little ball fell into the dirt.

"You . . . What are you doing?" he blurted out with fright.

The woman bent over and picked up the money.

"You have no conscience!" she said angrily and began to dig down into her purse. "To Vyselok it's ten rubles they take!"

"What are you talking about?" Bychkov cried out desolately. "Are you making fun of me?"

The woman found the bill she was seeking and handed it to him.

"Thirteen, I won't give any more!"

"Wait a minute . . ." Bychkov felt how his teeth were bared in a pitiful, awful smile which was chattering something. "Didn't you hear what I told you?"

"There aren't enough ears to listen to everybody. Are you going to take the money or not?"

"How can you?" Bychkov cried in desperation and cursed impotently.

"Don't try to misbehave here. It's not a highway here. I'll drag you quick enough to the militia."

Bychkov looked at her petty, angry face, which even in wrath did not become open. The closed, business-like face of a little, squalid, predatory female, and he understood that he had no one to blame except himself. He had thought the whole thing up himself. She had no concern with him. She was pretending that she was listening to him so that he would leave her alone and carry her further. And once she had understood that she had nothing to fear she had calmly gone to sleep.

He repeated her last words, mocking her mispronunciation with contempt and pain. "Learn to talk, witch!"

With a clank he put the truck in gear and started up so fast that the mud, pressed out from under the wheels, whipped across the gleaming black boots of the woman.

When he arrived at the supply base of the Fourth Sector there was no one except a sleeping guard in a thick sheepskin coat. Bychkov fell upon the old man. Why in heaven's name had they demanded the transformer if there wasn't even anyone to receive it? Sons of bitches and bureaucrats!

They didn't give a damn that a person risked his head in order to get the load through to them! The startled guard rushed to the telephone, and Bychkov climbed back into his cabin. He was all atremble. He buttoned up his quilted jacket, stretched out his legs right up to his stomach, collected in one knot the warmth of his whole body. Nothing helped. The feverish repulsive tremble penetrated to the ends of his fingers.

And then people ran up, many people, among them the chief of the Fourth Sector, an elderly, gray-headed engineer. With main force they dragged Bychkov out of his cabin, shook his hand, clapped him on the back, embraced him, and the chief of the Fourth Sector even wanted to kiss him. But Bychkov pulled away and the chief pecked him with cold, harsh moustaches somewhere beneath the jaw. And they all said at once that Bychkov was a heroic lad, and this, and that. It turned out that they had sent one of the employees ahead to warn the driver that he couldn't get through. And what a brave boy he was that he didn't listen and helped, yes, *saved* the Fourth Sector! Bychkov remembered the man who was waving his hand on the highway to whom he, immersed in his new happiness, had simply paid no attention ...

"Well I got here—and it's all right!" he said rudely. "Unload it faster, I'm tired ..."

The chief of the Sector tried to persuade him to go take a rest: there was a barracks right next to the base. The truck could be handled by the duty chauffeur. But Bychkov refused to listen to him: he needed neither sleep nor rest at that moment.

When the unloading was finished, he climbed into the cabin and took the truck through the gates. At the end of a long and already dark street—it was late—as before, there were bright lights over the entrance to a bar. Bychkov pictured to himself how he would enter the hot, close atmosphere pungently smelling of beer, how he would empty the cut-glass goblet of vodka gleaming green on its edges. He pictured how warmth would flow through his veins and how all of a sudden he would be hit in the head by the stupefying intoxication which would heat up the living memory and pain in a sweet drunken longing, and how there would gush out in this longing the song about the blue kerchief. And then he would entirely forget himself...

A light, hardly sensed, tender odor still remained in the cabin, but there was nothing of the odor of cheap eau de cologne, powder, and wet fur. It awakened in Bychkov the memory not of his recent traveling companion but of that other one whom he had still not met. Today he had made a stupid and pitiful mistake. Well, so what! At least he had discovered that she exists. She is inside him. She is already united with his existence. Just so as not to lose her in himself, and then she would appear in real life—on a daytime or a nighttime road—would make an appearance once and for always. He lightly and then deeply sighed, and the tremble which had tormented him quieted.

The enormous truck which was proceeding with determination toward its goal stopped all of a sudden with spitting brakes, veered sharply, went into reverse, and, sprinkling with the powerful light of its headlights the lit window of the bar, turned around and went back.

The Echo*

Sinegoriya, the seashore, empty in the afternoon hour, a little girl arising from out of the sea . . . It's almost thirty years ago!

I was looking for little stones on the wild beach. Earlier there had been a gale, and the hissing waves had rolled across the beach right up to the bright walls of the seaside sanitorium. Now the sea had quieted down and returned within its boundaries, exposing a broad, chocolate-colored shot-with-blue ribbon of sand, separated from the shore by a little bank of pebbles. That sand, moist and so firm that in walking along it one did not leave a track, was strewn with sugarlike round little shiny stones, light-green blue pebbles, smooth, rounded little pieces of glass like well-sucked sugar candies, with dead crabs, with rotten waterweeds, which gave forth a pungent odor of iodine. I knew that the big wave was bearing valuable little stones to the shore and patiently, step by step, investigated the sand deposit and fresh wash of pebbles.

"Hey, why are you sitting on my shorts?" I heard a thin little voice.

I raised my eyes. Above me stood a naked little girl, lean, with prominent ribs and thin arms and legs. Her long wet hair clung to her face. The water gleamed on her pale body—almost untouched by sunburn and all bluish and in goose pimples from cold.

The little girl bent down, pulled out from under me her striped, yellow and blue shorts, shook them, and tossed them onto the stones. She herself tumbled down prone onto a shoal of golden sand and began to dig down into it and shovel it off to the sides.

"You might at least put something on . . ." I muttered.

"Why? I can get a suntan better this way," answered the little girl.

"And aren't you ashamed?"

"Mama says it doesn't matter for little ones. And she doesn't let me bathe in my shorts. She says I'll catch cold if I do that, and she doesn't have any time to fuss with me . . ."

Among the dark rough stones all of a sudden something tenderly glistened: a tiny clean little teardrop. I pulled a cigarette box out and added the teardrop to my collection.

"Oh, show me!"

The little girl gathered her wet hair behind her ears, revealing

* Russian title: "Ekho," dated by the author 1960, published in his collection *Rannei Vesnoi*, pp. 440–56.

her slim face with dark spots, green catlike eyes, turned-up nose, and a mouth which was enormous, reaching almost to her ears. She began to look over my stones.

On a thin layer of cotton wool lay: a small oval, transparent, rose cornelian, and another cornelian—larger, but not worn by the sea and therefore shapeless and dull to the light; several stones in a porcelain-patterned exterior; two interesting fossils—one in the form of a star-fish, the other with the imprint of a small crab; a small "chicken-god"—a stone ring; and then the pride of my collection— a smoky topaz, mist dissolved in dark glass.

"You collected them today?"

"What do you mean? For all the time that I have been here!"

"Not much."

"Try yourself!"

"I should bother!" She jerked her lean peeling shoulder. "To crawl all the day long in the heat for lousy stones!"

"You're a fool!" I said. "A naked little fool!"

"You're a fool yourself! I suppose you also collect stamps?"

"Well I do collect them!" I answered with a challenge.

"And cigarette boxes?"

"I used to collect them when I was little."

"And what else do you collect?"

"I used to have a collection of butterflies . . ."

I thought that this would please her, and for some reason I wanted to please her.

"Foo, how nasty!" she jerked her upper lip, showing two narrow white fangs. "You smashed their heads and stuck them on pins?"

"Not at all, I put them to sleep with ether."

"It's nasty all the same . . . I can't bear it when people kill things."

"And do you know what else I collected?" I said thoughtfully. "I collected different makes of bicycles!"

"I don't believe you!"

"My word of honor! I ran through the streets and asked all those who had bicycles: 'Uncle, what make of bicycle is yours?' And he would say: 'Duks' or, maybe, 'Latvella' or 'Opel'! And so I collected all the makes. Only one was I missing—'Enfield Royal' . . ." I was speaking quickly, afraid that the little girl would interrupt me with some kind of a sneer, but she was watching seriously, with interest and even stopped tossing sand about from her fist. "Every day I ran all the way to the Lubyanka Square and once almost fell under a streetcar, but nevertheless I found an 'Enfield Royal'! You know it has a purple trademark with a large Latin 'R' . . ."

"So you're not such a bad type after all . . ." said the little girl, and she laughed with her big mouth. "I will tell you in secret, I also am a collector . . ."

"Of what?"

"Of echoes . . . I have always collected lots of them. There is an echo which is as ringing as glass. There's an echo which sounds like a copper pipe. There's a three-voiced echo. There's one which sounds as if peas were being poured out, and there are others . . ."

"All right, stop lying!" I angrily interrupted her.

The green catlike eyes pierced me.

"You want me to show you?"

"Yes, well, I would like it . . ."

"I'll only show you, no one else. And can you come with me? We have to climb all the way up to the Large Saddle."

"I can come!"

"So tomorrow we will go in the early morning. Where do you live?"

"On Primorskaya, with the Bulgarian."

"And we are on Tarakanikha."

"Ah, so I saw your mother! So tall, with black hair?"

"Uh-huh. Only I don't see my mama at all."

"Why?"

"Mama loves to dance . . ." The little girl shook her hair which was already dry and which was some kind of gray. "Come on, let's go swim once more!"

She jumped up, stuck all over with sand, and ran to the sea, her rosy narrow heels twinkling . . .

The new morning was sunny, without wind, but not hot. The sea after the gale was still breathing cold and did not allow the sun to heat up the air. And at times when a thin little cloud swam across the face of the sun—looking like cigarette smoke and erasing the blinding southern brilliance from the gravel of the pathways, from the white walls, and from the tile roofs—then the landscape grew gloomy as if before a long period of bad weather, and the cold draft from the sea immediately grew stronger.

The pathway up to the Large Saddle wound at first among not very high hills and then stretched upward straight and steeply through a thick and fragrant walnut forest. It was cut through by a shallow trough strewn with stones, the branch of one of those turbulent streams which pour down from the mountains after a rain, roaring and ringing throughout the whole district, but which dry up more quickly than do the raindrops on the leaves of the walnut trees.

We had already covered no small part of the way when I decided to find out the name of my acquaintance.

"Hey" I shouted at the yellow-blue shorts gleaming like a butterfly in the walnut grove. "What's your name?"

The little girl stopped, and I came up to her. The walnut grove at that point grew more sparse, parted, opening the view to the gulf and our settlement—a pitiful little handful of small houses. The enormous, mysterious sea stretched to the horizon, and behind it were misty dull-blue strips laid down in the heavens one upon the other. And in the gulf itself the sea pretended to be gentle and small, playing, stretching a white thread along the edge of the shore, biting into it and again stretching out . . .

"I don't even know what to tell you," the little girl said thoughtfully. "I have a silly name—Victorina, and everyone calls me Vitka."

"We could call you Vika."

"Tfoo, how nasty!" she exposed her sharp fangs in a familiar fashion.

"Why? Vika—that's a wild pea, vetch."

"It's also a mouse name. I can't bear mice!"

"Well, if it's Vitka, let it be Vitka. And my name is Serezha. Do we still have far to go?"

"Are you tired? When we get past the forester's house we can already see the Large Saddle . . ."

But we still twisted around for a long time in the stuffy walnut grove with its smells of tartness and honey. Finally, the pathway became a stony road, gleaming white with a thin sandlike powdered sugar and led us out on a broad gentle ledge. There, in a grove of apricot trees, nestled the forester's lodge, built of limestone composed of seashells.

Hardly had we approached the cozy little house than the quiet was disrupted by a mad barking. Clanking their chains, which were hung on a long wire, two enormous shaggy, dirty-white dogs dashed toward us, soared into the air, and, choked by their collars, rolled out their rosy tongues, wheezed, and fell to the ground.

"Don't be afraid, they can't reach us!" Vitka said calmly.

The dogs' teeth clicked just half a step away. I saw the burrs in their manes, their teeth, their dilated nostrils. Only their eyes were buried in their hair. It was strange that from the lodge no one emerged to take the dogs away. But no matter how they tried, no matter how they pulled on the wire, they could not reach us. And when I became convinced of this I was painfully glad. Our crusade was taking us to cliffs and caves inhabited by secret voices. The only thing we were lacking was dread guards, dragons barring daring people from access to the secret. And there they were, the dragons—the overgrown, eyeless dogs with their meat-red mouths!

And again we twisted and turned along the narrowing pathway in the walnut grove. There the walnut grove was not so thick as below. Many of the bushes had dried out, and on others the leaves had been eaten into a cobweb by a small shiny black beetle.

I was tired and I was angry at Vitka. Without paying attention to anyone or anything she was stepping ahead with her thin legs straight as sticks, with their slightly bowed knees. But ahead all of a sudden it grew light. I saw a slope overgrown with a low brown grass and in the distance a gray cliff stretched upward.

"The Devil's Finger!" Vitka said, still moving.

The closer we approached, the higher the gray rocky cliff rose —it seemed to grow disproportionately to our approach. When we stepped into its dark cool shadow, it became monstrously enormous. This was not the Devil's Finger, but the Devil's Tower, murky, mysterious, unattainable. As if she were answering my thoughts, Vitka said:

"Do you know many people have tried to climb it? None of them succeeded. Some fell to their death and others broke their arms and legs. But one Frenchman climbed it."

"And how was he able to?"

"Well, he was able ... But he couldn't get back down, and he went crazy up there and afterward died from hunger ... But, nevertheless, he was a brave man," she added thoughtfully.

We went right up next to the Devil's Finger, and Vitka, lowering her voice, said:

"Right there ...," she took several steps backward and softly called: "Serezha!"

"Serezha ...," a mockingly furtive voice repeated in my very ear, as if it had been born in the depths of the Devil's Finger.

I trembled and involuntarily stepped back a little from the cliff. And right there greeting me, from the sea, there ringingly washed upon me:

"Serezha!"

I froze and somewhere up above in a fatigued-bitter moan could be heard:

"Serezha!"

"The devil!" I pronounced in a suppressed voice.

"The devil!" rustled above my ear.

"The devil!" breathed from the sea.

"The devil!" answered from above.

In each of these invisible mocking voices there was felt a firm and awesome character: the whisper was a maliciously furtive, quiet lad; the voice from the sea belonged to a cold merry chap; in the heights there was hidden a hypocritical and inconsolable complainer.

"Well? Shout something!" said Vitka.

And in the ears, interrupting her voice there crept a whisper: "Well?" ringingly, with a laugh: "Shout" and, as through tears: "Something."

Overcoming myself with difficulty I shouted:

"Sinegoriya!"

I heard the three voices answer . . .

I shouted, talked, whispered many more words of all kinds. The echo had the keenest ears. Certain words I pronounced so quietly that I barely heard them myself, but they invariably found their answer. I no longer experienced fear, but every time when the invisible whispered in my ear my backbone grew cold and the sobbing voice tightened my heart.

"So long!" said Vitka and left the Devil's Finger.

I rushed after her but the whisper reached me, rustling venomously, insinuatingly, the words of farewell, and from the distant seascape came a giggle, and a voice from up above groaned:

"So long!"

We went in the direction of the sea and soon turned out to be upon a stony ledge overhanging a precipice. On our right and on our left rose spurs of the mountains, and beneath us yawned an abyss in which one's gaze drowned. If the Devil's Finger had fallen through the earth it would have left behind such an enormous awesome hole as this. At the bottom of the gap there stuck up sharp clammy stones like the fangs of a giant. And the dark sea, the shade of ink, beat against them like a battering ram. Some bird or other, stretching immobile, seemingly dead, wings slowly and in circles was falling into the abyss.

It seemed as if things were not yet finished here. There had not yet come into equilibrium the dread forces which tore from out the center of the earth the gigantic stone finger, which split the mountain mass into a monstrous well, which sharpened its bottom with the shapes of rocks, and which compelled the sea to lacerate its tender tongue on them. All of the stone mass around and below was unstable, unsteady, and in a state of hidden inner strain striving for a remaking . . . Of course, at that time I was unable to name that torturing, alarming sensation which seized me at the edge of the Large Saddle.

Vitka lay on her stomach at the very edge of the precipice and motioned me to her. I sprawled out next to her on the firm and warm smooth stone surface, and the sucking, chilling attraction of the chasm disappeared. It became quite easy to look downward. Vitka leaned over the precipice and shouted:

"Oho-ho!"

There was a moment of silence and then a thick whirring voice thundered like a trumpet:

"Oh-ho-ho-oo!"

In this voice there was nothing awful notwithstanding its force and density. Evidently, there lived down in the abyss a good giant who wished us no harm.

Vitka asked:

"Who was the first to deceive?"

And the giant, after thinking a little bit, answered with laughter: "Eve!"

"And do you know," said Vitka, looking downward, "No one has succeeded yet in descending from the Large Saddle to the sea. One man got to the middle and got stuck there..."

"And he died from hunger?" I asked, mockingly.

"No, they tossed him down a rope and dragged him up... But I think it's possible to get down."

"Let's try!"

"Let's!" Vitka replied immediately and simply, and I understood that she was serious.

"Some other time," I awkwardly laughed her off.

"Then let's go... To your health!" shouted Vitka into the abyss and jumped to her feet.

"Health!" cackled the giant.

I wanted to talk with him some more, but Vitka dragged me further. The new echo, according to Vitka, was "ringing like glass," and it was nested in a gorge which was as narrow as if it were a knife cut. The echo had a thin, piercing voice. It thinned out to a squeal even a word said in a deep bass. And what was even more repulsive: having squealed out its answer, the echo did not quiet down, but for a long time more squeaked like a mouse in some of its own cracks and crannies.

We did not stop for long at the gorge and went further. Now we had to scramble upward along a steep slope covered at times with a harsh brown grass and prickers and at times naked, polished, and slippery. Finally, we reached a ledge piled up with enormous boulders. Every boulder was reminiscent of something: a ship, a tank, a bull, the head conquered by Ruslan, a warrior in armor on his knees, a piece of shore artillery with its barrel broken, a camel, the maw of a roaring lion, and now and again the parts of the body of a giant who had been torn to pieces: a humped nose, an ear, a jaw with a beard, a fist which was powerful and unclenched, a naked foot, a forehead with curls of hair on it...

All of these stony beings—parts of beings, objects dressed in stone—tossed back and forth, as if it were a ball, any word which resounded among them, with momentary speed and sharp brevity reflecting the facets of the sounds. It was here that the "pea-like" or "bird-shot" echo lived.

But the most astonishing was the echo about which Vitka had said nothing. We didn't walk to it, but crawled along on a steep slope, taking hold of ledges, of lichens, of dry bits of bushes. Out from under our feet and hands little stones crumbled, pulling after themselves larger rocks. And behind us as a result there was an incessant thunder. When I looked behind myself I was surprised at the smallness of the height which had made us dizzy at the precipice. The sea from here no longer seemed to be a smooth mirror-like surface: boundless and unembraceable it merged with the heaven, forming together with it a single sphere—a cupola which reigned over all the visible expanse. And the Devil's Finger, stressing our altitude, had again diminished to a mere upright protrusion.

Vitka stopped at a half-round dark gap leading into the center of the mountain. I looked into it, and when my eyes had become a little used to the dark I could see an arched cave with the long beards of stone icicles. The walls shed a green, red, blue shimmer. From the cave seeped the muskiness of a crypt and, involuntarily, I recoiled.

"Hello!" Vitka shouted, sticking her head into the hole.

And it was as if empty barrels began to echo, bumping against one another beneath the arch: "Boom!" reverberated through the corners and with a low "oh" finally burst out to the open, just as if the mountain had emitted its spirit.

I looked at Vitka with respectful astonishment. Lean, freckled, with tousled grayish hair, with her sharp fangs in the corners of her lips, with her green gleaming eyes—she herself seemed at that moment just as fantastic as the secret world into which she had led me.

"And so shout!" Vitka ordered.

I bent down and gave forth into the small black mouth of the mountain. And again it reverberated inside there, began to roll about in a squeaky-squealy tone, and then breathed in my face with a rotten-smelling chill draft which was not of this world. All of a sudden I was seized by an awful loneliness, loneliness and defenselessness, among the peaks and ravines of this stony, cliff-dwelling world peopled by mysterious and wild voices.

"Let's go," I said to Vitka, expressing my confusion. "Let's go away from here!"

Our further path I perceived as an endless falling downward. On this path again there flashed past the stone cemetery, the Devil's Finger, the sick, thinned-out walnut grove, and the foresters' dogs

flying on their chains and gasping in suffocation, and another walnut grove—this one healthy and full of strength. Our fall was broken
by the dry gorge which skirted the settlement on the side of the mountain.

"Well, was it interesting?" Vitka asked when we stepped onto
our street.

I again felt myself in serene ordinariness, and Vitka no longer
seemed to me to be the fantastic mistress of the mountain spirits.
She was simply a bony, uncomely little girl. And in front of this little
girl I had played the coward!

"Interesting..." I said lazily. "Only what kind of a collection
is that?"

"And you only want the kind you can keep in a box, inside your
shirt?"

"No, why should I?... But echoes will answer to anyone, not
just to you yourself alone."

Vitka looked at me somehow strangely for a long time.

"Well, so what, I don't mind!" she said, shaking her head of
hair, and she went off home ...

Vitka and I became friends. Together we climbed up Temryuk-
Kaya and Svadebnaya Mountain. On Svadebnaya, in a grotto, we
found a croaking echo. But Temryuk-Kaya, with its spurs, its powerful slopes, and its peak sharply stuck up into the heaven, turned out
to be completely fruitless ...

We were almost inseparable. I grew used to the fact that Vitka
went swimming naked. She was a good sort, a comrade, and I didn't
see in her a little girl at all. Vaguely I understood the nature of her
lack of shyness: Vitka considered herself hopelessly ugly. I never ever
met a person who so simply, openly, with such clear dignity recognized her own uncomeliness. Telling me once about one of her school
girl friends, Vitka mentioned in passing: "She is almost as ugly a
thing as I am ..."

Once we were swimming not far from the fisherman's wharf,
when down from the high shore above there poured a band of small
boys. I knew them a little, but my shy efforts to get close to them
had led to nothing. This was not the first year these boys had spent
vacations in Sinegoriya. They considered themselves old inhabitants
and did not allow strangers in their band. The ringleader was a tall
strong boy named Igor. I had already come out of the sea and was
wiping myself with a towel; Vitka was continuing to gambol in the
water. Waiting for a wave, she jumped up high and slid on her
stomach down its crest. Her small buttocks gleamed.

The boys carelessly answered my greeting and were about to go past when suddenly one of them, in red bathing trunks, noticed Vitka.

"Boys, look, a naked little girl!"

Then the fun began: shouts, whistles, spoofing. I have to give credit to Vitka. She didn't pay any attention to the antics of the boys, but this only poured oil onto the fire. The boy in red trunks made a proposal: "To bend her legs up to her head." The proposal was met with glee and the boy in red trunks waddled out into the water. But at that moment Vitka with animal-like speed bent down, fished around in the water, and when she straightened up in her hand she had a weighty stone.

"Just try!" she said, baring her fangs. "I'll smash your whole face!"

The boy in red trunks stopped and tried the water with his foot.

"It's cold . . ." he said and his ears became redder than his trunks. "I don't feel like going in . . ."

Igor approached and sat down on the sand at the very edge of the shore. The boy in red trunks without any words understood his leader and sat down beside him. The remaining boys followed their example. With a chain they had cut Vitka off from the shore, her clothing, and her towel. Vitka tried their patience for a long time. At times she swam far out into the sea and then returned, dived, wallowed in the water, and then sat on an underwater stone, rolling waves onto herself with her arms. But the cold finally had its effect.

"Serezha!" shouted Vitka. "Give me my shorts!"

For all of this time I, without even noticing it, had been wiping myself with the towel. My well-wiped skin glowed, just as if from sunburn, and I was still wiping the dry surface as if I wanted to wear myself down to holes. In the pitiful and humiliated embarrassment which possessed me there beat only one precise desire: just not to participate in Vitka's shame.

"Serezha, give your lady her shorts!" in a joking voice squeaked the boy in the red trunks.

Turning about on his elbow, Igor said to me with a threat: "Just try!"

It was a vain warning: I wouldn't have moved from my place in any case. Vitka understood that she could not expect any help from me. Pitifully writhing, with all of her body sunken into her thin little stomach and covering it with her hands, purple and goose-pimpled from the cold, with a twisted face, she climbed out of the water and ran sideways to her shorts to the tune of the laughter and whistling of the boys. That to which, in the purity of her soul, she had not given any significance presented itself to her as nasty, humiliating, shameful.

Jumping on one foot and unable to get the other into the leg of her shorts, somehow or other she managed to get dressed, grabbed her towel from the ground and ran away. All of a sudden she turned back and shouted at me:

"Coward! Coward! Pitiful coward!"

From all existing words Vitka had selected the most vicious, hurtful, and unjust of all. She should have understood that it was not Igor's fists of which I was afraid. But she evidently wanted once and for all to shame me in front of the boys.

I don't know whether it was a caprice of the leader who did not want to follow her or whether something interested Igor in Vitka, but he asked me in a friendly and trusting tone:

"Listen, what is she, crazy?"

"Of course crazy!" I gave way completely in the face of this generosity.

"And why do you fool around with her?"

Not at all in order to make Vitka seem better, but only wishing to protect myself I said:

"It's interesting. She collects echoes."

"What?" Igor was astonished.

In a low outburst of grateful frankness I immediately set forth all of Vitka's secrets.

"Well that's something!" said Igor with delight. "I've been living here for three summers and I never heard anything like that."

"You're not exaggerating?" the boy in the red trunks asked me.

"Do you want me to show you?"

"All of them!" Igor said with authority, again becoming the leader. "You're going to take us there tomorrow!"

In the morning it was drizzling. The mountains stretched upward gray-white, like clouds of soapsuds. With the gloomy sound of the stormy sea, which was the color of mountain grass, there mingled the roar of the swollen streams and small rivers.

But Igor's gang decided not to give up. And once again the already familiar trail wound beneath my feet, and in its middle, rolling along the gravel, ran the dull yellow little bit of a stream. The walnut grove smelled—already not with a honey-sweet fragrance with a slight touch of bitter—of the rottenness of fallen leaves, the sourness of washed-away earth in which something is rotten, exhaling a wine-vinegar odor. It was difficult going. Feet lost their footing on the wet earth and slipped on the stones...

At the house of the forester we were met by the customary heart-rending bark of the watchdogs, but in the damp air their bark sounded softer, duller, yes, and they themselves did not seem so dreadful in their wet, bedraggled hair. Their black eyes which looked like olives were visible.

And there was the ailing walnut grove, infected with the beetle.

The wind and the rain had torn off the weak and eaten leaves. The grove stood naked, sad, and through it could be seen the dark gloomy shape of the sea.

The Devil's Finger, wound about in clouds, did not show itself for long. Then, at an unattainable height its peak shown out black, then hid, for a moment was exposed for the entire height of its trunk, and momentarily again disappeared in the whirling air. Strangely, the wind drove toward the sea, and the light clouds drove from the sea like steam from the mouth on a frosty day. They slipped along the very earth, covered us with a moist smoke and suddenly disappeared, settling a dew on the slopes.

Finally, from out of the cloudy dimness once more the Devil's Finger rose and barred our way.

"Well, let's see your miracle," Igor said without a smile.

"Listen!" I pronounced triumphantly, feeling how my back grew familiarly cold. I made my hand into a megaphone and shouted:

"Oh-ho-ho!"

In answer there was silence. There was neither the maliciously insinuating whisper nor the laughing splash from the sea nor the complaint from up above.

"Oho-ho!" I shouted once more, stepping nearer the Devil's Finger, and all of the boys separately caught up my cry.

The Devil's Finger was silent. We shouted again and again—but there wasn't the slightest answer! Then I rushed to the precipice—the boys after me—and with all my strength yelled down into the swirling depths. But even the giant did not answer.

In embarrassment I began to rush back and forth from the precipice to the Devil's Finger, from the Devil's Finger to the gorge, and again to the precipice, and again to the Devil's Finger. But the mountains were silent . . .

I pitifully began to persuade the boys to go up higher, to the cave. There we would beyond a doubt hear the echo. The boys stood before me, silent and severe, like the mountains. Then Igor opened his lips in order to say just one word:

"Blowhard!"

And, turning around abruptly, he went away, taking the entire gang behind him.

I dragged along behind, vainly trying to understand what had happened. I wasn't worried at this moment by the contempt of the boys. I only wanted to discover the secret of my failure. Could it possibly be that the mountains reacted only to Vitka's voice? But whenever I was with her the mountains obediently answered me also. Perhaps she really possessed the key which permitted her to lock up the voices in stony caves?

There came sad days. I had lost Vitka and even my mama condemned me. When I told her the mysterious story with the echo, Mama took my measure with a long, alien, examining stare and said sadly:

"It's all very simple: the mountains reply only to those who are pure and honest..."

Her words opened up much to me, but not the mystery of the mountain echoes.

The rains did not stop. The sea seemed to be divided into two parts. In the gulf it was dull yellow from the sand brought down by the rivers and streams. In the distance it shone clean. The wind blew incessantly. Daytimes, it shook the rain about like a gray sheet. At nighttimes—always clear, in small white stars—it was dry and black because it disclosed itself in black: in the rough branches, tree trunks, in coal-black shadows which ran across the lit earth.

Several times I saw Vitka in passing. She went to the sea in any weather and was able to get from the sparse, rare sun a thick chocolate sunburn. From loneliness and longing every day I now accompanied my mother to the market, where there was trading in local products: vegetables, apricots, goat's milk, *varenets*. Once I met Vitka at the market. She was alone. She had a woven basket in her hand. I watched how she walked among the hawkers' trays and milk cans in her yellow-blue shorts. She selected tomatoes with determination. She herself tossed a piece of meat on the scales. And I felt with pain that I had lost a good friend.

In the morning on the first sunny day I wandered around the garden, picking up fallen apricots with soft rotten spots, when I heard someone calling to me. At the gate there stood a little girl in a white blouse with a blue sailor's collar and a blue skirt. It was Vitka, but I didn't recognize her right away. Her grayish hair was smoothly combed and bound back with a ribbon. On her suntanned neck there was a string of coral beads. And on her feet there were deerskin shoes. I ran to her.

"Listen, we are going away," said Vitka.

"Why?"

"Mother is tired of it here... Here's what, I want to leave you my collection. I don't need it anyway and you can show the boys and make your peace with them."

"I'm not going to show anyone!" I cried out in heat.

"As you want, let it be for you yourself. Have you guessed why nothing happened with you?"

"And how do you know that nothing happened?"

"I heard... So did you guess?"

"No..."

"You must understand, the chief thing is from what place you shout." Vitka lowered her voice confidentially. "At the Devil's Finger—only on the side of the sea. And you probably shouted from the other side. There isn't any echo there. In the abyss you have to hang down and shout straight down the wall. You remember, I bent your head down then? In the gorge shout into the very depths so that your voice should go further. And then in the cave it always answers. Only you didn't get there. And among the stones also . . ."

"Vitka!" I began repentantly.

Her thin face twisted.

"I am going to run along because my bus is leaving . . ."

"Shall we see each other in Moscow?"

Vitka shook her head.

"We are from Kharkov . . ."

"And are you coming here again?"

"I don't know . . . Well, so long!" Vitka with embarrassment bent her head to her shoulder and immediately ran off.

At the gate my mother stood and with a long insistent stare followed Vitka with her eyes.

"Who is that?" my mama asked somehow with gladness.

"That is Vitka, she is living on Tarakanikha."

"What a lovely being!" with a deep voice my mama said.

"But no, that's Vitka!"

"I am not deaf . . ." Mama again looked in the direction in which Vitka had run off. "Ah, what a miraculous little girl! That turned-up nose, those ashen locks, those surprising eyes, that sculpturesque figure, her narrow feet, her hands . . ."

"What are you saying, Mama!" I cried out, disappointed with her strange blindness. It seemed to me somehow hurtful for Vitka. "You didn't see her mouth!"

"A beautiful big mouth! You don't know anything!"

Mama went to the house. I watched her back for several seconds and then rushed off and ran to the autobus station.

The autobus had still not left. The last passengers, loaded with their bags and suitcases, were storming the door. I immediately saw Vitka on the side on which the windows weren't open. Next to her sat a plump black-haired woman in a red dress, her mother.

Vitka also saw me and grabbed at the handrail of the frame so as to open the window. Her mother said something to her and touched her shoulder, probably trying to get her to sit down in her place. With a sharp movement Vitka brushed off her hand. The autobus roared and slowly climbed along the unpaved road, spreading behind a golden trail of dust. I ran along beside it. Biting her lip, Vitka tore at the handrail and the frame fell down with a bang. It was easier for me to consider Vitka beautiful when she was out of sight—her sharp fangs and her dark freckles scattered across her whole face spoiled the image which Mama had remade for me and in which I had come to believe.

"Listen, Vitka," I quickly said. "Mama said that you are beautiful! You have beautiful hair, eyes, a mouth, nose . . ." The autobus gathered speed and I ran. "Hands, legs! It's true, Vitka!"

Vitka only smiled with her big mouth, gladly, trustingly, loyally, opening in that big smile all of her good soul, and right there with my own eyes I saw that Vitka really was the most beautiful little girl in the world.

Settling heavily, the bus went onto a wooden bridge across a stream which was the boundary of Sinegoriya. I stopped. The bridge thundered, trembled, and rocked. In the window again appeared Vitka's head with her ashen locks waving in the wind and her sharp suntanned elbow. Vitka made a sign to me and with all her strength threw across the stream a silvery coin. The gleaming trail in the air was quenched in the dust at my feet. There was a superstition: if you throw a coin there, sometime you will without a doubt return . . .

I wanted the day of our departure to come more quickly. Then I also would throw a coin and Vitka and I would meet again.

But that was not destined to be. When we left Sinegoriya after a month I forgot to throw the coin.

Vladimir Tendryakov

An Introduction to Vladimir Tendryakov

Vladimir Fedorovich Tendryakov who has established himself in a firm position as one of the most important younger Soviet writers to emerge in the post-Stalin period was born in 1923. Like most of his contemporaries Tendryakov was in the war from its first days. He continued in military service till 1943. From 1944 to 1946 he was in Young Communist League work as a secretary of a district (Rayon) committee of the Komsomols (Young Communist League) in Kirov Province, located in a remote region of Northeast Central European Russia between the Volga River and the Urals. Thus it is no coincidence that many of his better-known stories are set in the wild, remote heavily forested country about the village of "Gustoi Bor." Tendryakov has been a member of the Party since 1948. He was first published in 1947. In 1951 he graduated from the Gorky Institute of Literature in Moscow, and within two years after his graduation his long stories—more properly novellas—began to appear in Russian literary journals: *Not Suited* in 1954, *The Fall of Ivan Chuprov* in 1956, *Tight Knot* in 1956, *Roadholes* in 1956, *The Miracle Worker* in 1958, *Three, Seven and Ace* in 1960, *The Judgment* in 1961, *Short Circuit* in 1962. In 1959 appeared his first novel, *In Pursuit of the Fleeing Day*. One of the Soviet literary journals has announced that a new novel by him is to be published.

Tendryakov was one of the editors of the almanac *Literary Moscow* in the year 1956—which contained short stories and essays (including one contribution by Tendryakov himself) constituting as a whole a sweeping indictment of Stalinism and a bold exposure of some of the seamy side of contemporary Soviet life. In the reaction against greater freedom of literary expression which set in after the suppression of the Hungarian revolution in November 1956 this publication—and its editorial board, including Tendryakov—was one of the principal targets of Party attacks.

Tendryakov came in for severe criticism also after publication of his story *Three, Seven and Ace* in early 1960. The newspaper *Pravda* published an article soon after the story came out entitled "Who is Being Accused?" It was signed with the name of a critic, Lukin, but clearly expressed the opinion of the paper's editors. Lukin attempted to demonstrate that Tendryakov in his story was attacking Soviet society.

That the writer had any such intention can certainly be very seriously doubted. Tendryakov is clearly a faithful communist, loyal to the regime. At times in his work, however, he arrogates to himself the privilege of looking beyond the immediate propaganda problems of the hour and attempts to discern deeper human truths. He is frank about this—and as he has progressed in his career he has carried his search further and further away from propaganda. He is one of the most informative of contemporary Soviet writers, and he treats serious questions and problems in a slow, serious, not to say even heavy-handed, manner.

Here is how one work on contemporary Russian literature, published in the Soviet Union, describes Tendryakov:

"Psychological depth of characters, dramatic tension and emotionality of story-telling, clear depiction of the Russian landscape—such are characteristics of the creative ability of Vladimir Tendryakov."

Stylistically, Tendryakov seems to have taken something from a Russian writer of modern times who is unknown in the West but who had much influence in the Soviet Union—Shishkov, the author of the Siberian epic, *Grim River*. There is in Tendryakov the same extreme vividness of imagery, the same attenuation of detail, the same continual tendency to overstatement, the same prolixity and conscious use of repetition as in Shishkov. Tendryakov belongs to that honorable tradition of Russian writing going back to Turgenev and beyond, of which Shishkov is a member and Yuri Nagibin as well, which looks to the Russian rural landscape and particularly to the forests and the hunters who haunt them for much of its scenery and inspiration.

It is typical of Tendryakov that his stories usually have a clear moral to them. And it is also typical of him that, so as to be absolutely certain that his moral does not escape his reader, he brings it out at some point, usually near the end of the story, and states it with stress so as almost to set it in italics.

All in all of the outstanding younger Soviet writers of today Tendryakov is perhaps farthest away from Western contemporary tendencies in terms of style. As a consequence some Western readers may find him slow-moving, perhaps even tedious.

Generally, one observes that among Western readers, including also Western students of Soviet literature and others who can read him in the original, there is the widest imaginable variety of opinions on Tendryakov. For example, H. T. Willets in *Survey*, for January 1963, declares: "It may be absurd that the sloppy novelettes of an Aksenov find their way into English, because they are considered revealing about the mood of Soviet youth, while exquisite stories by Tendryakov, for instance, are little known in the West." On the other hand another American scholar, equally versed in contemporary Soviet literature, has termed Tendryakov's stories overrated. After I had completed my translation of *Short Circuit,* included in this collection, I asked several individuals to read it and to give me their opinion of it. Some were enthusiastic and others felt it was pretentious.

Certainly Tendryakov is the most explicit of all contemporary Russian writers in his forthright expression of the new humanism in Russian literature, a humanism which is also to be found in some contemporary Western literature, and which therefore constitutes a bond in idea and emotion with creative expression in the West. Tendryakov's humanism has been put in its bluntest statement to date in his novella *Short Circuit.*

One of Tendryakov's stories best known in the West—partly because it has been available in English translation for some time and partly because at the time it first appeared in 1956 it was a rather bold condemnation of the heartlessness of bureaucracy—is "Roadholes." *

Tendryakov's best-known work to date is his story entitled *Three, Seven and Ace,* published in the journal *Novy Mir* in March 1960. † (The title was taken from the series of cards in Pushkin's "Queen of Spades," which the story's leading figure hoped would win him his fortune—but which did not.)

Tendryakov's novel, *In Pursuit of the Fleeing Day*—published in 1959—deals with quite a different scene and quite a different basic question—a Soviet school and attitudes toward education.

Tendryakov's story *The Judgment*—published in *Novy Mir* in March 1961—is a nearly novel-length account of a boisterous bear hunt at nighttime in the deep forests of the Gustoi Bor district and of the consequences which this hunt had in the lives of the three hunters who took part in it. Again in this story Tendryakov deals with universal questions. In his pioneering on this path, and in his well-developed and well-expressed sense of the humanism of our times, lie his considerable possibilities.

---

* Translated in *Soviet Literature,* No. 2 (1957); also in *Stories from Modern Russia,* edited by C. P. Snow and Pamela Hansford Johnson (New York, 1962).

† *Three, Seven and Ace* has been published in abbreviated form—about half length (translated by David Alger)—in the collection *Dissonant Voices,* edited by Patricia Blake and Max Hayward (New York, 1962). This translation omits important passages, including even the story's "moral."

Short Circuit[*]

Dramatis Personae

Western readers often find the Russian names in Russian literary works most confusing, particularly because a particular character may be addressed or identified in a story by different names, all of which sound nearly equally outlandish and alien to Western ears. In order to make things easier for the Western reader translators sometimes simplify the names of the Russian characters in the works they translate. I have no quarrel with this practice—but it inevitably results in some loss of the Russian flavor of the work, and in this story I have preferred to stick exactly to the names and nicknames used in the original. At this point for the benefit of the reader I list the names of the characters—full names, identifications, and nicknames:

Ivan Kapitonovich Sokovin: *manager (or director) of the Electric Power System of a large Russian city and its surrounding area. He is usually identified as* Ivan Kapitonovich, *but sometimes as* Ivan Sokovin *or simply by his wife,* Ivan. *As he reminisces to himself, he uses his nicknames as a village youth:* Vanka Sokovin *and* Vanka the Prince.

Nadezhda Sergeyevna Sokovina: *his wife—usually identified as* Nadezhda Sergeyevna—*called on occasion by her husband* Nadya.

Vadim Ivanovich Sokovin: *his only son—the chief electrical engineer of a large chemical factory—usually called* Vadim, *but also* Dima, Dimka, *and* Dimochka.

Galina Vasilevna Sokovina: *Vadim's wife, does not appear in the story because she is a patient in a maternity home awaiting the birth of her first child. She is the daughter of Vasily Vasilevich Stolyarsky and Bronislava Semyenovna Stolyarskaya and is referred to by a variety of nicknames and her given name:* Galina, Galochka, Galka.

Ignat Golubko: *the chief engineer of the Electric Power System and Ivan Kapitonovich Sokovin's righthand man. He is almost always referred to as* Ignat Golubko *or sometimes* Ignat *or* Golubko.

Yelena Ignatievna Golubko: *the not quite seventeen-year-old daughter of Ignat Golubko, who is called always by her various nicknames:* Lena, Lenka, Elka, *and, most frequently of all,* Elochka.

Vasily Vasilevich Stolyarsky: *the chief of the Control Room (chief*

[*] Russian title: *Korotkoye Zamykaniye,* first published in *Znamya,* No. 3 (March 1962), pp. 3–54.

dispatcher) of the Electric Power System—almost always referred to as Vasily Vasilevich, *also, by his wife on one or two occasions, as* Vasya.

Bronislava Semyenovna Stolyarskaya: *his wife and Vadim's mother-in-law. Always referred to as* Bronislava Semyenovna.

Boris Yevgenevich Shatskikh: *chief of the Planning Section of the Electric Power System, usually identified as* Boris Yevgenevich, *sometimes as* Shatskikh.

Victor Shapochkin: *a Control Room engineer or junior dispatcher in the Electric Power System, always referred to as* Vitya Shapochkin *or simply* Vitya.

Sanka Goryaev: *a worker referred to by this name or more simply as just* Sanka.

1

The clock over the entry to the city's main postoffice, the enormous clock in the tower of the railway station, street clocks mounted on lampposts, alarm clocks, and wall clocks in apartments—all read ten minutes to eight in the evening.

A sparse, dry snowfall lackadaisically and lazily drifted down on the city. And the city was aglow. The city was ablaze. Garlands of light bulbs, arches, varicolored cascades along the walls. Without a sound the signs exploded: "Happy New Year!" And as the signs flared the snow-covered roofs too blazed out in crimson flurries.

The indifferent little snowfall scattered over the flowing, pulsating, dancing city. Dry little snowflakes fell upon the broad paws of the firs. Standing out in the squares they seemed to be showered with glowing coals.

The snow fell on the passers-by. No one paid any attention, all were blinded, intoxicated, excited, possessed. All hurried to complete last-minute errands, to make posthaste last-minute purchases:

In the stores there was a crush:

"Four vodka . . . Red wine . . . Champagne . . ."

"We're really going to show in the New Year."

"It isn't just showing one in— It's also seeing one off. We're exchanging the old year for the new."

"Vodka, cognac, champagne . . ."

Snowflakes melted on the fur collars of overcoats, on hats, on foreheads.

The parks and the city stadium were filled up with school children. The New Year arrived at a late hour and children were supposed to be asleep by that time. But, after all, it was not a celebration to be missed, and they could get their share ahead of time. Standing there, too, as on the squares, were big New Year trees garbed in red, green, blue, and purple lights. Skates cut into the colored ice. Even the honorable Grandfather Frost (one of the first Grandfather Frosts to appear in this noisy, blinding city) was also on skates. In the rays of the searchlights, which gleamed silvery from snow dust, there whirled a carousel-like ring of skaters. The shadows danced. The music pealed.

In the Opera Theater there was going to be a costume ball for young people ...

In the University Club the students were getting ready to celebrate ...

In the club at the Red Toolmaker Factory a costume ball was about to begin ...

The best restaurant in the city, "The Sunrise," closed off one of its rooms. In this room they were not only going to show in the New Year but also honor a visiting guest. He flew to our country from across the ocean two weeks ago. The New Year found him here ...

The clocks showed ten minutes to eight ... In the lights there was a tangle of snowflakes.

2

At that moment guests were already gathering at the apartment of the manager of the Electric Power System, Ivan Kapitonovich Sokovin.

On New Year's Eve people sit down to the table only at midnight, but the master of the house had his own ideas: it's not good if only the dining table brings people together. The evening is free. It's possible to get together earlier, to chat, gossip, and dance. No need for things to be dull even before the drinking. The guests were told: come just as soon as you are free. Ten to eight and in the entrance hall there jingled the first rings at the door. The master of the house himself rushed to open it.

"Ignat! Oho! Brother, you're looking like an important character. Take off your boyar's coat this minute ... And Lenka! Look how she's blooming. Eh, no, darling, you're playing pranks. Don't turn away—put your cheek up here ... Oo, she's strict, strict, I tremble and retreat ..."

Ivan Kapitonovich was heavy of shoulder, large-chested, short-armed, mobile like a rubber ball. He wore triumphantly a thick pepper and salt head of hair, and his big-browed face was handsome with weighty male good looks.

Manager of the electric power system ... According to his social position he should have been among those present at the reception for the foreign guest, but he had declined the invitation. He had his own reasons.

In the first place, for the entire year he had been on the outs with his son, didn't see him, didn't talk with him. Three days before a reconciliation had taken place. It was only appropriate to celebrate the newly reestablished peace in the family on New Year's Eve.

And in the second place, his son Vadim had taken his young wife that morning to the maternity home.

During the day Vadim had bought flowers and waited at the entrance to the maternity home. He had pestered them with, "When? How is she feeling?" till they promised him to telephone just as soon as she had given birth.

Now the bouquet of hothouse roses stood on the blinding tablecloth in the center of the table. The green of the leaves and the unnatural splendor of the flowers reminding one that outside the dark windowpanes was the cold, that snow was drifting down, that winter was in full swing. Vadim, hunched over and squeezing his hands with his knees, sat beside the telephone.

He was twenty-nine years old and the chief electrical engineer of a big chemical factory.

Father and son much resembled each other—but in the way a photo negative resembles its positive print. Vadim was the same kind of person as his father: short, stocky, with the same large head, but with light hair, and without his father's sprawling brows. The father's face was of a hard mint, the son's soft, full-cheeked. The father was impetuous, energetic, the son inclined toward thoughtfulness, at first glance perhaps it might seem he was wilted.

Also waiting for the promised telephone call with Vadim was his mother-in-law, Bronislava Semyenovna Stolyarskaya. She was a shy woman, whose simple and exhausted face didn't in any sense go with her holiday dress of rainbow-hued taffeta—looking almost like a gasoline film on a puddle. She sat stiffly, since her dress was rustling immodestly. But with quiet fascination she told Vadim:

"My Galochka was born a weakling—we fed her from an eyedropper. One time we wondered whether she would live or not. And in a year's time no one would believe it: she was plump and playful and her eyes were bright. And what a restless character..."

In her quiet voice there was a gentle bewilderment. That same Galochka who was born such a weakling, who was fed from an eyedropper, was now herself giving birth.

Time passes and human life flows by. In four hours would come the new year and in that new year there would live a new human being, a new destiny would come into existence—and who knew whether it would be successful or unsuccessful.

Vadim listened to Bronislava Semyenovna and squeezed his palms between his knees. When will they phone? In one minute? In one hour? In two hours? Even though it was not far off it was still in the future, and the secrets of the future are sacred until their proper time.

3

Chief Engineer Ignat Golubko and his daughter came into the room.

Golubko was large, fat, dressed up in a black suit and a starched shirt. His daughter was a girl in the tenth or last year of secondary school named Lena, or Elochka. From out of a fluffy, airy skirt a narrow-shouldered, thin body, burdened with a stack of hair. Out from under the hair—two wide-open eyes ready to be enthusiastic or to hate with all the implacability of not quite seventeen years.

He, nodding his head to all present and puffing, dropped into a chair. She saw the flowers on the table and her brows quivered.

"Are those for Galka?"

She went up to Vadim, looked into his face, and asked quietly:

"Are you worried?" She sat down.

Vadim knew Lena from birth. She often half jokingly, half-seriously, called him brother.

Ignat Golubko's wife had died three years earlier, and in his time away from work he didn't let his daughter out of his sight. He even went with her to parties, listened to the disputations of young people, kept quiet, drank cognac which he brought along with him, and watched with a squint: "Eh, let them amuse themselves . . ."

Ivan Kapitonovich nudged Ignat.

"You're falling behind me, brother: I'm just five minutes away from being a grandfather. But don't lose heart—you'll soon catch up. Yours isn't going to be unattached for long."

"Just teach them to dance!" muttered Golubko. "What's the good—she'll take up and leave."

Bronislava Semyenovna, sitting at the telephone, trembled. But the telephone was silent. It was the doorbell that was ringing. Ivan Kapitonovich with a vibrant gait rushed into the entrance hall.

A minute later he led in a new guest and began to introduce him:

"Ignat you already know . . . And that's my son, Vadim . . . I beg you to love and welcome—Boris Yevgenevich Shatskikh . . ."

The new guest squinted from the bright light and awkwardly

held some sort of package under his arm. He bowed with an embarrassed air and shook hands. He was slightly humpbacked but not so much that it looked ugly. His dark blue suit fitted him very well. From out of his sleeves peeked snow-white cuffs. He had a curly head of hair, a dark, well-formed face, and was in his own way handsome.

Ivan Kapitonovich loved to advance people from the masses. Not long ago Boris Yevgenevich Shatskikh was an ordinary economist, a rank-and-file employee in the planning section. Ivan Kapitonovich didn't get along with the chief of this section, who had resigned ahead of time on a pension. And no one thought that his place would be taken by Shatskikh. But Ivan Kapitonovich wanted it this way. Ivan Kapitonovich, having promoted him, then began to extol him at meetings. Ivan Kapitonovich as a sign of his highest regard for him had invited him today to his family celebration.

"Nadya" Ivan Kapitonovich called. "Come and get acquainted!"

In the doorway appeared Nadezhda Sergeyevna, the wife of Ivan Kapitonovich, tall, red-cheeked from standing over the stove, with uncovered plump arms.

"I'm glad to see you. Oi, and what is that?"

"Forgive me, I think it won't be out of place at the table."

"Liquor? But we have so much . . ."

"Superspecial cognac—French . . ." Shatskikh was engulfed with a blush from embarrassment.

Ignat Golubko came to the rescue.

"Take it—don't refuse it. French cognac is a rare bird in our parts."

"Well, folks, let's celebrate," Ivan Kapitonovich rubbed his hands. "We're all friends here. The second grandfather-to-be is still on duty at the plant, but he'll no doubt get here before the New Year . . . New Year! And what sort of a holiday is it really, let me ask? Humanity pays tribute to the great god—Time! Time! What's more important than that?"

"Isn't that the truth," Shatskikh caught up. "Every holiday is in some degree or another a landmark of time, but it's only the ushering in of the New Year that is dedicated wholly, without any other motives, to time."

"Most of all I need time head of me. I'm now fifty-five."

"Let's be exact: fifty-six is just around the corner. Don't make yourself out to be younger than you are. We are the same age," Ignat Golubko prompted from his chair.

"True enough. The fifty-sixth—and I need the fifty-seventh, the fifty-eighth, the sixtieth . . . If I have them then everything else will work out. If there is just life ahead then we can organize it. If there is only Time ahead. We'll celebrate to the limit the birthday of the great god."

"For you and me it's a sad holiday," interjected Golubko again.

"Why is that?"

"Why because your great god and mine marches, the son-of-a-bitch, not to youth but to the grave. Little to be glad about."

"And I, my friend, don't want to return to youth. I consider that I have lived my life quite successfully. It would be dangerous to repeat it. I found myself and I might not have. I might, instead of being an electrical engineer, have become, let's say, a soft drink or beer vendor—skimping on my portions, extorting a kopeck, acquiring household property. If the great god Time serves me there is at the same time another god whom I truly serve. That god is energetics! Without it we are all moles, digging in the dark. Energetics—that's the chandelier up there on the ceiling! It's the loom which weaves the cloth for trousers! It's many-faced and omnipresent, that god. And I am his servant and master."

Ivan Kapitonovich stood in the center of the room, spreading his feet out broadly on the parquet floor, red-faced, thick—peasant-boned. Vadim, sitting at the telephone, looked up at his father sullenly.

"Servant and master of the chandelier?" he pronounced.

Ivan Kapitonovich turned sharply.

"Of chandeliers, of table lamps, street lights, high-voltage transmission lines, turbines, generators, boilers, streetcars, electric trains, lathes in the factories—is that so little? Don't ask me to list everything—otherwise we won't have time to celebrate New Year."

"It's too little."

"Ah, yes, I didn't remember—love for human beings! Hail big words! But words remain words. My love for machines is weighty, material."

"Machines can bear the weight of that heavy love—they're iron. But human beings falter."

Ivan Kapitonovich directed a lengthy stare at his son. Vadim sat, morosely, pressing his hands with his round knees, his stubborn, bulging forehead jutting out.

For a minute there was an awkward silence in the room. All understood that right then unwittingly the ancient, lingering quarrel between father and son which had lasted, to be sure, more than just one year had broken out again. The dispute was not quite clear for the rest; it was a hidden family war, unpleasant to witness.

And on the table covered with the gleaming tablecloth the fully opened roses bathed in the electric light. In the corner gleamed the holiday fir tree, hung with tinsel, drowning with its juicy, crude pine smell the delicate fragrance of the flowers. And from the kitchen came the clank of pots and pans . . . Ahead lay the holiday celebration.

And at that moment the telephone rang and Bronislava Semyenovna with a changing expression grabbed for the telephone.

"I'm listening . . ."

4

But it was not the call from the maternity home. It was Bronislava Semyenovna's husband, Vasily Vasilevich Stolyarsky, phoning from work. He was also worried about his daughter—wanted to know whether or not she had given birth.

Ivan Kapitonovich took the phone.

"How is it there? Everything all right . . . ? As soon as you finish up come right here. Dress uniform. Without you we can't begin. And don't worry about Galka. We have everything under control."

"Ivan Kapitonovich!" The wide-open eyes of Elochka had a look of censure. "Why didn't you provide a replacement for Vasily Vasilevich? He has valid reason—his daughter is giving birth."

"He's the chief of the control room, darling. He has to see to it that the holiday is not spoiled for everyone."

"If he's the chief then he must be certain his subordinates won't fail him. Otherwise he's the slave of his duties and not chief."

"Ha, ha, slave of his duties!" Ivan Kapitonovich, obviously pleased that the quarrel with his son had not continued, was again in a joyous mood. "Ignat, she lives on electric power and doesn't even know the first letters of the alphabet. Time to conduct some explanatory work."

"Teach them to dance," Golubko rumbled, looked at the window and raised his watch. "Ten minutes to nine," he announced.

Ivan Kapitonovich, Vadim, and Shatskikh involuntarily raised their eyes to the window and from there to the wall where the clock hung and then together turned their heads to the window. There, beyond the partly opened curtains, the city bathed in holiday light and noise. Their city, an active miracle, which spread out across the land for many kilometers. A city competing at nights with the starry heaven.

Already for many days the city had been in a fever.

The end of the year—factories and plants worked to complete the annual plan. The end of the year—fulfillment or nonfulfillment of the plan, reprimands or bonuses. The end of the year—race, race, race without let-up. The city was in a foam, the city was in a sweat, gasping, and in a chorus it wailed: "Help! Save us! We need kilowatts! Thousands of kilowatts! Hundreds of thousands!" The power

stations were squeezing out the last drops. The end of the year—
the finish line was close.

This is the way it had been for many days. And now Ignat
Golubko looked at his watch and announced:

"Ten minutes after nine."

Consider that time was up—for some with glory and for some
ingloriously. The lathes were coming to a halt. The lights were going out in factory shops and workers were departing for holiday
spreads. Time was up—and the city breathed out a first sigh of relief.
One more hour and the fever of so many days would be past. The
city would quiet down and rest. One more hour—but for the time
being the appetite of the city was still voracious.

Ten minutes after nine. In one hour plus a little bit at the
control room the intensified watch would come to an end. The chief
of the control room, Vasily Vasilevich Stolyarsky would make his
appearance in this room.

"To the departing year, friends!"

But until the clinking of the glasses there still remained nearly
four hours.

5

Ivan Kapitonovich started the phonograph. In the holiday atmosphere the sad sounds of the old waltz were heard:

> "Quietly all about,
> The mounds are covered with dark.
> From behind the clouds shone the moon.
> The graves guard the quiet."

In sad minutes of life Ivan Kapitonovich never remembered
music. Music was for good times, for enjoyment. But Ivan Kapitonovich's tastes went only so far as "There's a Bluff on the Volga" and
"The Burial Mounds of Manchuria." Every time he felt a holiday
upsurge of mood he started playing that waltz, long since forgotten
by everyone, and became sentimental.

"Now that's not your fashionable jingles: 'Marina, Marina, My
Signorina.' Such music is good to listen to."

He went up to Elochka and took her caressingly and firmly by
the arm.

"Do a favor to an old man."

And Elochka obeyed.

She, thin, light, with her narrow face thrown back, with her hair
flowing down her back and he, broad, thick, restraining the force
seeking to come to the surface but as if infected with her light-

ness, the two of them glided through the room, bypassing chairs and the corners of the table.

The phonograph wept about fallen heroes, about the graves resting among the mounds, of the shades of the past, of alien and distant grief. And in the well-lit room it was cozy and the decorated New Year's fir tree gleamed ... The sadness of long ago and the impending holiday—involuntarily one experienced the fullness of the moment.

And at that moment the phonograph sank into a low bass. Darkness flooded into the room which had been filled with bright light. For a second there were visible among the lamps of the chandelier and the dull peaks of the wall lamps the crimson, still breathing filaments of the light bulbs. For a second ... And then the light again gathered strength and flooded onto the frozen faces of the guests, the tablecloth with the bouquet of flowers, the gleaming fir tree, and then again dimmed, not to darkness but to the half darkness of sunset. The faces of the guests became bronze. The phonograph wailed in a smothered voice. The chandelier beneath the ceiling strained in its struggle against the darkness.

Ivan Kapitonovich let Elochka out of his arms and, stumbling over the chair, rushed to the telephone, and the telephone, as if it felt his presence, rang out appealingly. Ivan Kapitonovich grabbed it.

"What happened?"

For a minute which seemed to everyone present very long indeed he listened with stony face. During this minute the light became firm, and the wall lamps and the chandelier beneath the ceiling lit up the room, so it seemed, more strongly than before. Ignat Golubko moved forward in his chair, Shatskikh, bewitched, blinked his long eyelashes in the direction of Ivan Kapitonovich. Elochka smoothed out her skirt in the center of the room. Vadim who had jumped up from his chair stood at attention next to his father. The phonograph again acquired articulation and sang penetratingly:

> "Mothers weep
> Wives weep ..."

Ivan Kapitonovich listened. His face was turned to the chandelier. Slowly, hardly noticeably even for an experienced eye, the light bulb was losing current.

"So," exclaimed Ivan Kapitonovich as he put down the phone and turned on his heels to Ignat Golubko. "A nice New Year's present. The eastern power lines are out. The car is coming right now."

> "All as if in one voice weep.
> Evil fate and destiny cursing ..."

Crowding and knocking against each other Ivan Kapitonovich and Golubko drew on their overcoats. The latch clicked behind them.

Vadim dashed to the telephone and hurriedly dialed a number:

"Who is it? This is Sokovin speaking. Pass on the word that there has been an accident on the power line. It's possible there will be a cutback ... Cut off? Who says a cut off? Yes, not for certain ... things may be all right. It's not known ... Oh, the devil!" He threw down the phone and exclaimed: "The proverb is really right: Till the lightning strikes the muzhik won't cross himself."

He stood for a second over the phone. Bronislava Semyenovna with diffidence and hope sought out his eyes. Without saying a word, Vadim, shoving forth his jaw like his father, marched out to the entrance hall to the coat hanger.

Nadezhda Sergeyevna, corpulent, with majestic carriage, in an apron, unhurriedly came into the room, pushed the chairs up against the table, straightened out the tablecloth, moved over the flowers, sat down, put her hands on her knees and said without directing her remarks to anyone:

"Well, I guess we'll have to wait."

Bronislava Semyenovna began suddenly to seek jerkily her handkerchief:

"They may cut off the maternity home ... No light ... My Galochka ..."

"Oh stop it—they won't cut it off! And if they do it'll be only for a minute. And in general it's no tragedy. I was born in candlelight myself."

6

They had waited for the car several minutes.

Now Golubko was sitting in the rear seat, spreading himself out with the phlegmatic calm typical of him. Ivan Kapitonovich was beside the driver with a scowl on his face and a defiant decisive air.

They passed by autobuses and trolleybuses stuffed with people and light. The holiday lights winked, overflowed, jumped. Cars like the people, infected with preholiday bustle, crowded each other.

For hundreds of thousands of city dwellers, walking and riding along the streets or sitting in warm apartments, light is a gift of nature. It is and it must be: hardly anyone ever thinks of the people who give it to the city.

Ivan Kapitonovich lived in a new district. The control room was at the other end of the city. And the city was alive with the holiday. The streets were full of people and there was a wait at every traffic light.

In tsarist times, not long before World War I, on the shore of the river which at that time had not been shackled in concrete embankment they had built a power station—five small boilers which set in motion two turbogenerators. Five smokestacks shed their soot on the roofs of the buildings nearby and current flowed to the center of the city, to the homes of the wealthier merchants and to the provincial governmental institutions. At that time this power station had seemed a miracle of technology. Later, it had been three times rebuilt—the boilers changed, more powerful generators installed, and the station each time had received a new youth and become more powerful—three times, five times, ten times. And now this station, with capacity increased tenfold over its initial capacity, was a pygmy in comparison with the new ones. It was no longer possible to increase it, and it was retained only because it helped heat the apartment houses in nearby blocks—well that its boilers worked now not on coal but on gas—it didn't belch forth soot to spoil the city air.

Right up against its old walls leaned a three-story building with sprawling windows. Here was housed the management and here was the control room.

The electric light pole, made of pine timber just like the birch or the mountain ash, is a familiar part of the landscape. There are songs about birch trees and the mountain ash but no one sings about electric light poles—it would be considered funny, awkward. A naked trunk, stiff dryness, on rusty hooks the glass insulators—but nevertheless it would be worth while to sing of them, not of their beauty, for there is none, but of their abundance, their omnipresence. The plebes of the power industry, younger brother of the high voltage towers, they march along the snowdrifts in the open places in the forest, take small towns by storm, stand as unchanging guards of forgotten post offices and collective farm offices. One can say without exaggeration that wherever a human being appears he drags behind him an electric light pole. He stretches a wire—and it brings life.

The center of the earth, which is wound around with electric wires, its brain, is the control room, where the chief of the control room Chief Dispatcher Vasily Vasilevich Stolyarsky, is on duty. It was to the control room that Ivan Kapitonovich and Golubko were hurrying.

In the city so far the lights were burning . . . Hurry! Ivan Kapitonovich and Golubko were silent. The chauffeur raced the car . . .

7

Vadim leaped out of the entryway and ran right into a woman. A bag and a box of candy tumbled to the sidewalk.

"Excuse me!"

The man next to the woman, bending down over the dropped purchases, gave a piece of his mind:

"Don't try to look with the rear of your head."

From the side of the street a car pulled away—no doubt the one carrying Vadim's father and Golubko.

The sparse snowfall was powdery. The city was noisy. The air was permeated with freedom and holiday gaiety. The day was over and tonight the night was given over to merrymaking.

Girls, evidently schoolgirls walked hand in hand along the sidewalk, pushing passers-by to the side, singing, fooling:

"In the forest was a fir tree . . ."

They were sprinkled over with snow—and their eyes shone and their teeth glistened.

On the other side at the show window of the gastronome—the store selling fancy groceries, meats, drinks and delicacies—was a crowd of people gaping. In the window was an enormous champagne bottle, and from out of its mouth leaped a stream into a goblet the size of a small pail. On the roof, never weary, signs blazed out "Happy New Year!" "Happy New Year!" in green, red, blue versions.

A little bit of an old man with a frosty little beard, in big felt boots, was selling holiday fir trees which leaned against the wall. A few hours ago they were being eagerly grabbed. Now no one was buying. It was late. The little old man, the only workaday figure thereabouts, stamped up and down in the cold and, like a post rider, clapped sleeve against sleeve.

The man and the woman whose purchases Vadim had knocked out of their hands stood by an old Moskvich automobile.

"Don't you need a fir tree, good citizen? They're cheap—the price is down."

"The snowstorm sang her a song:
Sleep, my little fir tree, sleep . . ."

"Happy New Year!, Happy New Year!, Happy New Year!"— green, red, blue!

Everything was quiet. The city splashed with light. Yet Vadim was dragging himself off to the chemical combine. There was no need. Everything was calm.

Vadim stared at the window with the bottle of champagne. Behind the broad plate glass was warmth, light. The glazed tiles gleamed. The cold and the snow were shut out. But one second and then the next and Vadim noticed: The current fell ever so slightly and the window darkened ever so little. And in the street lamps which hung over the pavement there was a feeling of strain and fatigue. And the sign over the roof didn't simply splash out with strength its green, red, blue words. In it there could be felt a chilly tremble. And it was as if the city itself were slowly slowly shriveling, becoming more confined.

And Vadim jumped to the Moskvich and grabbed for the door handle.

"Comrades! . . . Please give me a lift!"

"This isn't a taxi."

"It's terribly important. I wouldn't ask . . ."

The man turned:

"Where is it you want to go?"

"To the chemical factory."

"Oh, no, not that! It's not on our way."

"There could be an accident there. Do you understand? An accident . . . Maybe there could even be loss of life . . ."

The man and the woman glanced at each other and then looked mistrustfully at Vadim: Fur cap askew, pulled down on his forehead. Directly over his right eye on the dark fur of the cap a gray wisp peeked through. And this gray wisp over the round, alarmed face had an untimely touching effect. The eye beneath it looked out eagerly, appealing—one could not doubt him.

The owners of the Moskvich hesitated momentarily in indecision. The woman had a well-worn rabbit fur cap, faded lips, and soft round eyes. He was a good-natured robust type in a new sacklike stiff coat.

"Even as it is we're late," said the woman diffidently. The man sullenly looked into his sleeve at his watch.

"Oh well—get in . . ."

Pulling up the stiff flaps of his coat he awkwardly crawled behind the wheel.

"How should I go? Through Prokhorovka or through the Square of the Commune?"

"However you want—but only faster."

The Moskvich slowly got under way.

They floated past the old man stamping up and down in his felt boots. The schoolgirls were crossing the street and blocked their way.

"Faster, faster."

They turned off the main street, and the Moskvich rolled along little side streets and alleys, conscientiously jolting the passengers on the bumps. Here the holiday atmosphere didn't strike the eyes. Here it was a run-of-the-mill night with swinging street lamps over the snow-covered pavement.

"Faster, faster."

And the owners of the Moskvich anxiously talked with each other:

"It sounds as if something is knocking in the differential. Do you hear it?"

"No, I don't hear it."

"There it goes again."

"It must be the wheel—there's ice on the fender."

"Faster, faster."

For five years Vadim had been working at the chemical plant and not once had the current been cut off. Night and day the current flowed without interruption, day and night, months, years, probably decades ... The plant did not have its own turbine. Even a turbine! And how badly it was needed.

A year ago the question had been raised of installing an independent power station or at least a turbine of four or six thousand kilowatts capacity at the chemical combine. Vadim's father had come out in determined opposition to the proposal: it would not be advantageous; it would not be profitable; in a year and a half from two sides the power lines from neighboring systems would reach the city. Their power system would become part of a gigantic electric power grid—and then accidents would no longer be frightening. It would be foolish to throw money away on building dwarfs. The majority kept quiet both because it wasn't wise to spoil relations with the omnipotent master of electric power and also because "it's none of my business"—the question did not affect many. Vadim came out in opposition to his father in the presence of all, and the directors of factories looked at each other gaily. His father sat with a face like a dark oak panel. After the session he went up to Vadim —his jaw jutting out and wrath in his eyes beneath his brows. There was a short conversation, and from that time the break between them had begun.

There was no reserve power! The lines from neighboring systems hadn't yet reached them. Cut off the power and the factory would start to burst out in smoke like a bonfire on which water was sprayed. Faster, faster! ...

"Why is it that it jerks?"

"The carburetor is playing tricks. I can't seem to set it right."

The car jumped out onto the broad, straight highway, lit on both sides by fluorescent street lamps. Two more kilometers to the combine.

Galya was giving birth ... The maternity home would be cut off before the combine ... He'd bought flowers ... The street lamps were burning—at the combine things were normal. Why was he rushing, breaking his neck? Turn back perhaps ...

"The valve isn't knocking any more."

"It isn't knocking."

"And the oil pressure is normal."

"Normal. The old boy is still holding up."

The little old Moskvich dashed down the straight highway exerting all its unmighty power. And the empty highway, lit by the faded light blue light of the fluorescent lamps seemed somehow dead, unreal—a fantastic road into the unknown.

The light burned and Vadim was torn in two parts. The factory and Galka! Forward, faster—he would make it. Back to the maternity home! There's nothing for him to do ahead at the factory.

The street lamps glow. The highway is empty. In the distance the lights of the factory gleamed out.

8

Today was a special day for Vasily Vasilevich Stolyarsky. Nothing had happened, neither good nor bad, nothing at all. As always early in the morning he had arrived at the control room, studied the supplementary schedule sent out before every holiday. He had called the station and confirmed: The Chernushinsky Power Station at 20:30 might stop two turbines for repairs. He went home and had lunch and then toward evening when the greedy appetite of the city for power had begun to rise again, second by second, he was already sitting in the control room. His work . . .

December 31 was a special day for Vasily Vasilevich because he had just before sent off his daughter to a maternity home and for the first time realized: he was about to become a grandfather.

He was of medium height, neither fat nor lean, rather balding back from his forehead, befitting his age. Some sort of a neutral expression had firmly joined itself to his normally formed colorless countenance—expressing perhaps polite reserve, perhaps his own natural timidity covered over by politeness which expressed nothing. He was always in a freshly laundered shirt, always in a necktie, and his workday suit was always pressed. He addressed everyone with the unfamiliar form of the personal pronoun, and he himself was always addressed respectfully. People after making the acquaintance of Vasily Vasilevich immediately forgot him. And on meeting him for a second time they asked: "Haven't we met before?"

He had worked in the electric power system for thirty years, a little less than Ivan Kapitonovich Sokovin. It wasn't quite that he was dissatisfied with his life, considered himself a failure—after all, the chief of the control room was a man of importance. No, he simply realized that so far he had not yet done what he had to do. He, for example, could, if he wished, point out things to Chief Engineer Golubko: for example the fact that out in the network districts the power capacities cut off by the automatic apparatuses for reducing load were too low. This was dangerous. It could lead to unpleasant consequences. He could have made some suggestions in the planning of the new district substation ... There was much he could have done, but Ivan Kapitonovich, the all-powerful manager, didn't always pay any attention even to Golubko's opinion, and he never asked advice of Vasily Vasilevich. To compel others to listen to him, to force his advice on others, was not at all in Vasily Vasilevich's character. For the time being he simply worked ... But chance—luck—was a great thing. The thought came to mind that it could raise up a quite undistinguished person in such a way that people would remember his name forever. Without luck geniuses mend shoes or work as meek little accountants.

He didn't dream of being a Napoleon. He simply waited patiently for something, for some set of favorable circumstances, which would help him develop his modest capabilities. Modest! Vasily Vasilevich knew their worth. Something bigger than he did every day, something surpassing his routine.

And on one occasion, or so it seemed, he encountered an opportunity. He was sent on an official trip to the Berestyanka River where at that time the construction of a big hydroelectric power station had only begun. He succeeded in discovering a miscalculation in the planning: a railway branch which was being hurriedly built to newly discovered ore deposits was in the zone of flooding. Vasily Vasilevich made a conscientious calculation, wrote a report, and took it to Ivan Kapitonovich. The latter with his influence had to convince still more influential people that the state stood to suffer losses in the millions. To save millions of rubles—here was the long-awaited opportunity, here was the destined hour of Vasily Vasilevich.

Ivan Kapitonovich read the report and was wrathful:

"The fools are sticking their necks out! Our construction project is bigger and it's not for us but for them to dance according to our rules." And he promised: "I'll press the thing and they'll dance."

And he did press it. The branch railway was moved—even though with some tardiness. Someone was fired, someone caught it. At high-level meetings where Vasily Vasilevich had no entry Ivan Kapitonovich was praised as a vigilant person who held close to his heart not only narrow and local interests but who had in good time saved millions for the state.

Vasily Vasilevich did not count on capitalizing on this opportunity, of rising on the strength of it, but the fact that they passed him by with indifference, didn't ask, didn't seek his advice, didn't remember his existence, was hurtful.

An hour of destiny had come, but not for Vasily Vasilevich. And patiently he began to wait for another hour of opportunity. He had been waiting till this very day.

And today in the morning he awakened and remembered his daughter, remembered that by New Year he would be called grandfather. Already grandfather—in other words life, as a matter of fact, was already lived. And he asked himself: all the preparation, all the getting closer to something more serious. Why? When? Fifty years already gone . . .

And on that day Vasily Vasilevich went his usual way to work, looked at people, at young people who had ahead of them all their life, and also at quite old people and at those of middle years—and at others still not old but feeling the approach of old age.

Were there many of them who in their lifetime had had an hour of destiny? The majority were the run-of-the-mill of boundless humanity. They would die and over their grave would be written numbers which say nothing: he was born on such and such a date and he died on such and such. Sixty, eighty, ninety years—and what filled them?

In essence hopes were dead and dreams had disappeared. And what was more awful than that? But Vasily Vasilevich did not feel disappointment. He was no exception. He was like everyone else. Not so bad to grab a star from out of the heavens, but nothing to be done about that . . . It was sad, of course.

There are days in life which will always be remembered not for special events, not for shocks, but for some kind of spiritual transformations. Such a transformation Vasily Vasilevich experienced at that moment, before the New Year. One more touch of maturity, one more discovery of oneself. How could it be called? A step toward old age? Maybe . . .

9

The control room was an expansive hall with windows from floor to ceiling. Within its walls two teams could have freely played at volleyball.

For Vasily Vasilevich, who had first crossed the threshold of the control room when the painters were still carrying away the trestles and stepladders after the building had just been built, everything here was as usual. With the years the system had grown. With the years the control room itself had changed. The control panels had been reequipped. New instruments had appeared. But all these innovations, like chance changes in the landscape for a rural dweller, had immediately become ordinary.

He pushed open the door which bore the strict and curt sign, "Entrance Forbidden," and saw the long table. In front of the table were instruments—voltmeters etc. He customarily took a look at the needles: they, as always, were frozen in positions to the right —a sign that everything was normal at electric power stations working hundreds of kilometers from this building at the city embankment, that everything was normal at substations and also on the power lines that march on gigantic towers through forests, fields, marshes, and rivers. Over the voltmeters there jutted out glassed-in cases of frequency meters. Beneath glass on a broad strip of paper pens drew out a wavering line. The line was straight, quiet—and that meant that at the different ends of the electric power district the heavy rotors of generators were turning simultaneously, like soldiers marching in time, and it meant that the turbines were making the assigned number of turns per minute.

At the table was an armchair. Each armchair had a switchboard with a set of switches, telephones and, on mobile legs, intercoms.

Back toward the wall was another table, if indeed one could call it a table. At it were neither armchairs nor ordinary chairs and no one ever sat behind it. There was no place on the table to put paper. On each square centimeter of it were buttons, switches, handles, which could blaze out like a light. This was the main control panel of the control circuit.

The control circuit ... An uninitiated person seeing it felt in his heart a triumphant chill: there it was, a secret thing which had come from science fiction into real life. The control circuit is a magic window to all the boundless power district, on a territory which was only a little smaller than France.

It occupied the entire enormous wall, a light blue, gay panel many meters long. From out of it stared round, square, triangular little eyes, burning, in the majority, with red, and in some places with green lights. They were like stars in the heavens, gathered into constellations. Every constellation had its own name—Chernushinsky Power Station, Vysokovsky Power Station, Berestyansky Hydroelectric Station, Western Substation, Eastern Substation ... Every constellation was an electrical object.

It was 300 kilometers to the Vysokovsky Station. On a train one had to count on almost a whole day's travel. But if at that station something went out of order—if the pressure fell in the boilers or a generator cut off, at that very second Vasily Vasilevich, sitting in front of the light blue panel of the control circuit would know about that situation often more quickly than those at the station. The telephone would be raised:

"What's wrong out there?"

The round, square, and triangular little eyes would begin to wink and instead of red, which means, "All O.K." there would shine out green, meaning "Take measures." It was not red but green lights which signaled alarm in this building.

Customarily at the panel in the hall only the control operator sat on duty. There was also the telephone operator. The control operator on duty on New Year's Eve was a certain Vitya Shapochkin, a young engineer who several years before had finished his studies. He was a lad like other lads. He was an enthusiastic soccer fan, a lover of operetta, gay at parties. One could meet such as him at every step on the street. But no more did he seat himself at his working chair than he became an omnipotent dictator whose word was law. The chiefs of electric power stations and substations, gray-haired electrical engineers, were obliged to obey him unmurmuringly, obey without thinking. The secretary of the Regional Communist Party Organization or the chairman of the Regional Governmental Organization, the most influential people in the region, would not take on themselves the risk of stopping a rolling mill at a steel mill on their own authority. They would have to get in communication with Moscow for permission from the center. But Vitya Shapochkin could order: Stop! And it stops. Try not to obey him—with him one doesn't fool. He could cut off from the line the entire mill together with its rolling mill. During the entire time he was on duty he was God and tsar, the enthroned sovereign in the control room chair. To be sure, Vitya Shapochkin had to use his sovereignty very carefully and not capriciously. He didn't have the right to be wrong since, for his mistakes, his control-room majesty, Vitya Shapochkin, would be severely punished.

Such sovereigns as Vitya, under Vasily Vasilevich, were five in number. Three of them in three daily duty shifts and two in reserve, for replacement on holidays and during vacations or in case of illness.

Today was an important day because Vasily Vasilevich himself sat on duty.

Three people in the spacious, brightly lit hall: Vasily Vasilevich, Vitya, the telephone girl in the corner at the switchboard.

Vitya Shapochkin had a stiff crew cut, and his face was in freckles which disappeared neither in winter nor summer. His strong neck was confined in the starched collar of his shirt, and his suit was the color of café au lait. The young man had gotten himself up today as if he were a bridegroom. Obviously, he would rush straight from work to celebrate New Year. Vitya leafed over the control room log, yawned, often looked at his watch. He was not very absorbed in his work today...

The telephone girl assiduously drew on long sheets graphs of the consumption of power. The graph lines dipped. The load was beginning to drop—the preholiday time was telling.

Vasily Vasilevich putting out on the table his hands with fingers intertwined together thought his own thoughts—of the New Year which promised him nothing new.

The needles of the voltmeters held steadfast within the correct range. The frequency meters quietly wrote their unending chronicle, every minute, every second. The control circuit which took up every little bit of the wall gleamed with ruby lights. Red light—all in order.

There was quiet in the hall, everyday working quietude. Vasily Vasilevich was used to it—it disposed one to thoughtfulness—and it calmed one.

10

In order for the needles of the instruments to stay within the necessary ranges, in order for the lights on the circuit to gleam with their comforting red glow, and in order for there to be working quietude at the control room, at a distance of hundreds of kilometers at power stations powerful mills ground pieces of coal into the finest coal dust. Mighty blowers blew it through roaring nozzles into the white hot burners of boilers—every boiler as large as a ten-story blast furnace. The steam from the boilers beat against the blades of the turbines, turned the enormous shafts and together with them the heavy rotors of the generators... All the rotors at all the stations turned in one tempo, all of them turned "in step," and there was trouble if anyone got off the beat.

There were five stations serving the city: four steam and one hydroelectric. Five stations, scattered in various places.

Two were on the east: Sobolyansky named for the village of Sobolyany which grew up together with the power station into a town with a highway, a railway branch, with a big club; the second called Rudnogorsky near the growing city of Rudnogorsk.

Two stations, two constellations on the light blue pattern of the control room. From them emerged red lines of 110,000 volts each. They rested up against a third constellation—Eastern Substation. From the substation along the board there stretched a yellow line— a 220,000 volt transmission line.

Side by side—two columns of the steel towers each carried three twisted cables the thickness of a young birch tree and more than

200 kilometers long across dales and fields, hills, and swamps. The densest forests respectfully gave way before them with broad rights of way as straight as a stretched string. Three massive twisted cables —a river of electric power flowed from the east to the city. And only because of that did the factories and plants work, only because of that did the throwing of a wall switch light up the lamp hanging from the ceiling. Only because of that did the streetcars and trolley-buses move and the electric train arrive at the station platform.

But the greedy city needed more than one electric river. There was a second just like it from the northwest—marked with a yellow line on the control panel circuit. This river was fed by three other stations—Chernushinsky, Vysokovsky, and the Berestyansky Hydro-electric Station. Two rivers, two power nuclei, not stopping day or night, winter or summer—the realm of Ivan Kapitonovich Sokovin.

Vasily Vasilevich remembered that the guests had begun to gather at Ivan Kapitonovich's apartment. He took the phone, dialed the number. His own wife, Bronislava Semyenovna, answered. No, Galochka hadn't given birth yet, they hadn't phoned from the maternity home . . . Then he heard the bass of Ivan Kapitonovich himself: "When you are free come here right away. Dress uniform . . ."

Vasily Vasilevich put down the phone and glanced at his watch: ten minutes after nine. One more hour here in all probability.

Vitya Shapochkin put aside his magazine and also reached for the telephone.

"Call Verochka to the phone please . . . Vera, hello! Are you getting ready? . . . How are things with me? I'm sitting here . . . No, not soon. The change of shift is at 11 o'clock . . . Nothing to be done about that: that's work. By 11:30 I'll be there. It's only a step away."

The telephone next to Vasily Vasilevich rang. The duty engineer at the Chernushinsky Station asked permission to stop two generators for repairs.

Within a few minutes on the board two round little eyes which till then had burned red blinked in green. The Chernushinsky Station had stopped two generators out of five.

Vitya Shapochkin, without hurrying, went up to the board, clicked a switch on the control panel and hung on each of the blinking little eyes a sign with the letter "T"—signifying "current repair." Then in the same unhurried manner he sat down at his place, rubbed his thick crew cut, and began to register this event in the log . . .

11

At the forty-first kilometer from the Eastern Substation, if one goes straight along the transmission line, at a distance of approximately fifty kilometers from the control room, there stood two transmission towers: one of them in the edge of a forest and the other in the middle of a field. These two towers were distinguished by absolutely nothing from thousands of their sisters. They rested just as reliably on concrete foundations and from them there hung awesome garlands of insulators. Like all the rest they carried three massive twisted wires, each of them the thickness of a good cable.

This night the wind swept snow upon the foundations, whistled through the steel frame, and swung the heavy wires. And even though through the field between these two towers there passed a roadway, an ordinary sledge road from one village to another, all around it was quiet and empty. Who would want to go out across country at night—and for that matter on New Year's Eve. Perhaps only the hares circled round about through the nearby drifts—or perhaps a hungry wolf was running past.

The ends of high voltage cables were held together by clamps. There was one such clamp swinging in the air between the two towers. It had been installed many years before and, it would seem, had weakened, but continued to hold.

And on this lonely New Year's Eve, as was determined later, the wind was not strong. It was not blowing up a snowstorm and not raging in a hurricane. An ordinary wind blew in gusts, raising snow dust from the drifts. But the clamp did not hold...

The thick cable fell with a crash, showering a handful of big sparks on the snow smoothed by the wind. The steel rod inside the twisted cable bent it up resiliently and the end lashed across the neighboring cables. There in the sleepy field deep in snow burst a peal of thunder, flames exploded into the thick darkness, and down on the snow there poured not a handful but a whole armful of big sparks.

Short circuit!

And at the substation standing forty kilometers from that place there stood on panels instruments which are not very large. The turbine shafts turned. The flame boiled in the boilers. Current flowed on the cables. The enormous system worked under tension. And these instruments slept quietly. For years, sometimes for decades, they were out of action—if everything about was working satisfactorily, if no accident had taken place.

But it had taken place—a short circuit! And at this second the automatic defense, the little instruments on the control panels of the substation awoke from their long sleep. They sent out the signal —cut off the line!

Cut off the line! Otherwise at the power stations the current would burn up the generator windings. Cut off the line! Otherwise the machines would be put out of operation. Cut off the line! So that the accident would not spread further like a conflagration from a carelessly discarded match. Cut off! An unconditional order.

And the switches ... No, they were not like those installed in the walls of apartments which under the pressure of a finger turn on or off a lamp. They were also not like the knife switches on a marble slab. It's by no means so simple to cut off a high-voltage line, to interrupt the flow of a powerful electrical river. A knife switch or a wall switch would simply burn up in a fraction of a second, turn into white-hot steam—and woe to anyone who held the handle of a knife switch or pressed the button of a wall switch in this circumstance.

The switches on high-voltage lines were bulky machines with cylinders half again larger around than a man's embrace. They towered higher than a small house. They were filled with oil or compressed air. There in the oil took place the severance of the powerful rushing current. There the bursting flame was quenched. Human hands did not touch it. The switch worked automatically.

An order: cut off! And the switches obeyed.

And at that moment new instruments came to life.

Maybe the short circuit was temporary. Maybe a kite with a twine tail flown by children got caught in the wires. Maybe a thin branch raised into the air by the wind fell across the wires and shorted them ... The kite tail with its twine tail would burn. The burned branch would fall. And in such cases there was no need to stop the work of the line, to interrupt for long hours the flow of the electric river, to wait until the repair crew arrived, discovered what the matter was. The line could be turned on again.

The apparatus for secondary trial of the line went into operation ...

But no—it was not a temporary short circuit—but a real one. And the automatic defense again sent its signal: cut off! And that time the order was final.

All of this happened so quickly that the first spark from the bursting flame had not succeeded in falling on the snow before the line had been cut off once, turned on again, and again cut off. The intelligent instruments had done their work—and then left it to human beings to get out of the mess by themselves.

12

It was exactly at this second that the lights had gone dim all over the city. The store windows had gone dark. The street lights had gone out. The holiday signs crying out with bright fire had choked up. Decked out holiday trees on the city squares, search-lights lighting up the skating rinks, chandeliers beneath the ceiling, table lamps—all of them had gone out, but only for a second.

And since the light had begun to shine again people did not pay any special attention to that.

"See! Someone's fooling around!" And again they went about their affairs.

13

At that second on the circuits in the control room there had begun a dance of lights. Almost the entire right side of the panel blinked and gleamed in warning green lights. The needles of the voltmeters dropped to the left. The pens of the frequency meters, instead of a straight line, began to draw out a line which was quavering and falling. In their chronicle was a signal showing that relaxed, quiet times were over, that troubled times had begun.

Two rivers of power fed the city and one had dried up. But the city was still gluttonous.

Vasily Vasilevich stepped on the pedal of the intercom beneath the table.

Up to that minute this spacious hall was separated from the stations, from the substations, by tens and hundreds of kilometers, by city blocks, forests, rivers, lakes—but now the distance disappeared. At every part of the entire system the voice of Vasily Vasilevich could be heard. He was the man sitting in the control room chair and his word was law for everyone. With one curt movement Vasily Vasilevich put himself in communication with his entire realm.

"R-1, R-2!" pronounced Vasily Vasilevich into the dark mouth of the intercom.

He named two city substations, those locations at the approaches to the city, to which the rivers of power flowed. "Regional-One" and "Regional-Two"—out from them in all directions stretched cables beneath the ground, lighting the city, nourishing its factories, plants, transport, radio stations, telephones, telegraph . . .

"R-1, R-2!"

And into the silence of the control room erupted two voices—one female, ringing and clear like that of a child, the other a modulating baritone.

"R-1 is listening!"

"R-2 is listening!"

"An accident on the eastern lines! . . . Cut off the first three series as per the accident plan. Don't touch the communal service feeders! Take off thirty thousand each!"

"Order being carried out!"—the female voice.

"Order being carried out to cut off thirty thousand!" the baritone replied in military form.

In a second or so the city would begin to consume sixty thousand kilowatts less. But even before Vasily Vasilevich stepped on the intercom pedal throughout the entire city hundreds of guard devices had gone into operation. Without any order they had cut off a number of insignificant objects.

And the lights had come back on. They were burning, or so it seemed, with their former brilliance there beneath the ceiling. But the experienced eye could note that the filaments of the light bulbs were oscillating in rhythm, as if they were breathing with effort, with strain. In the needles of the instruments there was not that friendly, quiet certainty that there had been a minute before. The frequency meters continued to draw a line falling to one side. Their chronicle continued to announce troubles.

"Eastern!"—called Vasily Vasilevich.

"Eastern Substation is listening . . ."

"Report—what's wrong there?"

14

The intelligent instruments completed their independent work, leaving it up to people to make heads and tails of the confused situation. And people took charge.

The engineer on duty at Eastern Substation with which Vasily Vasilevich had just talked immediately turned on a new piece of apparatus—"the line searcher" or, as it was known, the "LS"—a relative of the radar apparatus which sought out enemy planes in the air in wartime. "LS" sent out a wave—not in the air but in the cable. The wave hurtled through the cable—and came to a stop! . . . Instead of metal—there was air, a different medium. The wave struck it and reflected back like a ray of sunshine from off a mirror. On the "LS" screen at the substation danced a beam of light.

It hurtled out, struck emptiness, and returned backward—and all of this took only some imperceptible fraction of a second since an entire second for an electromagnetic wave is an eternity in the course of which it can more than seven times circle the world along the equator, travel to the moon.

The engineer at Eastern Substation, with the crudity of perception characteristic of all people, would not have caught the difference of time between the sending of the impulse by the apparatus and the dancing beam on the screen. But the apparatus told him: such and such an elapsed time. Time was translated into distance—

in all 40 kilometers and 600 meters to the break. The apparatus might make a mistake of from 50 to 100 meters, no more.

"The break in both lines is located in the 41st kilometer near the village of Mitkin Dvor, between the 162nd and 163rd tower . . ."

15

Time moved forward second by second and every second was one more jump toward catastrophe.

Three stations were now working for the city. Three stations were not capable of satisfying its appetite. The city was suffocating them and having suffocated them would die itself: the lights would go out, transport would come to a halt, water would cease to flow from the faucets, the pumps which drive heat into the radiators of apartments would stop working, and apartment houses would become numb with cold.

And in the city there were half a million inhabitants. Half a million in the city itself and half a million in the suburbs and at least two million in the smaller cities and towns nourished from these same electric power stations. Millions of people! And right now they were lightheartedly greeting each other: "To the New Year! To new happiness!"

Implacably—second by second. Time was the enemy. It was also a savior. In just an hour the greed of the big city would fall and then three stations could satisfy it without strain. The holiday illumination on the streets would burn brightly and the theater entrances would twinkle invitingly and the holiday trees on the squares would gleam with lights. Just to get past these dangerous seconds! They couldn't be stretched out. They had to be filled up with activity to the limit.

And Vasily Vasilevich was acting:

"Western Substation!"

There was an obedient reply from out of space:

"Western Substation is listening."

"Cut off the towns of Semyonovsk and Razvodino!"

"The order to cut off is being carried out!"

In the city of Semyonovsk were 100,000 people and in Razvodino 60,000. Without their knowing about it Vasily Vasilevich Stolyarsky with one word cast them into darkness. He cast them into darkness and immediately forgot about them. Action is necessary. Time is merciless.

And the needles of the instruments continued to fall. The big city, the chief devourer of power, was suffocating the power stations. The big city was stubbornly and blindly going to its own catastrophe.

Second by second. There was no time to ponder.

Vasily Vasilevich grabbed the supplementary plan.

It was a paper with several signatures. Right now in the entire region there was no more powerful human being than Vasily Vasilevich Stolyarsky, but the power of this paper was greater than his power. He could compel the hundred thousand people of Semyonovsk to sit in the darkness. He had the right to stop a factory. But to depart from what was written on that paper, to disregard its prohibitions—that, no, he could not. If he departed from its instructions he was a criminal. If he disregarded them he would be tried.

Vasily Vasilevich held it up in front of him. Among other signatures there was the signature there of Ivan Kapitonovich Sokovin ... Vasily Vasilevich looked at it closely ..

Second by second indifferent time marched by. The needles of the instruments crept to the left ...

And in the control room in which several minutes ago there was sedate calm there rang out shouts, cries for help, demands, questions. The feverish life of the broad system which was threatened by catastrophe had broken into the control room.

"Control room!" Chernushinsky Station is talking! Pressure is dropping. We can't keep going much longer! ..."

"Control room! The director of Red Toolmaker Factory refuses to shut down! ..."

"Chernushinsky is talking! Do you hear me? The pressure is dropping! ..."

Vasily Vasilevich kept staring at the plan.

Second by second ... Millions of people needed the decision of Vasily Vasilevich, right now, immediately, these seconds, but Vasily Vasilevich delayed.

Holiday plan ... Those lines which on ordinary days would have been shut down first were now on the forbidden list. He did not have the right to leave the chemical factory without power, but it was forbidden also to cut off the first feeder: on it was located the Sunrise Restaurant where they were preparing to receive the V.I.P. from abroad. All the provincial chiefs, and also the correspondents of newspapers, radio stations and television were gathering ...

Nothing was clear. Time was not waiting. The needles were falling to the left.

"Chernushinsky is speaking! The pumps are stopping! Cut off!" Vasily Vasilevich came to himself and answered in a creaking voice:

"Hold up as long as you can."

"The Red Toolmaker refuses to obey orders! ..."

"Cut it off!"

"Chernushinsky is speaking!" The voice in the intercom was

angry and determined. "In five minutes I'm dropping to zero!"

"To drop to zero" was a phrase equivalent to the word catastrophe.

Part of the power which each power station produced went for its own needs. The mills which pound the coal, the pumps, the fans, the compressors—everything worked with electric motors which required current. And if so much was being sucked out of the station that there wasn't enough current for itself it would go out like a candle covered with a can.

"I'm dropping to zero!" the voice raged. "I am cutting off myself, on my own responsibility!"

The engineer at Chernushinsky Power Station saved himself, and threw to the mercy of fate his crowned dictator. Unwilling treason—and he couldn't be condemned for it either.

New lights flashed out with the fatal green light. Chernushinsky Station had left the field.

In ten minutes Chernushinsky Station would regain its strength and return to operation. But by that time the Vysokovsky Station would have gone out of operation and, after that, having exhausted all its supply of water, the Berestyansky Hydroelectric Station. Thus, there commenced something which is most terrifying—the collapse of a power system, complete collapse! Long hours and maybe even days—darkness, a numb city with dead factories . . .

Green lights flashed on the circuit. Before Vasily Vasilevich lay the useless emergency plan.

And desperate thoughts jumped into the brain, thoughts without flesh: "What is there to be done? What do others do in such a situation? . . . The most likely thing would be to give an order to R-1 Substation to cut off everything! Cut off half the city . . . And what about the emergency plan?"

The sheet of paper was like a block on his path. He was powerless to step over it.

"Vasily Vasilevich! The frequency has dropped to forty-six and a half!" Vitya Shapochkin cried out with alarm.

His face was red and perspiring and his necktie was loosened. He likewise had not sat idly. He had called a car for the manager. He had phoned him at his apartment. He had spoken with the network branch and with the duty officer at the customer relations office.

A frequency of forty-six and a half instead of 50! At 49 the alarm already goes out. Catastrophe was close at hand. And a new voice on the intercom confirmed this:

"Vysokovsky is speaking! The pressure is dropping! Cut load immediately. I'm dropping to zero!"

"What do others do in such a case? And on the New Year . . . And my daughter is giving birth ... She'll have to give birth in the dark ... Maybe she already has given birth ..."

The door swung wide open from a shove, and with his coat wide open, his cap pushed back from his forehead, Ivan Kapitonovich burst in. Golubko squeezed through behind him.

Vasily Vasilevich stared at the manager in hope and desperation.

16

Vitya Shapochkin turned on the tape recorder. Later, these seconds would be examined with carping thoroughness. They would be reviewed again and again and every step would be weighed several times. Not one word, not one sound must escape—everything would be on the tape.

Vasily Vasilevich, getting up from his chair, began to report to Sokovin.

"A continuing short circuit ... The load is crushing ... Chernushinsky Station cut off on their own. I can't reduce the load. There's a prohibition on shutting down on every feeder. I can't decide to shut down whole substations ..."

Ivan Kapitonovich listened, his heavy jaw jutting forward, his shoulders elevated, his narrowing pupils piercing the drooping lids of Vasily Vasilevich.

Not one word of scolding or indignation. He was silent and this silence in the hot-tempered Ivan Kapitonovich compelled not only Vasily Vasilevich but also Vitya Shapochkin and the telephone girl in the corner to freeze.

Only Golubko alone, his broad back to the manager, was talking on the phone:

"Get in touch with the repair crew immediately. Tell them to light signal bonfires. I'm flying there!"

Ivan Kapitonovich with threatening calm pronounced distinctly a short phrase.

"I am taking the direction on myself!"

Such is the discipline of the control room—that holy of holies of electric power. Ivan Kapitonovich was the most responsible person present, but if he should undertake to run things then Vasily Vasilevich had the right to send him to blazes. Vasily Vasilevich was sitting at the control panel. He was responsible. And even in the presence of his own chief he remained a dictator. Only his word and no one else's would be taken into account.

"I am taking the direction on myself!"—this was a magic phrase. With it Ivan Kapitonovich cast down Vasily Stolyarsky from his position as dictator and became dictator himself.

Heavily stepping along the parquet floor he went up to the chair freed by Vasily Vasilevich but did not sit down. There was no time. Standing up he took the phone and pressed the lever on the switchboard.

"Customer relations office! Who is on duty? I'm taking off the entire load . . . Yes, all of it. Warn the consumers!"

He pulled to himself the mouthpiece of the intercom:

"R-1, do you hear me?"

"I hear you, Ivan Kapitonovich."

"The entire load!"

"Even the steel mill plant?"

"You heard: all feeders! Leave only the pumping stations."

Three pairs of eyes looked at him with respectful horror: Vasily Vasilevich standing beside him, Vitya Shapochkin, and the telephone operator who for a second raised her eyes from the switchboard.

The mouth of the intercom, pulled upwards on its mobile support, stretched toward the face of Ivan Kapitonovich, and his face was stony. On it were alive only the trembling nostrils of his short nose and his harsh voice . . . Ivan Kapitonovich was at that moment carrying out something which was frightening: he was cutting off the entire city, everything without discrimination.

"R-2!"

"R-2 is listening."

"Shut down all feeders."

"The chemical factory is on the fourth feeder."

"Shut that off too."

"Vysokovsky is speaking! Vysokovsky is speaking! I can't take the load! I'm dropping . . ."

"Vysokovsky!" Ivan Kapitonovich authoritatively interrupted the voice. "I'll begin to put on load again after fifteen minutes. Chernushinsky, do you hear me? Berestyansky! Fifteen minutes . . ."

Since the initial words, "I am taking the direction on myself," just one minute had passed. Golubko had just finished his conversation, put down the telephone, and turned about. In his massive body there had disappeared his customary corpulence. With a light step, adjusting his cap on his head, he moved toward the doors and on his way remarked to Ivan Kapitonovich:

"The helicopter is waiting. In 40 minutes I'll be at the scene of the accident."

Ivan Kapitonovich nodded.

At the door Golubko ran into a high, stately man in an overcoat, light for the season, with military bearing. This was the district accident inspector. In his profession it was considered reprehensible slowness to arrive on the scene later than the management and therefore he thrust forward his chest with special effort and significantly knitted his brows ahead of time.

"The causes are unknown?" he asked from the threshold.

"The causes of the accident are not here," Ivan Kapitonovich greeted him. "Golubko, take him with you, he can carry out his investigation there."

Golubko took the inspector by the elbow.

"Come along, brother, we won't hinder things here."

"The Secretary of the Provincial Party Committee is on the line!" the telephone operator called.

Ivan Kapitonovich took the telephone:

"Aleksei Mitrofanovich, I can't talk much. There has been a serious accident on the line. We're suffocating. I have to shut down the whole city for 15 or 20 minutes. We'll deal with the situation and I will phone you."

Outside the high windows the lights went out—not one gleam anywhere. Impenetrable murk poured upon the window glass. But the ceiling lights in the control room continued to burn as brightly as before. Right now the control room was fed by that power station nestled next door. The ancient veteran of the power industry continued to burn independently of all the rest.

17

Without warning, suddenly, like the punishment of God, like a whirlwind or an earthquake, medieval murk fell upon people of the twentieth century spoiled by technology.

On the streets flashing headlights of automobiles pierced the dark. Traffic signals stopped working. Traffic policemen who operated them lost their power.

The radio which was singing: "Oh you, my darling . . ." went silent in the middle of a word.

The screens of television sets, trembling with wavering blue light, rolled up like snails.

Trolleybuses came to a halt in the middle of the streets.

In stores crowded with customers a crush began: everyone rushed to the doors in the hopes of seeing there the customary well-lit city streets.

Suburban trains, till that moment lit up and swiftly tearing through the air, lay still on their tracks.

At the freight station the switch engine, powered by home-made steam and not by electricity, ran into a freight train. The engineer couldn't see the red light—the entire signal system of the railway had stopped working.

There was an accident on Spartakovsky Street also. A streetcar which was climbing a hill slipped back down and hit another street-car which was following behind it.

In the Sunrise Restaurant where the famous guest was awaited the director grabbed hold of his head and the leaders who had organized the reception rushed to the phones.

But at the central telephone station all telephones for the general public had been shut down, leaving in operation only the emergency lines. It was unknown how long the accident would continue —and they had decided to economize on battery current.

The flow of New Year greetings on the telegraph lines stopped.

The city was under siege. The city had been thrown back from the middle of the twentieth century into the darkness of the middle ages.

And in the entire murky city only the broad windows of the control room gleamed. Only there did the spirit of the modern age which marched upon the Earth remain alive.

18

Before Ivan Kapitonovich had issued the order to cut off the power of the city a conversation about him had been taking place in his own apartment near the decorated holiday tree.

Boris Yevgenevich Shatskikh was talking with Nadezhda Sergeyevna. Elochka, her hands clasped on her knees, was sitting quite still and listening seriously. Bronislava Semyenovna was hovering over the phone.

"I, for example, am always frightened by the surprises, the eccentricities of life." In the voice of Boris Yevgenevich was quiet, cozy inspiration and his meek eyes looked straight and openly at Nadezhda Sergeyevna. "Whenever something collapses doubts attack me like famished dogs: what if everything is not thus and so, what if I am mistaken, what will be the consequences? Right here we were assembled in order to drink and be merry and all of a sudden—an accident. Well-arranged life threatens to collapse. And there is Ivan Kapitonovich, for dead certain, while cursing in his soul, but without any particular hesitation, without superfluous doubts, attacking that danger. He is the responsible individual, the commander-in-chief, and he is the one who more than anyone else will be held responsible. But he is purposeful and doesn't even think about the consequences. Enviable boldness, and that, I would say, is nothing other than the mettle of a great personality. Only the bold move life forward."

"A great personality? Well, you've really overstepped a bit," Nadezhda Sergeyevna smiled.

"You smile, you think about me: he is a flatterer. But I just said mettle. And that's not a gate pass into immortality, not an official registration document for permanent residence in the last volume of universal history. For that matter history is often taken up with insignificant personalities. What kind of people, for example, were Tsar Mikhail Romanov and Empress Anna Ioannovna? If there are in history complete nonentities, it is also true that outside its field of vision remain armies of people who could on the basis of their character with full justice be called outstanding."

"You know him from the show side, but he is at times vain and he has been accused of narrow-mindedness."

"Vain? Perhaps. Balzac was also vain when he pasted onto his plebeian family name the aristocratic prefix, 'de'—but as for narrow-mindedness, forgive me but ... with narrow-mindedness I cannot agree ... Purposefulness can be mistaken for narrow-mindedness. On Ivan Kapitonovich's shoulders rests responsibility for, in one sense, the welfare of more than one million people. Is it a joking matter? Close up it is difficult to take in what is grandiose with a glance. People usually see particular traits, individual cases. Some Peter Sidorov has had his feelings hurt. Some Sidor Petrov has been bypassed unjustly. In running a big show Ivan Kapitonovich inevitably is going to push someone or other. There are going to be cracks in the fates of some people and the life of someone or another is going to be broken in two. Well, what can one do—shed tears over every case, wring one's hands, gather up the pieces to glue them together, fuss over things ..."

Elochka looked at Shatskikh with implacable searching eyes:

"Tell me ... But frankly, please ... And Papa ... My papa too?"

But just at that moment the lights went out.

The darkness was extraordinary, threatening, distinctive for some reason from the kind of darkness present when a fuse blows. For the first moment no one comprehended why it seemed so hostile till Bronislava Semyenovna declared in fright:

"The windows ... Even the windows are invisible."

Always outside the windows there burned some city lights or other—but right at this moment in place of the windows there were just dark, diffuse spots. The ordinary nighttime city which had seemed to be indestructible had disappeared without a trace.

"It would seem that this accident is no joking matter," Boris Yevgenevich declared.

There was a weak click in the dark. Bronislava Semyenovna had picked up the telephone.

"And the telephone is not working," she reported.

"The phone isn't working!" Boris Yevgenevich was surprised. "My, oh my! That means the whole city is without light. The whole city!"

"There's an official telephone in Ivan's study," Nadezhda Sergeyevna reported. "It's certain to be working."

Bronislava Semyenovna got up:

"I'll phone the maternity home..."

But Shatskikh stopped her:

"There's no use. If the telephone was shut off here then they won't answer at the maternity home also. Oh my! What a misfortune!"

The street came alive, but in a strange kind of way. Headlights roamed through the darkness, and there were angry honks of horns. Cars caught by surprise complained and rebelled.

Nadezhda Sergeyevna began to look for something by feel and some things fell onto the floor.

"I can't seem to find them... They should be right here somewhere. There were some left from the country house... Aha, here they are. And in one piece, too, it would seem."

A candle, standing crookedly in a glass on the table, flamed up. The elastic gloom retreated a step. In the dark corner the decorations on the New Year's tree glistened weakly. The powerless light emphasized the omnipotence of darkness. And it was impossible to believe that at one time people knew at nighttime no other form of light, that they worked and chatted in such a light and were not in despair from it but even experienced gladness.

For a minute or so all looked as if bewitched at the sickly little tongue of the flame.

Elochka, with a toss of her head, raised her eyes toward Shatskikh.

"I wanted to ask you... Do you consider that my papa is the same kind of a person as Ivan Kapitonovich?"

"Your papa..." Shatskikh for some reason looked with fright at the window where the lights from cars flashed past. "Your papa... Ivan Kapitonovich always takes everything on himself and therefore there aren't any people like him around him."

"And nevertheless, if my papa were in the position of Ivan Kapitonovich, would he act in the same way?" Elochka asked stubbornly.

"It's hard to say... He would have to act the same way..."

"No, he would not have to!" Elochka declared precisely.

Nadezhda Sergeyevna shook her head is distress!

"Oh, young people, young people... Vadim is older by a good deal but he's just the same..."

In the corner next to the phone there were sounds of sobbing.

"Bronislava Semyenovna, what is wrong?"

"I am afraid for Galina ... Suppose right at that minute she was there ... If Ivan Kapitonovich would just phone."

"Even though Boris Yevgenevich put Ivan high up in the heavens he is still not God. Everything will be all right. We just have to wait."

"Mis-fort-unes!" sighed Boris Yevgenevich and for some reason inappropriately reported: "There will have to be a scapegoat."

19

The Moskvich approached the chemical factory.

The factory stood in the middle of a broad field and even at nighttime its severe, stony nudity made itself felt—geometrical, regular squares of its buildings, its rising stacks, concrete, asphalt, steel, glass and not one little tree nearby, not one house. The city had not been built up in its direction and greenery was stunted on its approaches. From time to time when things accidentally went out of order the combine belched forth a cloud of sulphuric gas which had a fatal effect on everything living.

Right now it stood, illuminated with lights, among the snows, open to the winds. As always it led its own isolated life. Thirty two enormous ovens days and nights and on week-ends and in even the biggest holidays cooked out a hellish brew from pyrites. In high and many-jointed towers every hour and every minute there took place a simple chemical sacrament—gas, driven by fans from out of the ovens, was transformed into strong hydrochloric acid. The chemical factory was one of those untiring laborers knowing no rest.

Vadim and the chemical factory were the same age. They had both made their appearance in the world in 1930 and both were twenty-nine years old. But Vadim had just begun to enter his maturity while the combine was already counted as aged, as a veteran of industry. Vadim loved this monumental grim structure of the first years of the First Five Year Plan.

This love had its own remote history.

On the narrow little street of Malaya Prokhorovka, in the same apartment house in which little Vadim—Dimochka or Dima as he was also called—lived with his mama and papa there lived just one story below Sanka Goryaev. He was older than Dima by two years, short, frail of appearance, but feared for his bony fists by all the children in his courtyard. Dima caught it from Sanka particularly— because he was Sanka's neighbor, because he was a mama's boy, because at school he was held up as an example for everyone. Sanka beat up Dima, and Dima hated Sanka with an impotent frenzied hate. He hated his independent swagger, his narrow, turned up shoulders, the insolent look in his light-colored eyes.

In the second year of the war Dima had his twelfth birthday while Sanka became fourteen. Dima wore his school pupil's uniform, and his mother wrapped his lunch in a napkin for him every morning. Sanka departed for a vocational school.

At that time here into this area, far from the front lines, factories were being evacuated—from the Ukraine, from near Rostov-on-the-Don, from near Leningrad. Once Dima accompanied his father on a visit to such a factory. (His father was taking Dima to visit his grandmother and along the way decided to make a side visit.)

A factory? No, it was no factory. There in the middle of the field stood lathes—without walls or roof. Cold autumn rain was drizzling down from the heavens. To one side shivered a naked willow. Women lugged parts along plank flooring. Motors whistled. Metal bit into metal with a screech. The sticky rain drizzled down. There in the middle of the field was a refugee factory, a factory putting its roots down on the spot. Even the machines had an orphaned look. People stood at the lathes with earthy faces, with red, stiff hands, dressed some in greasy cotton jackets, some in canvas raincoats, some in ragged city overcoats. They didn't lift their eyes. They worked. And the rain drenched their backs and heads, and a dank wind whistled between the rows of lathes.

At one lathe there stood a boy. He was too short and in order to reach the metal blank gripped in the vice he stood on a wooden box. On his back had been thrown a piece of oilskin off which water was dripping.

"They can't get walls up by winter . . . Here in the snow in the frosts . . . I would raise a monument to these people after the war!" His father took Vadim by the arm. "Let's be going along."

Dima recognized Sanka. It was he standing behind the lathe, who didn't raise his head, who saw nothing. He had other things to think about than Dimka.

Till then Dima, like any other boy, had suffered and pined: time was passing and what a time! Girl partisans died proudly on gallows. Soldiers smothered machine guns with their chests. Pilots of shot-down planes dove into enemy troop columns. Every day brought new feats and new heroes. And he was growing up so slowly. Mornings his mother carefully wrapped a scarf about his neck and put his lunch into his pocket.

How unjust! Happiness for those older, but for him the doors were shut. A scarf around his neck and a piece of bread spread with margarine, wrapped in paper: "Be careful crossing the street . . ."

And there he had seen Sanka . . . His narrow, gray face, his sunken eyes, his aloofly stubborn bent of the head with cap pulled down over his eyes and that oilcloth... No, he was not like the heroes whom Dima had pictured to himself. There was neither a proudly thrown up head nor iron firmness in his look. He will work in the winter too, in the deep cold, in the snow... Monuments should be built to such people... It was Sanka—the same Sanka with whom he had fought in the courtyard, older than himself by just two years!

It was no longer childish envy of the lucky ones nor boyish intoxication with great feats. Vadim in those minutes for the first time felt a wrathful feeling of shame for himself. Why was he not standing next to Sanka? Sanka was there and he here. He watched from the sidelines. From the sidelines, out of it all! Was there any justification for himself?

Winter came and Dima continued to sleep in a soft bed. When he went off to school his mother, as always, wrapped him about the neck with a scarf and pushed his lunches into his pocket... He was only thirteen years old but his own life seemed to him to be unbearable, since somewhere nearby there was another life. Somewhere Sanka was standing behind a lathe in the snow.

Together with the new Sanka appeared a new overwhelming feeling—of painful responsibility for others—a feeling even at full maturity attainable not by any means by everyone. Vadim made its acquaintance in childhood.

He decided to run away from his soft bed and his mother's lunches. No, not to the factory. His father would seek him out there —but to the front, further away. He spent a night at the station, unable to get onto a train. In the morning a policeman brought him home.

He couldn't explain what he felt, put into words his disturbed state of mind, not to his father or mother or his friends. It was too complicated, not within his power. Dima became reserved. He didn't run away from home again, and carried his feelings within his soul: "I'll finish school and go into a factory—no one can stop me."

But then in the tenth grade—last year of school—he asked himself: would he be of greater use to others if he were to quit his schooling and go into the factory as a worker? He was not one to study just in order to grab off for himself in life a piece of fat. And education had never prevented anyone from becoming a decent person. So Vadim went on to an institute...

And then the chemical factory...

During his first week at work he had run into none other than Sanka in the acid tower department. Dry, sinewy body beneath heavily hanging oil-stained coveralls. Narrow face already touched with sparse wrinkles. Bulging light-colored eyes. An independent cast about his thin lips which seemed to say: "Just try and touch me with bare hands." Shabby, prematurely aged, already beginning to grow bald, but nevertheless alive and healthy Sanka, who had once stood on a box next to a lathe with only a piece of oilskin between him and the rain. The same Sanka who was constantly alive in Vadim's memory, who had given direction to Vadim's life.

On the outskirts of the city, where the streetcar turns back, stood a board pavilion, "Beer and Soft Drinks." There Vadim first got together with Sanka.

They began from a long time back—from Malaya Prokhorovka.

"Do you remember how you poisoned my life?"

"I beat you up, I suppose?" Sanka asked and laughed with the very corner of his thin lips: "I don't remember—after all I used to beat up many."

"Well I remember you all right . . ." and Vadim began to tell about the factory in the open field.

Sanka sipped his beer and looked with interest at Vadim, listening with curiosity as if the chat was about ordinary boyish affairs, no matter how close to the heart, on Malaya Prokhorovka.

"What happened happened. I also wanted later to run away to the front."

"Things were really rough?"

"In war it's always rough. I grew up, became tall. On the streets old women began to point—there's a shirker hiding a long way from the front. How could they know that things were rough there too?"

The fact that he once stood behind a lathe in deep cold he didn't consider a misfortune and he didn't consider a feat. Everyone who had worked side by side with him had done the same, experienced the same. And Sanka went away without understanding why Vadim was so enraptured about it.

All of them were like Sanka—and he too among them. He no longer felt any necessity of explaining to anyone the complicated cataclysms of the mind which had previously not given him peace. One need accomplish only what one can. There had been a fog and now it had been dispersed. It turned out that one doesn't have to get confused or complicate matters unnecessarily. One can live simply. At the chemical factory Vadim felt himself better than he had in his own family. Here at the factory he had acquired the precious sensation: you are not alone. Here had ended his seclusion.

Perhaps Vadim would have become at home in any other spot, but fate presented him with the chemical factory. It was unique and he made it his own.

Right now Vadim looked at the lights of the approaching factory with irritation and sadness: "Why the hell did I rush out here? As if they couldn't get along without me ... Oh, Galka, my Galka!"

He looked back at the city. The city spread out in the dark, broad as a galaxy—an uncounted field of big and little stars, a foggy accumulation of shining windows. And behind each window was a family: husbands and wives, fathers and mothers, sons and daughters. They love. They quarrel. They are glad. They suffer. Behind each window was a small world. The windows melted into a sparkling cloud, into the Milky Way. The worlds emerged into one giant world—a big city. The human galaxy floated in space and somewhere there in its heart there was cast the happiness of Vadim. Somewhere there was a window—just try and distinguish it—behind which his wife, Galka, was suffering right now with a suffering as ancient as life itself. She was suffering in order that there might appear a new human being, in order that a new fate might be woven, in order that in the boundless galaxy there might burn forth a new imperceptible little star. And that window was a window signalling a new family, a new little world in the human universe.

Oh, Galka, Galka!

The Moskvich, jolting its passengers, jumped across a railway crossing. There remained only some hundred meters more. Two lanterns, swaying in the wind, and the lighted window of the guard booth at the entrance were visible. Shadows lazily strolled along the bare asphalt and the snow piled along the sides of the road.

And all of a sudden the lanterns went out. The warming window of the guard booth became invisible. The whole factory drowned in the darkness. Over the pounding of the motor could be heard the whistle of the wind.

Vadim turned back again with all his body. The city, the human galaxy, had disappeared, just as if it did not exist on the earth. Instead of the cloudy accumulation of worlds there was mute, faceless blackness, instead of life non-existence.

The motor of the old car pounded in the darkness and the rush of the wind could be heard.

"Stop—we're there!" Vadim ordered.

He jumped out of the car and protecting his face from the wind jumped to the dark doors of the entrance.

20

And in the well-lit hall of the control room Vasily Vasilevich stood at his former place.

Somewhere a steaming sweating man—the duty officer in the customer relations department—was desperately serving out a sentence. Notwithstanding the fact that the majority of telephones in the city were silent he was being snowed under with a hurricane of phone calls.

"We're performing a complex operation. The patient is under the anaesthetic and the entire thorax lies open."

"The electric furnaces are freezing up!"

"The incubators are loaded! Tens of thousands of chicks are going to be lost!"

"The institute is breeding valuable varieties of bacteria. Without warmth in the nourishing medium they will perish. Ten years of work! A decade of work of the entire institute is being destroyed!"

Outside the walls of the control room at this moment every second there were a dozen accidents.

From time to time telephone calls even got through to it. The switchboard operator called Ivan Kapitonovich:

"The chairman of the Provincial Executive Committee!"

Ivan Kapitonovich took the phone:

"Yes, yes, an accident ... They're trying to find out. Something is wrong out on the transmission line."

"From the City Committee of the Party!"

"Yes, yes, an accident ... They're trying to find out. Golubko and the accident inspector are there on the spot."

"From the Provincial Police Department!"

"Yes, yes, they're trying to find out. I can't say anything more precise right now. Later ..."

Ivan Kapitonovich, Vitya Shapochkin, the switchboard operator—all were occupied. Only Vasily Vasilevich was standing there without anything to do. Having worked tens of years in this room he now turned out to be an outsider, an unneeded person. Ivan Kapitonovich who had not yet seated himself in the empty chair paced back and forth in front of the table walking around him as if he were a post.

Ivan Kapitonovich's face was heavy and dark, and his eyes were invisible beneath his frowning brows. And the fact that he did not burst into a rage, did not explode with wrath at Vasily Vasilevich, shouting at him such phrases as "You fouled up everything! You certainly messed up the system!" was a bad sign. He went around him and didn't even notice him ...

At the moment when Vasily Vasilevich got up from his chair time was an enemy. From second to second it was leading to catastrophe. And right now time was an ally. With every second the stations were gathering strength. Vasily Vasilevich was unable to turn time about—but Ivan Kapitonovich did. And so simply. No special perspicacity was necessary in order to reach the conclusion: you can't drain the sea with a spoon, and once it was impossible to save things with a partial reduction of load it was necessary to cut off the entire city. Simple . . . Vasily Vasilevich knew this. He knew it, but he couldn't make up his mind to do it.

Perhaps the power of Ivan Kapitonovich served to make him bold? But right now he was occupying his, Vasily Vasilevich's, place and making use of his, Vasily Vasilevich's, authority.

On the table, opposite the chair, lay a forgotten sheet, the emergency plan, an unnecessary piece of paper. There was the signature of Ivan Kapitonovich. But he didn't even take a look at it . . .

And this sheet of paper reminded Vasily Vasilevich that all his life from one day to the next he had always lived in apprehension, always been afraid of something—a sheet of paper with an official signature, a telephone call at home. And most of all he had feared the wrath of Ivan Kapitonovich himself. He had gone about glancing behind himself, afraid to step forward further than what was already measured off for him, and yet he had day-dreamed of his hour of destiny, about boldness, about manifestation of some slumbering powers. Boldness! He knew, but he couldn't make up his mind to act . . .

Unexpectedly, Ivan Kapitonovich stopped in front of Vasily Vasilevich. Short, broad, heavy like a stone on the steppes, hands in his pockets, cap down over his brows—cloudy, cold eyes.

It was strange—but Vasily Vasilevich even felt relief. Anything was better than to stand there like a post. Even wrath, even reproaches, even insulting scolding, even any end whatsoever to his painful and unnecessary existence within these walls. Let there be an end.

The word which Vasily Vasilevich awaited with his head involuntarily drawn back into his shoulders was heavy and crude like a cobblestone:

"Drrrrripp!"

Vasily Vasilevich threw back his face and met head on the pressing stare of the turbid eyes.

"Brain made out of dough! Wet behind the ears! Butterfingers! They shouldn't let you out of the house!"

It wasn't the rudeness. It could have been borne. But the rough blow fell right onto a fresh wound. Vasily Vasilevich had just been punishing himself for his lack of independence. He had been punishing himself without mercy. He felt himself spit on and humiliated. There was a limit to everything. He couldn't bear more humiliation.

Vasily Vasilevich did not drop his eyes:

"I have worked for you seventeen years. And what kind of independence can there be under you?" There was a challenge in his quiet voice.

He had objected. And this was the maximum of which he was capable. But even that surpassed the customary bounds.

The already dark face of Ivan Kapitonovich with the jutting jaw grew brown. He was silent and did not know what to answer. He had not expected to be resisted.

"Ivan Kapitonovich!" called out Vitya Shapochkin. "The customer relations office reports there's a discharge of acid at the chemical factory."

Ivan Kapitonovich turned.

And Vasily Vasilevich continued to stand at his former place. The conversation had not come to an end and was left up in the air. Vasily Vasilevich felt himself smashed. His legs were folding beneath him. His back was breaking...

21

On the streets an indifferent little snowfall floated down.

Passersby felt their way to the trolleybus and autobus stops and stood there as customarily in crowded queues. They waited—perplexed, depressed, deaf.

Auto headlights pierced in stripes the cave darkness. The lit autobuses in the dark city—gleaming islands of light—appeared to be apparitions from a distant, light-hearted, lost world. The passengers went to them, as if in attack, with noise and din.

On Spartakovsky Street, near the two streetcars which collided, people rushed about and slammed the doors of telephone booths. The driver of the streetcar was injured, but it was impossible to call first aid.

At the city airport a passenger plane arrived from Moscow. But the airport was dead—without one landing light. The plane made broad circles. The plane waited in the air. How long could it wait? No one could answer exactly. The passengers impatiently looked at the black plane windows. Below it was all dark. Below was an uninhabited land.

The dry little snowfall floated down, emphasizing the lack of coziness of the city. The wind wandered between buildings as if through crannies and cracks.

And already from mouth to mouth, from gateway to gateway, from one dark apartment to another, crept the rumor:

"They blacked out the city. They're expecting an air raid. War!"

Things were on edge in the uninhabited city.

And the little snowfall floated down...

22

In the dark entrance Vadim put his hand in his pocket and remembered immediately that he was in his best suit and had left his pass home.

"You can't enter, citizen. Entrance to the plant is forbidden to outsiders," the guard declared with polite firmness.

"I'm not an outsider."

"How do I know? Present your document."

"I am the chief electrical engineer of the factory."

"I know nothing. I am new here. Present your document. I'll light a match and I'll verify in good order. And without a document you are for me a suspicious character. That's our fate—to suspect everyone."

The guard pronounced with obvious satisfaction the word "suspect." Once in a lifetime he had the possibility of manifesting his vigilance.

"Hell, there's an accident in the factory and you are grabbing me by the sleeve! Do you want to be sent to trial?"

The voice of the guard immediately became guilty:

"Well that's the order . . . I would be glad to . . ."

"Get out of my way!"

The guard stepped aside.

On the territory of the combine they had already lit the emergency lights which was not the customary generous and abundant lighting but instead sparse, stifled light which only in places diffidently broke through the thick darkness.

At this minute the air was filled with the howl of the siren. An iron shriek in which a cry for help and an impotent threat joined into one. The choked factory, the pile, one upon another, of towers, ovens, sections, machines, called out in a soul-rending voice. And amid the half darkened courtyard, in the dim light, gray tufts of smoke, like fairy-story dragons after deep sleep, wearily stretched out, smoothed themselves out, gathered strength.

The ovens in which the powerful fans stopped, thirty-two ovens, filled with white hot sulphur broth from pyrites began to smoke. The straining siren called the workers from the ovens into the open.

Struggling with short legs against the flaps of his coat a man ran at Vadim. From the bobtailed figure an awkwardly long shadow danced obliquely along the asphalt walk. Vadim recognized Khomyakov, doctor from the combine's dispensary.

"What happened?" Vadim shouted.

"At the acid tower section . . . They just told me . . . Faster!"

Vadim should have gone to the factory's substation, but the

siren and then the broken cry of Khomyakov and his order, "faster!" gave Vadim a push. He rushed to run shoulder to shoulder with the doctor.

The siren cut off and deafening silence descended.

"What's happened there? A discharge of acid?"

"Worse . . . Nitric acid got into the drain wells, into the water . . . Oxides of nitrogen . . . In the acid tower section it turned out there weren't any gas masks handy."

Oxides of nitrogen were more awful than the cloud dragons which hovered at that moment over the dark courtyard.

"Criminal negligence!" Khomyakov raged on the run. "They didn't get the workers out in time. They didn't stop work. They're also good ones over there . . ."

Vadim remembered. His father had gone to the control room. He had cut off the entire city and with the city he had cut off the chemical factory too. But, as the old saying goes, while the sun is rising the dew will eat away the eyes. His father was a savior and not a criminal. He had no other course.

Vadim ran and kept quiet. It was not the place to dispute or prove something.

A railway branch line with a train of tank cars. Piles of sand and rubble, the blunt joints of pipe, snow—and over everything gray tufts of gas. The combine reminded one of a gigantic dying scene of fire devastation.

From out of the gas fog which floated over the snowy courtyard there leaped a man hung all over with gas masks. Vadim jumped to him and took from his hands several of the sets.

23

Near the tower section burned in a reflector just one small lamp bulb and the light from it was uncertain, greenish, somehow as if in an aquarium. And all about pipes, pipes, pipes, a tight interweaving of iron pipes—a battery of cooling installations. They were breathing out heat, reminding of the fact that only just ten minutes ago the factory was alive and operating. The riveted sides of the reservoirs were also like gigantic pipes growing into the ground. And from above there pressed down the murk of night in which the high walls of the building dissolved.

The gates to the department were wide open. One of them for some reason had been taken off its hinges and had been thrown down flat on the melting asphalt. Inside the building, beyond the open gates, was a dry, transparent mist. From out of it into the air, beneath the open oppressive heaven, people poured.

They stood, gathering in a group, coughing and cursing, and explained to Khomyakov who was still breathing hard.

"Answerable for all of us ... We got the hell out of there without stopping to think ... And he rushed to shut the oven doors, thought he could stop it. We didn't notice he was missing till we got here. And it's impossible to go back there with a naked snoot—you'll croak yourself."

Several hands grabbed at the gas masks which hung on Vadim. One he kept for himself.

"Whoever has burns—don't crowd around here!" Khomyakov ordered. "Straight to bandaging!"

Vadim hurriedly and awkwardly pulled the mask onto his face. They crowded around him and gave him advice:

"Hook it beneath the chin."

"One can see he didn't eat army chow."

"Check whether it's tight around the ears."

The glass began to mist up right away. The pipes and the people emerged for him foggily through a mist.

In the section, beyond the doors, two lamp bulbs loomed out like washed out spots. The jointed sides of the towers struck out of the darkness. In the drunken mist Vadim saw one back and another —of those who had succeeded in getting masks on before him and who already were moving about the section.

He struck his knee painfully on a pump screwed down to the cement floor and nearly fell down. He wiped off the glass in front of his eyes in the mask with his rubber finger. And the world acquired clarity.

The cement foundations, the pipes of the ventilators, shone greasily, enormous out of all scale. From them along the walls and the floor went crooked and determined shadows, murk overhead as on the street. Silence. Only in the tight rubber skull the blood beat.

In this concrete, sparsely lit world the inhabitants noiselessly loitered—instead of human faces muzzles awful with their stupidity, instead of eyes saucers. Their movements seemed languid, their backs bent—they looked down as if they were trying with their saucer-eyes to make a hole in the cement floor.

One of these inhabitants stopped and waved his arms in the direction of Vadim. And Vadim, limping on his injured leg, rushed to him.

On the side of a tower, behind the ventilating installation, writhed a human being. His oily quilted jacket was bunched up at his shoulder blades, showing his blue shirt. His face was pressed to the rough floor and his foot, in a rough work shoe, was turned awkwardly.

Vadim's comrade impatiently threw back his mask which was pulsating from breathing: "Grab ahold!" He himself took the shoulders and Vadim took the legs in their rough, work shoes.

They dragged him through the section, trying to keep in step with each other. And from all the nooks and crannies there moved in towards them other inhabitants with their inhuman faces.

Outside Vadim tore off the sticky mask. The cold air freshened his perspiring face. And the air, even though polluted by the gas, but nevertheless winter air, made his head swim for a second in intoxication.

They put down the victim flat on the gate panel. People rushed to him, pushed Vadim aside. But when he had caught his breath he also was impelled to look. He shouldered his way through.

With his narrow unshaven chin pointed upwards, his legs spread out, there on the broad door panel, in his unbuttoned quilted jacket, his besmeared blue shirt in plain view, lay Sanka Goryaev ...At that moment he seemed even shorter in height—almost a boy. His head was desperately thrown back. His puny body lay there in doomed strain. And his face was indifferent.

Beside him Khomyakov crawled on his knees, dragging along the dirty asphalt the end of his hanging scarf. He growled in the total stillness:

"Concussion of the brain ... He climbed up and fell down ... Hit himself on his head ..."

He carefully buttoned the quilted jacket on Sanka's chest and got to his feet frowning without the strength to take his stare away from the outstretched body.

"Will he live?" Someone asked diffidently.

Khomyakov cast a wrathful look at the voice and answered nothing.

From the broad reflector there poured the uncertain, aquarium-like light. The interwoven bent pipes crowded the people. Vadim stood and crumpled up the gas mask in his hands.

24

The husband and wife sat for a minute listening to the silence so untypical near a large industrial enterprise. The light of the Moskvich headlights illuminated a deaf concrete wall. Behind it no sign of life. The motor ran. The wind lashed snow dust against the window glass ...

And because of the silence, the darkness, the absence of life both felt out of sorts. Something was happening behind that blank wall, something out of the ordinary, incomprehensible. The wall hid the secret.

"You're going to run down the battery," said the wife.

He sighed, moved the gearshift and, with the beam from his headlight licking the wall and the tightly shut entry gate, turned the car around.

"Look there," he exclaimed with quiet astonishment in his voice. "It's dark in the city too."

She moved over closer to him.

Behind lay the secretive, silent, looming factory and in front of them the city was drowned in darkness. Snowflakes danced in the beams of the headlights and the windshield wiper fidgeted back and forth. Alone in the whole world. The snow drifted down and the world was visible for only a depth of some tens of meters in the beam of the headlights of the Moskvich with its worn-out generator.

The wind which swept about the windows and body of the car only intensified the silence. And its whistling reminded that all around lay a smooth, snowy, empty field. And suddenly in the silence a siren howled. The factory cried out with alarm behind their backs.

He reduced his speed. She moved even closer to him.

"What's that? What's going on there?"

"I don't know." His voice was dispirited. "They have chemistry there. Maybe something is going to explode."

"Oh my! Let's go faster!"

But he didn't step on the accelerator and she didn't insist. The Moskvich continued to roll along quietly.

They both lived a life which in the accepted terms is called, with praise, simple. And it was really simple, just like that snowy field through which they were riding at that minute. No matter how hard you looked ahead or behind there was nothing to take hold of. He was employed as head of the business and records department at an auto base—she as a clerk in accounting. All the strength of their soul, body, brain, and all their time to the last minute was occupied in earning, buying, amusing themselves. And the peak of their life the success which brought them both gladness and disappointment was the purchase of the Moskvich. Joy when they could go outside the city to swim, to picnic with a tablecloth spread out on the grass, to wash the car till it shone. Disappointments when some careless truck driver dented the bumper... They could think and worry about each other—but they never had to think and worry about others. And not because they were by their nature hard-hearted. No, no one demanded it of them and in fact no one in particular even needed their help, just as it never came into anyone's head to reproach them for the simplicity of their life.

And here behind their back the factory cried out. Now they, perhaps for the first time, were unconsciously gripped by a feeling for someone else's incomprehensible misfortune. Both were frightened by that misfortune, even though they knew it didn't threaten them with any dangers. Both felt the awkwardness of fleeing from that misfortune. The factory screamed out in the snowy waste. Ahead lay the dark, silent city. Something happened. Something had appeared at that minute infinitely more important than a knock in the transmission or a suspicious squeak in the axle.

The Moskvich went further but went slowly, uncertainly.

The siren fell silent and again there was only the beat of the motor, the gusts of wind, the emptiness, quiet, quiet.... Somewhere up ahead stood the city in all its dark enormity and they were going to it.

"And if there's no light how are we going to celebrate?" She declared in perplexity. "And to think that the Klyushkins made us bring a phonograph."

He didn't answer.

In their car there lay packages with cold cuts and appetizers, bottles of wine and vodka, and a phonograph. The were on their way to celebrate New Year in the society of others like themselves who were living a simple life. A group celebration had been arranged. Everyone would bring some appetizers and something to drink. They themselves were bringing the phonograph and the Klyushkins had promised to bring records. All this had been agreed on and calculated ahead of time. It was going to be a big party—in other words a gay party.

"The Fomichevs will begin to pester us: They'll say, 'We live outside of town and don't have a car but we got here on time—and you...'

"The Fomichevs won't get there," he interrupted angrily.

"How do you mean—they won't come?"

"If the city's without electricity that means the suburban trains are all stopped."

And she quieted down in fright—grasping for the first time the scale of the event.

The machine went even more slowly and finally stopped at the side of the road.

"What are you doing?" she asked in a whisper.

"And what if it's necessary to take someone to the hospital?"

"Oh, what a misfortune . . ."

In a few minutes they stood at their previous place, radiator next to the factory wall, headlights turned out.

"Something smells," she informed him.

"Chemistry. It means some kind of gas got out."

"And it can explode?"

"It's chemistry."

"Let's get farther away."

"There are people inside there," he gestured with his head in the direction of the wall. "Are we any better than they are?"

And then she was silent. The snow was drifting down. The wind swept it from the windshield. They waited patiently—pressed one to another in the cold car. And what they were waiting for they couldn't have told.

25

Vadim crumpled the gas mask in his hand.

On the plank panel of the gate, off its hinges, there on the ground lay Sanka with his head thrown back, his chin pointed upward and his face indifferent.

Sanka was lying there . . . The difficult history of the last years had entered into his short biography in a total way—cities smoking in ruins, tractors hauling cannon instead of ploughs. Victories do not come easily. Sanka Goryaev lay there, one of the victors, hardened at lathes beneath the open sky, his mature strength ripened on the ration cards of wartime. There lay a citizen in a greasy quilted jacket.

An awkward injustice: Vadim's father in order to save the city had to kill Sanka Goryaev. His father could not be blamed

It was unthinkable . . . But the human being lay there dead. Did his father think of that when he gave the order? His father was not a novice in electric power. He could guess. He knew. But to know —did that mean to think? He saved the situation, solved the problem. The problem—the problem is God! The problem is Moloch demanding from time to time human sacrifices.

At that minute when his father had issued his order—he was not to blame. It was a desperate minute. Just delay a bit, fail to decide, and one way or another it would have led to more serious catastrophes, perhaps to more serious sacrifice of life. But it wasn't just then right at that minute, but always, that his father considered that the problem came first of all. The problem was God! Who else was it but he who had opposed the installation in the factory of a power plant. And he had even opposed the installation of a turbine.

Inefficient! Not profitable! Not profitable? But what profits could buy back now the death of Sanka Goryaev? There Sanka lay, chin pointed upward.

The workers from all four sides raised up the gate panel and carried him away ...

Their boots clomped along the frozen asphalt and they moved along in total silence. Sanka, small, narrow-shouldered, rocked gravely on his too broad stretcher. Through the gas-laden mist there drifted a light little snowfall.

"Do you need your gas mask any longer, fellow?" someone asked reaching out for it. "Give it to me, I'll put it back in place."

Vadim silently took off the gas mask.

"And where is your cap?"

"Your cap?"

Vadim touched his head and felt the snow in his hair. He had probably lost his cap from his head when he had put on the gas mask.

Right then throughout the entire factory the lights went on. Immediately the night sky rose and the gas, floating in the air, became whitish instead of a dirty gray. It even seemed harmless to the eye.

Behind the brick wall of the building past which they were passing the fan began to howl.

And Vadim came to himself: the current had been turned on and who knows whether some new misfortune might take place. He rushed off ...

26

There wasn't yet light through the entire city, but the center already gleamed with fire.

The street lights illuminated the streets generously.

Green and red eyes of the traffic lights stared with commanding severity down on the streets.

And once again the holiday trees were all in lights, and once again over the rooftops gleamed the signs: "Happy New Year! Happy New Year!"

The trolleybuses came out of their deep sleep. The streetcars came alive.

The lights of the airdrome burst out. The plane from the capital which had been circling in confusion made its last turn and headed in for landing.

Majestic, strong, with its weight of many tons—this articulation of metal rushed with a roar over the little bit of a helicopter in which Ignat Golubko was awkwardly sandwiched.

The radio sang out.

The telegraph went back to work on all channels: "Happy New Year. I wish you happiness . . ."

The suburban electric trains again dashed along.

The screens of television sets burst into light and the announcer, a local beauty, the most popular woman in the entire city, announced with a bewitching smile as if nothing had happened:

"We continue our broadcast which was interrupted for technical reasons."

27

The light came back on in the Sokovin apartment. And amidst the abundance of this light on the gleaming tablecloth the slightly guttered candle continued to burn. It seemed embarrassing that its pale, painfully weak tongue of flame just one second before had been the center of a little world and had powerfully attracted to itself stares. The faces of all were as if after sleep—aloof, set, expressing nothing.

Bronislava Semyenovna was the first to come to life. She seized the telephone and hurriedly dialed a number.

"Maternity home? Is this the maternity home? Pardon me, I want to know—Galina Vasilevna Sokovina . . ." A strained and tragic expression. And suddenly she became soft and tears glistened in her eyes: "Thank you . . . Thank you . . . I'm very grateful."

She raised up her face which looked as if it had been washed and declared with happy fatigue:

"A little girl . . . Born in the light of a kerosene lamp . . . Six pounds . . ."

Nadezhda Sergeyevna smiled broadly with relief.

"And what did I say? It wasn't anything so terrible. I, for example, was born in the light of a peasant lamp."

"Bronislava Semyenovna, from me—the first present for the newly born," Shatskikh jumped from his chair.

And Elochka shyly exclaimed:

"Congratulations!"

The darkness had lain heavy. The darkness had been binding. The awkward in-between-time had come to an end and everyone felt calm and freedom and again the flowers on the table struck the eyes. And with the returned light had come glad news.

"Just think—a new human being. The human race has become richer by one unit, right now at this moment. In the birth of a child one involuntarily feels something historic," Shatskikh declared quietly.

Bronislava Semyenovna wiped away a tear.

"How good you all are. All of you. And you, Boris Yevgenevich, are wonderful."

Boris Yevgenevich was embarrassed:

"Thank you . . . The first present for the newly born."

The telephone rang. Bronislava Semyenovna hurriedly shoved her handkerchief up her sleeve.

"I am listening . . ." Her voice right away stopped short with confusion. "I don't know anything . . . Ivan Kapitonovich is at the control room . . . I don't know anything. Just a minute." Bronislava Semyenovna covered the phone with her hand. "You talk to them, Boris Yevgenevich."

Shatskikh took the phone reluctantly.

"Yes . . . This is Shatskikh, head of the planning section . . . Please understand—I am here just by chance . . . I can easily believe you . . . But I have nothing to do with it . . . I am not informed about anything . . . By chance. Why are you shouting? I have nothing to do with it."

Evidently at the other end of the line the party had hung up in anger. Boris Yevgenevich's face immediately became confused.

"Who was it?" Asked Nadezhda Sergeyevna.

"The director of the chemical factory, Kushchenko. Something very unfortunate happened there."

"Oh, how awful! And Dimochka is there . . . But why did he phone here?"

"They won't connect him with the control room—and he doesn't know where to turn. He threatens to bring Ivan Kapitonovich and everyone around him to justice. He attacked me . . . What do I have to do with it?"

"It's all right. He'll be angry and that's all there will be to it."

"No, that Kushchenko is an influential man, a member of the party bureau, a representative. He can make such a racket!"

"It doesn't concern you, Boris Yevgenevich."

"It ought not to. But when they cut down a forest the chips fly. And sometimes even a bystander gets something in his eye. He threatens to bring Ivan Kapitonovich to justice . . ."

"Ivan will answer. What are you so afraid of?"

Boris Yevgenevich went over to the holiday tree in the corner, farther away from the telephone. He sat down, raised his shoulders, and was silent.

"Let's talk about something else," Nadezhda Sergeyevna proposed. "We can find a subject which is more pleasant. Here is what I propose. The New Year is New Year and we have right now our own happiness. I'm going to bring a bottle and we'll sit closer together in a circle and drink to the birth of the granddaughter and at the same time make a guess what her name will be. Elka—it will be wine for you, but I want something stronger so Dima's daughter should grow up to be strong. What would you say if I were to open your cognac, Boris Yevgenevich? Such an occasion deserves it."

In a minute Nadezhda Sergeyevna put out on the little table next to the telephone the thickset bottle.

"Let's try it... Well, Boris Yevgenevich, move up closer... We'll see what French cognac is like. A bottle like a woman with a big behind... Boris Yevgenevich, how many times do I have to invite you?"

Boris Yevgenevich unwillingly moved up. His eyelids were drooping and his lips were tight.

"What's wrong with you?" Nadezhda Sergeyevna asked. "Someone shouted at you on the telephone and you went to pieces. You should be ashamed."

"Something really is wrong with me lately. I don't understand myself."

"What is it? Come on, let's hear your complaint. Men are stupid in such things. We, women, are more understanding."

"It's strange, Nadezhda Sergeyevna... Until Ivan Kapitonovich directed attention at me I lived like everyone else. I worked and I feared nothing. I went to work with a light heart. And then all of a sudden—I am chief of the planning section! All of a sudden Ivan Kapitonovich extols me to the skies. It seems to me as if everyone is looking at me in a special way. One would think—success, so go ahead and live and be glad. And I am all the time afraid that tomorrow Ivan Kapitonovich will come to himself and instead of praising me will say: "Eh, you're not the one I took you for! I am afraid that someone is going to say something out of envy to Ivan Kapitonovich. I am afraid to run into him in the morning. I am afraid when he calls me to his office and also when for any length of time he doesn't. And it's awful both when he praises me and when he speaks indifferently. I don't understand myself, Nadezhda Sergeyevna. Some kind of insanity. You will laugh, but I have become afraid even when a cat crosses the road... And right now? You are right, right a thousand times when you say that there is nothing to be afraid of, that I am not responsible for the accident. But nevertheless... All of a sudden the least likely thing will happen... Ivan Kapitonovich is a strong tree and it's not so simple to fell him. But if they do fell him? Under Ivan Kapitonovich it's awful and without him..."

Boris Yevgenevich squeezed his dry hands with his sharp knees. His head sank into his raised shoulders. His dark, moist eyes stared forth, pleadingly, at Nadezhda Sergeyevna.

Unexpectedly he stopped talking. The light eyes of Elochka looked at him attentively from the side. And under that look he immediately felt that all were embarrassed by his words—most of all Nadezhda Sergeyevna. She listened with eyes cast down.

"What have I said, Nadezhda Sergeyevna Forgive me! Stupidities ..."

"Let's better drink to the health of our granddaughter." Nadezhda Sergeyevna reached out her full hand to the bottle.

The face of Boris Yevgenevich suddenly pinched up into a grimace just as if he had eaten something sharp. He jumped up.

"Where are you going? Sit down."

"No, forgive me ... It's always this way with me. I am silent at first and keep it pent up inside myself. And then all of a sudden without any rhyme or reason I spit it out. Oh, what stupidities!"

"Oh, forget it ... Sit down ..."

"No, it would be better for me to leave. Forgive me, I can't."

Boris Yevgenevich, holding high his raised shoulders, hurriedly went to the door and stopped in the doorway.

"Bronislava Semyenovna, nevertheless, the first present for the newly born is to be mine. With all my heart."

'What a strange man!" Nadezhda Sergeyevna let drop.

"Not strange, just pitiful," Elochka objected.

Bronislava Semyenovna sighed and declared without any condemnation:

"He flew too high ... Thank God that my Vasya doesn't try to climb to big positions. Everything is always peaceful with him."

On the big table in the bright light the candle guttered. In the bustle they had forgotten to put it out.

28

Ivan Kapitonovich switched his telephone over to the duty officer at the maintenance and service department.

"Report!"

"At the freight station—a wreck. A switch engine ran into a train."

"Victims?"

"No victims."

"Thank God!"

"On Spartakovsky Street two streetcars collided."

"Victims?"

"The driver was slightly injured."

"Slightly ... Only half a misfortune. Further."

"But out there at the chemical factory, Ivan Kapitonovich."

"What?"

"A fatal accident with a fatal result."

"One died?"

"One."

Ivan Kapitonovich bit his lip.

"That's bad. What took place?"

"I haven't been able to find out yet. Presumably acid emission."

"Maybe it wasn't fatal? They're past masters at scaring everyone out there."

"I don't know. They can't make heads or tails of things out there yet themselves."

Vasily Vasilevich stood at his former place. For those fifteen minutes he had not moved. Very much like a school pupil put in a corner and told to stand there—and at his age . . . He was not needed. He was superfluous here. Superfluous! After so many years of work. And where, in fact, lay his blame? He couldn't make up his mind to exceed the instructions. And the instructions were not clear. Like a cyberneties apparatus given an inexact program—jammed up.

Fifteen minutes . . . Vasily Vasilevich became weak. His legs became numb. His head whirled. Nausea rose into his throat.

A machine without flights upward or falls downward, incapable of taking a risk, a machine with a calculated regime of operation. It failed to justify hopes set on it. And now it stood unnoticed. They hadn't yet had time to move it outside the door and for the moment reconcile themselves to the fact it still occupies space. They passed by the uninspired thing on the side.

Become angry? Rebel? Against what? I'm to blame. I failed to do the job. It was necessary long before this to have fought for the right to be a human being. To fight? With whom? With Ivan Kapitonovich? Was he really an enemy to him?

It would be good to sit down. There was no more strength to stand up any longer. But in this room there were no chairs for guests. There was only the chair in front of the control panel. Sit down at the panel in his old chair? Sit down in order to rest?

Ivan Kapitonovich had entrusted not him but Vitya Shapochkin with distribution of the load. The power stations gathered power but the accident had not come to an end with this. It had only begun. There had been a breakdown of the system. Three stations one after another must go into operation. Like soldiers who had left the column they had to fall into step immediately. The difference lay only in the fact that a soldier who failed to fall into step would not fall down seriously wounded, but at a power station the coils of the generators could burn out and the machinery go out of operation. And in that case it would already be a catastrophe with new force.

Load up to assured capacity...Vitya Shapochkin was not so experienced as he, Vasily Vasilevich. Ivan Kapitonovich had entrusted the task to Vitya Shapochkin, however, and didn't even wish to notice Vasily Vasilevich who was standing one step away from the chair in which he had sat for decades.

If he could only sit down in that chair and rest...

Ivan Kapitonovich was doing three things at once. He was talking on the telephone. He was watching the instruments with his round eyes. He was listening to the orders of Vitya Shapochkin on the intercom.

"Chernushinsky! Come in!"

Vitya Shapochkin showed both strain and bravery on his red face. He was proud that at such a moment he was entrusted with commanding the power station.

Ivan Kapitonovich watched him and grumbled into the telephone:

"Airport! Airport! Has Golubko left yet? He has already taken off? Good!"

Vasily Vasilevich stood near the chair and was hardly able to stand from fatigue. If he could only leave...Entirely...Impossible! Not working, superfluous, unnecessary, but nevertheless at work. He didn't belong to himself and it was not in his power to move from the spot on which he stood.

29

The light burst out over the tightly closed entrance to the chemical factory. The light burst out and the mysterious aura over everything immediately disappeared.

"We should go," she said uncertainly.

"I guess so," he agreed with an embarrassed air.

At this moment he was ashamed. He had turned back, panicked just because the power had been shut off for a few minutes.

But he did not succeed in turning the key in the ignition. Somewhere from the rear, from out of the darkness, there erupted a car gleaming with light-colored finish—an ambulance. Settling down onto its shock absorbers it braked sharply and demandingly and hoarsely screeched out at the bare gates.

The guard in his black great coat jumped out and helpfully started to open up. Tangled in his coat flaps he opened one side on the run, then the other, and stood at attention.

The ambulance started forward but the guard of a sudden waved in a fuss at the driver and the car stopped.

In the open gateway there appeared the backs of workers. Crowding one another and stepping uncertainly, looking at the ambulance, they carried some kind of a broad plank panel. The ambulance orderly, in a white smock with an overcoat over it, was fat but quick. From the bowels of the gleaming machine he pulled out a stretcher . . .

The owners of the Moskvich sat dismayed, sticking out their necks, watching. The workers surrounded the ambulance closely. Only backs dressed in quilted jackets and canvas could be seen. And among them an orderly in white hovered.

The doors of the ambulance shut with a crash. Giving out a hoarse honk of its horn the ambulance moved backward sharply, turned after a second in which its gleaming side was beneath the light of the gate lamp and dashed off into the darkness.

He awkwardly turned on the seat of the Moskvich, pushed against the door and got out.

The workers crowded about, getting a light from one another. On the asphalt powdered with snow lay the broad panel of the plank gates taken off its hinges.

He asked, nodding in the darkness where the ambulance had whirled away:

"Injured?"

A dark faced, grim worker unwillingly growled out:

"Wish he were."

"What is it—for good?"

The worker was silent, drawing on his cigarette. Others under their breath:

"He was still young."

"Young or not—two little ones on his neck."

"Just today he told me: he had agreed with his wife that she would come for him here at the end of his shift. I'll change my clothes, so to speak, and we'll go straight to the celebration."

"He's already celebrated his holiday."

"And his wife . . . A funeral instead of a holiday."

"She should be warned, prepared for it. Otherwise it will be like hitting her over the head. Not so nice."

"Do you know where he lived?"

"That's the thing. I don't know."

"Pishchenko knows—they are friends."

"Pishchenko is in the first shift today."

"What mean luck! Let's go, what do you say?"

"I pity the woman."

They threw their butts into the snow, raised the door from the roadway and leaned it up against the wall. One after another they wandered onto the territory of the combine. There remained the guard. Without hurrying he closed the gates, clanked the latch, loudly blew his nose and said significantly:

"That's the way it goes . . . There was a human being and now he is no more. Poisoned with gas, I hear."

Right next to the spot on which the ambulance had stood there was something dark lying, trampled into the snow. The guard bent over.

"Look—dropped his cap. Fell from the stretcher and they didn't notice."

The owner of the Moskvich looked at it and went up to it with determination.

"Show it to me."

"A stylish cap. I guess he must have earned good wages. They lost it . . . Well, he doesn't need it now."

He took it into his hands and began to look it over from all sides insistently. A good-quality woolen top, soft fur, wet from the snow which caressed the fingers like velvet.

"What are you feeling it for—as if you intended to buy it?" the guard asked.

"Come here to me! Look at this!" he cried out in a muffled tone in the direction of the Moskvich.

She took a long time getting out of the car, approached, took a look and got pale right away.

"It's his—there's the marking."

He continued carefully to feel the gray mark with his fingers."

"Do you know him?" the guard sympathetically inquired.

"We were just waiting for him."

No, he was not an acquaintance, not close. They had waited for him, worried about him. Again they were gripped by a powerful desire stronger than their will to do something, to help somehow. It wasn't possible for them to toss aside this cap, to turn about, to forget, and to go to their celebration.

"They just spoke here of his wife. They said she was intending to come here. She should be warned somehow so that it shouldn't stun her just like that . . ."

"But how? We don't know where she lives."

"Do you remember from what entryway he came out?"

"Well, yes, I do remember."

"Well, we're going to go there."

"But the apartment house is big. If we were only to know the number of the apartment . . ."

"They have two little children . . ."

The guard interrupted:

"Why bother. She'll come here. She'll find out. Plenty of time for her to suffer her grief."

"But she was going to celebrate the holiday."

"Well, so what? She'll wait and wait some more and then decide that they missed each other. And so she'll go and celebrate by herself. And let her ... Better that way."

To him at that particular minute the reminder of the holiday seemed blasphemous. Celebrate, when grief had entered the house! Make merry alongside misfortune! That merrymaking subsequently for a whole lifetime would seem a curse, a malicious mockery. No, he would not want such a holiday. Let the grief come right away. Let there be misfortune without merrymaking. And besides that he was *obliged* to do something. Although it was little still it was something. In the frosty air there reeked from the guard the smell of tobacco. On his crumpled up physiognomy, round like a pancake, there was neither sympathy nor concern. There was just casual interest: look here, you see, the human being is gone but his cap remained behind. And in the owner of the Moskvich there stirred an unpleasant feeling: "He wouldn't push you into a pit, but if you were to fall into one he wouldn't even reach out his hand to save you."

"We'll go from door to door through the entire entryway," he said with determination. "We'll show the cap—and they will recognize it ... The apartment house is big but the entry is not so very big."

She did not object. Only the guard shook his head with doubt.

In five minutes the Moskvich briskly sped towards the city.

30

One section of the city after another burst out in street lights and innumerable windows. At the skating rinks in the city parks the searchlights beamed down on the ice. The sprawling carousel-like ring of skaters began to get going again from out of the light crowd. Grandfather Frost on his ice skates raised over his high red cap his crook and made jokes.

From out of the boilers of apartment houses warmth moved to the radiators in apartments. The city had not become stiff with cold. It had not died. It returned to life.

The lines of passengers at the stops on municipal transport routes dispersed. Only at the coin telephone booths on the streets were there small groups of people. Everyone who had been caught by the onrush of darkness was hurrying to phone to explain:

"I got caught. I couldn't get out ... I'm coming ..."

Medieval murk collapsed. Again it was the middle of the twentieth century. The reborn light ended the alarm of the city's inhabitants. What blackout? What war? Fairy stories! To the New Year, friends! To new happiness!

And at the forty-first kilometer on the electric power transmission lines, at the span between two towers, numbered 162 and 163, the accident crew arrived.

In the middle of the field they began to build bonfires. The helicopter with Ignat Golubko was going to land by them at any minute.

31

At the control room Vitya Shapochkin jumped to the panel and at the back end of the yellow line on the circuit hung a small sign with zigzag marks—indicating that the line was grounded, that repair was under way.

Ivan Kapitonovich finally turned to Vasily Vasilevich and dryly ordered him:

"Sit down! Continue the distribution of the load!"

Vasily Vasilevich trembled. He was being invited to return to work, when everything had already been done, when they had finally remembered him, in order merely to keep things in their proper place. The chair ought not to be empty. He would sit down in this chair, and then . . . The power stations were working. The rotors of the generators were marching in step—the most dangerous part was already behind. Vitya Shapochkin had coped with the situation . . .

Vasily Vasilevich did not answer. He took in the hall with a glance: the frequency meters continued to write their chronicle and their chronicle reported that the time of troubles had passed. The needles of the voltmeters held firm. Everything round about was familiar and at the same time strange, somewhat like a railway station, boring to tears, a joke repeated for the tenth time.

"Maybe I didn't speak clearly? Sit down in your working place!"

"I can't . . ." Vasily Vasilevich answered quietly without moving his position.

The thick brows of Ivan Kapitonovich crawled with surprise there beneath his lambskin cap:

"Whaatt!"

"I can't. I must be . . . sick . . ."

"And what happened to you?"

His brows dropped, but his light-blue eyes looked out from under them suspiciously and in an unfriendly way.

What was wrong with him? Could one really explain! That man, evidently, had never experienced and would never experience anything like it. In other words, he would never understand.

"I am sick," Vasily Vasilevich repeated. He turned about and went to the door, feeling behind his back the stare of Ivan Kapitonovich.

Would he yell at him or not? Would he order him to stop? Would he compel him to work? If he were needed, if it were impossible to get along without him here in these walls, he would stop him of course and sit him down in the chair by main force. Vasily Vasilevich slowly went to the door, waited for the cry, but the cry did not come. Vasily Vasilevich unhindered went up to the door, pushed it open and went out...

And all of this was so extraordinary, so strange, that Ivan Kapitonovich did not even take umbrage.

"Well imagine that!" he said in astonishment.

And Vasily Vasilevich descended the stairway just as slowly, step after step, and waited... If he was necessary, of course, they would remember, catch up with him, tell him to return. But behind his back everything was quiet.

On the street the light snowfall drifted down. Passersby hurried. The street lights shone brightly. The city quickly returned to its former life.

In his overcoat, buttoned up to his chin, in his worn puffy cap, Vasily Vasilevich walked to his home, outwardly calm, slightly bent, a person of respectable age with dignified slowness. Very much like hundreds of other passersby.

32

In the first minute, as soon as the door had closed behind Vasily Vasilevich, Ivan Kapitonovich taken quite aback from surprise, thought; "Something is wrong. Something happened with him..."

Vasily Vasilevich's face had been reserved, without anger, fear, or disappointment. His voice, as always, had been quiet, polite, but his look was direct, unblinking. No one had ever discovered in him either nonsense or morbid vanity. During seventeen years everything had happened. He had received worse scoldings than that from Ivan Kapitonovich.

"Something is wrong. Something happened..." This was a simple thought, born of inability to understand: there was in it not pity, nor sympathy, only an involuntary desire to figure the man out.

But in the next minute Ivan Kapitonovich remembered: "But in fact he did leave! What right does he have? He left his post! He was insubordinate!" And already after that his thought, "What is wrong, what happened?" didn't interest him any more. He was face to face with disobedience, an outrageous departure from established norms. Just to think—he left... Maybe he should have taken him by the elbow and sat him down in the chair? Immediately everything became simple and comprehensible. Right away there was found easily a firm decision: "I won't fire him, but I'll demote him."

A decision was found. That was the end of it. There was no need to ponder any longer the eccentricities of Vasily Vasilevich. There was no need and, in fact, no time for it.

"Ivan Kapitonovich! It's Golubko talking!"

In the voice of Golubko who had flown half a hundred kilometers there was a familiar ring: "I am sitting in the lap of nature—snow up above, snow down below, snow on all sides . . ."

"Come on, come on, don't drag it out."

"As always, as the saying goes, a rotten piece of harness spoiled the marriage. A clamp weakened and one wire whipped across the others."

And this familiar grin in his voice, the calm of Golubko, which had always been pleasant to Ivan Kapitonovich, right at this minute aroused sharp irritation: he was cloudless and waggish. And here things had been allowed to fall apart into chaos. On the very holiday they were climbing out into the white world with naked backsides. You can't blame this one on an inadequate supply of technical equipment . . . He was standing there joking. Maybe he was thinking that Sokovin all by himself would get chewed up for everyone. Joking!

"Who's to blame?" drily asked Ivan Kapitonovich.

"The inspector hardly got here before he was off at a gallop. He's an eager beaver. He's digging up those who are to blame."

Ivan Kapitonovich exploded:

"And what about you? Aren't you to blame? Who was supposed to look after the apparatuses for unloading frequency? Maybe the good Lord God was supposed to install them and not the chief engineer! If there had been enough apparatus this misfortune wouldn't have happened."

"Careful, Ivan," Golubko interrupted him with undisturbed calm. "And who was it that grabbed me by the sleeve, who kept setting hopes on the fact that the main line was coming through from the Urals. We'll join the grid and be saved—we'll have anything we want. They were coming, but they didn't quite get here! Our neighbors have power lines with 500 kilovolts, and we got stuck on 220. And am I supposed to be to blame for that? We would do better not to point the finger at each other—it's an undignified occupation."

"Is that the way you're going to break out into song when the time comes to answer?"

"It's not so frightening in company. In one word, I am reporting to you: in one hour we are going to finish here! Yes, there's one more request: you aren't going to drive away the storm clouds with hysterics. So don't even think about calling off the celebration. I'm frozen. I need badly to warm myself behind a table. To your health—we're going to meet this year yet."

Without putting down the phone, Ivan Kapitonovich asked:

"Connect me with the provincial party secretary."

"I'm connecting you . . ."

"Aleksei Mitrofanovich, I'm reporting to you: We are loading the system. The city has been entirely reconnected. Semyenovsk and Razvodino are to be connected during the next ten or fifteen minutes. What about the Red Toolmaker Factory? Tell them not to make so much noise . . . Nothing happened to them . . . The chemical factory . . . Yes, I heard . . . Yes, it's unfortunate . . . There's nothing to be done about it . . . It could have been worse. Yes, there's an investigation underway . . . Yes, after the holiday we'll sort out the details . . . Yes, at Wednesday at the party bureau.

Vitya Shapochkin shouted into the intercom:

"Western! Western! Come in with the eighth feeder!"

The last echoes of the recent turmoil.

Ivan Kapitonovich stood as previously in his cap and his overcoat near the empty chair in which Vasily Vasilevich should have been sitting. The danger had passed. The expression of aroused determination had disappeared from the face of Ivan Kapitonovich. It had become grim, old, and tired.

"When the repairmen complete the line repair report to me. I will be at my apartment," he said, buttoning up his overcoat.

"Is the automobile ready?"

"It is waiting at the entrance, Ivan Kapitonovich."

Nodding his head in farewell, he went out unhurriedly.

He got out of the automobile and dismissed it two blocks away from his apartment building.

He no longer had to worry convulsively about what was taking place from second to second. Catastrophe no longer hung over the head. One could permit oneself the luxury of not paying any attention to time. One could be alone with oneself. Ivan Kapitonovich walked the city street with a tired gait . . .

And all about the lights stormed—signs burst out into light, cornices of buildings gleamed, garlands burdened with light hung over the streets. And the calm little snowfall drifting down from the heavens underlined the glad turbulence of the street. And people occupied with themselves and with their own affairs, people hurrying past in a rush, did not notice Ivan Kapitonovich. And one could be glad at the newly acquired common happiness, that there was no darkness on streets, that the holiday had not been spoiled. One could also regret that those minutes of darkness had stolen from all the people, on the street, part of their labor. And one could, last but not least, remember the man who perished at the chemical factory. Ivan Kapitonovich, no matter how one looked at it, was a victor who had won a battle at a heavy price. And indeed he could have thought of those for whom he had fought a battle. But Ivan Kapitonovich didn't notice anything, didn't experience anything, except fatigue and a bad mood . . . Why did all the cables break at once! One lashed the others . . . A double cable, evidently, would have been much more reliable. They almost, almost had succeeded by New Year in bringing up the main transmission line. Then—no longer would they have been isolated provincial princes but a particle of a great electric realm. The rotten piece of harness would not have spoiled the wedding . . . Almost, almost . . . And because of this "almost" you're going to catch it, Ivan . . . On Wednesday—a meeting of the party bureau.

Right there on a sidewalk, blocking the way for passersby, stood a group. A short chap, with a forelock peering out from under his cap, bleated on an accordian. The lacquered keys gleamed. The fingers lept up and down the keyboard. The serious face of the accordionist was raised haughtily. Two women, not so young, and a man ringingly counted out on the frozen asphalt a gypsy dance. The passersby went around them, looking at them with a smile.

But it's a bit early to begin to celebrate. Look here, brothers, you won't have anything left by the time the New Year arrives.

Ivan Kapitonovich went past without turning. Sadness gnawed at him: he was going to have to answer for an awkward unlucky accident. Just a little bit more . . . On Wednesday—the party bureau . . .

His mood spoiled even more when he began to climb up the stairway to his own apartment. The guests would sit around the table. He had to act as if he were merry: the celebration was a matter of obligation . . . Vasily Vasilevich would probably not come after their conflict. And that meant that Bronislava Semyenovna would sit as if she had been ducked in the water. That meant that Vadim would again begin to make a wry face . . . And Nadya, a good person, who all the past year long had been caught between her husband and her son, a patient mediator in both camps, would begin to dissemble in front of the guests . . . Everywhere it was a question of trifles. But they spoil life in a big way. Just try and avoid them. They say that for the elephant there is no beast more awful than a mouse . . .

On the stairway landing next to the open door into a neighboring apartment stood a strange man and woman. Ivan Kapitonovich went past them to his door. But the man stepped after him.

"Pardon me . . . Just a minute."

"Yes."

The man had a broad face with high cheekbones and a bunched up, badly fitting overcoat. He looked inquisitively into the face of Ivan Kapitonovich. The woman who was stretching her neck out from behind his back had a withered face and eyes round like an owl.

"By any chance do you know this cap?"

"Hm . . . How did you find it?"

"Does this cap belong to a relative of yours?"

"That is my son's cap. But what is the matter?"

The man and the woman looked at him with compassion. From a sick presentiment a chill ran to the ends of the fingers which held the cap.

33

Ivan Kapitonovich was already on the street when they caught up with him. He was rushing back and forth along the curb stretching out his hand toward automobiles which were flying past. The cars did not stop: everyone on a holiday evening was in a hurry and all the taxis were in great demand.

The man hesitated, approached, and hesitatingly touched Ivan Kapitonovich on his shoulder.

"We have a car . . . we can take you."

Ivan Kapitonovich looked with mad eyes, wilted perceptively, and obediently permitted himself to be led to the Moskvich.

"Where should we go?" asked the man, sitting down behind the wheel.

"Where?" Ivan Kapitonovich came to himself. He had rushed out in order to go to Vadim. Alive or dead—to him! Faster! Faster! He had not comprehended anything more than that. And now there was a sober question: Where to go? Where was Vadim? After all he was not at the chemical factory.

"To Deryabin Hospital."

He did not know with what clinic the chemical combine was connected, and he named the best-known hospital in the city where ordinarily they sent victims after all accidents. And again the lights moved by one after the other, passersby hurrying to celebrate flashed past, trolley-buses pushing off from their stops, store windows, cinema advertisements, holiday trees—a happy city unconcerned about a human being stricken with grief.

Ivan Kapitonovich had never given much thought to how much

he loved his son. In recent times Vadim had often aroused in him disappointment, even wrath. He considered: his son because of his youth did not understand him. Vadim, unlike his father, had not had to climb with effort each little step in life. He was born in a city. From the first day of his life electric lights had shone down on him. From his childhood he was used to the radio, to the telephone, to the fact that with the coming of winter the rooms in the apartment would become warm by themselves. He was born in the family of a well-provided electrical engineer. At his service were books, motion pictures, theaters, schools, an institute for his higher education. He had become an educated person just as naturally and easily as with maturity a beard appears on the cheeks of a man.

And he, Ivan Sokovin, had been born in the village of Lapshevka. The twentieth century had already begun. Somewhere the droshkies of Russian *izvozchiks* ran alongside automobiles. The first awkward airplane was already rising into the air somewhere. Motors of generators were turning somewhere. But in the peasant huts in Sokovin's village of Lapshevka peasant lamps using splinter wicks crackled. The Russian muzhiks scratched the land with the same wooden plow with which their ancestors had scratched the Russian earth many centuries before under Ivan Grozny and Vladimir Monomakh. The most clever piece of machinery known there was the mill which, with its joints creaking, turned its pitted millstone. Half of the huts were heated "in the black," in other words, by stoves which had no chimney. In the wintertime the village was covered all over with snow. Wolves howled on the outskirts. Even the rich peasants went about in birch-bark sandals. Even the rich peasants —and Vanka Sokovin, known on the streets as Vanka Prince, was from the itinerant poor. For seven of such they had just one homespun coat among them.

If elsewhere in the world the twentieth century had already begun, Lapshevka, let it be said, was living in the fifteenth. It was necessary to break through five centuries. Five centuries to be passed not in a whole lifetime, but during the course of several years! This meant something. Had it not been for the revolution he would have lived his whole life as an aborigine of Lapshevka village, Prokhorovsky District, Nikolsk County.

Vanka Sokovin was taken into the army. There they began to teach him the alphabet and the service rules, the multiplication tables, marching in step, political indoctrination, and the fortification of long-term fire positions. His teacher in the use of mines, in order to give at least some kind of a concept of electricity to these lads from all of the villages of the Russian countryside, brought to the class an electric motor. Two wires, thin as strings, were fastened by clamps to a bobtailed steel box the size of a birch cheese box. Inside the box there were neither levers, nor wheels, only coils of wires. The electric motor turned, filling the room with a restrained buzzing hum. The men in turn seized with their hands the whirling end of the shaft. They wanted to stop it, but the shaft turned, burning the palms of their hands. And the teacher grinned behind his army moustaches.

"You can't stop it, boys. In the motor there is five horsepower."

Five horsepower! In a bobtailed iron box! Five horsepower poured through two thin wires which looked to be dead. No joke—five horsepower! No levers, no muscles. What is flowing along the wires? What is storming inside the box, in emptiness, in the air, between some kind of spindles? A magic, unattainable to simple mortals. If he could only master it, become himself a wizard, get to the heart of that secret force—but he would sell his soul to the devil. He wouldn't even be sorry to pay with his life. But what could he possibly be doing, a bark-sandaled peasant with a homespun snoot on Kalashny Row? *

Ivan Kapitonovich became an ordinary worker at an electric power station. He worked next to an enormous machine, one shaft of which weighed several tons. There took place what appeared to be at first glance a trifle: someone opened the windows in the generator room. It was late autumn, the grass was touched with the first light frosts. A wind was blowing. And the machine "caught cold." In this there was nothing extraordinary. It is customary among electric engineers to say that a turbine "caught cold." The temperature fell only a few degrees. The convulsively living metal cooled off just a little bit. Just a very little bit, in the dimension of the thinnest hair, the clearances changed, just a little bit, but even this was enough. The powerful machine turned out to be a tender little baby. From the "cold" it became "sick" and the heavy shaft sagged. There was vibration. It was necessary to stop the turbine and "heal" it over a long period.

After this Ivan Kapitonovich experienced for all his life a fatherly feeling for capricious metal, made into a "living organism." No one could understand better than he the hidden caprices in the character of a turbine. No one quicker than he could foresee its whims. Like a father he was tender. Like a father he was demanding. And the machine answered him with gratitude. Even now, after becoming manager of a big power system Ivan Kapitonovich, looking from time to time at a high-voltage line, continued to experi-

* A Russian saying. Kalashny Ryad or Row—the finest and biggest of the marketplaces of old Moscow—therefore the ultimate in urbanity to be contrasted with the ultimate in provincialism—bark sandals and homespun.

ence his earlier sensation of the great secret which he had not attained. Three cables, not so very thick, in all the size of a rope, but
through them runs a force which turns heavy flywheels, thousands
of lathes, which hurls along loaded freight trains, which melts stubborn metal in furnaces, which raises freight the weight of a five-
walled village hut and all this all at once. Not five horsepower, but
a million. If these forces leaped from out of the cables which hang
overhead and were in fact to turn into horses, then countless herds
would fill up all the earth. There would remain no place for people.
No, all the same it is a secret which cannot be contained under the
skull. Alongside a secret there always lives a deification.

Weak man has become the master of the planet. The time is
not far distant when he will become the master of the solar system.
In this growing mastery is the high meaning of his life. And for
mastery there is needed—power. And this power human beings have
found in machinery. Without machinery man would vegetate on
the earth as a pitiful being with weak muscles and dull teeth. To
live for great mastery over nature—that means to live for power.
Not only the machine serves the human being, but also the human
being, if he wants to remain himself, is obliged to serve machines.
So thought Ivan Kapitonovich. And who can reproach him for that?
His own son reproached him. He said then at the meeting: "Every
economic advantage must retreat when the matter concerns the
preservation of health and life of a human being."

Ivan Kapitonovich after the meeting detained his son. "Listen,
you rotten humanist! Don't present me as a hater of the human race.
I have brought more good to people than all the poets, and phi-
losophers with whom you have stuffed yourself."

Vadim's look at this minute was absentminded. He answered
softly:

"I often think that if there had been no revolution, you would
have become in your little Lapshevka, if you please, a kulak, a rich
peasant. You yourself, perhaps, would be walking around with rup-
tures, but for certain you would have been driving your workers into
the grave."

This was too much. The snot-nose knew about kulaks only in
books. He had spit in his father's very soul. For a long time they
parted.

34

Deryabin Hospital. The famous professor, who founded it at
the end of the last century, had not even dreamed that it would become a city inside a city. Buildings, buildings, squat structures, little
streets and blind alleys, covered with virgin snow.

Ivan Kapitonovich, gripping in his hand his son's cap, wandered drunkenly, running into entryways, behind which there were no signs of life until he managed to drag himself to the door which had over it the sign "Reception Room."

The intern there, a lad in a white robe, with a professional equilibrium, stared at Ivan Kapitonovich who was covered over with snow. No, no one had been brought from the chemical combine. No, there could be no mistake. They would have informed him without any doubt.

He looked into the face of Ivan Kapitonovich and was embarrassed.

"Sit down, if you please . . . I will go right now and call. I will find out everything. Please sit down."

In ten minutes he returned.

"The Eleventh Polyclinic . . . that's on Second Kozhukhovsky . . ."

"Is he there?" Ivan Kapitonovich asked.

The doctor was a little hesitant with his answer:

"There . . . They brought one from the chemical factory."

They had brought one—and there had been one victim only—there could be no mistake.

And again the Moskvich dashed through the streets of the city. Again the holiday lights, people, people, machines . . .

At the chemical factory there had been one victim! At the control room he had received that news calmly. Of course, it would have been better without any victims at all, but if he had known ahead of time that there would be a victim all the same he would have given the order to cut off the power! One victim compensates for many misfortunes. One victim can save the situation . . .

And this victim—his own son!

Dimka . . . He stood on his knees in the middle of the room in just his nightshirt, frowning, rolling a tin can along the floor. He rolled it along just a little bit, and felt under his little hand that the can was not where it was before. It had moved. Again he rolled it and again he felt for it—and it wasn't there. And he, the father, looked at the concentrated little face: That three-year-old tyke was not amusing himself but pondering and not about ordinary things. The can was not there and a second ago it was here. It was possible to feel it with his hand. Now there was just an empty space. Into his childish mind began to enter a vague comprehension of space and time. A helpless human child-thing . . . Ivan Kapitonovich stood, astonished: This was it—a human being appeared, a thought appeared.

Dimka . . . soon afterwards he had fallen seriously ill of scarlet fever. They thought he would not recover. On one early sunny morning he had opened his eyes and with difficulty had opened his lips which had stuck together:

"Mama . . ."

But his mother, who hadn't shut her eyes all night, was sleeping. Ivan Kapitonovich could not restrain himself, took the baby in his arms and felt in them the strong, rough, heavy, brittle bones, the warm life. His son's head hung on his father's shoulder, and Ivan Kapitonovich carried about the room the light little body and grew cold from horror: What if he had died, what if he could never again feel with his hands the brittle little bones, could not experience happiness from the fact that the hot head of his son lay powerless on his shoulder, next to his rough cheeks?

Dimka . . . When he had grown up, gone off to school, they had grown apart from each other. Ivan Kapitonovich was constantly busy. Much therefore in his son had seemed to him incomprehensible. Incomprehensible why he had run away from home that time and spent the night at the railway station. Incomprehensible why he had not continued his studies in order to get an advanced degree . . .

One victim . . . Dimka! The little baby hand, which rolled the can, the thought which was born in the childish head, the brittle little bones, the life which lay warm underneath them, the incomprehensible acts—and all of this was wrapped up in one word "son."

No more life, no more thought, no more human being—in the world there was a breach, a gap! When there is a ring at the door Nadya will not say any more: "Here is Dimochka." He won't put in his appearance any more, rosy-cheeked, restrained, a small boy and a grown-up simultaneously. Just an hour ago he had sat at the telephone and waited for the call. He would have a child, but he would not know about it. A little more than an hour ago there had been a human being, and now he was no longer. Unbelievable! Impossible! A nightmare!

But his cap lay on his father's knees. His cap which fell from the stretcher. The fingers felt the caressing fur.

Dimka was no longer. At the price of his life, he, his father had saved the city from catastrophe. He was victorious, throwing to blind chance one victim, only one!

"To the New Year! To new happiness!"

For Dimka this year would not come. Reconcile yourself to it: he was a victim!

35

The office of the duty doctor gleamed comfortingly with white—a white table, white stools, a white couch, and on white walls posters:

"Protect yourself against grippe," "Hygiene is a guarantee of health" ... The woman doctor was dressed in a spotless white robe. Under the coquettish little cap, white as snow, there were dark deep eyes, eyes which could stop one on the street, which would then be long-remembered with a tearing feeling of loss: Why weren't these eyes always nearby, why did you not have the luck to see them every day? The eyes of a woman with a great talent of understanding, forgiving, loving, of self-sacrifice in the name of good. Beside them even the banal posters "Protect yourself..." touched the soul with their concern: protect yourself, good people, from the grippe, from lack of cleanliness, from infection, protect yourself and others.

The duty doctor immediately understood that questions were superfluous—an unnecessary cruelty. She called the nurse and quietly said:

"Accompany him, Tonya."

The nurse pulled on over her robe an overcoat, changed at the threshold from felt slippers to felt boots, and with a toss of her head invited Ivan Kapitonovich: "Let's go." The neat felt boots of the nurse loudly squeaked on the powdered snow of the hospital courtyard. Ivan Kapitonovich's entire body was disobedient, heavy as stones. He could hardly keep up with the nurse. "Squeak! squeak! squeak!"—he heard ahead of himself. One step, another step, still another. They are taking him to Vadim. In a moment he will see him. And Vadim just that day had brought a bouquet of roses... And in his childhood he had loved ice cream very much... "Squeak! squeak!" The courtyard came to an end and then a few steps further ..

And beyond the hospital wall, beyond the roofs of the neighboring buildings on some street or another, in sections there flashed out the persuasive sign: "Cross the street ... (pause) Only ... (pause) On the green light!" The sign held for a minute in all its shininess and color, and then went out.

The squeaking of the felt boots ahead stopped. Quiet. "Cross the street ... Only ..."

Steps leading down into the earth, a door into some kind of a cellar. The nurse stood and waited for Ivan Kapitonovich, hiding her face in the raised collar of her overcoat. She opened the door and shouted:

"Stepan!"

In the dim light someone's shadow staggered.

"Stepan, this person has come to see the one whom they recently brought." She pointed her head at Ivan Kapitonovich: "Go on in." She herself hurriedly turned back and her felt boots quickly squeaked along the snow: Quick, quick, to get away from someone else's misfortune, from someone else's grief.

Ivan Kapitonovich went down the stairway, he crossed the threshold and saw before him in the dark corridor a massive figure.

Even in the meager light of a dusty little lamp in its wire netting there was visible the unhealthy yellowness of a swollen face, red eyelids, a broad turned-up nose pierced with nostrils. And this nose was the only thing on that visage not covered with a rusty scum of tough beard. The cellar creature stared stupidly and indifferently at Ivan Kapitonovich.

Ivan Kapitonovich remembered the eyes of the woman doctor. Deep, sensitive, eyes which understood everything, compassion, the thoughtful posters: "Protect yourself . . ." All of that remained up there above. There, to the best of their ability, they struggled for life, for health, they protected human beings. Living people are forced to make a place for the dead—and it is here. And there before him was the doorkeeper of death. He was accustomed to human grief. There wasn't one drop either of sympathy or enmity on his watery physiognomy . . .

And then the improbable took place—the doorkeeper of death groveled: "Come in . . . Right here . . . Careful . . . There's a step there . . . Everything here is always in complete order. We know our business . . . We can carry out all the preparations so that everything will be fitting and proper . . ." He whistled and awkwardly crowded with his side Ivan Kapitonovich who shuddered from horror and repulsion. He understood: he had on a good quality overcoat, soft gloves, a cap made from expensive lambskin, and, by his experience, the guardian of the corpses knew that people stricken with grief are not miserly, are generous in their gifts.

"We'll wash him well, we'll prepare everything so that he'll look just as though he were alive . . . Noble . . ."

The employee opened the door. There was a low stone ceiling with peeling plaster, naked walls, and broad plank benches. On them there were two corpses in indifferent nakedness—one couldn't any longer call it shameless nakedness.

"Come over here. Come here, you can see better . . ."

The closer corpse to Ivan Kapitonovich was an old woman and the other . . . The other was not Vadim.

In the courtyard Ivan Kapitonovich lost his strength. He leaned against the rough frozen wall, overcoming the nausea which was rising upward toward his throat. And in the courtyard, sprinkled with snow, there was quiet. It was the steady, calm quiet which exists only next to where people are living, when you know that right beside you, behind thick walls, there are sitting happy people in warmth and coziness. Several lights were burning on various floors. There stood trees powdered with hoarfrost. Through the lace of the iron fence the light from the street lanterns was piercing.

And over the roofs in the heaven: "Cross the street . . . (pause) only . . . (pause) on the green light!" And somewhere the New Year lights were blazing at full force. Somewhere people in party clothes were celebrating: "To the New Year, to new happiness!" Nevertheless life was the master on earth . . . Could it possibly be that Vadim could return to this life? Could it possibly be that it had been a mistake?

Something fell at his feet. Ivan Kapitonovich bent over with difficulty. It was the cap . . . It was Vadim's cap which had fallen from his hand . . . And right away his weakness passed. His heart beat loud. Ivan Kapitonovich crossed the courtyard in a run, flew up the stairway in a run, rushed into the office of the doctor. With surprise and fear dark eyes stared out from under the white little cap.

"Per . . . please permit me to phone."

"Yes, if you please . . ."

Holding back his impatience, he carefully dialed the number. There was no answer for a long time and then finally:

"Yes, we're listening . . . Vadim Sokovin . . . Sokovin, if you please . . ." There was silence. His heart stopped.

"He was just here. I am afraid that he just went home . . . No, here he is! I'm giving him the phone."

A voice spoke out which was tired and ecstatically, painfully familiar: "Yes, who is this? Oh, it's you, father . . ."

"Dimka . . . Dim . . . I am coming for you right now."

When Ivan Kapitonovich appeared at the Moskvich waiting next to the hospital fence both the husband and the wife stared with horror at his face. During these minutes he had been transformed: His eyes were sunken, his cheekbones had become sharper, in his lips there had appeared something inarticulate, helpless.

On hearing that Vadim was alive and healthy, that a mistake had taken place, he and she, seating themselves back in the car, continued to look with fright at Ivan Kapitonovich.

36

And so they sat in the crowded machine. They sat and kept quiet. And there ahead in the cold night spread the city—an accumulation of countless lights.

"Sanka had two children already," Vadim let drop.

Ivan Kapitonovich painfully knitted his brows at these words.

Sanka had two children and a wife. Ivan Kapitonovich did not remember Sanka. He didn't know his wife at all. But he now knew what this woman must be suffering. She would come in first to the quiet white office of the duty doctor, see the posters on the walls—"Protect yourself . . ." —feel on herself the look of the doctor, the deep, good, helpless eyes. And then she would descend, and then

that person from the cellar would meet her . . . And she would swallow her grief to the last drop. She could not count on a mistake . . .
And the flashing sign over the rooftops of the apartment houses
would turn on and off, informing pedestrians that they should cross
the street only on the green light. And life all around would go forward, as it goes forward. And people, paying no attention to her
grief, would begin to have a good time, to drink, to raise a toast . . .
And she would have to worry about the children. There were two of
them . . .

He did not know how this woman looked. He had no idea what
kind of a face she had. He did not know anything about her character. *But he could have been in her place!* He understood her, he
ached for her. He understood her in the way in which one can only
understand oneself. He ached as one can ache only with one's own
pain. Neither an acquaintanceship of many years, nor a blood kinship, could have made her any closer. Close! Should he now step
aside from her, going no further than compassion, even though it
was sincere, even though it was warm. No, all his life long, remembering this, he would knit his brows the same way. A close person
in an understood misfortune! How could she be helped? With what?
Should she be sought out, visited, should something be done for her?
Something . . . What a philanthropist! Ivan Kapitonovich was silent.
He did not know whether Vadim would understand. Maybe he was
thinking: the old man has gotten sentimental . . .

And on the front seat the owners of the Moskvich had their own
conversation: "Something is rattling."

"It's the handbrake, I already told you."

"Ah, the brake . . ."

The city grew in front of them. The lights fell into contours.
The outlines of the first apartment houses emerged in front of them.

All four got out at the entrance. The owners of the Moskvich
had happy relief on their broad faces. The mistress of the Moskvich
had an embarrassed face, shy and also happy. One after the other
they pressed the hand of Vadim. He gripped it strongly and she
gently. They had done everything that they could for this person,
they were proud of him, just as if they had saved him with their own
hands. Ivan Kapitonovich had the wish to ask: where they worked,
how they live, did not they need help? But right there he stopped
himself: to help, to thank, to reduce everything to calculation—you
scratch our back and we'll scratch yours, or we won't let you be sorry.

"Thank you," said Ivan Kapitonovich and he shook their hand.
The Moskvich dove behind an enormous autobus and again made
its appearance, already in the middle of the street. Inside it, in all
probability, again there had begun the worried conversation about

brakes, about shock absorbers, about the fact that "the cams are knocking . . ."

A chance encounter, and neither Ivan Kapitonovich nor Vadim would ever, in all probability, see them again.

In front of the door Ivan Kapitonovich suddenly stopped.

"I have to go and see a certain person."

"Whom?"

"I have to . . . You go on in—I'll be back right away."

He opened the door and pushed Vadim into it lightly and heard in passing:

"Here is Dimochka!"

37

The women sat at the little table, in front of the bob-tailed bottle. Bronislava Semyenovna had a red, softened face. His mother had across her cheek a young crimson blush. Elochka stared with a shining look.

"Dimochka, what happiness there is . . ." Bronislava Semyenovna blinked in deep emotion and looked for a handkerchief in her rustling dress.

"Well, my son, I congratulate you." Nadezhda Sergeyevna took hold of Vadim's head and drew it to her and kissed him on the forehead.

"Did she give birth?" Vadim guessed. "A son? A daughter?"

"A little daughter, Dimochka, a little daughter . . ."

"We were already looking for a name for her. Here let me pour something for you. Hold the liqueur glass for me." But instead of being glad Vadim sat down on the chair, holding with trembling fingers the liqueur glass filled to the brim.

"And at the plant . . ." he began, and his voice broke, "one of our workers perished . . . one . . . Sanka Goryaev. I knew him from childhood . . ."

And immediately awkwardness was felt—as if Vadim had said something rude, quite indecent. Bronislava Semyenovna who had still not found in the rustling folds of her dress her handkerchief dropped her eyes ashamed. But it could be felt: she was ashamed not for herself, not for her immodest happiness, but for the lack of tact on the part of Vadim. In the eyes of Nadezhda Sergeyevna there appeared a soft rebuke: "Why this right now?" Only the narrow face of Elochka became still more elongated and on it appeared a curious watchfulness bordering on confusion.

A daughter had been born—this gladness was sacred, a gladness alien to selfishness. His mother and Bronislava Semyenovna were happy not so much for themselves as for Vadim, but he . . . They didn't want to know what he said. They didn't want to hear about some other person's unhappiness. What if there were in the world death, injuries, ruined fates—it was impossible to embrace the infinite. They wanted to keep, preserve their modest gladness which they had just experienced at this table. They had hoped that he would share it, that he would respond to it...

Nadezhda Sergeyevna answered:

"You can't help him... Why?... Just empty suffering."

You can't help? Empty suffering? It was really impossible to help Sanka with anything. But sufferings never pass without leaving their mark. They compel one to think. They make a human being more soft, more responsive, deeper, and was this really so little? Was this empty? To step aside from sufferings, to be ashamed of them— that is to steal from oneself and together with oneself from everyone else also.

But Vadim did not object to his mother's statement. She, that sober woman, brave in her own way, whom he loved, lived within four walls, and she considered it her obligation to guard these walls from the hostility of that boundless world that surrounds them. Someone else perhaps might understand, but not she. She had always divided happiness into her own and that of others.

Vadim raised his liqueur glass and said:

"For Galka's health."

He drank it down. And the women were joyful. They were quite willing to believe that he had understood his mistake, that he had recognized his lack of tact. They talked about the name. Nadezhda Sergeyevna proposed that the daughter be named Tanya.

Elochka moved her chair up to Vadim, attempting to look from below up to his eyes. She was quiet for a time and finally asked in a whisper:

"You were a friend?"

"With whom?"

"With him."

"I never had the chance, Elka... But I would have liked to be."

"You knew him from childhood and didn't have a chance to be friends with him?"

"That's the way it turned out. Probably I wasn't quite up to him. I hadn't grown up that much."

"You are up to anyone," she objected with conviction. "I will always be your friend."

The narrow face, surrounded by luxuriant locks of hair, her thin features and her broadly opened light-colored eyes, questioning, waiting with alarm, devoted with straightforward, clear, immeasurable childish loyalty.

"You—yes. I know that."

"But that's too little for you?"

Yes, loyalty alone is too little for friendship but Elochka could not yet give more. Could she occupy that place which Sanka had occupied in his life?

"I would like to be for you just what he was for me," he answered her in all seriousness.

And Elochka was quiet, thinking about the man whom she had never known.

Vadim also was thoughtful. Nadezhda Sergeyevna and Bronislava Semyenovna talked about what kind of infant clothes should be made and how best things could be arranged for Galka after the maternity home. Vadim thought to himself . . .

Death and birth—in this there is not only the firm strength of life, it's incessancy, the undeviating steadiness of its development. In this is also the complexity of being. If there were no birth there would be no death, there would be no grief, but there would be nothing then by which to measure happiness. It would be absent. The world consists of crying opposites. In the universe alongside cosmic cold—there is the white-hot plasma of the stars. Vadim had nothing to complain about: he had work, he had friends, he had a wife, beautiful, lovely, beloved by him. And now there was a daughter—he had everything, but there were Sanka's children left without a father . . . He, Vadim, is a part of that world which consists of firmly connected opposites. To consider himself happy would mean to shut himself up into himself. And even Bronislava Semyenovna lives not for herself alone but her daughter and her husband. Even she does not shut herself up in herself.

Let there even be only sufferings if there is nothing else left. Let there be sufferings. They do not pass by without leaving their trace.

38

Something had taken place with Vasily Vasilevich, that unobtrusive complacent person. Something was tormenting him. Something had destroyed his equilibrium. Could it possibly be that this secret something would so remain inside him, impinging on no one?

During the hour since they had parted, there had taken place an earthquake. Some kind of strata in his soul had been shaken and had been exposed.

Vasily Vasilevich sat in front of Ivan Kapitonovich in his old faded pajamas. Through the unbuttoned collar could be seen his flat white chest, his prominent collarbones. His face was out of the ordinary. His expression was not the one he wore at work. Over his right brow was a bitter wrinkle. His eyelids were heavy. Under them his eyes gleamed dryly.

Vasily Vasilevich kept quiet. And behind his back the window covered with a tulle curtain brightened and then darkened. And it was as if someone were beating in time on white-hot iron, soft as wax, powerful blows which could not be heard. Finally Vasily Vasilevich said sadly:

"If you had only come to me earlier with such a question."

"When earlier?"

"Well, ten years earlier, even five. Now it's too late."

"Why?"

"Why . . . I just phoned the maternity house . . . You and I are grandfathers."

"Which?"

"A granddaughter . . . We are grandfathers, but we are different. You succeeded in doing at least something, but I just realized that my life has already been lived, yes, and not in the way I wish it had."

"Don't say that . . ."

"Oh please don't say those trite words and phrases: you'll say to me it's early to retire into the reserves, or that we have many cords of wood left to cut . . . But I just today understood: no matter how I try to deceive myself it's nevertheless a fact that somewhere inside myself I am an unsuccessful person. And if you had come to me earlier and asked me: open up your soul . . . Maybe my life and my character also would have come out differently."

"Why did you wait till someone came to you? Why didn't you open up your soul yourself? Why didn't you do it yourself without waiting?"

Vasily Vasilevich grinned ironically.

"One can open up one's soul only to someone who sympathizes with one. And if that person doesn't have any sympathy for you you aren't going to open it."

"I have in my system hundreds of engineers and employees and several thousand workers. Even if I wanted to I couldn't become a friend to all of them. I couldn't get inside the soul of all of them."

"And I don't even insist that you personally should get into my soul . . ."

"You can kill me, but I don't understand—for what are you reproaching me?"

"Well a week ago you said that at the Chernushinsk power station the second turbine should be stopped—because one of its blades is unsteady."

"Well?"

"The fact that the blade is unsteady in the turbine you know, and who is it that works on this turbine?"

"I know them also: Zolotyuk and Shevtsev . . ."

"And how much do you really know about that Zolotyuk? You know his last name, his first name and his patronymic, that he is careless or assiduous, skilled or unskilled in his work. But beyond an evaluation of him as a worker you know nothing. And indeed that is only a little bit of a particle of one human being. Just a little bit! Everyone of us has his attachments, his views, his thoughts and his opinions. Does, for instance, the opinion of Zolotyuk or, let's say, my own, interest you? No Ivan Kapitonovitch, what concern do you have with someone's views and opinions. The blade is unsteady —that is in every way more important. And your indifference does not remain only in you yourself. It is like an infection. It is catching among others as well. The manager Sokovin takes no interest in what constitutes the life of engineer Skoptsev. Skoptsev in his turn doesn't care a damn for the turbine mechanic. Indeed, the only thing that's asked from him is that the blade of the turbine should not be unsteady. And the turbine mechanic Zolotyuk is indifferent to the ashman Ivanov. An e-lek-tric pow-er sys-tem! A *system,* the word itself speaks for itself—meaning something that is in common, mutually connected. The machines are really connected with each other and united. They live organically in the system. But people? People —they fend for themselves . . . They call you an iron-willed organizer. Your steel talent has forged a steel chain. It is sufficiently strong. It doesn't break often. But human nature in its steel rings, forgive me for saying it, is cramped. And the most unpleasant thing of all is the fact that sometimes this is not suspected, considered to be normal. I also considered it so . . . Only today I understood something."

Ivan Kapitonovich sat there with his head bowed. The window flashed and darkened. The New Year sign on the roof of the house next door flashed and died down.

Twenty minutes later they were walking along the street. Both were silent. Both were looking backward into the past, each into his own, both were dissatisfied with it.

And there was the holiday table. The china sparkled. Peppers flamed on their dish. Bottles were pointed in a friendly way at the chandelier which was shining with a steady, reliable light. And there in the middle of the table a hymn to family prosperity, a monument to gluttony, a sacred sacrifice to the holiday—on a broad platter lay a piglet with parsley in his teeth.

Ignat Golubko arrived in time. After the frost and the wind his face burned with crimson. He carried on himself the delicious odor of the smoke of bonfires. Under the table he hid his feet in warm knitted stockings which he borrowed from Nadezhda Sergeyevna: he had rushed out in his best shoes and he had had to walk in the snow up to his knees. Over him as over Ivan Kapitonovich there hung a threat. They faced a grim period of accountings, justifications, scoldings, and official rebukes on their record. And perhaps there would be even greater complications for them. And the chief engineer would not be on the sidelines in this. But Golubko was good-humored . . .

He thought to himself: "Teach them to dance . . . What will happen will happen. One cannot die twice . . . Why distress oneself when others will do it for one . . ."

He looked greedily at the table and wrung his hands. Elochka slyly watched everyone. She jealously observed the expression on each face: how they regarded her father, why did no one consider him a hero? After all, he had to do more than anyone else. He flew off somewhere, he froze, he wandered around in the snow—the first savior. She didn't guess about everything else that had taken place. Sometimes her glance met the glance of Vadim.

For Vadim everything today looked different than it did yesterday. He looked at Elochka with new eyes. She was going to become a human being. It was still not known: what she had in her, whether nature had endowed her with a great mind or a special talent. But one thing was indubitable—her need sincerely to have compassion for others, not to remain indifferent. Ordinary, not so much. But even this not so much people sometimes lose with age. He, Vadim, had the responsibility as a friend, as an ordinary acquaintance, as a human being. He was responsible for her for the memory of Sanka.

The laden table—through the amber of the jelly around it there oozed the tender meat of the sturgeon, the broad soupbowl was filled with salad made with mayonnaise, green peas and crimson carrots rested upon it like jewels—not a salad, but a jeweled crown.

Nadezhda Sergeyevna walked anxiously around her creation, moving something a little bit one way, changing something a little bit—the last brush strokes of the artist.

Bronislava Semyenovna with hidden alarm watched the men: They were not themselves, neither Vasily Vasilevich nor Ivan Kapitonovich. They sat there, making wreaths of smoke with their cigarettes, silent, as if it were not a holiday ahead but a formal meeting. Well, it was understandable: Such an unexpected turn of affairs —and right on New Year's Eve . . .

The laden table. Above the bottles rose bowls with tangerines. They had in them the sun of the south, the odor of unknown ports, and romance of books read in childhood. Nadezhda Sergeyevna looked at her watch and threw up her head like a trumpeter getting ready to give the signal for an attack.

"To the table! To the table!"

But right then the doorbell rang. Who was it that was there, uninvited? Ah, it was Boris Yevgenyevich Shatskikh. He entered sideways looking with embarrassment at the floor, moved away from Nadezhda Sergeyevna and made his way into a corner, in passing glancing at Ivan Kapitonovich.

"To the table! To the table! We're going to be late! Five minutes are left before the New Year!"

Five minutes before New Year and upon Ivan Kapitonovich there descended dishes—the fish in aspic, the tsar's crown of a salad, the bottles, the piglet with the parsley in his mouth and there popped into his mind the passing thought: "Drinks... How indeed it is strange, however." The time which flows down upon one is too significant a thing to be greeted only with piglet baked in the oven and a whole row of bottles to be emptied.

In five minutes the New Year, three hundred and sixty-five new days. How shall one live them? It is worth pondering.

Bibliography

Contemporary Russian Literary Works Available in English Translation—with Brief Descriptions and Annotations

This Bibliography makes no claim to completeness of coverage, but it is a fairly full list of Russian literary works written in the 1960's and the latter part of the 1950's which have been published in English translation either in England or America—or by the Russians themselves in Moscow. There has been no effort to discriminate in selection of items for inclusion on the basis of quality of translation. There are some excellent translations of high literary quality—all too few—and also some pedestrian, hurried, even execrable translations—all too many—as well. There has been no particular effort to discriminate in the selection of items for inclusion on the basis of the quality or importance of the works either. There are excellent works to be found in this list, and also much run-of-the-mill "socialist-realism," and some outright trash. Certain categories of writing have been largely omitted—but not entirely: works for juveniles, science fiction, literature about Lenin, and by and large the works of Soviet authors who do not write in Russian as their native language, in other words, literature of national minorities.

At any rate it is hoped that the Bibliography will be of some assistance to students and others who may be interested in particular writers or particular subjects in contemporary Russian literature. And to this end some brief annotations on particular works and writers have been included wherever they seemed relevant.

The names of Russian authors are transliterated into English in varying ways by different translators and editors. Thus one can find such varying versions as Vasilii Aksenov, Vasily Aksyonov, and Vasili Aksyonov. And the same variety is true of virtually every other Russian writer who has been plentifully translated. Ordinarily, in this Bibliography I have adhered in my listings to the spellings of writers' names used in the particular works listed, giving the various versions as given. This is useful in order to facilitate the task of readers who may wish to look up individual writers and works in library catalogues. However, it was obviously not practical to do this when, as in the case of Yevgeny Yevtushenko, it would have meant that works by him would have been listed, some of them, under the letter *E*—for Evgeni Evtushenko—and others under *Y*. The reader should therefore be advised that in the case of Yevtushenko (or any other writer whose last name begins with *Ye*) listings in library

382

or periodical catalogues or other bibliographies may be found instead under the letter *E*.

Titles included in the Bibliography are those published or scheduled for publication up to the end of 1962 in the United Kingdom and up to mid-September of 1963 in the United States.

I wish to express gratitude for the assistance given me in collecting titles for this Bibliography and for running down details on individual items to Mr. Peter Collins, of George G. Harrap & Co. in London, and to Mrs. Elizabeth Shub, of New York City.

Abramov, Fyodor, *The New Life: A Day on a Collective Farm,* translated by George Reavey. New York: Grove Press, 1963.
A short novel, published as a special book-length supplement in *Evergreen Review,* No. 30, 1963, paperbound. On contemporary farm life—the seamy side included. Originally titled *Around and About* in Russian.

Abramov, Fyodor, *One Day in the "New Life,"* translated by David Floyd. New York: Frederick A. Praeger, 1963. 174 pp.
Same as the previous with a slightly different title.

Adamovich, Alexander, *War Under the Roofs,* translated by N. and A. Johnstone, in *Soviet Literature Monthly,* No. 8, 1962, pp. 90–119.
A novel by a Belorussian writer: this selection consists of individual chapters.

Agapov, Boris, *Beginnings,* translated by Asya Shoyett, in *Soviet Literature Monthly,* No. 8, 1963, pp. 111–22.
In essence an article, or documentary story, on Soviet science and scientists.

Akhmadulina, Bella, *Volcanoes,* translated by W. H. Auden, in *Encounter,* April 1963, p. 53.
She was Yevtushenko's first wife. She is one of Russia's most talented younger poets, more talented, some consider, than her better-known ex-husband.

Akhmatova, Anna, *From the White Flight,* translated by S. Burnshaw, in *Poetry,* September 1961, p. 377.
A poem.

Akhmatova, Anna, *Two Russian Poems,* translated by Babette Deutsch, in *Columbia University Forum,* IV, 3, 1961, pp. 19–20.

Akhmatova, Anna, *Two Verses (1956–57),* in the *Penguin Book of Russian Verse,* edited by D. Obolensky, Harmondsworth, and Baltimore, Md.: Penguin Books, pp. 324–25.
The original Russian and a prose translation. The selection from Akhmatova also includes half a dozen of her earlier works.

Aksenov, Vasilii, *Colleagues,* translated by A. Brown. London: Putnam, 1962. 240 pp.
A short novel about three contemporary young Russian doctors.

Aksenov, Vasilii, *A Starry Ticket,* translated by A. Brown. London: Putnam, 1962. 224 pp.
A short novel about contemporary Moscow high-school graduates seeking a way in life.

Aksenov, Vasilii, *A Ticket to the Stars,* translated by Andrew R. MacAndrew. New York: Signet Books, 1963. 176 pp. A paperback edition.

Aksyonov, Vasily, *Colleagues,* translated by Margaret Wettlin. Moscow: Foreign Languages Publishing House, undated. 317 pp. Paperback edition. Also in *Soviet Literature Monthly,* No. 4, 1961.

Aksyonov, Vasili, *Halfway to the Moon,* translated by Ronald Hingley, in *Encounter,* April 1963, pp. 59–68.
A short story about a Soviet lumberjack on a strange kind of a vacation.

Alexeyev, Mikhail, *Cherry Pool,* translated by Hilda Perham, in *Soviet Literature Monthly,* No. 6, 1963, pp. 40–53.
A short story published first in 1962. About wartime on a collective farm.

Alyoshin, Samuil, *Alone,* translated by Hugh McLean and Walter N. Vickery, in *Year of Protest, 1956.* New York: Vintage-Random House, 1961, pp. 37–115.
A play posing an acute family dilemma—divorce and a woman alone.

Amlinsky, Vladimir, *Late-Night Picture Show,* translated by Ralph Parker, in *Soviet Literature Monthly,* No. 12, 1961, pp. 103–16.
A short story about the virgin lands.

Andreyev, Vladimir (pseudonym), *Gemailis, and Other Tales from Stalin's Russia,* translated by Fred P. Berry. Chicago: Regnery, 1963.
The author was a former Soviet secret police officer.

Antonov, Sergei, *Alyonka,* translated by Robert Daglish, in *Soviet Literature Monthly,* No. 10, 1961, pp. 50–103.
A story about the virgin lands—and a long truck trip.

Antonov, Sergei, *It Happened in Penkovo,* translated by O. Shartse. Moscow: Foreign Languages Publishing House, 1959. 209 pp.

Arbuzov, Alexei, *Irkutsk Story,* translated by Rosa Prokofieva, in *Soviet Literature Monthly,* No. 7, 1960, pp. 84–146.
A popular play, somewhat in the Thornton Wilder style (*Our Town*), on the contemporary Soviet East and ordinary young people.

Ardamatskii, Vasilii, *No Rosy Haze,* translated by L. Kolesnikov. Moscow: Foreign Languages Publishing House, 1958. 118 pp.
A story. Original Russian title was *Orphan.*

Argunova, Nora, *Brassy,* translated by Jacob Guralsky, in *Soviet Literature Monthly,* No. 2, 1961, pp. 124–29.
A short story about a Russian colt.

Arzak, Nikolai, *This is Moscow Speaking,* translated by John Richardson, in *Dissonant Voices in Soviet Literature,* edited by Patricia Blake and Max Hayward, New York: Pantheon Books, 1962, pp. 262–306.
This is a satire on the Soviet government's attitude to public opinion—and was allegedly sent out of the Soviet Union illegally by a professional writer using a pseudonym. It was initially published in the Polish newspaper in Paris, *Kultura.*

Aseyev, Nikolai, *Verses: The End of Summer; Romeo and Juliet; The Blue Hussars Are Riding; The Sky,* translated by Herbert Marshall, in *Soviet Literature Monthly,* No. 5, pp. 116–20.

Asayev, Nikolai, *Verses: Lenin's Time; Bullfinches; Happiness; A Couple Goes By; The Nightingale,* translations by Irina Zheleznova, Dorian Rottenberg, Herbert Marshall, in *Soviet Literature Monthly,* No. 4, 1962, pp. 109–15.

Astafiev, Victor, *Stories: Geese on the Ice; Zlodeika,* translated by George Hanna, in *Soviet Literature Monthly,* pp. 104–10.
Two short stories about animals.

Auerbach, Elizaveta, *K. S. Stanislavsky, Children, I Believe in Love,* translated by Asya Shoyett, in *Soviet Literature Monthly,* No. 2, 1963, pp. 123–28.
Short short stories—or perhaps they are reminiscences—of an actress-writer.

Azhayev, Vasily, *Prologue to Life,* translated by Ralph Parker, in *Soviet Literature Monthly,* No. 9, 1962, pp. 3–136.
A novel—production and chemistry.

Baklanov, Grigori, *The Cost of War,* translated by Margaret Wettlin, in *Soviet Literature Monthly,* No. 5, 1962, pp. 95–106.
A story about Germany immediately after the war.

Baklanov, Grigorii, *The Foothold,* translated by R. Ainsztein. London: Chapman and Hall, 1962. 221 pp.

Baklanov, Grigori, Yuri Bondarev, and Vladimir Tendryakov, *Forty-Nine Days,* translated by Margaret Wettlin, in *Soviet Literature Monthly,* No. 7, 1962, pp. 3–56.
A screen play on the subject of Soviet sailors on a barge adrift in the Pacific and of their rescue by Americans.

Bedarev, Oleg, *Grazing the Horses at Night,* in *Soviet Short Stories,* edited by Avrahm Yarmolinsky. New York: Doubleday-Anchor, 1960, pp. 258–70.
Story of a boy on a collective farm.

Bedny, Boris, *Lovers' Seat,* translated by Gladys Evans, in *Soviet Literature Monthly,* No. 4, 1962, pp. 93–102.
This is an episode from a novel entitled *Girls,* dealing with contemporary Russians.

Bek, Aleksandr, *Berezhkov, the Story of an Inventor,* translated by B. Isaacs. Moscow: Foreign Languages Publishing House, 1957. 519 pp.
A novel about a contemporary Soviet inventor and the psychological problems of technical creativity—originally published in Russian in 1956.

Bek, Aleksandr A., *Volokolamsk Highway,* translated by Eve Manning, in *Soviet Literature Monthly,* No. 6, 1963, pp. 53–79.
The original novel, *Volokolamsk Highway,* published in 1943–44, has been recently supplemented or completed with additional stories from which this selection represents some chapters.

Belyaev, Aleksandr, *The Amphibian,* translated by L. Kolesnikov. Moscow: Foreign Languages Publishing House, 1959. 285 pp.
Russian title: *The Human Amphibian.*

Belyaev, Vadim, *Musya and Masha,* translated by Gladys Evans, in *Soviet Literature Monthly,* No. 4, 1962, pp. 104–14.
A story about contemporary factory workers.

Berggolts, Olga, *Daytime Stars,* translated by Eve Manning, in *Soviet Literature Monthly,* No. 12, 1961, pp. 26–91.
Daytime Stars is a book of the author's notes on her own life from childhood up to the siege of her native Leningrad. This selection is the third or last of the three parts completed up to publication of this translation. A sequel to it was being written at the time.

Bikchentayev, Anver, *Short Stories: Once a Teacher; Keep the Lights Burning,* translated by Natalia Lukoshkova, in *Soviet Literature Monthly,* No. 4, 1962, pp. 102–9.
A Bashkirian writer who writes in Russian—his two stories here translated appeared in his book *Keep the Lights Burning* in 1961. They are about contemporary Bashkiria.

Blynsky, Dmitri, *Bird-Cherry, Debut,* translated by Margaret Wettlin, in *Soviet Literature Monthly,* No. 7, 1960, pp. 149–50.
Two short poems.

Bogomolov, Vladimir, *First Love,* translated by Mary Mackler, in *Soviet Literature Monthly,* No. 6, 1963, pp. 112–15.
This is a short story about love in war.

Bokov, Victor, *Winter. An Anthology of Russian Verse, 1812–1960,* edited by Avrahm Yarmolinsky. New York: Doubleday-Anchor, 1961, pp. 231–32.
A poem dated 1956.

Bondarev, Yuri, *Artillery Support,* translated by Hilda Perham, in *Soviet Literature Monthly,* No. 6, 1963, pp. 92–112.
The excerpt here translated represents one chapter from a war novel published in 1957.

Bondarev, Yuri, *The Last Shots,* translated by Natalia Lukoshkova, in *Soviet Literature Monthly,* No. 8, 1960, pp. 3–134.
This is the full text of a novel dealing with the last months of the war.

Borodulin, Rygor, *Winter,* translated by Joe Wallace, in *Soviet Literature Monthly,* No. 8, 1962, p. 146.
A short poem.

Borzenko, Sergei, *Taking a Chance,* translated by Gladys Evans, in *Soviet Literature Monthly,* No. 11, 1961, pp. 109–14.
A short story about the building of a hydroelectric station.

Brovka, Petrus, *Verses: Why Did I Become a Poet; The Leaf; Pledge of the Heart,* translated by Tom Botting and Irina Zheleznova, in *Soviet Literature Monthly,* No. 8, 1962, pp. 135–39.
Poems by a Belorussian poet.

Bryl, Yanka, *The Birches White with Hoar-Frost,* translated by George H. Hanna, in *Soviet Literature Monthly,* No. 8, 1962, pp. 5–20.
A Belorussian farm story by a Belorussian writer.

Bubennov, Mikhail, *Eagle Steppe,* translated by Eve Manning, in *Soviet Literature Monthly,* Nos. 4, 5, and 6, 1960.
A novel about the virgin lands.

Bykov, Vasily. *The Third Rocket,* translated by Robert Daglish, in *Soviet Literature Monthly,* No. 8, 1962.
A war novel which came out in early 1962—by a Belorussian writer. This is an excerpt.

Bykova, Elena, *Ordynka Street,* translated by Eve Manning, in *Soviet Literature Monthly,* No. 5, 1963, pp. 113–20.
A sketch of a well-known Moscow street by a woman writer and chemist.

Chakovskii, Aleksandr, *A Year of Life,* translated by S. Rosenberg. Moscow: Foreign Languages Publishing House, 1958. 254 pp.
A novel about the arctic.

Chakovsky, Alexander, *Light of a Distant Star,* translated by Ralph Parker, in *Soviet Literature Monthly,* No. 7, 1963, pp. 3–97.
A novel, about Russia in the postwar period—a search for a missing person. The writer is editor of the *Literary Gazette,* and this novel was highly praised by official critics.

Chaplina, Vera, *Zoo Babies,* translated by I. Litvinova. Moscow: Foreign Languages Publishing House, 1956. 208 pp.

Chaplina, Vera, *Scamp and Crybaby,* translated by I. Litvinova. Moscow: Foreign Languages Publishing House, 1959. 24 pp.

Chukovsky, Kornei, *From Two to Five.* Berkeley: University of California Press, 1963.

Chukhovsky, Kornei, *The Pied Piper of Peredelkino,* translated by M. Morton, in *Horn Book Magazine,* Oct. 1962, pp. 458–68.
Chukovsky is a renowned children's writer.

Chukovskii, Kornei, *The Telephone,* translated by D. Rottenberg. Moscow: Foreign Languages Publishing House, 1960. 16 pp. Juvenile.

Chukhovskii, Nikolai, *Baltic Skies,* translated by R. Daglish. Moscow: Foreign Languages Publishing House, 1957. 632 pp.

Chukhovsky, Nikolai, *The Tramp,* translated by Walter N. Vickery, in *Dissonant Voices in Soviet Literature,* edited by Patricia Blake and Max Hayward. New York: Pantheon Books, 1962, pp. 158–85.
A story published in 1956 about a would-be capitalist in the period after the Revolution.

Dudin, Mikhail, *Verses: A Song of Bridges; The Lake Enframes the Dawn-Lit Sky; I Watched With You the World Go By,* translated by Archie Johnstone, in *Soviet Literature Monthly,* No. 5, 1960, pp. 108–12.
Short poems.

Dudintsev, Vladimir, *A New Year's Tale,* translated by Gabriella Azrael. New York: E. P. Dutton, 1960. Paperback.
This is a short story packaged as a separate book. It is remarkable and interesting as a fantastic allegory with political meaning. The same work was published in England, in a different translation: V. Dudintsev, *A New Year's Tale,* translated by Max Hayward. London: Hutchinson, 1960. 48 pp.

Dudintsev, Vladimir, *Not by Bread Alone,* translated by E. Bone. New York: E. P. Dutton, 1957. 512 pp.
Also published in England by Hutchinson in the same year. This sensational novel became a *cause célèbre* in the Soviet Union in late 1957. It is a bitter attack on the brutality of bureaucracy—in the form of a tale of the trials and tribulations, including exile in Siberia, of a lone inventor named Lopatkin, who had pitted himself against the mandarins of Soviet science and a prominent official named Drozdov. Loptakin triumphed in the end, but Drozdov and his crowd were not defeated. The struggle will continue, the author indicates.

Ehrenburg, Ilya, *A Change of Season,* translated by Manya Harari and Humphrey Higgins. New York: Alfred A. Knopf, 1962. 297 pp.
This edition brings together two related novellas of Ehrenburg, *The Thaw* and *The Spring.* The first of these gave its name to the whole post-Stalin epoch to 1957. Published in Russia in 1954 it was a depiction of the atmosphere in early 1953 among the Russian intelligentsia in a provincial industrial city—with stress on the hopes for change in the air immediately after Stalin's death. It blazed trails in that it was frank and outspoken about many things previously unmentionable in literature. It was severely criticized, but Ehrenburg stuck to his guns and published the sequel, entitled *Spring,* the next year, 1955. *The Thaw* was first published in America, in a different translation, by Regnery in Chicago. The English edition of *The*

Thaw was published by Harvill Press, 1955, and of *The Spring* by Macgibbon and Kee, 1961.

Ehrenburg, Ilya, *Chekhov, Stendhal and Other Essays,* selected and with an Introduction by Harrison E. Salisbury, translated by Anna Bostock, Yvonne Kapp, and Tatiana Shebunina. New York: Alfred A. Knopf, 1963. 291 pp.
Included in this well-organized, well-selected, and edited volume are nearly a dozen of Ehrenburg's important literary essays, etc., of the post-Stalin period, in which this senior Russian writer sets forth his liberal platform. Individual essays from among these have been published elsewhere in other translations.

Ehrenburg, Ilya, *People and Life, 1891–1921,* translated by Anna Bostock and Yvonne Kapp. New York: Alfred A. Knopf, 1962. 434 pp.
This volume contains the first two parts of Ehrenburg's valuable and interesting literary memoirs, which have been severely attacked by official critics in the Soviet Union but whose publication nevertheless continues. It is the publisher's intention to bring out the rest of the memoirs as soon as possible. There is an appendix of names mentioned and an index.

Ehrenburg, Ilya, *People, Years, Life,* translated by I. A. Langnas, in *Odyssey Review,* vol. 2, no. 4, December 1962, pp. 9–127.
These excerpts from Ehrenburg's memoirs, taken from the installments published in *Novy Mir* in May and June 1962, contain some of the most interesting parts of the work—describing the civil war in Spain, the great purge or *Yezhovshchina* in Russia in 1937 and 1938, and the years preceding the Nazi attack on Russia in 1941.

Fedin, Konstantin, *The Bonfire,* translated by Ralph Parker, in *Soviet Literature Monthly,* Nos. 1 and 2, 1962. Selected chapters.
This novel by a distinguished Russian writer is the third volume of a trilogy which began with *Early Joys* and continued with *No Ordinary Summer. The Bonfire* deals with the same characters in the summer of 1941. The *Soviet Literature* selections include a large number of chapters of the work.

Fedoseev, Grigorii A., *Mountain Trails,* translated by G. H. Hanna. Moscow: Foreign Languages Publishing House, 1958. 494 pp.

Feuerabend, Yevgeni, *Verses: The Foundry District; New Cities; The Rainbow,* translated by Tom Botting and Dorian Rottenberg, in *Soviet Literature Monthly,* No. 8, 1960, pp. 135–36.

Firsov, Vladimir, *The Sun Appeared,* translated by Dorian Rottenberg, in *Soviet Literature Monthly,* No. 7, 1960, pp. 154–55.
A short poem.

Fomenko, Vladimir, *The Earth Remembers,* translated by Robert Daglish, in *Soviet Literature Monthly,* No. 5, 1962, pp. 3–76.
Chapters 14 through 20 of a novel about the problems of rural people being forced to move because of a hydroelectric dam.

Forsh, Olga, *Palace and Prison,* translated by F. Solasko. Moscow: Foreign Languages Publishing House, 1958. 261 pp.

Fyodorov, Vasily, *Art,* in *An Anthology of Russian Verse, 1812–1960,* edited by Avrahm Yarmolinsky. New York: Doubleday-Anchor, 1961, p. 238. A very brief poem dated 1958.

Fyodorov, Vasili, *There is My Home Country,* translated by Jack Lindsay, in *Soviet Literature Monthly,* No. 2, 1962, pp. 96–98. A poem.

Fyodorov, Vasily, *Two Verses: Wreckage of War; The Sculptor,* translated by Margaret Wettlin, in *Soviet Literature Monthly,* No. 6, 1960, pp. 122–24.

Fyodorov, Vasily, *Hearts: The Wrathful Fear Not . . . ; To My Verse; And This I Saw . . . ,* translated by Louis Zelikoff, Gladys Evans, and Irina Zheleznova, in *Soviet Literature Monthly,* No. 7, 1962, pp. 103–7. Poems.

Ganina, Maya, *Matvei and Shurka,* translated by Natalia Lukoshkova, in *Soviet Literature Monthly,* No. 1, 1962, pp. 105–23. A story on Siberian workers.

Garshin, Vsevolod, *The Scarlet Flower,* translated by B. Isaacs. Moscow: Foreign Languages Publishing House, 1959. 279 pp.

Gernet, Nina, and Grigori Yagdfeld, *Katie and the Crocodile,* translated by Margaret Wettlin, in *Soviet Literature Monthly,* No. 9, 1960, pp. 3–56. A cinema story for children. Also published by the Foreign Languages Publishing House as a separate book—translated by F. Solasko, 1959. 92 pp.

Gladkov, Fedor, *Restless Youth,* translated by R. Parker and V. Scott. Moscow: Foreign Languages Publishing House, 1958. 266 pp.

Glebov, Anatoli, *Pravdokha,* translated by Eve Manning, in *Soviet Literature Monthly,* No. 10, 1962, pp. 87–118. Memoirs of a journalist about a remarkable man—from a collection of similar stories entitled *Tales of the Strong.*

Gonchar, Oles, *Man and Arms,* translated by George Hanna, in *Soviet Literature Monthly,* Nos. 6 and 7, 1961. Boys, girls, and war—a novel.

Gonchar, Oles, *Usman and Martha,* translated by Asya Shoyett, in *Soviet Literature Monthly,* No. 10, 1960, pp. 110–16. A war romance.

Gorev, Gleb, *In a New Suburb of Moscow,* translated by Leonid Lamm, in *Soviet Literature Monthly,* No. 8, 1961, pp. 114–30. A series of brief vignettes of contemporary life in a new Moscow housing development.

Goryshin, Gleb, *Hullo, Sister!* translated by Dorian Rottenberg, in *Soviet Literature Monthly*, No. 7, 1962, pp. 112–20.
A forester's story—on the Soviet East.

Gouzenko, Igor, *The Fall of a Titan*, translated by Mervyn Black. New York: W. W. Norton and Co., 1954. 629 pp. Published in England by Cassell, 1954, and Hamilton, 1960.
This novel advances the thesis, as the foundation of its plot, that Maxim Gorki was assassinated on the orders of Stalin.

Granin, Daniil, *Those Who Seek*, translated by R. Daglish. Moscow: Foreign Languages Publishing House, 1956. 538 pp.
A novel.

Granin, Dmitri, *A Personal Opinion*, translated by Valentin Eyre, in *Bitter Harvest*, edited by Edward Stillman. New York: Frederick A. Praeger, 1959, pp. 260 ff.
A story of a bureaucrat in science who has irrevocably lost his personal integrity. Also included in *Year of Protest, 1956*, edited by McLean and Vickery.

Grekova, Irina, *Beyond the Gates*, translated by Eve Manning, in *Soviet Literature Monthly*, No. 4, 1963, pp. 61–86.
A story about young scientists and their uninhibited, free-thinking lives "inside the gates" of their guarded institute, in which they have complete control over access of the outer world—and its political controls—to them.

Gribachev, Nikolai, *August Stars*, translated by R. Bobrova and others. Moscow: Foreign Languages Publishing House, 1957. 74 pp.

Gribachev, Nikolai, *Poetry: Evolution; Summer Rain, Happiness; Never!*, translated by Gladys Evans and Tom Botting, in *Soviet Literature Monthly*, No. 1, 1962, pp. 123–27.

Gutsalo, Yevgen, *Klava, Queen of the Pirates*, translated by Natalia Lukoshkova, in *Soviet Literature Monthly*, No. 3, 1963, pp. 96–103.
A story.

Ilin, M., and E. A. Segal, *Do You Know?* translated by F. Solasko. Moscow: Foreign Languages Publishing House, 1956. 278 pp.
Ilin ranks as an outstanding writer for young people and adults on science and technology from the point of view of popularization. The Russian edition of this work was issued by the Children's Publishing House.

Inber, Vera, *For Ever*, translated by Dorian Rottenberg, in *Soviet Literature Monthly*, No. 12, 1961, pp. 119–20.
A short poem by a distinguished Leningrad poet on the Soviet spaceman.

Inber, Vera, *Verses: Razliv, or Water Meadow Halt; Two Lives in One*, translated by Tom Botting and Archie Johnstone, in *Soviet Literature Monthly*, No. 12, 1960, pp. 105–10.

Isayev, Yegor, *Memory's Judgement,* translated by Gladys Evans, in *Soviet Literature Monthly,* No. 6, 1963, pp. 118–25.
The poet is said to have taken six years to write this poem about a German. His poem has been described as "thoroughly propagandist in the best sense of the word." Propagandist it certainly is. The translation is an excerpt from the full work.

Ivanov, Vsevolod, *Off to Meet the Southbound Birds,* translated by Margaret Wettlin, in *Soviet Literature Monthly,* No. 10, 1963, pp. 3–72.
Notes on a journey to Siberia.

Kassil, Lev A., *Early Dawn,* translated by S. Rosenberg. Moscow: Foreign Languages Publishing House, 1957. 361 pp.
Kassil often writes for children or young people.

Kassil, Lev, *The Hero's Brother,* translated by F. Solasko. Moscow: Foreign Languages Publishing House, 1957. 79 pp.
Primarily for young people.

Katayev, Valentin P., *The Small Farm on the Steppe.* London: Lawrence and Wishart, 1958. 286 pp.
This work is also available under the title of *The Cottage in the Steppe,* translated by F. Solasko and Eve Manning, Moscow: Foreign Languages Publishing House, 1957, 379 pp. Katayev is an outstanding writer for young people, and this work was published in Moscow by the Children's Publishing House.

Katayev, Valentin, *The Jar of Jam,* translated by G. Azrael, in *Atlantic,* June 1960, pp. 92–95.

Kaverin, Veniamin A., *Open Book,* translated by B. Pearce. London: Lawrence & Wishart, 1955. 637 pp.

Kazakevich, Emmanuil, *By Light of Day,* translated by Darya Efremova, in *Soviet Literature Monthly,* No. 6, 1963, pp. 4–40.
One of the last completed works of an outstanding Russian writer. A story about bad news from the front.

Kazakevich, Emmanuil, *The Blue Notebook,* translated by Ralph Parker, in *Soviet Literature Monthly,* No. 11, 1961, pp. 7–78.
A novella on the theme of the revolution and the image of V. I. Lenin.

Kazakevich, Emmanuil G., *Heart of a Friend,* translated by R. Dixon. Moscow: Foreign Languages Publishing House, 1956. 247 pp.

Kazakevich, Emmanuil G., *The House on the Square.* Moscow: Foreign Languages Publishing House, 1958. 520 pp.
Occupied Germany.

Kazakov, Yuri, *Adam and Eve,* translated by Manya Harari, in *Encounter,* April 1963, pp. 39–51.

A story about a modern Russian artist on a "creative" trip in the Far North with a girl friend—his thoughts and his problems.

Kazakov, Yuri, *Autumn in the Oak Woods,* in *Esquire,* October 1963, p. 133.

Kazakov, Yuri, *The Derelict,* translated by George Gibian, in *Odyssey Review,* vol. 2, no. 4, December 1962, pp. 128–41.
This is a story about a buoy-keeper on the Oka River with a beautiful voice. Another available translation is by Walter N. Vickery entitled *The Outsider,* published in *Dissonant Voices in Soviet Literature,* edited by Patricia Blake and Max Hayward. New York: Pantheon Books, 1962, pp. 188–203. The Vickery translation is also in *Esquire* for November 1962, pp. 96–98.

Kazakov, Yuri, *Kalevala,* translated by Hilda Perham, in *Soviet Literature Monthly,* No. 4, 1963, pp. 105–14.
An account by Russia's most promising young author of a trip to a remote and historical district of the Northland.

Kazakov, Yuri, *The Smell of Bread,* translator unstated, in *Esquire,* September 1963, pp. 81 and 154.
The eternal peasant comes to the surface in an erstwhile city woman—published originally in *Pages from Tarusa.*

Kazakov, Yuri, *There Goes a Dog,* translator unstated, in *USSR Soviet Life Today,* issued by the Soviet Embassy in Washington, for March 1963, pp. 26–27.
A fisherman so eager for fishing that he misses romance.

Kazakova, Rimma, *By the Sea of Okhotsk; The Road,* translated by Dorian Rottenberg and Margaret Wettlin, in *Soviet Literature Monthly,* No. 7, 1960, pp. 146–49.
Two short poems.

Kazakova, Rimma, *Verses: Love Me Coyly; We Cursed War; The Pattering Rain Set Runlets Flowing,* translated by Herbert Marshall and Tom Botting, in *Soviet Literature Monthy,* No. 3, 1963, pp. 116–19.

Kazaktsev, Aleksandr P., *Against the Wind* (short stories), translated by S. Apresyan. Moscow: Foreign Languages Publishing House, 1955. 191 pp.

Ketlinskaya, Vera K., *Days of Our Life,* translated by A. Bostock. London: Lawrence and Wishart, 1956. 832 pp.

Khalov, Pavel, *Calling All Ships,* translated by Ralph Parker, in *Soviet Literature Monthly,* No. 8, 1961, pp. 61–104.
A contemporary story about Russian men and women at sea by a young Soviet Far Eastern writer—his first prose work.

Kharabarov, Ivan, *Untrodden Path,* translated by Walter N. Vickery, in *Dissonant Voices in Soviet Literature,* edited by Patricia Blake and Max Hayward. New York: Pantheon Books, 1961, pp. 185–87.

A poem by a young poet who got into serious trouble for his adulation of Pasternak.

Kholopov, Georgi, *Stories of the War,* translated by Natalia Lukoshkova, in *Soviet Literature Monthly,* No. 2, 1962, pp. 88–94.
Vignettes from a book with the same title—published in 1960.

Kin, Viktor P., *Across the Lines,* translated by R. Parker and V. Scott. Moscow: Foreign Languages Publishing House, 1960. 253 pp.

Kirsanov, Semyon, *In the Beginning,* translated by Tom Botting, in *Soviet Literature Monthly,* No. 2, 1961, pp. 143–44.
"You are creation's finest work"—verses.

Kirsanov, Semyon, *Once Upon a Tomorrow,* translated by Margaret Wettlin, in *Soviet Literature Monthly,* No. 8, 1963, pp. 123–37.
A selection of 14 short poems.

Kirsanov, Semyon, *The Seven Days of the Week,* translated by Hugh McLean and Walter N. Vickery, in *Year of Protest, 1956.* New York: Vintage-Random House, 1961, pp. 132–46.
A poem-allegory which is a strong protest against the heartlessness of bureaucracy. Published in 1956, it caused a sensation at the time.

Knorre, Fedor F., *Stories,* translated by E. Felgenhauer and L. Navrozov. Moscow: Foreign Languages Publishing House, 1955. 143 pp.

Knorre, Fyodor, *The Good Ship "Cormorant,"* translated by Archie Johnstone, in *Soviet Literature Monthly,* No. 10, 1962, pp. 126–42.
A story—a boy's reminiscence.

Kochetkov, Victor, *The Battle Raged* and *Quatrain,* in *An Anthology of Russian Verse, 1812–1960,* edited by Avrahm Yarmolinsky. New York: Doubleday-Anchor, 1961, pp. 240–41.
Brief verses dated 1960.

Kondrashova, Mariya M., *After the Day's Work.* Moscow: Foreign Languages Publishing House, 1958. 72 pp.

Korneichuk, Alexander, *Where the Dnieper Flows,* translated by P. Yefremova, in *Soviet Literature Monthly,* No. 8, 1961, pp. 3–61.
A play about a contemporary collective farm.

Korneichuk, Alexander, *Wings,* translated by John Gibbons. Moscow: Foreign Languages Publishing House, 1954. 131 pp.
A play which received much notoriety at the time it was originally put on because it depicted an unjust arrest under Stalin.

Korostylev, Vadim, *Baby Camel,* in *An Anthology of Russian Verse,* edited by Avrahm Yarmolinsky. New York: Doubleday-Anchor, 1962, p. 230.
A brief poem dated 1956.

Korshunov, Mikhail, *Riverine Ferry Service,* translated by Eve Manning, in *Soviet Literature Monthly,* No. 3, 1962, pp. 129–36.
A juvenile short story.

Kozhevnikov, Vadim, *Comrade Volkin,* translated by Ralph Parker, in *Soviet Literature Monthly,* No. 6, 1960, pp. 3–31.
A story about a war hero named Volkin—in peacetime.

Kozhevnikov, Vadim, *Gone the Day,* translated by D. Efremova, in *Soviet Literature Monthly,* No. 8, 1963, pp. 9–60.
A short novel—or long short story—about a construction and highway engineer who had once written a letter to Stalin and who, as a result, had spent some time in concentration camps, yet emerged as loyal a communist as when he went in.

Kozhevnikov, Vadim, *Meet Baluyev,* translated by Eve Manning, in *Soviet Literature Monthly,* No. 11, 1960, pp. 3–83, and No. 12, 1960, pp. 3–105.
A pipeline saga.

Kozhevnikov, Vadim, *Strength,* translated by Asya Shoyett, in *Soviet Literature Monthly,* No. 1, 1963, pp. 86–96.
A short story on the arctic.

Krivtsov, Vladimir, *The Time of Lightning,* translated by Eve Manning, in *Soviet Literature Monthly,* No. 7, 1963, pp. 97–112.
A story about a man who ponders on the road and becomes better.

Kuleshov, Arkadi, *My Songs; The Corn; The Evergreen Grove,* translated by Margaret Wettlin, Tom Botting, and Dorian Rottenberg, in *Soviet Literature Monthly,* No. 8, 1961, pp. 130–35.
Three poems from various periods of a Belorussian poet and writer.

Kuranov, Yuri, *Sketches,* translated by Vladimir Talmy, in *Soviet Literature Monthly,* No. 6, 1962, pp. 148–53.
Short vignettes from a first book—entitled *Summer in the North*—of a young author.

Kuznetsov, Anatoli, *Young Hearts,* translated by Vladimir Talmy, in *Soviet Literature Monthly,* No. 3, 1961, pp. 99–122.
Contemporary young people on a construction project—a story.

Kuznetsov, Anatolii, *Sequel to a Legend,* translated by R. Bobrove. Moscow: Foreign Languages Publishing House, 1959. 301 pp.

Lavrenev, Boris A., *The Forty First,* translated by M. Wettlin and N. Jochel. Moscow: Foreign Languages Publishing House, 1958. 190 pp.

Lipatov, Vil, *Wild Mint,* translated by Robert Daglish, in *Soviet Literature Monthly,* No. 5, 1961, pp. 3–116.
A to-do in a Siberian pine woods among lumberjacks—a novel.

Lipatov, Vil, *The Wisdom Tooth,* translated by Darya Efremova, in *Soviet Literature Monthly,* No. 4, 1963, pp. 3–39.
A story about a man and an automobile.

Lisovsky, Kazimierz, *In the Forest,* translated by Margaret Wettlin, in *Soviet Literature Monthly,* No. 9, 1960, pp. 124–25.
A brief poem.

Lugovskoy, Innokenti, *Daughter of the Orochons,* translated by Dorian Rottenberg, in *Soviet Literature Monthly,* No. 9, 1960, pp. 123–24.
A short poem.

Lukonin, Mikhail, *Verses: Those Who Returned from the Wars; Stalingrad Theatre; So Long; To Kolya Otrada; In Search of a Gentle Human Being,* translated by Herbert Marshall, Joe Wallace, in *Soviet Literature Monthly,* No. 3, 1961, pp. 122–31.

Markov, Georgi, *Salt of the Earth,* translated by Ralph Parker, in *Soviet Literature Monthly,* Nos. 2 and 3, 1961.
A novel about Siberia.

Marshak, Samuel, *Poetry: Quatrains; Immortality; Time and Eternity; Lily of the Valley; Seeing and Perceiving; A Lesson in Russian; My Country's Emblem,* translated by Dorian Rottenberg, in *Soviet Literature Monthly,* No. 4, 1963, pp. 114–19.
Poems by the leading Russian poet for children, one of the most distinguished translators into Russian from English (Barnes and Shakespeare), and a great lyric poet.

Martynov, Leonid, *Into the Cosmos Surged a Human Being,* translated by Herbert Marshall, in *Soviet Literature Monthly,* No. 10, 1961, pp. 106–8.
A poem by an outstanding senior poet.

Martynov, Leonid, *Power,* translated by Joe Wallace, in *Soviet Literature Monthly,* No. 2, 1961, pp. 145–46.
Verses on the theme of lightning tamed.

Martynov, Leonid, *Traces,* translated by Peter Tempest, in *Soviet Literature Monthly,* No. 5, 1962, p. 118.
A brief poem.

Matusovsky, Mikhail, *Pennant of My Nation,* translated by Marlina Tarlinskaya, in *Soviet Literature Monthly,* No. 2, 1960, p. 99.
A poem on Lunik.

Matveyeva, Novella, *Ode to the Pepper,* translated by Margaret Wettlin, in *Soviet Literature Monthly,* No. 2, 1961, pp. 147–49.
Verses to a vegetable.

Maximov, Vladimir, *A Man Survives,* translated by Anselm Hollo. New York: Grove Press, 1963. 106 pp.

This is a story—packaged by the American publisher as a novel—about a human being in the lower depths. Received some enthusiastic reviews in America. Was published in the magazine *Oktyabr* in the Soviet Union in October 1962.

Meleshin, Stanislav, *Encounter in the Taiga*. Moscow: Foreign Languages Publishing House, 1958. 139 pp.

Metter, Israel, *Major Dry-as-Dust*, in *Soviet Short Stories,* edited by Avrahm Yarmolinsky. New York: Doubleday-Anchor, 1960, pp. 271–301.
A story about locating a missing person.

Mikhalkov, Sergei, *The Store-Room*, in *Soviet Literature Monthly*, No. 12, 1962, pp. 112–16.
Several pages from the notebooks of a famous Russian writer for children.

Mikhalkov, Sergei, *Turntail's Trip*, translated by Archie Johnstone, in *Soviet Literature Monthly*, No. 3, 1962, pp. 105–14.
Juvenile—a short story.

Nagibin, Yuri M. *Dreams* (short stories), translated by R. Daglish and others. Moscow: Foreign Languages Publishing House, 1958. 162 pp.

Nagibin, Yuri, *Echo,* translated by Natalia Lukoshkova, in *Soviet Literature Monthly,* No. 6, 1961, pp. 110–24.
A short story.

Nagibin, Yuri, *The Khazar Ornament,* translated by Hugh McLean and Walter N. Vickery, in *Year of Protest, 1956*. New York: Vintage-Random House, 1961, pp. 233–55.
Along with this the editors include their translation of *A Light in the Window,* also by Nagibin. *The Khazar Ornament* deals with some of the facts of life in the Meshchera region southeast of Moscow—frequented by hunters (and writers)—as they are discovered by a newly appointed Soviet official there.

Nagibin, Yuri, *A Light in the Window,* translated by Elizabeth Marbury, in *Bitter Harvest,* edited by Edward Stillman. New York: Frederick A. Praeger, 1959, pp. 166–77.
This story about a bureaucrat director of a rest home is also included in *Year of Protest, 1956,* edited by McLean and Vickery.

Nagibin, Yuri, *The Newlywed,* in *Soviet Short Stories,* edited by Avrahm Yarmolinsky. New York: Doubleday-Anchor, 1960, pp. 196–212.
A story of a happy man on a lifetime honeymoon.

Nagibin, Yuri M., *The Pipe* (stories), translated by V. Shneerson. Moscow: Foreign Languages Publishing House, 1955. 112 pp.
This includes three stories: *The Pipe, Winner, The Winter Oak.*

Nagibin Yuri, *The Talk,* translation by Natalie Bienstock, in *Odyssey Review,* vol. 2, no. 4, December 1962, pp. 158–68.

A story about a hunter who had difficulty in communicating his feelings and thoughts.

Neiman, Julia, *1941,* translated by Walter N. Vickery, in *Dissonant Voices in Soviet Literature,* edited by Patricia Blake and Max Hayward. New York: Pantheon Books, 1962, pp. 156–57.
A brief and startling verse.

Nekrasov, Viktor, *Front-line Stalingrad,* translated by D. Floyd. London: Harvill Press, 1962. 320 pp.
A famous war story, written immediately after the war in its initial version, by a very talented author.

Nekrasov, Victor, *Kira Georgievna,* translated by Walter Vickery. New York: Pantheon Books, 1962. 183 pp.
Originally published in *Atlas, The Magazine of the World Press,* in 1961. This is a story—packaged by the publisher as a book—about a Russian sculptress and her choice between her elderly, prosperous artist husband, her young lover, and her ex-husband returned from a concentration camp.

Nekrasov, Victor, *On Both Sides of the Ocean,* in *Current Digest of the Soviet Press* (editor, Leo Gruliow), March 27 and April 3, 1963.
These translations consist of very extensive excerpts from the travel notes of Nekrasov on trips to Italy and America, in which he freely expressed himself about a number of different things from modern architecture to the system of Soviet tourist "guides" attached to tourist groups in the United States. As a result of these articles Nekrasov was nearly expelled from the Communist Party.

Nikolayeva, Galina E., *The Newcomer,* translated by D. Skvirsky. Moscow: Foreign Languages Publishing House, 1955. 168 pp.

Nikolayeva, Galina, *Talent,* translated by M. and S. Johnstone, in *Soviet Literature Monthly,* No. 10, 1962, pp. 72–87.
A story about a faithful wife by a talented woman writer.

Nilin, Pavel F., *Comrade Venka,* translated by J. Barnes. New York: Simon and Schuster, 1959. (Paperback: Marzani and Munsell, Inc.)
Published in England by Hutchinson, 1959, 304 pp. The same work was also issued under the title *Cruelty* (its original Russian title), translated by J. Guralsky. Moscow: published by the Foreign Languages Publishing House, 1958. 254 pp.
A novel—cops and robbers in Siberia.

Obruchev, Vladimir A., *Kukushkin,* translated by V. Bowen. London: Constable, 1962. 228 pp.
A geographer's tales.

Obruchev, Vladimir A., *Plutonia,* translated by F. Solasko. Moscow: Foreign Languages Publishing House, 1957. 327 pp.

Obruchev, Vladimir A., *Sannikov Land,* translated by D. Skvirsky. Moscow: Foreign Languages Publishing House, 1957. 372 pp.

Obukhova, Lydia, *Goodness of Heart,* translated by Eve Manning, in *Soviet Literature Monthly,* No. 5, 1962, pp. 76–95.
A story—drama in a remote hospital.

Obukhova, Lydia, *A Tale of Polesie,* translated by R. Parker. Moscow: Foreign Languages Publishing House, 1957. 363 pp.

Okudzhava, Bulat, *Good Luck, Schoolboy!,* translated by John Richardson, in *Encounter,* April 1963, pp. 73–87.
This is a partial translation of a lively war story by Russia's guitar-strumming poet, who is a sensational success among young people and a sensational failure with partyline critics and officials. The original was published in *Pages From Tarusa.*

Panova, Vera F., *Span of the Year,* translated by V. Traill. London: Harvill Press, 1957, 282 pp.
Vera Panova is one of Russia's most sensitive and talented writers.

Panova, Vera, *Time Walked.* London: Harvill Press, 1957. 177 pp.

Panova, Vera F., *Summer to Remember.* New York: Yoseloff, 1962.

Parkhomov, Mikhail N., *I Speak from the Grave,* translated by E. Manning. Moscow: Foreign Languages Publishing House, 1959. 196 pp.

Pasternak, Boris, *Beast in an Enclosure,* in *Bitter Harvest,* edited by Edward Stillman. New York: Frederick A. Praeger, 1959, pp. 254–55.
A very short verse reportedly expressing the poet's feelings over the Nobel Prize scandal in 1958.

Pasternak, Boris, *Doctor Zhivago,* translated by Max Hayward and Manya Harari. New York: Pantheon Books, 1958.
This famous novel was also published in paperback—by Signet and is in the Modern Library of Random House. The English edition was brought out by Collins, 1958. 510 pp. And there is the Russian edition published by the University of Michigan Press, Ann Arbor, 1958. The full edition includes a set of poems, some of which were published in *Znamya* in the Soviet Union in 1954.

Pasternak, Boris, *I Remember, Sketch for an Autobiography,* translated by David Magarshak with preface and notes, including also the essay *Translating Shakespeare,* translated by Manya Harari. New York: Pantheon Books, 1959. (Paperback edition: Meridian Books, 1960. 192 pp.)
This is not the only Pasternak autobiography—there is one written much earlier entitled *Safe Conduct,* published in 1931 (published by New Directions, 1958, and by Signet in paperback). But in this one he says many things he could not have said in any work published in the Soviet Union. Like *Doctor Zhivago* this too was sent out of the Soviet Union for publication.

Pasternak, Boris, *In the Interlude: Poems, 1945–1960,* translated by Henry Kamen with facing Russian text. London and New York: Oxford University Press, 1962. 250 pp.

Pasternak, Boris, *Poems*.

Many different individual translations of poems or groups of poems of Pasternak by various translators have appeared in journals and magazines. Among them: *Miracle*, translated by E. M. Kayden, *Christian Century*, September 23, 1959, p. 1081; *Dawn*, translated by B. G. Guerney, *The Atlantic*, June 1960, p. 40; *Hamlet*, *The Reporter*, June 23, 1960; *Snow Falls*, translated by George Reavey, *Good Housekeeping*, December 1959, p. 19, *Snow Storm*, translated by S. Stepanchev, *The Nation*, November 14, 1959, p. 362; *M.Ts*, translated by George Reavey, *Partisan Review*, May–June 1961, pp. 416–17; *Without Love*, translated by Max Hayward, in the same issue of *Partisan Review*, pp. 363–71; *Seven Poems, a New Version*, translated by R. Lowell, *Harpers*, September 1961, pp. 44–47.

Pasternak, Boris, *Poems*, translated by Eugene M. Kayden. Ann Arbor: University of Michigan Press, 1959. 210 pp.

Pasternak, Boris, *The Poetry of Boris Pasternak*, translated and edited by George Reavey, with a 100-page introduction to Pasternak's life and work. New York: G. Putnam's Sons, 1959. Paperback (Capricorn), 1960. 257 pp.

Paustovsky, Konstantin, *The Drozdovs*, translated by Hugh McLean and Walter N. Vickery, in *Year of Protest, 1956*, New York: Vintage-Random House, 1961, pp. 155–60.

This bitter attack on Soviet philistines by a distinguished liberal Russian writer was delivered during the course of the discussion of the novel *Not by Bread Alone* by Vladimir Dudintsev. It was published in *L'Express* of Paris, but not in the Soviet Union.

Paustovsky, Konstantin G., *The Flight of Time*, translated by L. Navrozov. Moscow: Foreign Languages Publishing House, 1956. 99 pp.

Paustovsky, Konstantin G., *The Golden Rose*, translated by S. Rosenberg. Moscow: Foreign Languages Publishing House, 1957. 238 pp.

Subtitled "literature in the making." Paustovsky is a fine writer. He often writes about nature, but this particular book is about mastery of literary skill.

Paustovskii, K., *A Little About Myself*, in *Voks Bulletin*, 1 (xcvi), 1956, pp. 19–21.

Paustovsky, Konstantin, *Reminiscences of Babel*, in *Partisan Review*, XXVIII, 3–4, May–June, 1961, pp. 383–90.

This fragment from Paustovsky's *Time of Great Expectations* is also included in *Dissonant Voices in Soviet Literature*, edited by Patricia Blake and Max Hayward.

Permyak, Evgeni, *The Tale of the Grey Wolf*, translated by Valentina Scott, in *Soviet Literature Monthly*, No. 10, 1960, pp. 3–110.

A novel about a Russian-American who returns to his native village in Russia—and what happens next.

Pervomaisky, Leonid, *The Simpleton,* translated by Pauline Rose, in *Soviet Literature Monthly,* No. 10, 1960, pp. 116–23.
A story by an Ukrainian poet—or is it a reminiscence?

Pilyar, Yuri E., *It All Really Happened,* translated by L. Persy. Moscow: Foreign Languages Publishing House, 1960. 188 pp.

Polevoi, Boris N., *He Came Back,* translated by O. Shartse. Moscow: Foreign Languages Publishing House, 1956. 138 pp.

Polevoi, Boris N., *Shores of a New Sea,* translated by I. Zheleznova. Moscow: Foreign Languages Publishing House, 1955. 143 pp.
Stories.

Pomerantsev, V., *Sincerity in Literature,* in *Soviet Studies,* V, 4, 1954, pp. 434–45.
This famous critical article on Russia literature, calling for honesty in writing, was published less than a year after Stalin's death. Its repercussions still reverberate.

Prishvin, Mikhail M., *Ship-Timber Grove,* translated by D. Fry. London: Lawrence and Wishart, 1957. 192 pp.
Prishvin, who wrote about nature and people close to nature, died in 1954. This is one of his last works.

Privalov, Boris, *Her First Bouquet,* translated by Pauline Rose, in *Soviet Literature Monthly,* No. 6, 1960, pp. 119–22.
A short short story.

Prokofiev, Alexander, *Down Where the Bankline Arches: Song,* translated by Marina Tarlinskaya and Archie Johnstone, in *Soviet Literature Monthly,* No. 2, 1960, pp. 97–98.

Prokofiev, Alexander, *Verses: Songs of Russia; Rhymes and Rhythms! No Peace Have I of You; The Heart of the Soldier; The Second Day; Again the Breeze Wafts Autumn's Scent,* translated by Margaret Wettlin and Joe Wallace, in *Soviet Literature Monthly,* No. 7, 1961, pp. 127–31.

Proskurin, Pyotr, *The Road,* translated by Ralph Parker, in *Soviet Literature Monthly,* No. 3, 1963, pp. 103–13.
A story.

Rakhmanov, Leonid N., *Restless Old Age,* in *Soviet Weekly,* London, 1958. 38 pp.
A play in four acts.

Rekemchuk, Alexander, *Callow Youth,* translated by Ralph Parker, in *Soviet Literature Monthly,* No. 12, 1962, pp. 3–110.

A novel by an Ukrainian who has lived in the far north—in the area near Vorkuta—for many years and who writes of the arctic. The story was made into a motion picture.

Rodimtsev, Alexander, *Mashenka,* translated by Eve Manning, in *Soviet Literature Monthly,* No. 8, 1963, pp. 61–103.
The author is a colonel-general who fought with distinction in Spain and in World War II—and this is a war story about a gallant girl at the front named Mashenka Borovichenko.

Rozhdestvensky, Ignati, *Lake Ingol; In the Polar Urals,* translated by Dorian Rottenberg, in *Soviet Literature Monthly,* No. 9, 1960, pp. 125–27.
Two brief poems—geographical in inspiration.

Rozhdestvensky, Robert, *Morning,* translated by Hugh McLean and Walter N. Vickery, in *Year of Protest, 1956,* p. 148.
An appeal for truthfulness—in the form of a short poem. The poem is also in *An Anthology of Russian Verse, 1812–1960,* edited by Avrahm Yarmolinsky, pp. 232–35.

Rozhdestvensky, Robert, *Requiem,* translated by Archie Johnstone, in *Soviet Literature Monthly,* No. 5, 1962, pp. 120–21.
Dmitri Kabalevsky, composer, wrote a symphony to this work which pays homage to war dead.

Rozhdestvensky, Robert, *Song of the Mainland,* translated by Jack Lindsay, in *Soviet Literature Monthly,* No. 2, 1962, pp. 95–96.
A poem.

Rozov, Viktor, *In Search of Happiness,* translated by N. Fround. London: Evans, 1961. 72 pp.
A play.

Rusetsky, Alexei, *Lift Up Your Eyes,* translated by Joe Wallace, in *Soviet Literature Monthly,* No. 8, 1962, pp. 144–45.
A poem.

Rybakov, Anatolii N., *The Bronze Bird,* translated by D. Skvirsky. Moscow: Foreign Languages Publishing House, 1959. 293 pp.

Rylenkov, Nikolai, *Another Autumn Combs Her Auburn Tresses: To Try Out Words for Colour, Weight and Worth...; Silence of August,* translated by Jack Lindsay and Dorian Rottenberg, in *Soviet Literature Monthly,* No. 2, 1962, pp. 64–95.
Three poems.

Rylsky, Maxim, *Coachman's Cottage; Yasnaya Polyana; Airways; The War of the Roses,* translated by Dorian Rottenberg, in *Soviet Literature Monthly,* No. 10, 1960, pp. 123–26.
Verses by a well-known Ukrainian poet.

Semyonov, Vladimir, *Documents,* in *An Anthology of Russian Verse,* edited by Avrahm Yarmolinsky. New York: Doubleday-Anchor, 1961, p. 239. Verses dated 1958.

Semyonov, Yulian, *New Year's Eve,* translated by Natalia Lukoshkova, in *Soviet Literature Monthly,* No. 5, 1962, pp. 106–16.
A story about a geological expedition in Siberia.

Sheinin, Lev. R., *Diary of a Criminologist,* translated by F. Solasko. Moscow: Foreign Languages Publishing House, 1959. 205 pp.
Evidently this translation consists of a few excerpts from the more substantial and interesting original work in Russian.

Shim, Edward, *The Queen and Her Seven Daughters,* translated by Eve Manning, in *Soviet Literature Monthly,* No. 1, 1963, pp. 50–86.
A story about a boy named Alyoshka on a tugboat named "Grozny."

Sholokhov, Mikhail, *Harvest on the Don,* translated by H. C. Stevens. New York: Alfred A. Knopf, 1960. Also in Signet Books (paperback), 1962. 333 pp.
This same translation was published in England by Putnam, 1960. Another translation is that of Robert Daglish, in *Soviet Literature Monthly,* Nos. 1, 2, 3 and 7, 1960, under the title *Virgin Soil Upturned, Book Two.* This is the novel—a continuation of his previous *Virgin Soil Upturned, Book One,* by the famous author of *And Quiet Flows the Don*—about the rural revolution in his own Cossack country consequent on collectivization of agriculture.

Sholokhov, Mikhail, *One Man's Life,* translated by Peter Henry, in *Stories from Modern Russia, Winter's Tales 7,* edited by C. P. Snow and Pamela Hansford Johnson. New York: St. Martin's Press, 1962, pp. 108–62.
The same story as that translated under the title of *The Fate of a Man.* It has been published in a translation by R. Daglish, as a separate volume by the Foreign Languages Publishing House in Moscow: *The Fate of Man,* Moscow, 1958, 67 pp. and the Daglish translation was also published in *The Atlantic,* November 1959, pp. 41–55. This story is about a man and a boy —both derelicts from the war—who found in each other a solace for their bitter wounds and losses. It is touching and tender. And in 1957 it was seized upon by Soviet authorities, including Khrushchev, as a model for other Soviet writers and elevated—somewhat beyond its real level—to the status of one of the allegedly major literary works of all time.

Sholokhov, Mikhail, *Tales of the Don,* translated by H. C. Stevens. New York: Alfred A. Knopf, 1962.
The English edition of this translation was published in 1961 by Putnam.

Simonov, Konstantin, *The Fourth,* translated by Ralph Parker, in *Soviet Literature Monthly,* No. 9, 1961, pp. 73–113.
A full-length play by a leading poet, dramatist, novelist, and journalist. Its subject is an "imperialist" plot against Russia involving a U-2-like flight,

antiliberal hysteria in America, and the soul-searchings of an American journalist who had long since "sold-out" to the "imperialist warmongers," but is presented with a chance to redeem himself by "exposing" the plot. Some Russians interpreted the play with a reverse twist—as a frank confession by Simonov of his own "sell-out" to the "personality cult" of Stalin and of his avowal of a change of heart.

Simonov, Konstantin, *Inozemtsev and Ryndin,* translated by Eve Manning, in *Soviet Literature Monthly,* No. 6, 1963, pp. 79–92.
A new war story by a famous Russian writer.

Simonov, Konstantin, *Letter from Tashkent,* translated by G. L. McGovern, in *The Atlantic,* June 1960, pp. 67–73.

Simonov, Konstantin, *The Living and the Dead,* translated by R. Ainsztein. New York: Doubleday, 1962. 552 pp.
Written in the period from 1955 to 1959, this war novel deals with the opening phases of the German invasion of Russia from June 1941 through the Russian victory in the battle for Moscow. As a novel it has been criticized for failure in character delineation. But it is an important historical document in its vivid depiction of the chaos in the Russian lines in the opening phase of the war.

Slutsky, Boris, *A Footnote to the Debate about Andrey Rublyov,* translated by Max Hayward, in *Encounter,* April 1963, pp. 71–72.
A short poem.

Slutsky, Boris, *Housing Construction,* in *An Anthology of Russian Verse, 1812–1960,* edited by Avrahm Yarmolinsky. New York: Doubleday-Anchor, 1961, p. 240.
A brief poem dated 1960.

Slutsky, Boris, *The Sea of Dreams,* translated by Joe Wallace, in *Soviet Literature Monthly,* No. 2, 1961, pp. 146–47.
A poem about an old map on his wall.

Smelyakov, Yaroslav, *The Early Shift,* translated by Archie Johnstone, in *Soviet Literature Monthly,* No. 1, 1960, pp. 107–9.
Two poems—exercises in communist declamation.

Smelyakov, Yaroslav, *Verses: Heroines Unsung; When I Fall Ill . . . ; Suburban Dining Halls; Winter Night; For Me the Past Was All Forgot,* translated by Margaret Wettlin and Dorian Rottenberg, in *Soviet Literature Monthly,* No. 5, 1963, pp. 122–28.

Smelyakov, Yaroslav, *Propaganda,* translated by Louis Zelikoff, in *Soviet Literature Monthly,* No. 10, 1961, pp. 105–6.
A brief poem appropriately titled.

Smirnov, Sergei, *Song of the Wind,* translated by Joe Wallace, in *Soviet Literature Monthly,* No. 2, 1961, pp. 144–45.
A poem in memory of Vladimir Lugovsky.

Snegov, Sergei, *Looking for the Way,* translated by Ralph Parker, in *Soviet Literature Monthly,* No. 4, 1962, pp. 29–93.
A short novel about factory production by a Russian writer who is a scientist himself and who usually writes about science and engineers.

Sobolev, Leonid, *General Overhaul,* translated by Eve Manning, in *Soviet Literature Monthly,* No. 11, 1962, pp. 3–92.
This novel was begun thirty years ago, and the first volume was only recently completed. It is about a tsarist naval vessel in 1914. This selection consists of Chapters 12 to 15.

Sobolev, Leonid S., *The Green Light,* translated by R. Parker and V. Scott. Moscow: Foreign Languages Publishing House, 1956. 223 pp.

Sofronov, Anatoli, *The Cook,* translated by P. Yefremov, in *Soviet Literature Monthly,* No. 11, 1960, pp. 83–137.
A play.

Soloukhin, Vladimir, *The Dew-Drop,* translated by Valentina Scott and Ralph Parker, in *Soviet Literature Monthly,* No. 9, 1960, pp. 56–123.
A Russian writer describes his native village of Olepino in Vladimir Province and the people who live there. This translation consists of chapters from the book.

Soloukhin, Vladimir, *The Grievance,* translated by Mary Mackler, in *Soviet Literature Monthly,* No. 2, 1963, pp. 117–23.
In essence a reminiscence of his childhood, in the village of Olepino in Vladimir Province.

Solovev, Leonid, *Adventures in Bokhara,* translated by T. Shebunina. London: Lawrence and Wishart, 1956. 256 pp.

Solovev, Leonid V., *The Enchanted Prince,* translated by B. Isaacs. Moscow: Foreign Languages Publishing House, 1958. 449 pp.

Solzhenitsyn, Alexander, *One Day in the Life of Ivan Denisovich,* translated by Thomas P. Whitney. New York: Crest Books, 1963 (paperback).
A novel. This edition contains an introductory essay and, as an appendix, the full text of an interesting attempted interview with inaccessible Solzhenitsyn by a Soviet newspaperman early in 1963. There are three other translations of this work available: By Max Hayward and Ronald Hingley (Praeger), available both in hardcover and paperback; by Ralph Parker (E. P. Dutton), available both in hardcover and paperback and also published in *Soviet Literature Monthly,* No. 2, 1963, and in installments in *Moscow News* in December 1962 and January 1963. The Hayward-Hingley translation was also carried in considerably abbreviated text in the *Saturday Evening Post.* There is another paperback translation by Jacques Katel. The great interest in this novel in the West was primarily political—because it was the first work of fiction to be published in the U.S.S.R. dealing in full and vivid detail with conditions in Stalin's concentration camps for political prisoners. However, the work also has great literary merit, and the modest writer, a

schoolteacher who was catapulted into national and international fame as a result of publication of this novel, is both talented and forthright.

Solzhenitsyn, Alexander, *Matryena's Home,* translated by H. T. Willets, in *Encounter,* May 1963, pp. 28–45.
A story about a Russian peasant woman with saint-like qualities which are exploited by her neighbors.

Sosnora, Victor, *Dolphins,* translated by Max Hayward, in *Encounter,* April 1963, p. 71.
A brief poem.

Stadnik, Ivan, *People are Not Angels.* New York: Praeger, 1963.
This is a revealing novel of collective farm life in the 1930's.

Stein, Alexander, *Ocean,* translated by Margaret Wettlin, in *Soviet Literature Monthly,* No. 6, 1962, pp. 81–148.
A play about navy officers on peacetime duty.

Surkov, Alexei, *Verses: Memories; Brotherhood; Stars Overhead; Our Strength; A Space-Flight Song; Saturday in Sidney,* translated by Peter Tempest, Gladys Evans, and Louis Zelikoff, in *Soviet Literature Monthly,* No. 11, 1962, pp. 101–7.

Surkov, Alexei, *My Contemporary,* translated by Dorian Rottenberg, in *Soviet Literature Monthly,* No. 10, 1961, pp. 105–6.
A brief poem.

Svetlov, Mikhail, *Three Verses: Horizon; Spring Morning; A Fable,* translated by Archie Johnstone and Margaret Wettlin, in *Soviet Literature Monthly,* No. 3, 1960, pp. 141–45.

Tank, Maxim, *The Sundial,* translated by Irina Zheloznova, in *Soviet Literature Monthly,* No. 8, 1962, pp. 139–40.
A poem.

Tarasenkova, Natalia, *Two Stories: The Distant Relative* and *The Chief,* translated by Ralph Parker, in *Soviet Literature Monthly,* No. 1, 1963, pp. 96–110.
Two very short stories from her collection entitled *Through the Forest,* published in 1959.

Tarsis, Valery, *The Bluebottle,* translated by Thomas Jones, in *Show, The Magazine of the Arts,* for August and September 1963; also published as a book—New York: Alfred Knopf, 1963.
This is allegedly an illegally exported story by a Soviet writer who was said to have been imprisoned in an insane asylum for sending it abroad for publication.

Tendryakov, Vladimir, *Potholes,* translated by Peter Henry, in *Stories from Modern Russia, Winter's Tales 7,* edited by C. P. Snow and Pamela Hansford Johnson. New York: St. Martin's Press, 1962, pp. 185–265.

A story—bureaucracy kills a man, the victim of an auto accident. This same story has also been translated under the title *Roads,* included in *Soviet Short Stories,* edited by Avrahm Yarmolinsky. New York: Doubleday-Anchor, 1960, pp. 213–58.

Tendryakov, Vladimir F., *Son-in-Law,* translated by Y. Rebrov. Moscow: Foreign Languages Publishing House, 1956. 163 pp.

Tendryakov, Vladimir, *Three, Seven and Ace,* translated by David Alger, in *Dissonant Voices in Soviet Literature,* edited by Patricia Blake and Max Hayward. New York: Pantheon Books, 1962, pp. 204–34.
This story which left a deep impression on Russian readers is about the devastating impact of a card sharp on a quiet, peaceful lumber camp in the northwoods. Unfortunately, this version is heavily cut, the author's moral to the story included.

Tertz, Abram, *Fantastic Stories,* translated by Max Hayward and Ronald Hingley. New York: Pantheon Books, 1963.
Tertz is allegedly the pseudonym of a Russian writer who is supposed to have illegally sent his work to the West for publication.

Tertz, Abram, *On Socialist Realism, Dissent,* VII (1960), pp. 39–66. Also translated by George Dennis—New York: Pantheon Books, 1961.

Tertz, Abram, *The Tenants,* translated by Vera von Wiren-Garczynski, in *Odyssey Review,* vol. 2, no. 4, December 1962, pp. 169–82.
From the series called *Fantastic Tales*—consisting allegedly of literature smuggled out of Russia by a Soviet author said to be writing under a pseudonym.

Tertz, Abram, *The Trial Begins,* translated by M. Hayward. London: Collins, 1960. 128 pp.
Originally published in *Encounter.* Also published in New York: Pantheon, 1960.

Tertz, Abram, *Unconquered, Time,* December 1961, pp. 29–30.

Tertz, Abram, *You and I: A Story, Survey,* April 1962, pp. 151–62.

Tevelev, Matvei G., *Hotel in Shegovets,* translated by O. Shartse. Moscow: Foreign Languages Publishing House, 1957. 176 pp.

Tevelev, Matvei G., *"Verkhovina, Our Land so Dear,"* translated by S. Rosenberg. Moscow: Foreign Languages Publishing House, 1955. 528 pp.

Tikhonov, Nikolai, *The Mists,* translated by George H. Hanna, in *Soviet Literature Monthly,* No. 2, 1961, pp. 142–43.
Brief verses by a distinguished elder poet.

Tikhonov, Nikolai, *Stories of Childhood,* translated by Ralph Parker, in *Soviet Literature Monthly,* No. 1, 1963, pp. 39–50.
Reminiscences of a poet's childhood.

Tkachenko, Anatoli, *Crater Bay,* translated by J. Lynott, in *Soviet Literature Monthly,* No. 2, 1963, pp. 107–17.
Tkachenko usually writes for young people.

Trifonov, Yuri, *There's Use in Checking Up Each Fact,* translated by Tom Botting, in *Soviet Literature Monthly,* No. 8, 1960, pp. 134–35.
A short poem.

Tvardovsky, Alexander, *Death and the Hero,* and *To My Critics,* translations by M. Wettlin and B. Deutsch and A. Yarmolinsky, in *The Atlantic,* June 1960, pp. 64–66 and p. 109.

Tvardovsky, Alexander, *No, Life Has Not Denied Me My Share,* prose translation by D. Obolensky, and Russian text, in the *Penguin Book of Russian Verse,* Harmondsworth, Essex, and Baltimore: Penguin Books, 1962, pp. 423–26.

Tvardovsky, Alexander, *Siberia,* translated by Tom Botting, in *Soviet Literature Monthly,* No. 11, 1960, pp. 137–41.
An excerpt from the long poem *Distance, Beyond Distance.*

Tvardovsky, Alexander, *The Stovemakers,* translated by Robert Daglish, in *Stories from Modern Russia, Winter's Tales 7,* edited by C. P. Snow and Pamela Hansford Jones. New York: St. Martin's Press, 1962, pp. 1–47.
A story.

Tvardovsky, Alexander, *The Two Smithies,* and also *About Myself,* in *Soviet Literature Monthly,* No. 4, 1961.
The first of these is a selection from his famous poem, *Space Beyond Space* or *Distance Beyond Distance* and the second a brief piece on himself.

Uspenskaya, Elena B., *The Town's Firstborn,* translated by O. Shartse. Moscow: Foreign Languages Publishing House, 1956. 64 pp.
Stories.

Vanshenkin, Konstantin, *Verses: Life, I Love You, I Do; The Boy; Nightingales,* translated by Dorian Rottenberg, Irina Zheleznova, and Tom Botting, in *Soviet Literature Monthly,* No. 2, 1963, pp. 131–36.

Vigdorova, F., *Diary of a Russian Schoolteacher,* translated by Rosa Prokofieva. New York: Grove Press, 1960. 256 pp.

Vinokurov, Yevgeni, *The Fleeting Days Delight; Such Fascination Lies,* translated by Peter Tempest, in *Soviet Literature Monthly,* No. 5, 1962, pp. 116–17.
Two delightful lyrics.

Vinokurov, Yevgeni, *A Poem,* translated by W. H. Auden, in *Encounter,* April 1963, p. 53.

Virta, Nikolai E., *Alone,* translated by O. Shartse. Moscow: Foreign Languages Publishing House, 1957. 472 pp.

Vladimov, Georgi, *The Real Stuff*, translated by Ralph Parker, in *Soviet Literature Monthly*, No. 3, 1963, pp. 3–86.
This novel about the exploitation of the Kursk iron ore deposits is by a promising young Russian writer. The original title in Russian was *The Big Ore*

Vlasov, Yuri, *The Imbroglio*, translated by Ralph Parker, in *Soviet Literature Monthly*, No. 10, 1962, pp. 118–25.
A short story about a weight lifter by a world's champion weight lifter.

Voznesensky, Andrei, *Accordions on Holiday*, translated by Margaret Wettlin, in *Soviet Literature Monthly*, No. 7, 1960, p. 151.
A short poem.

Voznesensky, Andrei, *First Ice*, translated by George Reavey, in *Mademoiselle*, December 1962, p. 113.
A poem.

Voznesensky, Andrei, *Parabolic Ballad, Fire in the Architectural Institute, Autumn, The Skull Ballad, Foggy Street, Anti-Worlds, Leaves and Roots, Evening on the Building Site, You Live at Your Aunt's*, translations by W. H. Auden, Stanley Kunitz, Richard Wilbur, Robert Conquest, in *Encounter*, April 1963, pp. 52, 54–58, 69–70.
Short poems—brilliantly written and here rendered with serious attempts to convey their artistry in translation.

Voznesensky, Andrey, *Six Digressions from the Poem, "The Tri-Cornered Pear"; Architectural; Night Airport in New York; Introduction; Another Introduction; Strip-Tease; New York Bird; Guitar Partita*, translations by Natalie Bienstock, in *Odyssey Review*, vol. 2, no. 4, December 1962, pp. 142–57.
Verses—impressions of America.

Voznesensky, Andrei, *Three Poems: Who Are You? Where Are You? You Sit There*, translated by A. Hollo, *The Nation*, December 22, 1962, p. 454.

Voznesensky, Andrei, *Verses: From a Siberian Notebook; Georgian Bazaars; Mountain Springs; In the Mountains; Earth; Wings*, translations by Dorian Rottenberg, Louis Zelikoff, Joe Wallace, Irina Zheleznova, in *Soviet Literature Today*, No. 1, 1963, pp. 110–14.

Wasilewska, Wanda, *Three Stories: Fame; Fellow-Passengers; The Shepherd*, translated by George Hanna, in *Soviet Literature Monthly*, No. 3, 1961, pp. 3–27.

Yakolev, Yuri, *The Boy with the Skates*, translated by Ralph Parker, in *Soviet Literature Monthly*, No. 2, 1962, pp. 66–68.
A story about a contemporary Russian boy by a writer who usually writes for young people.

Yashin, Alexander, *Levers,* in *Soviet Short Stories,* edited by Avrahm Yarmolinsky. New York: Doubleday-Anchor, 1960, pp. 180–95.
This same story—about the meeting of the Party cell on a collective farm—has been included in other collections including *Bitter Harvest,* edited by Edward Stillman and *Year of Protest, 1956,* edited by Hugh McLean and Walter N. Vickery.

Yashin, Alexander, *The Orphan,* published in *Soviet Literature Monthly,* May 1963, pp. 3–91.
This is a story about a new kind of Soviet parasite—a war "orphan" who makes his way through life by living off the goodwill and generosity of others. And it is also about an "orphan" collective farm which likewise lives off the generosity and goodwill of others. A trenchant satire on paternalism and its consequences. A Soviet *Tobacco Road* in some respects.

Yefremov, Ivan A., *Andromeda,* translated by G. Hanna. Moscow: Foreign Languages Publishing House, 1959. 445 pp.
"A space-age tale." Yefremov is a prolific writer of science fiction.

Yegorov, Nikolai, *After the Rain,* in *An Anthology of Russian Verse, 1812–1960,* edited by Avrahm Yarmolinsky. New York: Doubleday-Anchor, 1961, p. 231.
A brief poem dated 1955.

Yesenin-Volpin, Alexander S. (also spelled: Esenin-Volpin), *A Leaf of Spring,* translated by George Reavey, Russian text included. New York: Praeger, 1962. 173 pp.
Poems: Yesenin-Volpin is a son of the famous Russian lyric poet, Sergei Yesenin. His poetry has attained notoriety outside the Soviet Union largely on a political basis, because it was illegally sent out of the Soviet Union—where it was unpublishable because of its bitter antiregime character—and published in the United States. Yesenin-Volpin has been in an insane asylum in Russia. The question is whether, as frequently charged, this is a form of punishment for his sending his writing abroad or whether he is genuinely deranged, as official Soviet sources declare. For individual Yesenin-Volpin items see also *Time Magazine,* December 8, 1961, pp. 29–30, and *Notes from the Underground* by Patricia Blake, in the *Saturday Review,* November 11, 1961, p. 27.

Yevdokimov, Nikolay, *Light from Other People's Windows,* translated by Helen Rapp, in *Stories from Modern Russia, Winter's Tales 7,* edited by C. P. Snow and Pamela Hansford Johnson. New York: St. Martin's Press, 1962, pp. 163–84.
A story about an unambitious housemaid, contrasted with one who is ambitious.

Yevseyeva, Svetlana, *A Poem: No Berry, I, Sad with Wishes,* translated by Tom Botting, in *Soviet Literature Monthly,* No. 3, 1963, pp. 119–20.

Yevtushenko, Yevgeny, *Babi Yar,* translated by Max Hayward, in *Dissonant Voices in Soviet Literature,* edited by Patricia Blake and Hayward. New York: Pantheon Books, 1962, pp. 260–61.

These famous verses—about the ravine outside Kiev where the Nazis massacred Jews—have been much translated elsewhere and much publicized.

Yevtushenko, Yevgeny (transliterated here as Evgeni Evtushenko), *Four Poems,* translated by George Reavey and F. D. Reeve, in *Encounter,* April 1963, pp. 88–90.
Titles are *A Knock on the Door, Through the Crowded Streets, Humour, Secrets,* all short.

Yevtushenko, Yevgeny, *I'm of Siberian Stock, I Lie Upon Damp Earth, You Whispered, To Me You Are As a Ship,* in *An Anthology of Russian Verse,* edited by Avrahm Yarmolinsky. New York: Doubleday-Anchor, 1961, pp. 241–44.

Yevtushenko, Yevgeny, *Moscow.* New York: Crown, 1963.

Yevtushenko, Yevgeny, *Our Communist Faith,* translated by Archie Johnstone, in *Soviet Literature Monthly,* No. 7, 1960, pp. 152–54.
A political declamation, a poem.

Yevtushenko, Yevgeny, *Poems from Cuba,* translated by J. Lynott, in *Soviet Literature Monthly,* No. 10, 1962, pp. 142–49.

Yevtushenko, Yevgeny, *A Precocious Autobiography,* translated by Andrew R. MacAndrew. New York: E. P. Dutton and Co., 1963. 124 pp.
Also in the *Saturday Evening Post* in August 1963. The account of his meteoric career, and a report of his attitudes and thoughts written for a French newspaper. The work got him into hot water at home.

Yevtushenko, Yevgeny, *Selected Poems,* translated by Robin Milner-Gulland and Peter Levi. New York: E. P. Dutton, 1962. 92 pp.; also: Harmondsworth, and Baltimore, Md.: Penguin Books, 1962, with brief introduction.
This is the most comprehensive edition of Yevtushenko's poetry published to mid-1963 in the West.

Yevtushenko, Yevgeny, *Stantsia Zima,* translated by Hugh McLean and Walter Vickery, in *Year of Protest, 1956.* New York: Vintage-Random House, 1961, pp. 122–32.
Excerpts only. This same poem, entitled *Zima Junction,* is also included, in its full text, in the Yevtushenko collection entitled *Selected Poems,* translated by R. Milner-Gulland and P. Levi.

Yevtushenko, Yevgeny, Various poems.
Individual poems and groups of poems, translated by various translators, have appeared in many different magazines and journals in America and England. Among them are: *They Tell Me,* translated by George Reavey, in *Harpers,* November 1962, p. 68; *Pioneers,* translated by Babette Deutsch and A. Yarmolinsky, in *Atlantic,* June 1960, p. 73; *Our Mothers Depart,* translated by George Reavey, in *Good Housekeeping,* October 1962, p. 153; *Freshness, Freshness!* translated

by George Reavey, in *Mademoiselle,* December 1962, p. 13*; Babi Yar* (excerpt), in the *Saturday Review,* May 5, 1962, p. 11; *Babi Yar,* translated by Max Hayward, and *Irreconcilable,* translated by George Reavey, in *Life,* April 19, 1963, pp. 32–33.

Zabolotsky, Nikolai, *Five Poems,* in *An Anthology of Russian Verse, 1812–1960,* edited by Avrahm Yarmolinsky. New York: Doubleday-Anchor, 1961, pp. 235–38.
These date from 1936 to 1956—four of them from the 1950's.

Zadornov, Nikolai, *Captain Nevelskoi,* translated by Ralph Parker, in *Soviet Literature Monthly,* No. 5, 1963, pp. 91–112.
This is a chapter of a historical novel about a Russian navigator of the 19th century who made important discoveries in the Far East.

Zaligin, Sergei, *Bob,* translated by Helen Rapp, in *Stories from Modern Russia, Winter's Tales 7,* edited by C. P. Snow and Pamela Hansford Johnson. New York: St. Martin's Press, 1962, pp. 68–107.
A story about a colorless academician who makes his career simply because no one has the guts to stop him.

Zavgorodny, Gennadi, *Rendezvous,* translated by Natalia Lukoshkova, in *Soviet Literature Monthly,* No. 3, 1963, pp. 86–91.
A story.

Zhdanov, Nikolai, *The Trip Home,* in *Great Soviet Short Stories,* edited by F. D. Reeve. New York: Dell, 1962, pp. 433–47 (paperback).
This story is about a bureaucrat who goes home to his native village and begins to learn the facts of rural life in distinction from the fictions he deals with as an official and who quickly flees back to his sheltered office in the big city to escape. It has also been translated and included in *Bitter Harvest,* edited by Edmund Stillman, and *The Year of Protest, 1956,* edited by McLean and Vickery.

Zubavin, Boris M., *A New Start,* translated by H. Altschuler. Moscow: Foreign Languages Publishing House, 1958. 110 pp.